Terri Reed
and
New York Times Bestselling Author
Lenora Worth

Protect and Defend

Previously published as *Scent of Danger* and *Lone Star Protector*

⟨H⟩ **HARLEQUIN**® LOVE INSPIRED®CLASSICS

Special thanks and acknowledgment are given to Terri Reed and Lenora Worth for their contribution to the Texas K-9 Unit miniseries.

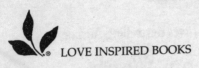

LOVE INSPIRED BOOKS

Recycling programs for this product may not exist in your area.

ISBN-13: 978-1-335-14768-4

Protect and Defend

Copyright © 2018 by Harlequin Books S.A.

First published as Scent of Danger by Harlequin Books in 2013 and Lone Star Protector by Harlequin Books in 2013.

The publisher acknowledges the copyright holders of the individual works as follows:

Scent of Danger
Copyright © 2013 by Harlequin Books S.A.

Lone Star Protector
Copyright © 2013 by Harlequin Books S.A.

www.Harlequin.com

Printed in U.S.A.

CONTENTS

Terri Reed's romance and romantic suspense novels have appeared on the *Publishers Weekly* top twenty-five and Nielsen BookScan's top one hundred lists, and have been featured in *USA TODAY*, *Christian Fiction Magazine* and *RT Book Reviews*. Her books have been finalists for the Romance Writers of America RITA® Award and the National Readers' Choice Award and finalists three times for the American Christian Fiction Writers Carol Award. Contact Terri at terrireed.com or PO Box 19555, Portland, OR 97224.

Books by Terri Reed

Love Inspired Suspense

Military K-9 Unit

Mission to Protect

Classified K-9 Unit

Guardian
Classified K-9 Unit Christmas
"Yuletide Stalking"

Northern Border Patrol

Danger at the Border
Joint Investigation
Murder Under the Mistletoe
Ransom
Identity Unknown

Visit the Author Profile page
at Harlequin.com for more titles.

SCENT OF DANGER

Terri Reed

The Lord is my light and my salvation:
Whom shall I fear? The Lord is the strength
of my life: Of Whom shall I be afraid?
—*Psalms 27:1*

Thank you to my fellow Texas K-9 authors,
Shirlee McCoy, Margaret Daley, Sharon Dunn,
Valerie Hansen and Lenora Worth.
You made working on this series fun.

Chapter One

Detective Melody Zachary halted abruptly at the sight of her office door cracked open. Unease slithered down her spine. She'd locked the door last night when she left the Sagebrush Youth Center. She always did.

Pushing back her suit jacket, she unlatched her weapon from the holster at her hip and withdrew the Sig Sauer. She pushed the door wide with the toe of her heeled boot. Stepping inside the darkened room, she reached with her free hand for the overhead light switch and froze.

A shadow moved.

Not a shadow. A man.

Dressed from head to toe in black. Black gloves, black ski mask…

Black eyes.

Not just the irises, but the white part of his eyes, as well.

Her heart stalled.

Palming her piece in both hands, she aimed her weapon. "Halt! Police!"

The intruder dove straight at her. She didn't have

time to react, to pull the trigger, before he slammed into her chest, knocking her backward against the wall. Her head smacked hard, sending pain slicing through her brain. The air rushed out of her lungs.

The man bolted through the open doorway and disappeared, leaving only the echo of his black, rubber-soled tennis shoes squishing against the linoleum and bouncing off the walls of the hallway.

Ignoring the pain pounding in her head, Melody pushed away from the wall. For a moment, her off-balance equilibrium sent the world spinning.

The exit door at the end of the hall banged shut. She grimaced. He was escaping.

Forcing herself to move, Melody chased after the intruder. As founder and co-director of the youth center, she'd come in this morning expecting to get a little work done before heading to the police station to start her shift. She hadn't been prepared for a smackdown and footrace.

The blood surging through her brought the world into a sharp focus she didn't experience anywhere else in her life except on the job. It had been a while since she'd had to chase a perp. And never from the youth center.

This place was supposed to be safe, for the kids who sought help and for the volunteers who ran the center.

Out on the sidewalk, she searched for the trespasser. Sagebrush Boulevard was empty. There was no sign of a person dressed in black. At seven in the morning on a Tuesday, Sagebrush, Texas, was barely coming to life.

At the end of town, the spire of the white community church gleamed in the early morning May sunlight, like a beacon of hope. A stark contrast to the dark figure who'd assaulted her. She sent up a silent prayer of protection, for herself, for the youth center and for the citizens of Sagebrush.

A cynical voice in her head taunted, *Would God listen?*

As much as she hated to admit it, she didn't know. He certainly hadn't listened to her pleas when her marriage fell apart and her ex-husband abandoned her to go "find himself."

Holstering her weapon and pulling her tailored jacket closed, she retraced her steps and entered Sagebrush Youth Center's single-story brick building.

She stopped in her office doorway surveying the scene. Irritation raced through her. The place had been ransacked. The filing cabinet had been emptied, the files strewn all over. The pictures of her family had been knocked off the desk.

Her heart squeezed tight at the sight of her sister's face smiling up at her from one of the images. Her arm was slung over her then twelve-year-old son's shoulders. A time when they'd been happy. Alive.

Forcing back the sadness, she continued her perusal. Books ranging from popular fiction to nonfiction teenage psychology had been pulled down from the shelves and lay haphazardly on the floor. The open desk drawers appeared to have been rifled through.

A cardboard box lay toppled upside down, the contents spilling out. Her nephew's name was written across the side in big bold letters. She didn't need a paper inventory of the box. She had the contents memorized. The files full of witness testimonies, and Daniel's effects at the time of his death had been in that box. All that was left of a life cut too short.

A sense of violation cramped her chest. She was

used to investigating this sort of vandalism, not being the victim herself.

She was no one's victim. Her fist clenched.

She would find the person who broke in, and discover what they'd wanted. She tapped her foot, impatient to get in there and see what had been taken.

But protocol had to be followed.

Yanking her cell phone out of the backpack-style purse she always carried, she dialed the Sagebrush police dispatch non-emergency number.

"Sagebrush Police Department." Cathy Rodriquez, the day dispatch operator answered in her no-nonsense tone.

"Cathy, it's Detective Zachary. I need a crime-scene unit at the youth center. My office has been broken into."

"Were you hurt, Melody?"

"I'm fine." She wouldn't mention the throbbing headache. The last thing she needed was to be coddled. She'd find some pain reliever in the nurse's station once things settled down. "I surprised the intruder, but he got away."

"I'll let the higher ups know what's going on."

"Thanks, I appreciate it." Melody hung up and leaned against the doorjamb. Despite the doubts that at times tried to rob her of faith, she sent up a silent prayer of thanksgiving that the intruder hadn't been armed. This scene could have gone down very differently.

The sound of footsteps sent a fresh wave of adrenaline pumping through her veins. She whipped around, her hand going to her weapon.

"Melody?"

At the sight of her volunteer co-director and fellow Sagebrush police officer coming toward her, she let out a tense breath. Jim Wheaton always wore the navy blue Sagebrush Police Department uniform, claiming the visual reminder of authority helped keep the kids in line.

Nearing fifty and single, Jim spent more time at the center, whether he was on duty or off, than any other volunteer. He claimed it was because he didn't trust the teens not to cause trouble, but Melody suspected he liked the company even if he wouldn't admit it.

"You're here early again today," he said, coming to a halt a few paces away.

She usually stopped by Arianna's Diner for a pastry and cup of coffee before heading to the station, but ever since her nephew's grave had been desecrated last month, she hadn't had much of an appetite. Keeping herself occupied gave her less time to think.

Besides, the diner was closed now that the owner, Arianna Munson, had been killed after being linked to the crime lord, known only by the police as The Boss.

For the past several years, a crime wave had terrorized the citizens of Sagebrush. The mastermind behind the crime syndicate was a faceless, nameless entity that even the thugs who worked for The Boss feared.

This man was at the top of the police department's most-wanted list. Especially after the crime syndicate kidnapped Rio, the three-year-old German shepherd partner of the K-9 unit's captain. The whole department was on high alert looking for the canine.

She could have used a dog like Rio today. Maybe she should look into getting a K-9 partner for the center. A nice big dog with sharp teeth. "Hey, Jim. I interrupted someone breaking into my office. They made a mess of things."

His gray eyes clouded with concern. "You okay?"

"Just a bruised ego." And a knock to the noggin. Nothing she couldn't handle.

"Let me see." He tried to push past her.

Her arm shot out and blocked him from entering. "I'm waiting for the CSU team."

He scowled. "It was probably a kid looking for some loose change."

Melody shook her head. "Guy was too big, too strong to be a teen."

"You get a look at his face?"

"I didn't."

The center's front door opened. A small dog with his black nose pressed to the ground entered. Melody recognized the beagle as Sherlock, part of the K-9 unit. He wore a vest with the Sagebrush Police Department emblem over his light brown and white coat. A harness attached to a leash led to the handsome man at the other end. Melody blinked.

What were Narcotics Detective Parker Adams and his K-9 partner doing here?

The dog was adorable with his floppy ears and big round eyes.

Much like his handler.

She didn't know the narcotics detective well. She worked for the homicide division, mostly cold cases, while he was part of the Sagebrush's elite K-9 unit. Their paths hadn't crossed much, though she'd noticed him at the police station.

Hard not to take notice when he filled out his uniform nicely with broad shoulders and trim waist. She liked the way he wore his dark hair swept back from his forehead and his warm brown eyes appeared kind whenever he glanced her way.

He wasn't much taller than she, but he had a commanding presence that she found disconcerting. Though why, she wasn't sure. Growing up the daughter of a cop, there were few people who intimidated her. But something about the handsome officer made her pay attention.

Two crime-scene-unit techs filed in behind Parker carrying in their equipment. Considering the police station was at the other end of the block, Melody wasn't surprised how quickly they'd arrived. She just didn't understand why Parker had responded to her call.

The CSU team approached, each member wearing a dark blue Sagebrush Police Department windbreaker. Parker hung back, letting his dog sniff the floor, the thresholds of the closed classroom doors, the lockers.

"Hey, Melody," said Rose Bigsby, a stocky woman with short blond curls and wire-rimmed glasses perched on her short nose. "Report came in that you had a break-in."

Melody gestured to the open door of her office. "In there."

Clay Gregson nodded to Jim and then smiled shyly at Melody as he moved past her to enter her office. The tall and lean CSU technician wasn't much on small talk, something the officers of SPD were used to. Rose, on the other hand, made up for her partner's lack of conversation just fine. Rose followed him in and started the process of looking for anything that would lead them to ID the intruder.

"Any idea who broke in?" Parker asked as he and his dog approached. "What was he looking for?"

Melody frowned. "I have no idea who the guy was or what he was after."

"What are you doing here, Adams?" Jim asked.

"Captain McNeal thought it'd be a good idea for Sherlock here to check out the center," Parker replied evenly. "Considering."

Her defenses stirred. "Considering what?"

He met her gaze. His dark eyes intense, probing. "The rumors of drugs being dealt out of here."

Her hackles rose like the feathers of a peacock on high alert. She'd been battling that particular thread of gossip since the center opened. She routinely searched the building and kept a close eye on the kids. She was certain there were no drugs on the premises. "We have a strict no-drugs policy. Any offenders will be prosecuted to the full extent of the law."

Parker shrugged. "Then there's nothing to worry about. Sherlock shouldn't find anything. He's got the best nose in the state, and it's never wrong."

"I've got to go to the station," Jim said abruptly and headed for the exit.

Watching him hustle out the door, Melody frowned. He'd just arrived. She shrugged off her coworker's strange behavior. Even though she was fond of Jim, she'd long ago decided she would never figure out the male species.

Or teenagers. Starting the youth center had been her attempt to help the kids of Sagebrush so they wouldn't end up like her nephew. At sixteen, Daniel had gotten mixed up with drugs, dealing and using, by all accounts. He'd ended up dead because of it. During a standoff with the police, he'd been wounded in the leg by Captain Slade McNeal and then shot in the heart by an unknown sniper. The assassin was never caught.

Saving other teens from Daniel's fate had become her mission in life.

However, that didn't mean she understood the teens or their thought processes. Thankfully, there were tons of books on the subject. If she could prevent even one teen from ending up addicted to drugs like Daniel, she'd feel she succeeded.

Her gaze strayed back to the mess in her office. Rose knelt beside the lamp and dusted black powder over the surface. The flash of a camera momentarily brightened the room as Clay photographed the crime scene.

What had the intruder been looking for?

"Did you get a look at the perp?" Parker asked, drawing her attention.

"No, he wore a ski mask."

"With blacked-out eyes?"

Surprise washed through her. "Yes. Very freaky. How did you know?"

"We've had a run-in with a guy wearing a ski mask and some kind of eyewear that blacks out the whites of his eyes. Did he take anything?"

Absorbing that information, she turned her gaze once again to the box labeled with her nephew's name. Would she find something missing? Did the vandalism to her office have anything to do with last month's desecration of Daniel's grave? A lump of anxiety lodged in her chest.

It had been five years since Daniel's death. Five years of searching for answers and coming up empty. What had recently changed to make someone dig into the past? And Daniel's grave?

The questions intensified the headache pounding at her temples. She didn't believe in coincidence. Daniel's grave, now her office. Were the two events connected? Maybe it was time to re-question some of Daniel's old buddies. Someone had to know something useful.

Her heart squeezed. Five years wasn't nearly long enough to have healed some wounds, though.

Realizing Parker was waiting for her to respond, she said, "I only did a cursory look, but I didn't see anything obvious missing. Perp rifled through all my files, drawers and books. Seemed to be searching for something."

"Interesting." He seemed to be thinking about something. "I wonder if this was the same guy who searched the station last night."

"What?" She hadn't heard about that.

"Someone searched the station house, concentrating mostly on the K-9 unit and Captain McNeal's office."

"Do you have any idea why? What were they looking for?"

His expression turned cagey. "We think it has something to do with the crime syndicate plaguing Sagebrush. But the station house wasn't broken into per se. The culprit came from within."

Surprised, she widened her eyes. "You think a fellow officer is working for the crime syndicate?"

"That's one theory. Though I can't help but wonder if the two incidents somehow connect to Captain McNeal's missing dog, Rio."

"Last month, K-9 Officer Jackson Worth spotted a masked man clad in black who was walking a dog matching Rio's description. We also have a witness who saw someone dressed like you've described kill a man in cold blood."

A shiver of dread worked its way over Melody's

flesh. She was thankful the intruder had decided to just knock her down rather than kill her.

What was he searching for? And would he be back? Maybe this break-in had nothing to do with her nephew's grave. Or maybe it had everything to do with it.

She intended to find out, regardless of the danger.

At four that afternoon, Parker's captain summoned him to his office. He knocked lightly before opening the door.

Captain Slade McNeal sat at his desk. He held the file with Parker's notes from the day. "So tell me what you think about this break-in at the youth center."

Only four years older than Parker, Slade had slightly salted dark hair and a square jaw. Lines of stress bracketed his blue eyes.

Stepping fully into Slade's office, Parker said, "The perp who broke into the youth center matches Nicki Johnson's description of the man who killed Gunther Lamont last month. The CSU techs didn't find anything useful." Not that he expected them to. So far the ski-mask guy had been very careful. No prints, no clear description identifying him.

"Did Detective Zachary find anything missing?"

An image of the pretty dark-haired, blue-eyed woman rose in Parker's mind. He didn't know Melody well. She kept pretty much to herself and devoted most of her free time to the Sagebrush Youth Center. A supposed alternative to the drug scene for the teens of Sagebrush.

But Parker was dubious of any place where teens with drug habits gathered. Though he appreciated the intention behind the youth center, he just wasn't convinced any place was safe from the invading poison.

Rumor had it that too many kids were partying on the center grounds.

Nothing had ever come of the internal investigation their captain had initiated. But that didn't mean it wasn't happening, which was why Parker and Sherlock had headed over to the center when the news came in that there'd been a break-in. The crime syndicate overrunning Sagebrush had their hands in the drug trade and would no doubt see the youth center as a viable outlet for their product.

Painful memories of his younger brother raced unbidden to the forefront of his mind. A deep sadness welled. Followed quickly by the anger that always chased after thoughts of Ethan.

His brother had died from tainted drugs.

Forcing his own personal torment back to the dark recesses of his mind, he answered, "No, nothing missing. Perp ransacked her office. She has no idea what he was looking for."

Slade narrowed his blue eyes. "The code?"

Parker shrugged, baffled by this turn of events. "Maybe. But why her office? She's not a part of our unit."

"Assuming that the masked perpetrator and The Boss are the same person, he must be getting desperate," Slade said.

Parker's cell buzzed, and he checked the caller ID. He didn't recognize the number. "Parker Adams."

"You better hustle over to the youth center. There's a drug deal going down."

Parker recognized his confidential informant's gruff voice. "What kind of drugs?"

"How should I know?" The man hung up.

Parker blew out a frustrated breath. Sometimes Harry Trenton was a pain in the neck. But his intel was usually worth the stipend Parker regularly doled out to him. Which meant the youth center wasn't what it seemed. An image of the lovely Melody rose in Parker's mind. He sure hoped the pretty detective wasn't involved in dealing drugs. He didn't like the idea of arresting her. But he would in a heartbeat. Getting drugs off the street was his number-one priority.

Meeting Slade's questioning gaze, Parker said, "My CI claims there's a drug deal going down at the youth center."

Visible tension tightened Slade's jaw. "You didn't find any drugs this morning?"

"No. Sherlock followed a couple of false trails. Could have been trace amount brought in on a shoe." He hoped that were the case.

McNeal stroked his jaw. "Check it out. If you find something concrete, let me know. I'll have to inform Captain Drexel."

The captain of the homicide division and Melody's direct boss.

"Will do." Parker headed out the back door of the brick one-story building and jogged the short distance to the K-9 Training Center on the adjacent lot. Parker had dropped Sherlock off a little earlier with the training staff because, being a two-year-old beagle, the dog needed some time to run around and burn off his excess energy so he'd be ready to focus when needed.

Callie Peterson, the lead trainer for the Sagebrush

Special Operations K-9 Unit, greeted Parker with a smile and a wave as Parker approached the training yard.

"Sherlock's in kennel one," she called out as she worked with Justice, a good-looking bloodhound, and his handler, Austin Black.

"Hey, Parker," Austin called out.

Parker lifted his hand acknowledging his friend and fellow team member.

Continued training for all the dogs of the K-9 unit was mandatory and necessary to keep the dogs and their handlers fresh and working well together. Justice was an integral part of the unit, his specialty search and rescue. Thanks to Austin and Justice, seven-year-old Brady Billows had been found unscathed after two thugs working for The Boss nabbed the boy because he'd been a witness to the assault on Captain McNeal's father and Rio's kidnapping.

Now if they could only find the captain's beloved dog. Even a twenty-five-thousand-dollar reward offered by the captain's good friend, Dante Frears, hadn't yielded any results. Everyone was working hard to bring Rio home.

Going to the kennel door, Parker grabbed the nylon leash from the nearby hook. Sherlock's short legs kicked up dirt as he jumped at the door clearly wanting to be set free.

"Settle down, boy," Parker said softly as he opened the dog-run door.

Instantly, Sherlock sat, his tail thumping the ground, his big brown eyes staring at Parker.

Love for the little beagle filled Parker as he clipped

on the leash and led the dog toward his vehicle. "Come on, boy, we've got work to do."

With his lights flashing, Parker drove the few blocks to the youth center with Sherlock inside his special crate mounted in the back passenger area of the SUV. Parker glanced in the rearview mirror at Sherlock. Affection rushed to the surface. The dog was the closest thing to family Parker had in Sagebrush. His parents had moved to San Antonio not long after his kid brother's death.

The sharp pain of loss stabbed at him. Parker's life plan had changed that day. He vowed to keep the streets drug free. A tall order for just one person, but Parker figured for every drug dealer he put behind bars, more kids would have a chance to live.

He'd gone on to the local college, but instead of majoring in business as he'd planned, he'd majored in criminal justice. As soon as he'd graduated, he joined the police academy, setting his sights on becoming a narcotics detective. When he'd been offered the job to work with the K-9 unit, he jumped at the chance. Sherlock was the best drug-sniffing beagle in the whole state of Texas.

They both proudly wore the Sagebrush Police Department emblem.

Parker brought the official K-9 unit vehicle to a halt at the curb, climbed out and opened the back door for Sherlock. The beagle jumped out. Immediately, his nose went to the ground, sniffing for a trail to follow. Reining in the leash, Parker walked toward the front of the Sagebrush Youth Center.

A squeaking sound drew Parker's attention. An old man, dressed in ragged clothing, pushed a shopping cart full of his possessions down the sidewalk. Their gazes met. Surreptitiously, Harry, the confidential informant who'd called Parker, pointed one gnarled finger toward the rear of the building.

Without acknowledging the old man, Parker veered Sherlock away from the front steps and hurried toward the back of the building where a wire fence, erected to keep in stray balls from the basketball hoops, dug into the cement of an old parking lot. Voices echoed off the sides of the center.

"Look, you don't scare me."

Parker recognized Melody's voice. The words were spoken evenly enough but a faint tremor of fear underscored them.

"You should be scared, lady. You're all alone. We can do whatever we want with you."

The pretty detective was in trouble.

Chapter Two

Parker quickened his pace, anxious to help his co-worker before anything bad happened.

"Tell me what you know about Daniel," Melody insisted. "Why was his grave desecrated? What was he into before he died?"

This didn't sound like a drug deal. Parker rounded the corner. A rough-looking character brandishing a knife had Melody backed up against the brick wall.

His stomach muscles tightened. Concern spread through his chest.

Two other equally seedy-looking thugs stood nearby leering at her. Melody's hands were up in a placating way, but she seemed far from cowed. In fact, she looked downright impressive in her tailored pantsuit, crisp white blouse and black boots. Her dark hair was gathered up at the nape of her neck by a gold clip. Truth was, he'd never seen her appear more collected.

She stared at her assailant with hard blue eyes and pressed her questions. "Was Daniel dealing drugs? You were his friend back then, so you have to know something. What was he doing in the woods the night he died?"

"I'm not telling you nothing," the knife-wielding guy said. To emphasize his point, he stepped closer and pressed the knife to her throat. Melody didn't flinch.

Either the woman was incredibly brave or had a death wish. Parker wasn't going to wait to find out which. He put his hand on the Glock at his side and stepped inside the fence. "Sagebrush PD. Drop your weapon. Back away from the officer."

The two thugs immediately bolted as if their feet had been lit on fire. They ran past Parker and disappeared around the corner of the building. Sherlock barked and pulled at his leash, wanting to give chase. The hoodlum with the knife backed up a step but didn't lower his weapon.

Now that Parker got a better look at him, he realized he knew the young man—Zane Peabody. He'd locked him up a couple of times on drug-possession charges.

Sherlock continued to bark and strain at his leash. He pawed the ground, showing signs of aggression reserved for when he was on the scent of drugs. Parker didn't doubt Sherlock smelled some cocaine or weed or something else illicit on the younger man. Zane was a user. Parker had come here to bust a junkie and his dealer. But that wasn't the situation here. Right now Parker's concern was to ensure his fellow officer's safety.

"Don't be stupid, man," Parker said. "Drop the knife."

Melody scowled at Parker. Then turned back to her assailant. "Zane, come on, talk to me. You guys were friends. Doesn't that mean anything to you?"

Zane wiped at his nose with his free hand. "He's gone. You can't help him now."

"I can find out who killed him," she said.

Parker inched closer, keeping Sherlock at his heels.

Zane backed up more. His gaze darted back and forth between Melody and Parker and then dropped to Sherlock. "If I talk to you I'm as good as dead. Just like Daniel."

"I can protect you," Melody insisted, taking a step forward.

Zane shook his head. "You can't protect me." Fear twisted his features. "The Boss owns these streets. He'll know. He knows everything." He backed up even more. "You better watch out, lady. Asking questions could get you killed." Then he ran.

His words hung in the air. A warning. A threat.

Every protective instinct Parker possessed came to life.

But one look at Melody's determined face made Parker's stomach drop to the heels of his black steel-toed leather uniform boots. The cold-case detective wasn't going to back down, even if that meant putting her life in the crosshairs of the mysterious and brutal crime syndicate.

"Thanks a lot," Melody groused as they watched Zane disappear around the corner. "You scared him off."

Figures she'd go on the attack. He'd heard that she was a tough lady. She'd have to be to deal with teens as much as she did.

"I saved your life," Parker said, falling into step with her as she marched toward a flight of stairs leading to the basement door of the youth center. Sherlock trotted alongside of him, his black nose close to the ground.

"I had it handled."

And he could sing like Sinatra. Not. "That situation could have turned bad in a heartbeat."

She stopped at the top of the stairs and faced him. Her bright blue eyes flashed with indignation. "I wasn't in trouble. And I don't need a white knight to save me. Zane wouldn't have hurt me. He'd been a friend of my nephew's."

Sherlock lay down on the cement, with his head on his paws. Clearly the dog didn't smell anything worth tracking.

"Familiarity breeds compliancy," Parker commented.

She grimaced. "Cute."

"What do you mean 'had been a friend?'"

Sorrow darkened her expression. "My nephew was Daniel Jones."

A sad case. A cold case. Or was it? Parker had seen the damage done to Daniel Jones's casket last month when it had been forced open and searched. "I hadn't realized you two were related." Empathy wove its way through him. "I'm sorry for your loss."

She nodded, acknowledging his sentiment. "Was there a reason you showed up?"

"I received a tip a drug deal was going down." He braced himself for her reaction.

Her mouth pressed in a firm line as annoyance darkened her eyes. For a long moment she stared at him. "What will it take to convince you the center is legit?" she finally asked.

Good question. One he didn't have an answer for. There was no reason not to believe the pretty detective was all she seemed. Hardworking, dedicated and professional.

Maybe he was letting his own issues cloud his judgment. But that didn't explain why she had a known drug user on the youth center's property. "What was Zane doing here? And why were you asking him about your nephew?"

Melody sighed and struggled to put her thought process into words. "I reached out to him. I admit it was a long shot, but it occurred to me since Daniel's grave had been defiled last month that maybe the break-in had something to do with his case. Since I have the files and evidence from that night in my office, it made sense."

She sighed and leaned against the railing. "I was hoping Zane would have remembered something or would say something to help me figure out what happened and why Daniel's grave had been tampered with after all this time." Instead she was left with more unanswered questions.

"I'm sure it must be hard not knowing who killed your nephew." Sympathy tinged Parker's voice.

"It is." Stinging sadness swept through her like a cold wind. "It shouldn't have happened. If only something like the youth center had been around when Daniel had been alive, maybe he wouldn't have gotten mixed up in drugs. Maybe he wouldn't have been in the Lost Woods that night."

"I was there the night Daniel Jones was killed," Parker confessed quietly.

She sucked in a sharp breath. She knew that from the reports, but his statement hadn't been any different than the other officers'. A burst of hope shot through her. Maybe he remembered something he hadn't put in his report. Would he have the answers she sought? "Tell me what you remember. What did you see?"

"Sherlock was on the trail of a scent, leading us

through the woods." Hearing his name, the dog rose to his feet, tail wagging, his big brown eyes on Melody. Parker adjusted his grip on the leash. "We found Daniel amped up on drugs and waving a gun around."

Melody tried to picture her nephew out of his mind and out of control, but the only images that came to her were of the quiet kid who always seemed slightly sad. Her heart ached for him.

"Daniel shot at the captain."

She winced. "I'd read that in the reports."

"Captain McNeal put a bullet in the kid's thigh as a means to stop him."

It had been the right move, considering he was firing on the police. What had he been thinking?

"I know the reports said no one saw the shooter. But can you remember anything that might ID him?" Hope swelled, anticipation surged. She wanted to find and arrest the man who'd pulled the trigger.

"No. I never saw him."

Disappointment flooded her veins.

"It happened so fast. Whoever fired was good. We scoured the woods for shell casings. The sniper left nothing behind except the bullet that killed Daniel."

"And there were no prints on the .308 caliber bullet," Melody stated flatly, adding to Parker's assessment that the gunman had been careful.

He shook his head. "Unfortunately not."

Melody's fingers curled. Whoever had done the deed thought they'd gotten away with it, but she wouldn't give up looking for the shooter, or finding out why Daniel was in those woods that night. "I've been working his case since I came on board. I wasn't in Sagebrush at the time. I was a detective for the Austin P.D. But after that night…" She swallowed.

Parker touched her hand. The warmth of his skin spread through her, chasing the cold away.

"Your sister, Sierra Jones, died that night, as well," he recalled gently.

Sierra. A wrenching pain gripped Melody as it did every time she thought about her older sister. "The ME ruled Sierra's death a suicide. She'd purposely over-dosed on sleeping pills."

It was still so hard to accept. Her sister had been so full of life, so fiery.

"What about Daniel's father?"

Melody shook her head. "Sierra would never say who he was."

"She didn't know or just didn't want to tell you?"

"I think she knew." It still hurt that her sister wouldn't confide in her. Melody consoled herself with the fact that they were nine years apart in age.

Compassion darkened his brown eyes. "I can't imag-ine losing both of them in the same night."

"It was devastating. For both my mother and me." As far as Melody was concerned, whoever killed Daniel was just as responsible for driving Sierra to end her life.

His gaze took on a faraway look. "When my brother died I remember thinking how cruel life could be some-times. How senseless."

Empathy twirled in her chest. He'd lost someone, too. "How did he die?"

His gaze sharpened. "Drugs."

Her heart sank. "Oh, no. Was he an addict?"

"No. He was fourteen and experimenting. The kids

he was hanging with were on the edgy side, not overly bad kids but…it only took one time."

She sucked in a sharp breath. "One time?"

"Yes." Bitterness laced his tone. "He'd taken a hit of ecstasy that was bulked up with a lethal dose of MCPP, a pesticide."

She reached out to take his hand, the warm contact comforting. "I'm so sorry."

She didn't know what else to say. His comment about the senselessness of life echoed in her head. She wanted to refute his words, tell him that with God, everything made sense, everything had a purpose, but how could she say that in the face of his brother's pointless and painful death?

Deep inside her, restless doubts stirred.

Lord, increase my faith, her heart whispered as it did every time uncertainty reared its ugly head.

Parker's hand slid over hers, the pressure firm as if he needed to hold on. "So you can see why even the mere hint of drugs sets me off."

"I do understand. I feel the same way. I started the center to honor Daniel's memory. But my hope is to give kids a chance to find happiness without getting high," Melody explained. She had to make him see the importance of the youth center. "We've done good work here. My vision has always been to keep these kids off the street and out of trouble."

"I'm sure your sister would be proud of you," Parker said.

She appreciated his saying so. Now if only he stopped thinking the worst of the center… Maybe if he became more familiar with the center and the teens, he'd see that the rumors about drugs here were unfounded. That they *were* making a difference. "Why don't you and Sherlock come in? The teens are starting to arrive, now that school has let out for the day. Take a look around. Meet the teens. See for yourself that the rumors are untrue."

He seemed to consider her offer and then nodded. "Sounds like a plan."

She led them inside the basement entrance. "When we took over the building, we renovated and turned the basement into a gym. There's a full-size basketball court in here," she said, pushing open the double metal doors to the gym on the right. Several teenage boys were shooting hoops. "Real hardwood floors and regulation-height baskets."

"That must have cost a pretty penny," Parker said as he pressed close to look through the open doorway.

The scent of his aftershave teased her senses. Spicy and tangy, like cinnamon and clove. She breathed in deep, liking the smell. Liking him.

Despite saying earlier she could handle Zane, there'd been a moment or two where she'd experienced qualms about the wisdom of questioning him alone. Even though she hadn't obtained the answers she was looking for, she was grateful Parker had arrived when he did. She'd known the minute Zane had opened his mouth, he was high on some drug. Who knows what he would have done.

Contrition churned in her tummy. "I owe you an apology and a thank-you."

Amusement danced in his dark eyes. "Okay, I'm listening."

He wasn't going to make this easy for her. Served her right.

"I shouldn't have snapped at you earlier," she said.

"I know you were only doing your job. I appreciate that you came to my aid."

"You're welcome. And forgiven."

She gave him a grateful smile. She led them out of the gym and down the hall. The beagle's nose was to the ground as he walked a crooked path at the end of his leash.

"The center used to be an office building," she explained. She stopped in front of a set of gender-marked doors. "We have two full locker rooms down here as well, complete with showers."

Sherlock pawed at the door to the boy's locker room. "Mind if we go in?" Parker asked.

"Sure."

They disappeared through the door. A few moments later they re-emerged. Parker's expression had turned pensive. The dog sniffed her boot.

She stepped away. "Everything okay?"

He shrugged. "Not sure. Sherlock lost whatever had him going."

Melody's stomach muscles squeezed. She had a strict policy against any and all contraband. Any violators would be arrested. If one of the teens had brought drugs into the center, it would only provide more fuel to the rumors circulating about the center. And give Parker more reason to be suspicious of her and the work they did.

"How did you come up with the funds for the center?" he asked.

She started them walking again. "Several patrons gave the center's initial start-up money. The Athertons, Dante Frears, Mayor Hobbs and several other business owners. We hold an annual fund-raiser in the fall for the community and usually raise our operating expenses for most of the year. There are two paid staff members and the rest volunteer their time, so the overhead is manageable."

They took the stairs to the main level. Her office was at the far end near the front door. "This floor has all the classrooms. Jim…you know Officer Jim Wheaton, right?"

Parker nodded. "Yes. I know Jim."

"He teaches woodworking classes. There are also cooking classes and craft classes. We have a game and TV room with all the latest electronic gaming systems. The local high school basketball coach holds clinics on the weekend as well as supervising open gym time." She took a breath. "A local nurse gives a free basic health-care class and a couple of women from the Sagebrush Christian Church lead a teen Bible study twice a week. On Sunday evenings, the youth pastor holds a teen worship night."

"Impressive."

Sherlock started pulling at his leash. Melody raised an eyebrow.

"What is it, boy?" Parker asked and let the leash drop. Sherlock took off with his nose to the ground. He headed straight for the bank of lockers situated against the wall between two classrooms. He started pawing and jumping at the last locker on the left.

Parker's expression darkened. "Can you open this locker?"

She grimaced and gestured to the combination lock hanging from the lock mechanism. "The key to the lock has been missing for…oh, at least six months. And no one seems to know the combination. I keep meaning to have the locksmith come out to rekey it, but haven't. There's nothing in there."

She hoped. But watching the way Sherlock was attacking the locker, a lump of dread dropped to the pit of her tummy. It occurred to her Sherlock hadn't smelled anything in the locker this morning so whatever had him agitated now had been placed in it recently. Not good. Not good at all.

The door next to the lockers pushed open and Jim Wheaton walked out. The heavyset officer's gray eyes narrowed on the dog. "What's going on?"

Beside her, Melody felt Parker stiffen. "Sherlock smells something," Parker said in a neutral tone that belied his physical posture.

"We need to get in this locker," she said, her voice tight with anger.

Jim frowned. "Why? Nobody uses it. Hasn't for months."

Several teens crowded around Jim in the doorway.

Melody's fingers curled with anxiety. "Can you break it open, please?"

Jim sighed heavily. "Yeah. Let me get something." He turned and groused, "Out of my way."

The teens scattered, some stepping into the hall, others moving back into the class.

Jim disappeared back inside the room and reappeared a moment later with a pair of bolt cutters, which he used to cut the lock. The locker door swung open.

Melody gasped. "Oh, no."

She stared at the pile of baggies filled with white powder and recoiled as if a rattlesnake was about to strike.

Someone had a stash of cocaine in the locker. Shock

punched her in the gut. Drugs in the youth center. This was her worst nightmare.

She met Parker's gaze. The accusation in his eyes stung worse than a snake's bite ever could. Did he actually think she had something to do with this?

"I'm shutting you down," he said, his eyes cold, his voice hard. "As of today, this place is off-limits."

Chapter Three

"You don't have the authority to do that," Melody protested.

"I'll get it." Tension tightened Parker's jaw as he stared at the drugs sitting on the shelf in the locker. It figured the youth center would be too good to be true. Guess the rumor mill was correct.

Was Melody dealing drugs out of the center? Disappointment flooded his system, yet he had a hard time reconciling those thoughts with the woman standing next to him. The shock in her eyes, the distress on her face couldn't be an act. Could it?

If she were guilty of dealing drugs through the center, she'd have thought up some excuse to refuse opening the locker. But there'd been no excuses, no hesitation.

He'd give her the benefit of the doubt. For now.

Sherlock jumped up, the nails of his paws scratching the metal locker, then the beagle let out a series of loud barks.

"Good job, boy," Parker said, absently withdrawing a small white towel from the leather pack around his waist. The towel had been scented with various drugs, which helped train the beagle to sniff out a wide variety of illegal substances and was the dog's reward for finding the correct stashes.

Distracted by the toy, Sherlock clamped his teeth around the end and tugged. Holding on to the other end, Parker played tug-of-war as a reward for a job well done.

"Who put this here?" Jim exclaimed, staring into the locker.

"That's what I'd like to know," Parker said, his gaze searching each person in the vicinity. "I want the locker and the bags printed."

Melody nodded her agreement. "Jim, would you call the station and have them send over Rose and Clay?"

Jim grunted his assent and disappeared back inside the classroom.

Pleased with her take-charge attitude, Parker shifted his attention to the kids huddled in a group watching the action unfold with wary expressions. "We'll need to get a court order to have the techs print everyone who's had access to the center."

Frowning, Melody followed his gaze. "Let's take it one step at a time, okay? See what prints the CSU team finds on the baggies and the locker and run them through IAFIS to see if any of the prints pop."

IAFIS—the FBI's Integrated Automatic Fingerprint Identification System—would only show those already in the system.

One way or another Parker would find whoever was using the center as a clearinghouse for their drugs. He wasn't going to let what happened to his brother happen to someone else.

He didn't think Melody was involved. At least he hoped she wasn't because he really liked her. Liked her determination and seeming dedication. She appeared sincere and genuine in her earnest attempt to effect some change in the lives of the kids in Sagebrush. His gaze skipped over her lush dark hair and her beautiful face. In all honesty, he liked a few other things about the detective, too. Sherlock jerked on the towel, bringing him back to his senses. The woman had a locker full of drugs. Now was not the time to be noticing her appeal. He shifted his focus to Sherlock. "Drop it."

The beagle let go of the towel and sat, his tail thumping softly against the floor. Parker put the toy back into his pack, glad for something to do so he could regain control of his emotions.

A young woman with long blond hair came down the hall. When she saw the locker and its contents, her face paled. "Oh, wow. Is that what I think it is?"

Melody took the woman's hand. "It is." To Parker, Melody said, "This is Ally Jensen, my assistant." She turned back to the young woman. "Do you have any idea how that got there or who's been using this locker?"

Ally shook her head. Her gaze darted to the group of kids and back to the locker. "No. No, I don't."

Parker narrowed his gaze on the girl. Could the drugs be hers? "Are you sure?"

Her green eyes shimmered with anxiety. "I'm sure."

The doors at the end of the long corridor opened and the crime-scene techs walked in.

"Called to the youth center twice in one day," Rose Bigsby said as she approached. She pushed up her wire-rimmed glasses with her free hand. "Did you have another break-in?"

Melody grimaced and looked as if she might be sick. "Not a break-in this time." She gestured to the drugs.

Clay whistled through his teeth.

Rose held up a staying hand. "Hold your horses, everyone. With all due respect to Sherlock's awesome track record for sniffing out the real stuff, we need to test it first, especially considering the whos and wherefores around here…" Her gaze slid to Melody. Parker could hear the unspoken thoughts about respecting coworkers. Rose set the duffel bag she carried on the ground and pulled on rubber gloves. "Everyone back up and give me room to work."

She opened her bag and withdrew a vial, then carefully opened a baggie, taking a tiny sample and putting it into the vial. The color the substance turned when mixed with the chemical agent in the vial would determine the type of drug.

"Cocaine," Rose announced, holding up the vial to reveal the purple-colored bottom.

Parker had figured as much. Rose and Clay set to work on fingerprinting the baggies and the locker.

Melody went to the group of kids and talked to them in a low voice. Frowning, Parker walked over.

"If any of you know anything about the drugs, I need you to tell me. You won't get in trouble for telling the truth," Melody said.

Parker's eyebrows rose. Was Melody really that naive to think these kids would reveal anything? If one of them was involved, they certainly wouldn't confess. And they *would* get in trouble.

Was she making this show of trying to find the culprit to throw suspicion off herself? His gut clenched.

What did he really know about her? She could very well be on the crime syndicate's payroll. Or her partner, Jim, could be. Parker needed to have both officers' finances looked at, see if either of them had money troubles, because that would be the only logical reason why someone like Melody, who was so smart and competent, would ever betray the oath she took to protect and serve.

As much as he hated the directions his thoughts were taking, he needed to report this to his boss.

And her boss.

They were supposed to be on the same team. If Melody had something to hide, then she'd have to pay the price. That thought didn't settle well with him at all.

Melody watched Parker step away to make a call. Tension coiled through her. She needed a plan of action. Get the kids to talk, and then track down the culprit. She would get to the bottom of this situation and prove to Parker the center wasn't being used for drug dealing. This was a one-time incident. It had to be. But the unease in her stomach taunted her.

"I saw John Riviera hanging around that locker," Joy Haversham said, drawing Melody's attention back to the question she'd asked the group of teens gathered in a nervous circle around her.

"Joy!" Tony Roberts made a slicing gesture across his throat.

Melody would be talking to John ASAP. If he were the culprit, then he would pay the price for his bad judgment and illegal activity.

"What? I did," Joy said. The fifteen-year-old girl twirled a brown curl around her finger. "He was standing there, leaning against the lockers last Thursday night."

"Doesn't mean those are John's drugs," Tony countered. "They could be anybody's. This place is easy to get into."

Melody arched an eyebrow. "Oh, really?"

Tony shrugged. At nearly eighteen, the kid was more man than boy. Had he been the one dressed in black this morning?

She eyed the width of his shoulders and decided no, he wasn't the man who'd rammed into her and knocked her against the wall. That man had had broad shoulders as hard as bricks. "What do you mean this place is easy to get into?"

A guilty, sheepish look crossed his face before he carefully masked it with insolence. "The windows in the locker room are never locked."

That was a surprise. Well, they would be from now on. The locker-room windows were at street level since the locker rooms were in the basement. She'd make sure Jim secured them every night.

Parker returned, pocketing his phone. He leveled her with an inscrutable look. "Our captains want us over at the station house as soon as Rose and Clay wrap things up."

"You two can go," Jim volunteered. "I'll stay and keep an eye on the place."

Parker shook his head. "They want to see you, as well."

A flash of annoyance shot through Jim's gray eyes. "I don't know anything about this. I'm just a volunteer."

Melody frowned. Technically, he was her co-director. "Jim, we'll both go. The center is both of our responsibility."

"Yeah, well, I keep telling you these kids are trouble," Jim groused. "Wouldn't surprise me if the captains decided the youth center was too much of a liability."

His words sent a shaft of apprehension sliding straight to her core. Jim knew how much this place meant to her. He and his late wife had taken Melody under their wing when she'd first arrived in town. Jim had tried to talk her out of opening the center.

But she wouldn't be dissuaded. And so he'd stepped up to be her co-director.

She suspected he'd volunteered to help her in order to protect her. But would Jim take this opportunity to help Parker convince the captains to close the youth center doors for good?

She sent up a silent plea for God's protection over the center. They were doing good work here. It would be a shame for everything they'd accomplished and all they could do in the future to end now. There were still so many kids who needed the help, the guidance the center offered. She'd made a promise to herself she'd do all she could to see that teens like Daniel were given every opportunity to choose a path other than drugs.

"I'll keep an eye on things," Ally assured Melody.

Melody wanted to trust Ally. The young woman had been a faithful volunteer from the beginning. They shared the bond of grief. Ally had been Daniel's girlfriend. After that horrible night, Ally had pulled her act together and had been clean ever since. At least Melody believed so. But at the moment, she wasn't sure what to think or who to trust. Someone with access to the center had stored his or her drug contraband in the locker.

"That's okay, Ally. I think it will be best if we close the center for the rest of the evening," Melody said, hating to cancel the classes and programs scheduled for the night. But Parker was right. The place had to be shut down. At least temporarily. "Would you mind posting a note on the doors?"

Ally sighed. "No problem."

Melody caught Parker's gaze. She detected a hint of approval mingled with the surprise in his brown eyes. Her hackles rose. She wasn't doing this for his sake. "Best to close now and sort this out than…"

Let you close us down for good. She let the unspoken words form in her mind.

He nodded as if he'd heard and understood.

Rose put all the bags of cocaine into a large evidence bag. "We'll take all this to the station. There's too much to print to do a good job here."

"I'm done," Clay added. "I got everything I could off the locker."

He and Rose gathered their things and exited the center. Jim followed closely behind.

Melody ushered the teens out the door. Hating to see the disappointment and confusion on the kids' faces, she said, "You all can come back tomorrow."

She could only hope and pray she'd be able to keep that promise. Would God come through for her? She'd find out soon.

"I'll give you a lift to the station," Parker said as he and Sherlock followed her while she locked up.

She shook her head. "I can manage to walk over there by myself."

"I've no doubt you can," Parker said. "But the captains are waiting."

"True." Realizing that it would be quicker to accept the offer of a ride, she followed Parker and Sherlock to the SPD vehicle.

The thick tension between her and Parker made her shoulder muscles tighten. Despite what Parker might think, she knew she'd done a good job with the youth center. And she'd do whatever it took to find who the drugs belonged to. She couldn't allow these kids to be in harm's way.

She rolled her shoulders, trying to release the tightness. Someone had breached the center with their poison.

After arriving at the station house, they went straight to the conference room. An oval table with leather chairs dominated the center. A floor-to-ceiling window stretched across one wall while the far wall was lined with shelves full of procedure books.

Jim was already there as were Rose and Clay. They'd filled the captains in on the situation. Captain Drexel stood by the window. A tall, African-American man in his late forties, he had his hands clasped behind his back as his dark eyes assessed them.

Captain McNeal sat at the table, his piercing blue eyes no less intense than his colleague's. He waved her and Parker in as Rose and Clay exited. "Any ideas who stashed the drugs?" he asked.

Melody shook her head and answered honestly. "No, sir. But the kids did give me a name of someone to question. Another boy that wasn't there tonight."

"It could belong to any one of those teens or even one of the other volunteers who come in," Jim stated. His gaze shifted from Melody to Parker and back to the captain.

The idea that one of the adult volunteers who came to the center to help the kids would be involved with drugs made Melody cringe. "I can't believe that."

"Can't? Or won't?" Parker's voice held a note of cynicism. Sherlock sat at his master's heel. He seemed to be staring at her with the same cynical look as his handler. Great. Now a dog was judging her, too.

"Both," she shot back, resenting his insinuation. She understood where his animosity stemmed from, but it didn't stop her from wishing he had some confidence in her. Though why she felt the need for his approval, she didn't know. She hardly knew the man. His opinion shouldn't matter in the least.

She turned her attention back to her captain because his opinion did matter. "Sir, I'll make sure it doesn't happen again."

"How do you propose to do that?" Drexel asked, stepping forward until his thighs hit the edge of the table. His sharp gaze speared through her.

Good question. She racked her brain for ideas. Her gaze landed on the bookshelves behind where Captain McNeal sat. "More education. More security measures."

"Like?" Drexel pressed.

Before she could answer, she felt something nudge her ankle. Sherlock had moved closer. His nose pushed at her pant leg, hiking the material up until he could lick her skin. His wet tongue was warm and rough. She lifted her eyes to meet Parker's.

Mild surprise reflected in his chocolate eyes. "He likes you." He gave a slight tug on the leash, bringing the dog back to heel.

An idea formed. "A formal demonstration of how easily drugs can be detected by the police would be a start."

Parker's eyes widened, then a grin tugged at the corners of his mouth and knocked some of the air out of Melody's lungs. Boy, talk about devastating.

"Sherlock and I could do that," he said.

"That takes care of the education part," McNeal conceded.

"We could search the kids as they come in," Jim suggested.

Melody's gaze snapped to Jim in disbelief, then to Captain Drexel. "We can't treat the kids like criminals. That will only drive them away. We'll keep a closer eye on things and manage the facility better."

With a thoughtful expression, Drexel exchanged a glance with McNeal. "Okay. For now. But there can't be a repeat of this incident."

"I'll do everything in my power to see that drugs never make their way through the doors of the teen center again."

"And I hope, Officer Zachary," Drexel intoned with a good dose of censure, "that you will think twice before confronting known drug addicts alone."

"Yes, sir," she assured him with a sidelong glance at Parker. Obviously, he'd informed them of the need to run off Zane and his buddies when he'd called the captain earlier.

"Drug addicts?" Jim interjected harshly. Clearly he was affronted that his partner would act without him. "What's this?"

She slid him a glance. "I was asking Zane Peabody questions about Daniel."

"Your nephew?" He shook his head. "You need to let that go."

Anger bubbled and threatened to explode like a geyser. This was an old argument. He'd made his position clear on her quest to find her nephew's murderer a long time ago. "I can't."

The empathy in Jim's gaze made it clear he thought she was working a lost cause. "You've done everything you can and still haven't been able to solve this crime. You need to accept the fact that you're not going to."

"You don't know that," she shot back, hurt by his lack of faith in her abilities. Captain Drexel had given her permission to work her nephew's case on her own time when she'd hired on with the department. "This case isn't unsolvable. No case is," she said. "It just takes time and effort. It's not a waste."

"Time and effort away from your responsibilities," Jim reminded her with a pointed look.

She gritted her teeth. Meeting her captain's arched eyebrows, she winced. The fact that she'd done some investigating today during working hours was something she was going to have to answer for, she knew, but letting Jim's negativism influence the captain wasn't something she planned to let happen.

"With the exception of today, I've only worked on Daniel's case after my shift."

Captain Drexel held up a hand. "I trust you'll use better judgment from now on."

The gentle chastisement hit its mark. "Yes, sir."

"Good. I understand you closed the youth center for the night," Drexel said.

"Yes, sir." Aware of Parker's gaze on her, she added for his benefit, "Just for the night. It seemed the prudent thing to do given the circumstances."

Her captain nodded. "Agreed. And it will give you time to do a thorough search of the facility to make sure there are no other drugs hidden on the premises."

"We can help with that," Parker spoke up.

Remembering how Sherlock acted at the boys' locker-room door, Melody decided having the super-sniffing dog's help would be a good idea. "We'd appreciate the help, Officer Adams."

If there were more stockpiles of drugs in the center, she wanted to know. Parker Adams and his dog, Sherlock, were the best means of uncovering any illegal substances. Even if spending time with the handsome detective and his police dog put her on edge.

"Parker, a word?" Slade said as Melody and Jim filed out of the office. Captain Drexel paced back to the window.

Parker nodded and waited until the others were out of earshot before saying, "Yes, boss?"

"What are your thoughts on the center?"

Aware of Drexel's scrutiny, he replied honestly, "Mixed. I know the center fills a need and provides a safe place for the teens. But finding those drugs leaves me with a bitter taste. Something's going on over there."

"Do you think Officer Zachary is involved?" Drexel asked, his deep voice reverberating through the room.

Remembering how upset she was when they opened the locker gave him hope she wasn't. "I don't think so. But I know not to come to any conclusions without more information."

"And Officer Wheaton?" Slade asked.

"Again, without evidence to the contrary, I have to believe both officers are on the up and up."

The two captains exchanged another look. Drexel gave a slight nod. Slade turned back to Parker. "Given the break-in this morning and now the drugs, I want you to stick close to the center. If something illegal is going on, and if either Officer Zachary or Officer Wheaton is involved, we want to know about it ASAP."

"Yes, sir."

With the captain's backing, he hoped she would accept his protection more easily. Though he had a feeling easy wasn't going to apply when it came to Melody Zachary. The detective seemed to have an independent streak as wide as the Rio Grande.

Parker started to leave but then turned back to ask, "Any word on Rio?"

Distress clouded Slade's blue eyes. "No. Not since Jackson spotted him last month in the Lost Woods."

Fellow K-9 officer Jackson Worth and his dog, Titan, a black Labrador, were the unit's explosive-detection team. They'd been working on another case when Jackson had seen Rio.

"Melody said the man who had broken into her office this morning was wearing a ski mask," Parker said. "From her description it's the same guy Jackson saw in the Lost Woods with that German shepherd."

Unfortunately, the pair had gotten away while the K-9 unit was in the midst of tracking them.

Slade's expression hardened. "All the more reason for you and Sherlock to become a presence at the youth center. If this guy in the black mask returns, I want him taken down."

"Roger that." Anticipation revved through Parker. This creep was a menace to society and needed to be brought to justice.

Chapter Four

Parker and Sherlock headed back to the center. He found Melody in one of the classrooms opening drawers and cupboards. The overhead lights hit her hair, making the strands gleam. Her slender back was to him. Sherlock gave a little yelp of greeting when he saw her.

She whipped around. Her gaze raked over him, then landed on Sherlock. She arched an eyebrow. "Does he smell something already?"

Parker chuckled. "No. He's saying hello to you."

She blinked. "Oh. Okay."

When she didn't move, he asked, "Would you like to pet him?"

She hesitated, and then tucked her hands behind her back. "No. I'm not much of a dog person."

"Did you have a bad experience with one?" That was usually the case. A badly behaved dog ruined the reputation of all dogs.

She shook her head. "No, it isn't that. I never had a dog growing up. I'm more of a cat person."

He'd never seen a cat earning its keep on the force. To each his own, though. "Shall we get to work?"

"It would be quicker to let your dog do his thing."

Parker took the special white towel from his leather waist pack and dangled it for Sherlock. The dog immediately latched on to one end. For a few minutes Parker played tug-of-war. Then he gave the command, "Drop it."

Sherlock released his end. Parker turned his back to the dog and stuffed the towel into his pack. Then releasing his hold on the leash, he pointed. "Find it."

With an excited bark, Sherlock took off, his nose to the ground.

Parker smiled at Melody's incredulous expression. "He is a smart dog, really."

She laughed softly, her expression relaxing into a smile that lit up her whole face. Their gazes locked. The pleasing sound of her laugh lifted in the air and wrapped around Parker, making him aware of her in a way he hadn't been before. She was a beautiful lady when she wasn't scowling at him or eyeing him like he was the enemy.

He cleared his throat, forcing away the attraction arcing between them. "Come on, let's see what he finds."

Sherlock had disappeared by the time they hit the hall. But his frantic barking led them to another classroom. They entered the woodworking room to find Jim holding a chair with the legs pointed at Sherlock in a self-defense posture.

Sherlock had his teeth bared as he barked angrily, but kept a distance.

"What did you do to him?" Parker demanded, grabbing the leash and looking Sherlock over for signs of injury.

"Me?" Jim sputtered. "I didn't do anything. I was in

here minding my own business when that mutt nearly
bit me."

Fisting his hands, Parker said, "He doesn't react like
this unless provoked."

"Jim, maybe you should go home." Melody rushed
to Jim's side. "We'll take care of the search."

"Fine." Jim set the chair down. "I've already searched
this room. It's clean."

"Great. Thank you." Melody smiled and put her hand
on his arm.

Jim gave her hand a pat before he skirted a wide
berth around Sherlock and Parker and escaped out the
door. As soon as he disappeared, Sherlock quit barking. His nose went to the ground and he started moving,
straining against the leash. Parker let go. Sherlock followed a scent straight to a cabinet. He pawed at the door.

Parker's adrenaline spiked. Melody walked over to
the cabinet and flung the doors open. Sherlock sniffed
the shelves of tools and lumps of wood, lost interest
and moved away.

Parker let out a breath mixed with relief and disappointment. He almost wished Sherlock found something in the room to implicate Wheaton. But Parker also
knew how devastating that would be to Melody. The
man was her partner, they'd worked together for four
years. Whatever his faults, she relied on him. Parker
had to respect that.

Over the next hour, they followed Sherlock through
the center. There were several false alerts, like at the
cabinet in the woodworking room.

"I suspect Sherlock's picking up on minute traces of
drugs that were left behind by whoever had stashed the
cocaine in the locker."

"We have to find out who it is," Melody said, her voice ringing with determination.

"Agreed."

When the culprit returned, Parker and Sherlock would be ready, even if it meant permanently shutting down the center and hurting Melody.

"Sherlock, attention!"

At his master's command, the little brown and white beagle jumped to his feet on the hardwood gymnasium floor of the Sagebrush Youth Center. His black nose lifted, his big brown eyes going on alert and his tail raised straight up.

From her place at the back of the room behind the sea of teens gathered to watch Sherlock and Parker's demonstration, Melody heard a couple of teenage girls sigh. A smile tugged at her mouth. The dog was adorable with his floppy ears and short little legs.

But Melody had a feeling, knowing the girls in question, they were most likely sighing and giggling over the dog's equally adorable handler, Parker Adams.

She didn't blame them.

For the past two days, he'd become a regular fixture in the center. Great as a deterrent to any illegal activities, which, any way you cut it, was a good thing for the kids. And, boy, Sherlock was a big hit.

But Parker's presence was wreaking havoc with her concentration.

The man could make even the most jaded of women look twice. With his brown hair swept away from his face, he exuded a warmth and vitality that drew people to him. His kind brown eyes and charming smile melted even the hardest of hearts.

Melody wasn't immune to the guy's appeal.

But getting involved with him in any way other than on a professional level wasn't going to happen.

She wasn't interested in a relationship with him or anyone else. After the disaster of her marriage, she still wasn't ready to try again. The last thing she needed was to have her heart trampled on. Once in a lifetime was enough. She had no intention of putting herself in a position where she could end up hurt and lonely and heartbroken again.

And Parker Adams had heartbreak written all over him.

She'd heard other women in the police department talk about him over the years. Parker was considered one of the town's most sought-after catches. The fact that he didn't date anyone more than a few times made Melody think he liked to play the field.

Being another name in some hunky guy's little black book wasn't one of her ambitions. She had enough on her plate without complicating things by getting emotionally involved.

"Detective Zachary is going to help me with a demonstration."

Hearing her name, Melody snapped back to attention and wheeled out the cart full of items she'd gathered from around the center. Parker held up his hand, indicating for her to stop a few feet away.

"Somewhere within one of the items in the cart is a towel doused with the scent of cocaine," Parker said. "Sherlock is going to locate the towel."

A ripple of unease ran through the teenagers sprawled on the floor watching. Melody's gaze searched the kids' faces, wondering if the anxiety she saw in several of their expressions meant they were carrying some type of the drug on them and were afraid the beagle would head their way.

"Detective Zachary, if you'd scatter the items…" Parker said with a smile.

Nodding, Melody pushed the cart around the basketball court and began dropping various different items on the gym floor. A backpack here, a shoe there, a purse over here, a jacket beneath the basketball hoop. She'd hidden the towel and then washed her hands as Parker had instructed. Though honestly, she hadn't smelled anything on the towel. Parker must have used pure cocaine because usually if cocaine had a scent it was of whatever the drug had been cut with.

When her cart was empty, she moved off to the side.

"Find it," Parker commanded.

Sherlock immediately turned his nose to the ground and moved toward the closest item, sniffed, then moved on. Holding on to the canvas leash attached to the dog's harness, Parker followed, allowing the dog a long lead.

Within moments, Sherlock started pawing and digging at the jacket beneath the basketball hoop. Melody chuckled softly. The dog was spot-on. She'd stuffed the towel down the arm of the jacket.

Parker picked up the coat, fished out the white hand towel and immediately allowed Sherlock to latch on to one end. For a moment they jostled over ownership of the towel. The kids laughed at the dog's obvious enjoyment of the game.

"Drop it," Parker commanded softly. Sherlock released the towel and sat, his tail thumping gently against the floor. Parker stuffed the towel into the black pack at his waist. He turned his attention to the group of kids. "Questions?"

Melody took that as her cue to pick up the items she'd spread out.

The kids knew, just as the dog had, that playtime was over. "Can he smell other drugs?" one of the teens called out.

Parker nodded. "Yes. He's been trained to detect cannabis, heroin, crack and crystal meth. Sherlock's sense of smell is a hundred thousand times stronger than a human's."

An appropriate murmur of awe swept through the room.

"How did you get him to detect the smell of dope? Did you drug him?" Tony Roberts asked with a smirk, as if he'd said something funny.

"No, stoned dogs aren't very helpful," Parker replied patiently. "Sherlock went through very intense and specialized training to become a narcotics officer. We have a training facility here in Sagebrush with some of the state's best trainers."

"Does he bite?" Misty Quinn asked.

The sixteen-year-old smiled coquettishly at Parker. Melody rolled her eyes as she picked up the last item. Misty flirted with every male she came in contact with, no matter his age. Melody was afraid her need for male attention would be the girl's downfall.

"No. Sherlock's job is to find drugs. Not hurt people."

Parker fielded several other questions from the kids, his patience never wavering. Melody liked that about him. Liked his calm demeanor and the way he focused on each kid, giving them his full attention when addressing them. The same way he was with her.

Every time they talked, he seemed to really listen, to really take an interest in her thoughts. It made her feel special. Which was ridiculous. There was nothing special about her. He treated everyone courteously.

Finally, it seemed the teens had run out of things to say. Melody set the full cart aside and came to stand beside Parker. "Okay, kids. Please thank Officer Adams and Sherlock for coming to talk to us today."

The teens clapped and started to disperse. Ally and Jim stood by the door with handouts inviting the kids to Friday night's free pizza and movie party.

"Thank you, Parker, that was great. Very informative," Melody said. "I think the kids really learned something."

"I'm glad you thought of this," he said, his gaze direct and friendly. "I should take Sherlock out for a break. Would you like to come with us?"

The thought of getting outside for a bit in the May sunshine sounded wonderful, almost as wonderful as spending more time with Parker. She hesitated. She wasn't sure spending time with him outside of the center was a good idea.

Her sister had always said sometimes you had to take chances even if they seemed risky. Otherwise, life was too boring.

"I'd like that," she finally answered, deciding there was no risk in going for a walk. "Would you mind if we found a latte to go while we're out?"

"Sounds good to me. We can stop at the Sagebrush Diner."

"Let me grab my purse from my office." She sure

could use the fresh air. After all, she'd been cooped up in her office at the station for the majority of the day, going over the case file for Captain McNeal's missing dog, Rio. A new set of eyes, he'd said when he'd handed her the box full of information.

Reading through the notes and witness statements made one thing clear to Melody. Her nephew's death and the kidnapping of the captain's dog had to be connected. A dog matching Rio's description had been spotted near the place where Daniel had died. That couldn't be a coincidence.

Parker and Sherlock followed her to the small office she used when working at the center. She unlocked the door and stepped inside. Her heel slid on a white sheet of paper lying on the carpet.

A strong hand gripped her elbow. "Steady there," Parker said.

The light pressure of his hand sent her senses racing. His other hand caught her around the waist. She leaned against him, inhaling his aftershave, a pleasing scent of spice and man.

She caught his gaze, the warmth in those dark depths made her feel light-headed.

Disconcerted by her reaction to him, she eased out of his hold and bent to pick up the paper. The side facing up was blank. But the other side had writing on it.

As the block letters registered, she released her hold on the sheet of paper as if she'd been zapped with electricity.

The roar of her heartbeat sounded like rapid-fire gunshots in her ears.

"Melody, what's wrong?"

The concern in Parker's voice wrapped around her,

taking the edge off the fear spiraling through her system. She pointed to the paper now laying faceup on the floor and managed to read the words aloud.

"Stop snooping where you don't belong or you'll end up in a grave next to your nephew."

A chill chased down Melody's spine. She couldn't believe this was happening. Standing in the doorway of her office, she watched as the crime-scene-unit tech, Rose, bagged the offending note.

Parker stood silent beside Melody with his hawklike eyes focused on her. Weighing her reaction.

She wrapped her arms around her middle to keep from trembling. She didn't want him to know how upset the note made her.

The ominous message kept flashing through her mind. Someone didn't like her digging into Daniel's murder. After five years of no leads, what had changed to make his murderer nervous now? And why unearth Daniel's grave? Did this have anything to do with the break-in to her office three days ago? To the drugs they'd discovered in the locker? So many questions with no ready answers. Her head felt like it might spin right off.

Rose finished up and left.

"You okay?" Parker asked.

The concern in his voice acted like a poker, making her straighten. She lowered her arms. She would not allow herself to show any weakness. Since she was a woman in a man's world, she had to be as tough, if not tougher, than her male counterparts. "Yes. I'm fine. Thank you."

He frowned. His warm brown eyes searched her face

as if trying to put together a puzzle. He'd find out a piece, maybe two, were missing. She tried to keep her expression neutral, but under his intense regard, found herself faltering, wanting to confide in him that, no, she wasn't okay. Hadn't been okay for many years.

It all harkened back to when her father walked out, leaving his two daughters to care for their distraught mother. Melody had lived in a constant state of hyperalertness since that fateful day. Always waiting for the next shoe to drop. And it had, many times over.

Each time leaving her with a gaping wound that took longer and longer to heal.

She dropped her gaze to the beagle at her feet. Sherlock sat at attention, his head up, his ears alert. Leave it to a dog to be the one to sense her anxiety. People, at least most of them, only saw what they wanted to see. If you said you were okay, they believed it.

"Let's go get that cup of coffee," Parker said, placing his hand at her elbow and sending an entirely different sort of shiver racing along her limbs.

Grateful to have a direction, she allowed him to lead her from the office. Beside them, Sherlock's nails clicked on the linoleum as they headed for the exit. Teens filled the classrooms along the corridor.

The smell of a baking confection drifted from the cooking class to her left. A group of teens learning to knit could be seen through the door of the class to her right. The muted whine of a jigsaw blade clearing cedar blocks came from the woodworking room.

Jim and his students regularly made birdhouses and other wood pieces to sell at the Saturday market.

Everyone was going about their business, unaware that Melody's life had been threatened. She sent up a silent prayer that this danger hanging over her head wouldn't touch any of the innocent kids or volunteers who came to the center. The last thing she wanted was for someone to get hurt because of her.

Outside, Melody blinked in the bright May sun. She shrugged off her backpack-style purse, pulled open the sides and rummaged around for her sunglasses. Her hand momentarily closed around the chunky watch at the bottom. Her reminder of the nephew and sister she'd lost.

Grief stabbed at her heart.

She blew out a breath. This happened every time she allowed herself to remember. She released the cheap trinket and snagged her glasses. She put the dark shades on and slipped the backpack into place.

Parker took a pair of mirrored glasses out of his pocket and slid them over his eyes. The effect gave him a dangerous edge.

She caught a glimpse of herself reflected in the mirrored lenses. She looked calm, collected. Chin up, shoulders squared. Professional. Just the way she wanted Parker to see her. She ignored the humid heat ratcheting up her body temperature and making her want to strip off her tailored jacket.

They made their way down Sagebrush Boulevard to the heart of the medium-size metropolis. The town was a buzz of activity on this late afternoon. A mixture of cowboy and trendy, up-and-coming affluence made the dress boutiques, businesses and restaurants appear not only quaint, but also appealing.

Melody had liked the town the moment she'd arrived, despite the tragic circumstances that brought her to Sagebrush from Austin. Though Sierra had moved to Sagebrush a few years after giving birth to Daniel, Melody had never visited. Regret that she hadn't known her older sister better before her suicide lay heavy on Melody's heart. If they'd been closer, maybe Sierra would have turned to Melody with her anguish instead of taking a lethal dose of sleeping pills.

As they arrived at the Sagebrush Diner, Parker paused near an outside table. "Do you mind if we sit outside?"

"Of course not." Even though Sherlock was a police dog, he might not be welcome inside.

Parker tied Sherlock to the leg of a chair.

Putting her hand on the glass door handle, Melody said, "What can I get you?"

In two strides, Parker reached her side and put his hand over hers. A tingling warmth shot up her arm and wrapped around her like a light blanket. "I'm buying. You sit. I'll order."

Retracting her hand, she shook her head. "Not necessary. This isn't a date."

Though the words were true, a small part of her wished this were a date. It had been so long since she'd gone on one, she wasn't sure she'd even remember how to act.

When he grinned, her heart thudded.

"I know. But humor me, okay? Let me be a gentleman and buy you a cup of joe."

Appreciating his chivalry, she relented. "All right. Thank you."

She told him her drink preference and then settled in a chair at the table. It had been an eternity since she'd allowed a man to buy her coffee. Ever since her failed marriage, she hadn't had the stomach to date. Not even for a cup of joe, as Parker put it.

She hadn't been enough to make Roger stay. What made her think she'd be enough for anyone else? Certainly not a man like Parker, who could have his pick of women. Going through the painful exercise of loving and losing again wasn't on her bucket list.

Not that she was thinking, in any way, that she and Parker…

Theirs was a professional relationship. Though it started a bit rocky, it had become more amenable the past few days. She could see why so many of the single females in town thought him a great catch. As long as she wasn't the one doing the catching.

The slight brush of something cold against her ankle startled her. She scooted her chair back, the metal legs scraping on the concrete sidewalk, creating an irritating noise. She bent slightly to see Sherlock had moved closer. He stared at her and she could almost see a caption over his head saying, "What?"

Parker pushed through the glass door with his hip, carrying a tray with both hands. He set the tray on the table and handed her a white porcelain mug full to the brim with frothy cappuccino. He set an equally foam-laden coffee drink in front of the empty chair across from her and then placed two plates with scones on the table.

He set a full bowl of water on the ground for Sherlock. "I wasn't sure if you'd like the lemon poppy seed or the blueberry, so I got both," he said as he took his seat.

"Thanks. Very thoughtful of you. I like both."

He handed her a fork. "Good. Me, too. We'll share, then."

She blinked. "Okay."

A little intimate for a professional relationship, but she could go with the flow.

"Who do you think wrote the note?"

Parker's question settled on her chest like a lead weight. "If I knew, I'd arrest them."

He nodded and forked a chunk of blueberry scone. "Best guess?"

Frustration tapped at her temple. "I don't have a guess."

"Daniel's murderer?"

"Well, obviously."

"Why obviously? Couldn't this be related to something else? Another case you're working on?"

"Maybe. Captain McNeal asked me to look at Rio's case file."

"Okay. That could be it. Though the whole department is searching for Rio, so why single you out?"

A ribbon of unease twisted through Melody. "Why, indeed."

Chapter Five

Parker gestured with his fork. "Seems like the threat could be coming from whomever left the drugs in the locker."

"True." Using more force than necessary to slice her fork into the scone, Melody tried to contain her frustration. "And like I've told you before—I don't know who the drugs belong to."

"But you have been asking around, right? You've talked to all the teens individually over the past few days."

She hadn't realized he'd noticed. She'd started her interviews with John Riviera, the teen seen hanging around the locker. He'd denied any knowledge of the drugs. As did all the kids. Not that she was surprised by their denials. Who in their right mind would confess without a very compelling reason? She sipped from her coffee. "The syntax of the note doesn't suggest a kid wrote it. It's too…formal."

"Good observation." He sat back, his broad shoulders canted slightly. "So if not a kid, then…there are plenty of adults going in and out of the center."

The thought that someone in a position of authority would abuse his or her power made her sick to her stomach. "You sound like Jim."

Her partner had been full of suspicions about everyone at the center lately, not just the kids.

Parker snorted. "I'm just saying, you never know what's really gone on with anyone. We all have a persona we want the world to see and it doesn't always reflect the actual nature of who we are."

"Too true." She used her public persona constantly to cover the heartache, the grief she worked hard to keep tapped down inside. Over the rim of her cup she watched him and wondered if he was really as kind and grounded as he appeared. What sort of person was Parker when he wasn't in uniform?

"What are your plans for this weekend?" she asked, steering the conversation away from the disturbing note and the many unanswered questions swirling around them.

"I'm heading to a classic car show over in Odessa on Sunday after church."

"So you're a car buff." And he went to church. Unaccountably that pleased her. It wasn't like she was a regular attendee. The few times she'd made it to the Sagebrush Christian Church, she'd sat in the back and didn't stay long enough to mingle when the service ended. To say she and God had a bit of a strained relationship was an understatement.

"Big time. I restored a Mustang Shelby GT 350 a few years ago. Now I'm working on a 1965 Sunbeam Tiger."

She could picture the white and blue Mustang. She'd seen it in the police station parking lot. Though she hadn't realized he owned it. "I don't know what a Sunbeam Tiger is."

"The Sunbeam Tiger was the first British-made car to win a Grand Prix race."

For the next half hour, Melody listened to Parker talk about his car. Hearing the excitement in his voice as he gave her the historic details of the car company made her smile, and his enthusiasm for cars was endearing. She wondered if he put that much passion in other areas of his life. She'd already witnessed his devotion to Sherlock. She doubted the beagle wanted for anything. Would Parker treat a woman with as much care and devotion? Was there a woman in his life? Someone who shared his love of cars and dogs?

She had no business wondering anything about Parker's love life seeing how she would never be a part of it. She forced back the questions as they cleared their empty mugs and plates and headed back to the youth center.

At the door to the center she stopped. "Thank you for the coffee."

He held the door open. "You're welcome."

Entering the center, she glanced back at him. "You've been here all day. Don't you have to be somewhere?"

He shook his head. "Nope. Sherlock and I will stick around until closing. Then we'll make sure you get home safely."

Surprised, she tucked in her chin. "You don't have to do that. I'm perfectly capable of seeing myself home."

"I know you are," he said, his voice pleasant, his expression neutral. "Still… Someone threatened your life today. I'm not taking any chances with your safety."

His concern was sweet, even if she knew it wasn't warranted. "As sweet as that is, I don't need protection."

He shrugged off her protest. "We're staying."

The adamant tone of his voice grated on her nerves. However, she doubted she'd change his mind. The man seemed to have a stubborn streak as wide as the state of Texas. "Fine. I'll be in my office."

Aware of him following her, she stalked to her office. Taking a deep breath, she hoped there wouldn't be any more surprises inside. All appeared fine as she entered.

She sat at her desk and turned her attention to the case file on Rio's disappearance. Lifting her gaze to Parker, who stood in the doorway, she said, "This case is so baffling. Why would someone steal Rio?"

He leaned against the doorjamb. "That's a question we've all been asking ourselves." He moved inside and closed the door. Sherlock lay down, his head resting on his paws, his eyes on her. "We received intel that Rio was taken to track something valuable in the Lost Woods."

She nodded. "Right." She looked down at the notes in the file. "Pauly Keevers, an informant, had provided that information. The police department has scoured those woods, though."

"True. However, we're still no further with our investigation."

"I can't imagine how hard this is on Captain McNeal and his son." Everyone knew how attached Captain McNeal's son had become to the German shepherd after the boy's mother died two years ago. A car bomb meant for Captain McNeal took his wife's life instead.

"It is hard." Parker looked down at Sherlock. "I don't

know what I'd do if anything happened to Sherlock." The dog's ears perked up at hearing his name.

Tenderness squeezed Melody's heart. She had no doubt Parker loved his K-9 partner very much. The dog was more than a tool to be used on the job. Sherlock was Parker's constant companion. A bond as close as any blood relation. All the K-9 unit dogs were beloved, and any loss stung as badly as if they were human. "You two work well together."

"We do. But it takes a lot of training." He gave her a wry smile. "For both of us."

She held his gaze, liking his humble admission. Liking him. Her heart thumped against her breastbone. She dropped her gaze to the file and forced her focus on the case and not on how handsome and appealing she found Parker. "How is Captain McNeal's father?"

When Rio was kidnapped, the thugs responsible had beaten Patrick McNeal senseless. He'd been in a coma for a month before regaining consciousness.

"Doing better. He's up and around, moving slow, though."

Some of the tension in her eased a bit at the news. "That's good to hear. I'm sure recovering from something so horrific would be hard. Especially for a man of his age." Her gaze snagged on a notation written in the margin of the report. "What is the code?"

When Parker didn't immediately answer, she glanced up. He stared at her with a curious mix of wariness and speculation.

"Is there something in that file about it?"

"A hand-written note," she said.

He strode across the office, rounded the desk and peered over her shoulder. He braced himself with one hand on the desk. His scent wrapped around her, making her acutely aware of his proximity. Her senses ignited. It took effort to point to the words scribbled in black ink and not let her hand shake with the effect of his nearness.

"We're not sure."

"You're working the case, too?"

"We all are."

That made sense. It was their beloved captain's partner missing, after all. She cocked her head and peered up at him. She could see the stubble of his beard on his strong jawline and the well-defined shape of his lips. His warm brown eyes met hers. She could spend all day staring into those chocolate-colored orbs. Worry that she was getting too close, too emotionally involved churned through her. She refocused on the topic. "Care to elaborate on what you do know?"

"We first heard about the code when Adrianna Munson, aka The Serpent, died." His voice dropped to a low tone. "Her dying words were, 'Cousin. Code. Danger.'"

Arianna had owned the posh diner in town, one that Sierra had sometimes worked at, which was why Melody had started frequenting the place before the diner shut down. Somehow going there every morning had given Melody a sense of connection to her sister.

The police recently discovered that Arianna was a middle-level manager in the crime syndicate invading Sagebrush. A fact Melody was sure Sierra hadn't known.

A few months ago, Arianna—The Serpent—had tried to kill Valerie Salgado, another K-9 officer, after Valerie had witnessed Arianna leaving the scene of a murder. Arianna had been killed in the process of taking her down. "Was Arianna's cousin involved?"

He straightened but didn't move away. "Nicki Johnson isn't involved with the syndicate. Arianna threw her under the bus by telling a syndicate lowlife named Derek Murke that Nicki had the code. Murke tried to kill Nicki to gain the code, but Nicki didn't have it. Officer Salgado and FBI Special Agent Lewis got to her in time. Murke was arrested and taken into custody. He lawyered up and won't talk. So we have no idea what the code refers to."

"But it has something to do with the crime syndicate," Melody said, her mind working to connect the dots. She picked up a pen and fiddled with it to distract herself from Parker's closeness. His energy hummed through her like a low-voltage current. "If Rio was kidnapped to find something in the Lost Woods, maybe this code has something to do with whatever's in the woods."

"That's what we think. In an effort to protect the citizens of Sagebrush and hoping to expose the villains, Slade sent out a press release stating the K-9 unit was in possession of 'the code,' hoping it would make the crime syndicate back off. Too many people have died trying to obtain it."

"Did the ruse work?"

He hesitated a moment, his expression contemplative. She arched an eyebrow and twirled the pen again.

Seeming to have made a decision, he said, "We think that's why the police station was searched."

A sick feeling kicked up in the pit of her stomach. "Which supports the theory that the crime syndicate might have one of our own on its payroll."

"Unfortunately." He placed a hand on her shoulder. The pen froze. A hot spurt of molten lava erupted at the point of contact and spread through her. "That's why you have to be very discreet with your investigation."

She hated the idea that someone within their ranks would be working with the crime syndicate. Given that Captain McNeal had handed her the file and Parker had confided in her about the subterfuge, she guessed they didn't suspect her. Which was gratifying. And ratcheted up her determination to help bring Rio home.

A soft knock on the office door drew her attention. "Come in."

Ally Jensen stepped in. Her gaze widened when she saw Parker, her eyes clearly landing on his hand atop her shoulder. "I'm sorry. I didn't realize you were busy... I'll come back."

"No, stay," Parker said. He squeezed Melody's shoulder before moving away. "Come on, Sherlock, let's allow Melody to get some work done." At the door, he paused to say, "What time do you want to leave?"

Aware of Ally's curious glance, Melody said, "Seven."

He nodded and disappeared out the door with Sherlock trailing behind him.

"Are you and *him* going on a date?" Ally asked as soon as they were alone.

A blush worked its way up Melody's neck. "No, nothing like that." But the thought grabbed a hold of her imagination. She shoved it away. "I do not date people I work with," she stated firmly, for her own sake as much as for Ally's.

"Why not?"

"Relationships are messy and complicated enough

without adding the pressure of working together to it." Besides, once he decided to move on, as he'd inevitably do because that was what men did, it would make working and living in Sagebrush awkward. She liked her life uncomplicated and peaceful. Or as peaceful as death threats and unsolved murders could be.

"Sounds like an excuse if you ask me," Ally said.

Melody refused to acknowledge any truth in the younger woman's words. "So...what can I do for you, Ally?"

At seven, Parker returned to Melody's office. Her door was open and he stepped inside. Sherlock tugged at the leash wanting to go to her. Funny how much the beagle liked her. Though Parker had to admit there was much to like about the detective. Even though Sherlock's breed was affectionate by nature, the dog didn't seek out others, preferring to stick close or follow a scent. Drug training had made him wary. Or maybe one too many bad guys kept Sherlock suspicious. Maybe like owner, like dog. One relationship gone haywire and he ran for the hills anytime he started to fall for a woman.

Melody sat at her desk poring over what looked like an accounting ledger. Earlier today she'd had her hair clipped back in her usual sleek style. Now her dark tresses were loose and cascaded over her shoulders in a straight, silky sheet. He much preferred it down.

Her face was a study in concentration, her lids lowered slightly over her blue eyes, her mouth pursed just a bit. His gaze snagged on her lips. Lush and full and a pretty shade of natural pink. He'd never seen her wearing too much makeup. Just a light coating of mascara to darken her thick lashes.

She didn't try hard to impress the way some women did.

She didn't need to. She was impressive any way you looked at her. From her professionalism to her earnest desire to make a difference in the lives of the teens of Sagebrush.

He admired her poise under pressure. Though he'd seen the flash of fear in her eyes when she'd read that note this afternoon, she'd quickly pulled herself together. She wasn't about to let anyone get the better of her. Which he'd already seen in action the day she'd faced down Zane and a nasty-looking blade.

The woman had guts. And that was precisely why he wanted to escort her home. If she found herself in a dangerous situation, she wouldn't think twice about plunging in. There would be no retreat. He didn't want her to get hurt. Or…killed.

His need to protect her stemmed from professional courtesy. He couldn't allow there to be any other reason.

He cleared his throat.

Her gaze jerked up, her eyes widening a fraction. "Is it seven already?"

"Yep." Sherlock strained at his restraint when he heard her voice. Parker let go of the leash. The beagle trotted to her side and sat, staring at her.

Melody smiled softly, but didn't reach to pet him. "Hi, there, Sherlock."

Still leery. The best way for her to get over her fear of dogs was more exposure. Parker had no doubt Sherlock would wear her down and she'd end up loving the dog. Just as long as she didn't turn that tender emotion on him. "How soon do you want to leave?"

"Now's perfect." She tidied up her desk. "My car's out back."

"I know." He'd seen her driving the light green VW Beetle, so he knew which was hers. "I parked next to it when I arrived. Sherlock and I will follow you to your place."

They left the youth center and drove across town toward a residential apartment complex flanking the Sagebrush Shopping Center. She led him and Sherlock through the entryway and up two flights of stairs. The building was older with fraying carpets, but it appeared clean. Her apartment was at the end of the hall.

When they approached her apartment door, she froze. "Melody?"

With her key in hand, she pointed to the lock where there were scratches in the door and on the gold metal.

Parker reached for his weapon. Someone had tried to break into her apartment.

"This is getting to be a regular thing with you," Rose teased lightly as she finished up dusting Melody's apartment door for fingerprints.

"Not something I hope to get used to or want to continue," Melody replied. She hated the sense of violation that crept through her. Her door hadn't been breached, but the feeling of invasion still managed to squeeze her lungs tight.

"No doubt," Rose said, pushing her glasses up with the back of her gloved hand. "You should double bolt this door. Just in case."

"We'll get that done tonight," Parker stated.

Melody's eyebrows shot up. *Oh, really.* He was now making decisions for her?

The crime-scene technician left and Melody turned to look at Parker, ready to tell him to butt out but the words didn't come.

Shadows from the dully lit apartment-complex hallway deepened the contours of his face but couldn't hide his concern. Knowing he worried about her touched something deep inside and made her ire dissolve like ice on a hot sidewalk.

He stood a few paces back, holding Sherlock's leash while the dog sniffed the crack of apartment 4C. The dog was probably attracted to the smell of Mr. Hendrix's gourmet cooking. The widowed older gentleman routinely invited her over to share a meal he'd prepared. She suspected he liked having the company and purposely made larger quantities than needed for one person.

The apartment door across from her apartment opened. Ethan Ryling and his wife, Kenzie, stepped out. Tall with close-cropped hair, Ethan was a pharmacist at the local drugstore while Kenzie, petite with short red hair and a big smile, was a nurse at Sagebrush General Hospital. The couple had moved in not long after Melody. Though Melody didn't know them well, she'd found them pleasant on the occasions that they met in the hall and chatted.

Kenzie rushed to Melody's side and put a hand on her arm. "Is everything okay?"

Not wanting to spook the couple, yet knowing they had a right to know, she answered honestly, "Someone tried to break into my apartment today."

"I knew I should've called the police," Ethan said, his voice rife with self-recrimination. "When I came home at lunch earlier, I saw a grungy guy at your door. He saw me and made a big show of knocking and then high-tailed it out of here. I didn't think much of it at the time."

"Can you describe this guy?" Parker asked.

"Tall, scraggly hair to his shoulders. He wore ripped jeans and a T-shirt."

Melody met Parker's gaze. The speculation in his brown eyes made her think he'd also come to the conclusion that Zane Peabody had tried to break into her apartment. But why? Did the hoodlum know more than he was telling her? Had he been the one to slide that threatening note under her office door?

"Should we be worried?" Kenzie asked, her green eyes wide. "I mean, do you think it was random? Should we talk to the super about getting some kind of security for the building?"

"That's a good idea," Parker said as he stepped forward.

"Is your dog friendly?" Kenzie asked Parker.

"He is. His name's Sherlock."

Kenzie bent to pet the beagle. Melody wondered if the dog's coat was as soft as it looked. Someday she'd have to work up the courage to see. The dog sat patiently for a moment then walked away, his nose hovering above the ground.

Kenzie stood. "He's so cute."

Melody nodded her agreement. Sherlock, and Parker, were cute. Too cute for comfort. A fact she'd been trying hard to ignore the past few days but was failing miserably. Every time she looked at him her insides turned to mush. Not the best reaction to be having to her coworker.

The couple said goodbye and left.

Alone again with Parker and Sherlock, Melody debated inviting them inside. She couldn't remember what state she'd left the apartment in.

"We should go to the hardware store and get that extra dead bolt," Parker said, drawing her from her thoughts.

"I can do that tomorrow." She didn't need him to take care of her. She was capable of installing a dead bolt on her own.

"I'd rather you didn't wait," he stated, stepping closer. His gaze touched her face like a caress. "Your safety is important."

His words reverberated through her. He sounded like he really meant what he'd said.

Of course he did. He'd care about anyone whose life was in danger. He was a kind and compassionate man. An officer with fierce protective instincts. And she was being ridiculous to think otherwise.

If she were in Parker's shoes she'd be telling herself not to wait, but to get the second dead bolt tonight, too.

"Just don't get used to bossing me around, okay?" Though if she were honest with herself, it felt kind of good to have someone else call the shots.

He held up his hand in mock surrender. "I wouldn't dream of it."

Feeling contrite for snapping at him, she said, "Sorry. I'm used to being the one in charge."

"I'll bet your parents had their hands full with you as a kid."

She stiffened. He didn't know what she'd endured growing up. And now was not the time to enlighten him. "Let's go get that dead bolt."

Chapter Six

Parker followed Melody back to her apartment from the hardware store. As they entered her hallway, the most amazing smell hit him, making his stomach growl with hunger. Garlic and spices. Someone was cooking and it made him aware that he hadn't eaten dinner yet. Neither had Melody. He was about to ask her to dinner when the door to 4C opened and a big burly man stepped into their path, wearing a bright orange apron, smudged with red sauce, over his jeans and T-shirt.

"Ho there, Detective Zachary. How are you this evening?"

Melody stopped to smile at her neighbor. "I'm good, Mr. Hendrix. And you?"

"Good, good." Curiosity gleamed in his hazel eyes as he took in Parker and Sherlock. "Who's this?"

"This is a coworker, Parker Adams. Parker, my neighbor, Stan Hendrix."

Parker offered the man his hand. Stan's grip was firm but not crushing. He looked to be in his mid-sixties, average height and build, with a bushy white mustache and little hair on the top of his head. His girth spoke volumes of his cooking.

"Mr. Hendrix, someone tried to break into my apartment earlier this evening," Melody said.

Concern rippled across the older man's face. "That's not good."

"I wanted you to know so you'd be careful."

Parker appreciated her thoughtfulness toward her neighbor.

Sherlock sniffed at Mr. Hendrix's shoes, then his little pink tongue darted out to taste the top of his left loafer.

"Leave it," Parker admonished the beagle and tugged the dog back.

Mr. Hendrix chuckled. "Guess he likes my pasta sauce. I spilled a bit on the floor. Must have tagged my shoe."

"Mr. Hendrix is a chef by trade," Melody explained.

"Retired," Mr. Hendrix clarified. "Though I have been thinking about opening a new place. I heard that Arianna's Diner has been put on the market."

"I'm sure you'd have a successful restaurant if you decided to dive into the business," Melody said. "I'd frequent the place for sure."

She started for her apartment when Mr. Hendrix asked, "Have you two eaten yet?"

"No, sir," Parker answered. "Whatever you're making smells delicious."

Stan grinned. "Well, then you're in luck. I made an extra batch of manicotti. Hold on a sec," he said, and disappeared inside his apartment.

"Oh, now you've done it," Melody said with mirth dancing in her eyes.

"I didn't mean…" Embarrassed, Parker let the words dangle.

She waved off his dismay. "He loves to show off his cooking."

When Stan returned, he carried a pan of delicious-looking manicotti. Tubular pasta shells stuffed with rich ricotta cheese. The sauce made of spices, tomatoes, basil and garlic. Parker's mouth watered.

"You don't have to do this," Melody protested when he offered her the pan. Though her protest didn't have much vehemence to it. Made Parker think they've been through this routine before.

"I know I don't," he huffed. "But I made way too much."

She kissed his cheek with affection. "Thank you."

He transferred the pot holders and pan to her hands and winked. "Enjoy."

It was obvious Stan thought something was going on between them. Before Parker could disabuse him of the idea, Mr. Hendrix disappeared back inside his apartment.

Parker noted the slight pink hue to Melody's cheeks and couldn't help being amused and a bit intrigued. He had to admit if he were in the market for a relationship, she'd be an excellent candidate. Smart, pretty, thoughtful and enjoyable company. But he wasn't. His focus was on the job. There was no time or energy to pursue a love life or to risk failing one. Though he could be a friend to Melody.

Friends didn't put unobtainable expectations on each other, which seemed to be part and parcel of romantic relationships.

"Does he often offer you food?" Parker asked, taking the key from her hand and unlocking her apartment door.

"Usually he invites me in to eat with him," she replied as she moved past him and entered her apartment. She went straight to the kitchen bar and set the pan of manicotti down.

Parker closed the door and looked around. The apartment was small, but comfortable. And surprisingly feminine. With her tailored suits, sleek hair and minimal makeup, he'd expected a more austere or modern place in maybe a black and white monochromatic scheme or in a neutral palette. Not so.

The walls were painted a light dusty blue, the carpet a thick-cut pile in a soft eggshell. A cozy sitting area was the centerpiece of the living room. Two floral-printed love seats sat across from each other. A glass table between the couches looked weighted down with numerous women's magazines. The built-in cabinetry in a light wood grain was filled with books, trinkets and DVD cases. However, he didn't see a television. Must be in her bedroom. He had to admit he was curious to see what her inner sanctuary was like. Would her private space be flowery and girly, too?

Steering his thoughts from that dangerous land mine, he noted that plants topped every available surface. Large feathery ferns stuffed between rows of books. Fresh roses on a round table by the window. A potted, big leafy plant stood on a stand in the corner. "Nice digs."

"Thank you. It's a work in progress."

She offered him an almost shy smile, which he found charming. He had a feeling she didn't let many people see this side of her. He felt honored and fascinated.

There was more to this woman than met the eye. He wanted to know what made her tick. Yet, he was sure delving deeper wouldn't be wise because he might find himself caring for her in ways he shouldn't.

She shrugged off her purse and hung it on a peg near the refrigerator. He stationed Sherlock by the door. "Down."

The beagle lay obediently.

Parker joined Melody in the kitchen. Oak cabinets and cream-colored tile appeared straight out of the eighties. But touches of whimsy softened the effect. Apparently, Melody had a thing for Disney. There were knickknacks and pictures of various different animated characters scattered throughout the living areas. Including a stuffed version of the Cheshire Cat that sat on top of the refrigerator. Definitely a multifaceted woman. And the more he discovered about her, the more fascinating she became. He'd better be careful or he'd find himself sliding from fascination to affection pretty quickly.

She handed him a bowl of water. "For Sherlock. I don't have any dog food."

The thoughtful gesture touched him deeply. "Thank you. Do you have any carrots?"

With a nod, she fished a bag of baby carrots out of the refrigerator. Parker took a few and set them on the entryway floor alongside the bowl of water. Sherlock went to town on the orange sticks and lapped at the water.

While Melody set out plates and utensils on the bar, Parker's gaze was drawn to the fridge door. Several magnets dotted the surface, holding up various different things. A thank-you note card, a receipt and an invitation he recognized. He had the same invitation sitting on the counter of his own kitchen.

The Founder's Ball was the social event of the year for Sagebrush. Everyone who was anyone in town attended. The whole department was expected to go, except for the lowest ranking least-senior officers. The Founder's Ball was an annual fund-raiser, the money going to a different cause each year. This year the money was going toward a new pediatric wing of the hospital. Was Melody going? If so, with whom? The thought that she'd have a date darkened his mood. Did he dare ask? In the interest of her safety, yeah, he should ask.

"Are you attending the ball on Friday?"

"I didn't know *not* going was an option," she commented as she deftly chopped up lettuce for a salad and scooped the pieces into a bowl.

He chuckled. "It's not." The question burning a hole through his mind popped out. "Are you going with anyone?"

She glanced up at him and then looked quickly away. "No. I'm planning on making an appearance and then scooting out."

"You'll have to stay for the entertainment," he said, without acknowledging how her answer lightened his mood. "I sing in a quartet and we're performing." As if she'd find that an enticement. *Cool it, Adams.*

"You sing?"

His chest puffed up a bit. "I do."

"Interesting." She tossed a handful of baby carrots and cherry tomatoes with the salad. She carried the bowl to the table.

Using the pot holders, he transferred the pan of manicotti to the table, as well.

"Interesting enough to tempt you to stay for the whole shindig?"

"Maybe," she said noncommittally.

"We could go together," he offered, surprised by how much the idea appealed to him. And not just because if she came with him to the event, he'd be able to ensure her safety.

She stilled. "I don't know about that. I don't really think it's a good idea for us to... I mean outside of work..."

The rejection in her words dug into him like the sharp tip of a skewer. Bothered by his reaction as much as by her words, he strove to reassure her. "We'd be going as friends. Nothing more," he said as much to convince her as to convince himself.

The anxious expression on her face eased a bit. "Oh, I see. I'll have to think on it." She filled two glasses with water and set them at the table. "If you'd like to wash up there's a bathroom down the hall on your left."

Feeling that he'd pushed the subject of the ball as far as she was willing to go for now, he followed her directions. The bathroom was an explosion of sunny yellow—walls, area rugs, towels and curtains. But what caught his attention were the sticky notes covering the edges of the mirror, each with a different scripture written in neat handwriting.

"God is our refuge and strength, an ever-present help in times of trouble," he read softly aloud. *"Delight yourself in the Lord, and He will give you the desires of your heart. For I know the plans I have for you, declares the Lord, plans for good, not evil."*

It pleased him that she had a kindred spirit of faith. He washed his hands and returned to the kitchen to find the table set and the dinner waiting. He took the seat across from her.

"Shall we say grace?" he asked, wondering where she stood in her faith given the scripts stuck to her bathroom mirror.

She inclined her head. "That would be nice."

Pleased she said yes, he bowed his head. "Father, thank You for this food we are about to receive, bless it to our bodies and our bodies to your service. Amen."

"Amen." She offered him a basket full of rolls.

He took one and buttered it. "That was very generous of your neighbor to share his food."

"He likes to cook. I think he's lonely. His wife died about three years ago. Right before he moved into that apartment."

Impressed with her generous heart, he said, "It's kind of you to spend time with him."

"I like to help where I can."

"Like at the center."

"Yes. Like at the center. If I could afford it, I'd quit the department and work full-time at the center. Keep it open during the day. Right now we're only open during the evenings and weekends." She sighed. "Mostly because we can't afford a full-time staff, but also because one of the board-of-directors conditions when we opened was that an officer be present at all times."

"Have you approached the board about paying you full-time to be there, rather than splitting your time with the department?"

"Not formally. Though I think the center's budget could handle it."

"It's a very honorable thing you've done by opening the center."

"Thanks." She dropped her gaze to her plate.

They ate in silence for a moment. Parker's thoughts turned once again to the danger surrounding Melody. Who would be targeting her and why?

"Tell me more about your nephew," he asked. "What was he like before that night?"

Sadness entered her eyes. "I didn't see a lot of him and Sierra. She and Daniel moved to Sagebrush a few years after he was born. And I went off to college."

"So she never married Daniel's father?"

"No. Sierra thought marriage antiquated and not worth the trouble." She let out a dry laugh. "I should have listened."

He frowned, not liking the bitterness in her tone. "Why's that?"

She shook her head. "Sorry. That was… I didn't mean to bring that up."

"You were married once?" Which explained why her last name didn't match her sister's.

"For a brief time." She averted her gaze and took a sip of water.

He had the sense she'd been hurt badly. Divorce did that to people. His heart ached for her. Surprisingly he wanted to push, to delve into what happened. But he didn't. He had his share of old wounds and wouldn't appreciate anyone digging into them.

She met his gaze, her expression shuttered. "I never understood—why Sagebrush? Of all the places she could have moved to. But I think…" She bit her lip and set down her fork. "I think Daniel's father must live here."

"Really? Why do you think that?"

"Sierra lived way beyond her means. She waitressed sometimes at the Sagebrush Diner but not enough to afford her lifestyle."

Turning the information over in his head, he asked, "So…what? You think Daniel's father was providing for them?"

"Or paying her off."

"Blackmail? Maybe the guy is married and liked having a separate family on the side?"

"Except Daniel didn't know until close to his death who his father was, so they weren't playing house on the side."

"How can you be sure?"

"Because Daniel called me a few months before that night and asked me all kinds of questions about his birth, questions about his mother, who she was seeing when she became pregnant. He asked point-blank if I knew who his father was. I told him the truth—I didn't."

"But you think he found out."

"Yes. I received a text from him the day he was killed. He said he'd figured it out and the guy was going to pay."

Parker sat back and stared at her. "Did you tell Slade this?"

"I reported it. Doesn't make a lick of difference, though. Daniel and Sierra took the secret of Daniel's father to the grave with them."

"How did Daniel get mixed up with drugs?"

Her mouth scrunched up. "I wish I knew. The first time he was arrested for possession, I should have pushed Sierra to get him some help. But she shrugged it off, saying he was experimenting."

"Just like my brother," he stated as a knife twisted in his chest.

She reached across the table and covered his hand with her own. "His death must have devastated your family."

He turned his hand over and laced his fingers with hers. It felt so good to have someone to hold on to as he rode the tide of anguished emotions that thoughts of his young brother brought. She understood his grief, his anger. "In so many ways. I wasn't sure my parent's marriage would survive. They both blamed themselves and each other."

"Like you blame yourself," she stated softly.

He fell into her compassionate blue gaze. "Yes."

"Are your parents still together?"

"They are. It was a difficult road to travel but through faith and love they are stronger now. When Dad retired from the company he worked for, he and Mom started traveling, mostly mission trips to third-world countries. I think it helps them to help others."

"I understand."

He knew that she did. The youth center was her way of helping others, just as being a narcotics detective was his way of making a difference. Maybe atonement wouldn't be found in this life, but he prayed God would be pleased with his efforts. And hers.

Drawn to her, he leaned forward, needing to be closer, wanting to be closer. The table butted against his middle, slamming him to reality. This bond he felt, though real, wasn't something he could nourish to full bloom.

Work and romance didn't mix.

The names of couples whose relationship did work

tore through his mind, blowing holes through that excuse. Several of the other K-9 officers were either married or engaged.

Okay, maybe it could work. But he wasn't going down that road. He'd traveled that bumpy path once before and ended up scarred for his trouble. He had no intention of reliving that kind of pain again.

He cleared his throat and released her hand. "After we clear these dishes, I'll install the dead bolt."

She blinked. "Sounds like a plan."

Yeah, it did. Everything was perfect. So why was he feeling so off-kilter, as if they had unfinished business?

Two days later, Melody locked her two dead bolts before heading to the youth center. She was glad Parker had insisted on doing the installation since it turned out to be more complicated than she'd thought it would. He'd had a few tools in the pack he wore at his waist and then he'd borrowed a drill from Mr. Hendrix.

Parker was a man who was always prepared and who always did the right thing.

Which was refreshing for her, since most of the men in her life all seemed to do the wrong thing. Her father, her ex-husband. Daniel. All had made bad choices that left those who loved them hurting.

Would Parker turn out to be the same? She hoped not.

Sharing an enjoyable meal with him had also shifted their interactions into a comfortable, growing friendship. He was easy to talk to, easy to be with. A dangerous combination. But she couldn't deny how nice it was to have someone other than herself to rely on. She'd been on her own for so long...

She'd almost spilled her guts about her failed marriage, just barely managing to hold back. And he'd been polite enough not to push, though she knew he was curious. It was in his eyes every time he looked at her. But she didn't need to burden him with her past. It was enough that they shared the bonds of grief over two young boys with lives cut short by drugs.

She exited her apartment building and walked toward the parking lot where she parked her car. A movement in her peripheral vision snagged her attention. Stopping, she spun to her right in time to see Zane Peabody duck behind a tree. What was he doing? Did his presence here this morning confirm he was the one who'd tried to break into her apartment two nights ago? If so, why?

Drawing her weapon, she yelled, "Zane Peabody, show yourself."

Chapter Seven

Adrenaline rushed through Melody. She couldn't believe this was happening here at her apartment building. That someone was after her, wanted to kill her. And that someone could be Zane.

Zane dashed from behind the tree and took off down the street, escaping.

Melody chased after him, fueled by a mix of anger and distress. She sped up and rounded the corner. The street in front of her was empty. No sign of Zane. She'd lost him.

Frustration pounded at her temples as she drew to a halt, catching her breath.

There was no sign of him among the cars or the trees lining the street in front of the buildings. Why was Zane hanging around her apartment? What did he hope to accomplish?

A prickling sensation at the back of her neck sent a fresh wave of alarm cascading down her spine. Someone was watching her. But the street was quiet. Not a soul in sight. Not even the birds chirped. Her hand tightened on her sidearm.

She retraced her steps to the front of her apartment building. The feeling of being observed intensified. She glanced over her shoulder. No one was there. A car engine roared. Melody's heart rate accelerated. She whipped around to see a white and blue striped Mustang pull to the curb a few feet away. Parker climbed out from behind the steering wheel. She exhaled a relieved breath. Sherlock stuck his head out of the open back window and gave a long, howling bark of greeting.

Parker strode toward her, a big smile on his handsome face. Her pulse tripped over itself for an entirely different reason. His dark eyes gleamed in the morning sunlight, and his brown hair, still damp from a recent shower, was swept back from his forehead and curled slightly at the ends. A flutter of interest stirred low in her abdomen. She fought the reaction. He wore black snakeskin cowboy boots, dark blue jeans and a light gray suit vest over a black dress shirt open at the collar. The man exuded charisma and self-confidence whether in uniform or out. Which didn't bode well for her peace of mind.

"Morning," he said as he came to a halt at her side.

"What are you doing here?"

"I came to see you, of course."

Of course. Like that made sense. "Seriously."

He tilted his head. "I'm serious. I thought I'd swing by and see what you were up to." His glance raked over her. She resisted the urge to adjust the tailored suit jacket or to make sure her slacks weren't wrinkled. "It's your day off, right?"

Narrowing her gaze on him, she answered, "Yes, it's my day off. How did you know that?"

"I checked the schedule."

Not sure how to feel about his attention, she murmured, "Checking up on me?"

He flashed her a devastating grin. "Kinda."

Okay, now she was really confused. "Why?"

He arched an eyebrow. "Someone threatened your life a few days ago. Just because you're off duty doesn't mean we should take the threat lightly."

She supposed that was true. Or maybe he still thought she was somehow involved with the drugs they found in the center. Or perhaps he was interested in her personally. She dismissed the latter. Though he'd been polite and charming, he'd never indicated his behavior was anything more than a cop doing his job. "I'm headed over to the youth center. Saturdays we open at ten in the morning."

He looked at her hip where her gun rested. "You always carry when you're at the center?"

She arched an eyebrow. "Like you said, just because I'm off duty doesn't mean I shouldn't be armed."

His mouth twisted in a wry smile. "That's not quite what I said, but okay."

"Zane Peabody was watching my building."

Parker's stance changed, turning protective as he searched the area. "What?"

"He's long gone. He ran away when I confronted him."

A fierce frown deepened the small lines around his eyes. "You confronted him? Alone?" He shook his head. "What were you thinking?"

"In case you've forgotten, I'm a police officer. I carry a badge and a weapon."

"I haven't forgotten. But you should have called for backup."

"There wasn't time."

Shaking his head, he gestured toward his car. "I'll drive you to the youth center."

"I thought you were going to a car show this weekend."

"Tomorrow after church." He cocked his head and considered her a moment. "Would you care to join me?"

"Go to a car show?" She couldn't say she was much interested in looking at cars, but the idea of spending the day with Parker away from work sent a thrill of anticipation racing along her limbs.

"Yes, to the car show. And church," Parker confirmed.

Uncertainty filled her. "I'm not sure that's a good idea—"

A loud explosion by the street jolted Melody. Sherlock's frantic barks pierced the air.

Parker reacted swiftly, grabbing her by the waist and practically throwing her to the ground. His big body covered hers. The spicy scent of his aftershave crowded her senses. Heart pumping wildly, Melody tried to breathe through the sudden fear flooding her system.

A car engine turned over. Another loud bang filled the air. This time the sound registered. A tailpipe expelling a shot of exhaust. Not gunfire.

Hot spots burned at every point of contact between her and Parker. Sensations zipped through her. She liked the feeling of his muscular body pressed close. Much more than she should. "Uh, Parker, you can get off me now."

He eased to the side and then helped her to stand as he rose. An old car rambled past, black smoke spewing from the tailpipe.

Melody let out a relieved laugh. "I hope no one caught that on video."

Parker chuckled, a deep rumbling sound. "Me, too. I didn't crush you, did I?"

"Hardly."

He captured her hand. Warmth seeped into her bones. "I'm glad that turned out to be nothing."

Staring at their joined hands, she thought there were some dangers that didn't announce themselves with the force of a bullet. Like finding herself way too attracted to her coworker. She extracted her hand. "I better get going."

"I'm driving you," he stated in a tone that said he wouldn't be swayed otherwise. "And on the way to the youth center we can talk about tomorrow."

He could talk all he wanted. She wasn't going to go. Her reaction moments earlier confirmed one thing. Fraternizing with him outside of the job would be a bad idea all the way around.

Melody couldn't believe Parker had turned her no into a yes, but his constant persuading yesterday had changed her mind without her actually realizing she'd agreed.

Now she sat next to Parker in the fifth pew at Sagebrush Christian Church letting the voices of the congregation rising in song wrap around her like a comfortable, familiar old blanket.

It had been too long since she'd attended a service. She'd found reasons not to over the past few years, but Parker wouldn't heed her excuses.

The man was way too charming. She'd better watch

herself around him, or she'd find herself charmed right into heartache.

She had to wonder, though, why he was so determined she accompany him to church. Was it only because he felt he needed to keep her close to protect her? Or did he think she needed church in her life?

Was he out to save her both physically and spiritually?

She smiled with wry amusement. Her grandfather would have approved. But Parker didn't have to worry. She had accepted Jesus as her savior when she was a young girl. And even though the relationship was strained, she hadn't completely turned her back on God.

A slight breeze came through the open window and ruffled her hair, like fingers teasing her nape. She glanced at Parker. His profile was strong and confident.

Her breath caught for a second.

He turned his head slightly, catching her gaze, and smiled. He sang in a deep baritone that she found herself listening to rather than joining in the singing.

When the hymn concluded, Pastor Eaton stepped to the pulpit. Tall with graying hair and kind eyes, the pastor reminded Melody of her grandfather on her mother's side. They'd lost him years ago to cancer, but Melody still thought fondly of the summers she spent at his ranch in north Texas. Her grandfather, like Pastor Eaton, had been a man of God.

As the pastor read from the book of Isaiah, Melody recognized the passage and remembered her grandfather teaching her from the same verses. She missed those more carefree days with her grandfather and grandmother.

When the service ended, Melody followed Parker out

of the church building. He stopped to talk to people, introducing her to those she didn't know as his coworker. A stark reminder that there was nothing personal between them. A vague disquiet lodged itself beneath her breastbone.

They returned to Parker's car where Sherlock sat waiting for them in the backseat with the window down to allow airflow. Parker never went anywhere without his partner.

Once they were on the road heading to Odessa, Parker said, "Thank you for coming with me today."

"You're welcome. Thank you for inviting me." The hairs at the back of her neck stirred as Sherlock's hot breath fanned over her. He had his paws on the back of her seat and his nose close to her ear. She shifted away from him.

"What did you think of the service?" Parker asked.

"It was nice. Pastor Eaton is passionate about God."

"Yes, he is. Did you like the message?"

"I did." She was surprised since she hadn't considered whether she'd enjoy the sermon or not. "It made me think of my grandfather."

He glanced at her. "How so?"

"My grandfather was a minister of a small congregation before he passed on."

"Ah. Now they make sense."

She cocked her head. "What makes sense?"

"The scriptures you have posted all over your bathroom mirror."

A flush of embarrassment heated her cheeks. She'd forgotten about those. Of course he'd seen the Post-it notes when he'd used the sink to wash for dinner. "You didn't mention them the other day."

"I didn't want to pry. Besides, I think it's a good practice. Start and end your day reading scripture."

"That's what my grandfather would say."

The pleased expression on his face made her think of her earlier suspicion. He had thought she needed faith. And in truth, she did. She wanted a deeper faith. She just wasn't sure how to go about it.

"The verse Pastor Eaton taught from today was one of my grandfather's favorites," she said. "'But those who trust in the Lord will find new strength. They will soar high on wings like eagles. They will run and not grow weary. They will walk and not faint,'" she recited, having committed the words to memory so long ago.

"The verse paints a vivid visual," Parker said.

"Yes, it does. Grandfather would say, 'Put those words in your heart, Melody, girl. God will move in your life. He will be there for you always. But first you have to actively trust Him. It won't be enough to say it. You have to act on it.'"

"And do you?" There was a wealth of curiosity in his tone. "Trust God, that is?"

The question dug deep, into places she rarely delved. "I try. When my father deserted us, I took my grief and anger to God." Her throat burned with the anguish of that time in her life. "When Mom slipped into depression, I turned to God again, seeking comfort." Those dark days haunted her dreams still. "Time and again, I've turned to God just like Grandfather instructed." Her fingers curled, her nails digging into her palm. "I've asked a hundred times *why?* Why had someone killed Daniel? Why would Sierra take her own life? Why, why, why?"

Why had her husband, Roger, abandoned her?

"But answers—solace—never came," she said, wincing slightly at the bitter note in her tone. "Only more heartache and more questions."

Still, she tried to hang on to the faith of her grandparents because the seeds of faith had been planted deep.

Some days were harder than others. Today? Today was a good day. She wanted a renewed strength.

"It's not a sin to question God, you know. If you're asking from a sincere and humble heart," Parker said quietly.

She blinked. Her pulse sped up. A flutter of anxiety hit her tummy. Could she honestly say her questions had stemmed from a humble and sincere heart?

"Can I ask why you don't attend church regularly?"

Grateful to be pulled from the direction her thoughts were headed, she slanted Parker a glance. "I usually work the Sunday shift."

But this week, she'd been given two days off in a row. And was spending the time with Parker. She wasn't sure how she felt about that. "Did you have anything to do with me having this weekend off?"

A grin tugged at the corner of his mouth. "Maybe."

Suspicion flared. "Why?"

"You work too much."

She frowned as mild irritation flared. "That's not your call."

He shrugged, totally unrepentant. "No, it isn't. It's Captain Drexel's."

Aghast, she stared at him. "You talked to my captain?"

"He wanted an update on the center. And when he heard about the threatening note…"

"He decided to have you babysit me?" Her fingers

curled around the seat-belt strap. She wasn't sure if she was angrier that they thought she was incapable of protecting herself, or that Parker was spending time with her only because he'd been asked to. And why was she taking offense? He was doing his job.

"Not babysit. Protect."

"Right." Just as she'd thought. "Look, Parker, I can take care of myself. I've been doing it my whole life."

He pulled back. "But you don't have to. You're part of the Sagebrush Police Force. We take care of our own."

His words slid through the barrier she'd erected around her heart, piercing her in vulnerable places. He was talking about cops who belonged, not those like her who existed on the fringe. He had no idea what it was like for her. And she couldn't fault him.

"Come on, don't look so down. Spending the day with me and Sherlock isn't that bad, is it?"

Forcing a smile, she admitted, "No, it's not that bad." Not bad at all.

"Good. Now relax."

Right. Easy for him to say. She couldn't relax when she was so acutely aware of him next to her. His vitality vibrated in the air around them. Her senses hummed. Great. How was she going to spend the whole day with him and ignore her attraction to him?

"That was surprisingly fun," Melody said.

Parker nodded in agreement as he drove them back to Sagebrush. Though he wasn't that surprised the day had been pleasurable. He enjoyed spending time with Melody. She was inquisitive and intelligent. Not many women would put up with a whole day of looking at classic cars. "I was impressed by how much you know about muscle cars."

She laughed, the sound soft and pleasing. "My dad was always a car buff. He'd had a 1970 Plymouth Barracuda. He spent a lot of time working on that car. I would sit in the garage with him while he tinkered with it. I hadn't realized how much information I'd absorbed until today."

"Does he still have the car?"

"I don't know. I haven't spoken to him since right after Sierra died. And it didn't come up in the short phone conversation."

Appalled, he stared at her. "Didn't he come for her funeral?"

Melody gave a dry laugh. "No. He couldn't be bothered."

The hurt and bitterness in her tone made Parker ache for her. "That stinks."

"Yes, well, once he left, he left. No looking back."

Dismayed, he tried to wrap his mind around her words. "You never saw him again? Not even when you got married?"

"Nope." Bitterness laced the word. "For a while Sierra and I received gifts at Christmas and birthdays but that eventually ended." She let out a scornful laugh. "He started a new family. Didn't want to be bothered with the old."

Parker's fingers flexed on the steering wheel as anger at her father ripped through him. He couldn't imagine a father walking away from his children. He knew it happened all the time, but the selfish act still boggled his mind. He would never do that to anyone he loved.

One of the many reasons he wasn't prepared to be in a relationship. Families took work, time and energy.

Until he was ready to be one hundred percent in, he'd stay far away from that kind of commitment. He'd let his brother down all those years ago, his parents, too. He didn't ever want to feel that kind of regret and hurt again. "Who gave you away at your wedding, then?"

She turned her face toward the passenger window. "No one. I walked down the aisle alone." She let out a humorless laugh. "Which pretty much sums up how the marriage went."

He glanced at her, hating to see the anguish etched in her profile. "I don't follow."

"I was as alone in my marriage as I am now. Six months after we said our 'I do's', Roger decided he needed to *find himself*." The words seemed torn from her as if she were trying to hold back. "He took off for Europe and never returned. A year later I was served divorce papers."

Heart twisting with empathy, Parker reached over and took her hand, offering what little comfort he could. "You're not alone anymore."

"Thanks," she said softly, but there was no conviction in her tone.

"I mean it. You have the whole Sagebrush P.D. behind you," he said, careful to keep the support general. Though he wanted to say she had him, too, but he didn't dare make any sort of promises that he couldn't keep.

"It's nice of you to say. Other than Jim and Kaitlin Mathers, I don't really spend time out of the office with anyone." Her mouth tipped up at the corner. "Except you, of course."

"Why is that? You've been with the department a

long time." Surely by now she'd have developed a network of friends.

"I've been very focused on the youth center and solving Daniel's murder. There hasn't been time for much socializing."

He heard longing in her voice. "Kaitlin's good people." Kaitlin Mathers was one of the K-9 unit's dog trainers. "Friendships take time and effort."

"True." She shrugged. "I'm not good at forming relationships. Or keeping them."

She had to be referring to her ex-husband. "You shouldn't blame yourself for you ex's desertion."

"I try not to. But there must have been something wrong with me to make him leave."

"No." Parker hated that she'd think that. "There's nothing wrong with you. He was an idiot to leave you."

Her grip tightened. "You're kind. You know that?"

"I'm telling the truth."

She looked away. "It's not just that. Even when I lived in Austin, I never really felt like I belonged."

"But you were on the Austin Police Force for a while, right? You must have friends there?"

"Acquaintances," she said. "But I never really learned how to make connections. Growing up I was so busy caring for my mother, I didn't have anything to give to anyone else."

Sympathy clenched his gut. "Your mother was ill?"

Melody met his gaze. Her blue eyes were shiny as if she was fighting her emotions. "She fell into a despondency after my father left. It was years before she finally came out of it. By then I was an adult."

"I'm sorry. That must have been rough." He swallowed hard. "When my brother died, my parents suffered, but they got help through our church."

"That's good they reached out. My mother wouldn't let anyone help her."

"But she came out of her depression."

Melody nodded. "She did. She's working now for a department store in Austin. She likes to keep herself busy so she can't dwell on the past."

"The past can't be undone. No matter how much we wish we could change things," he said.

"What do you wish you could change?"

"I'd have paid better attention to my brother. Not let him get sucked into trying drugs."

She gave his hand a gentle squeeze.

For the rest of the drive they remained silent.

Parker pulled onto the street of Melody's apartment building. Two Sagebrush police cruisers were parked in front, lights flashing.

Beside him, Melody stiffened and agitation radiated off her in waves adding to his own level of concern. He'd barely brought the car to a halt before she was out and running toward the building.

Sherlock let out a howl of protest at her departure.

Chapter Eight

"Come on, buddy, let's go see what's going on," Parker said as he harnessed the dog. They hurried to where Melody was talking with two patrol officers.

"There's been a break-in," the taller of the two men stated. His badge read Sanders. "You'll have to wait until the CSU team arrives to go inside, ma'am."

"Detective," Melody corrected. "I'm Detective Zachary, homicide. And this is Detective Adams with the K-9 unit."

The younger patrolman nodded to Parker. "I recognize you. What's the K-9 unit's interest here?" The K-9 unit shared the same space as the regular police force.

"Detective Zachary lives in this building," Parker said. "Do you know which apartment was broken into?"

Though he had a suspicion he knew what the answer would be.

"Apartment 4F," Sanders replied.

Melody inhaled a sharp breath. "My apartment."

Sanders blinked. "Oh. Sorry."

"Are there any witnesses?" Parker interjected.

"One of the neighbors. He sustained a minor injury from the perp. A guy in a ski mask."

Melody's gaze met Parker's. The same guy who'd ransacked her office at the youth center. "Could Zane and the ski-mask guy be working together?"

"Worth picking up Zane to find out," Parker said. He turned to the younger patrol officer. "I need you to put out a BOLO for Zane Peabody." They walked toward the cruiser as the crime-scene unit van turned the corner and came to a halt a few feet away. Rose and Clay climbed out. Rose was already shaking her head when she stopped beside Melody.

Melody held up a hand. "Don't say it."

"I wasn't going to say anything, except I'm sure glad to see you in one piece."

Affection for the CSU tech spread through Melody. "Thanks. Someone apparently managed to break into my apartment after all."

They filed inside and headed up to the fourth floor. Mr. Hendrix sat on the floor holding a bag of ice to his forehead. A dark bruise showed beneath the ice.

Melody rushed forward. "Mr. Hendrix. What happened?"

He took her hand with one of his. "I come out of my apartment just in time to get smacked in the face by a guy dressed like a ninja."

Rose inspected the dead bolts. "These have been punched through." She stepped inside. "Melody."

Dread made her sick to her stomach. She walked into her apartment and grimaced. The ransacking was worse than at her office. She hadn't been around this time to stop the masked man from destroying her property. The cushions of her love seats were ripped open. Her plants had been toppled over and potting soil spread across the floor. Her books were pulled from the shelves and scattered haphazardly about. Her many Disney character figurines were smashed to bits. Her gaze shot to the refrigerator, to the empty place where her treasured keepsakes once sat and her heart sank. Shreds of pink and purple material littered the kitchen floor.

The destruction seemed pointless. The feeling of violation stabbed at her worse here than at her office because this was her private space. Her fingers curled into fists.

A hand on her shoulder startled her. Parker stood beside her with worry in his eyes. "What could he be looking for?"

"I don't know," she answered truthfully. "But I hope he found it."

"You can't stay here," Parker said.

She turned to face him. "I've nowhere else to go."

"A friend's?"

She supposed she could ask Kaitlin. Though she didn't like the idea of intruding on her or putting her in any danger. "I'll go to the Sagebrush Hotel."

"That sounds like a good idea," Parker said. "As soon as Rose is done, pack a bag."

It didn't take long for Rose to finish up and give Melody the go-ahead to start packing.

Her bedroom had been tossed. Her clothes yanked from the drawers and closet and flung onto the floor with little regard. Impotent rage reared. Someone had not only ransacked her place but they'd robbed her of control. And she hated not being in control of her own destiny.

* * *

The Sagebrush Hotel had an old-world feel to the place, like stepping into a luxury hotel in Europe rather than southwest Texas. Melody felt strange entering the establishment with Parker at her side, like a couple coming to stay for a vacation when in fact she was hiding from some unknown danger that had thrown her life into chaos.

She had stayed at the Sagebrush Hotel for a few nights when she'd first arrived in town five years ago, right after Sierra and Daniel's deaths. Those days were a blur now. She hadn't stepped foot inside the mammoth hotel since.

Gleaming brass, marble floors and crystal chandeliers set an elegant tone. A large vase filled with exotic and expensive-looking flowers set atop a vast, round marble pedestal dominated the entryway. The hotel looked pretty much the same as she remembered.

Parker had called ahead and secured a room. They picked up the key from the reception desk. The hotel staff didn't blink an eye when they saw Sherlock. Of course the dog had on his police vest with the Sagebrush Police Department emblem.

Her room was the last one to the right on the tenth floor. The suite was airy and lit with low-wattage lamps, casting glowing circles of warmth to dispel the shadows.

Awareness of Parker so close behind her shimmied over her like silk sliding over her skin. The feeling left her a little breathless.

Needing to gain control of her reaction, she walked to the window and gazed out at the sweeping view of Sagebrush at night. Lights twinkled downtown and extended in the distance, then abruptly ended. A vast blackness stretching as far as the eye could see marked the Lost Woods, the thousand-acre forest on the edge of town.

She shivered. Daniel was killed in those woods. Those woods hold the answers. Answers she needed to uncover.

In the reflection of the window, she watched Parker set her suitcase on the floor near the door leading to the bedroom. He straightened and stood watching her. She studied his face, the angles and planes, liking the way his hair fell over his forehead, the way his mouth curved slightly at the corners. The way he made her feel. Protected. Cared for. Special.

Dangerous feelings that confused her heart and her mind.

A flutter hit her tummy when their gazes met. She turned away from the window with a sigh to cover the peculiar way he made her feel, plopped down on the leather couch and into the soft, luxurious cushions. "I'm not sure I can afford to stay here more than one night."

"You'll stay until the threat to your life is neutralized."

"Easy for you to say. It's not your checkbook taking the hit."

"Don't worry about the cost," he said. "The department will pick up the tab."

She arched an eyebrow. "You can't promise that."

"It's already been arranged."

A mix of annoyance and gratitude surged through her. "You think of everything, don't you?"

"It's my job."

Hers, too. Only she wasn't the one calling the shots. She watched him inspect the place, opening doors and cabinets. Peering under the couches, running his hands along the edges of the tables, chairs and around the inside of the lamps. She couldn't help but watch the play of muscles under fabric as he turned and reached, bent and flexed. The room grew warm. She remembered herself and why they were there. "Looking for drugs?" she teased.

"Maybe. Or bombs or snakes or anything that might pose a threat to you."

His words touched her, making her think he was really worried about her well-being. His attention warmed her from the inside. "No one knows I'm here. I'll be fine."

He strode toward her, stopping at the edge of the couch. "With everything that's happened, we can't be sure you're safe."

An arrow of anxiety shot through her. "I wish we knew what this was all about."

"Me, too. Until then, I'm staying with you."

Her heart jolted. The very idea of him remaining in the suite with her, alone, had her mind racing with equal parts anticipation and alarm. She shot to her feet. "No. Absolutely not. It wouldn't be appropriate."

Understanding dawned in his dark eyes. "I suppose you're right."

A vague sense of disappointment coursed through her. "You got that straight. I can take care of myself." With purposeful steps, she headed to the door. "I think we should call it a night."

He snagged a chair from the dining table and carried it to the door. "I'll be right outside the door."

"What?" Disbelief raised her voice an octave. "That's not necessary."

"Yes, it is. I'm not leaving you unprotected."

She couldn't let him sit out in the hall where the other guests would see him and ask questions. "What about Sherlock?"

"I'll kennel him at night at the training center."

Stunned that Parker would be willing to do that, she didn't know what to say. That was beyond the call of duty. Her gaze dropped to the dog sitting at Parker's feet. Sherlock stared back at her, his big, brown eyes adoring. "I can't ask you to do that."

"You're not asking."

Stubborn man. "There has to be a better solution."

He thought for a moment. "Officer Patty Truman."

A vague image of one of the female patrol officers came to mind. "Yes. That would work."

"Good. Tomorrow we'll make the arrangements with her."

Her heart skipped a beat. "And tonight?"

He grinned. "There's an extra blanket and pillow in the closet. I'm sure the hotel can handle Sherlock staying here for one night."

He was staying? Melody's palms started to sweat. She wiped them on her pant leg. Yeah, maybe the hotel could handle the beagle sticking around for the night, but could she handle Parker staying?

He replaced the dining chair and disappeared into the bedroom, returning a moment later with the pillow and blanket in his hand. He dumped them on the leather couch.

For a long moment they stared at each other from across the room. She couldn't deny there was a part of her that was glad he was staying. For protection's sake only, of course. Yet she couldn't get used to having him look out for her, because sooner or later, having him around would be a thing of the past.

Forcing back her agitation and growing attraction, she gave him a sharp nod and bolted for the bedroom. With the locked door separating them, she sat on the bed and planted her hands against her hot cheeks.

How on earth was she supposed to get any rest with him in the next room?

"What do you mean you've been staying at the Sagebrush Hotel? Why?"

"Shhh," Melody hissed to Jim Wheaton. She quickly glanced around to make sure no one was within earshot. Thankfully, the youth center wasn't busy yet. "Someone broke into my apartment last Sunday night."

Jim stopped midstride and faced her. "And you've waited five days to tell me? I'm your partner. I should've been told."

Guilt flooded through her. The thought of telling Jim hadn't crossed her mind. There was no reason for him to know. And the fewer people who knew where she was staying, the better. She was only telling him now because he'd wanted to swing by her apartment on his way to the Founder's Ball tonight and pick her up. "You're right. I should have told you."

"Adams knows though, doesn't he? That's why he's been dogging your steps all week. And why you've seemed distant."

The accusation in Jim's eyes made her wince. She didn't have to justify herself to him, yet he was her partner and friend. They'd been working together for a long time. She owed him the truth. She told him about the note and then about coming home and finding her apartment ransacked.

"And you told Adams and not me."

"Parker was with me when I got to the apartment."

Jim's eyebrows shot up. "You're dating Adams?"

"No. We're not dating. Captain Drexel asked him to provide some protection, that's all."

"Like I couldn't?" Jim stalked away, his heavy boots ringing through the hall.

Melody hustled to keep up. "Of course you could. It's just the way things worked out. That's all."

"Is he staying there with you?"

Heat crept up her neck. Not now. "No."

"Good. Parker's not good enough for you," he huffed.

She blinked, not sure how to respond. His words were something a father would say. Affection tightened her chest.

"So what did they take?"

The change of subject threw her for a moment. "Nothing as far as I could tell. I don't own anything of monetary value."

The items she treasured were only special to her because of the memories attached to them. Photos of her family, Daniel's Timex watch, the ring her mother gave her on her sixteenth birthday. The stuffed Cheshire Cat from her father. Her fingers curled with anger at the loss.

Jim pushed open the door to the woodworking room and paused. "I hope if anything else happens you'll come to me."

Pushing back her turbulent emotions, she nodded. "Of course, Jim."

He gave her a dubious look then went inside and shut the door behind him.

Melody blew out a breath, hoping to ease the constriction in her chest. Jim would get over his upset. He couldn't stay mad at her forever. They were partners.

But lately she hadn't confided in Jim the way she used to. The way she recently had with Parker.

With a bit of a start she realized she'd put a lot of trust and faith in Parker.

Guilt slithered through her. For the past two weeks, Parker was the one she went to when she wanted to talk out a thought or bounce around an idea, whether it was a case or something to do with the youth center.

Parker and Sherlock showed up at the hotel every morning to escort her to the station and then would walk to the youth center with her at the end of the day. And then again showed up to take her back to the hotel at night and wouldn't leave until Officer Truman arrived.

During the working day, they'd spent countless hours together searching for Zane. They'd tried all his usual haunts and canvassed the streets. But he'd gone to ground.

Melody hoped it meant the danger had passed, as well. This weekend she wanted to move back into her apartment. But tonight, she had a ball to attend. A quick glance at the clock hanging on the wall said she'd better get a move on. She needed to find Ally and give her some last-minute instructions about closing up.

Melody found Ally in the women's locker room. The young woman sat on the bench, her slim shoulders shaking. Tears streamed down her pretty face.

Concern tore through Melody. "Ally, what's wrong?"

Ally wiped at her tears. "I found this." She held up a yellowed, crumpled sheet of paper.

Curious, she took the note and quickly read the words scrawled across the paper.

> *Ally,*
> *I love you and know you deserve better than me.*
> *One day soon everything will work out and I'll*
> *be able to take care of you. I hope you'll always*
> *be my girl.*
> *Daniel*

Tears pricked Melody's eyes. "Where did you get this?"

"An old purse. I'd forgotten I even had it, until I discovered it in the back of my closet. I started using it." She sniffled and wiped at her nose with the sleeve of her shirt. "I was looking for some change for the vending machine and found that shoved in the bottom of a compartment."

"What do you think he meant, 'everything will work out?'"

Ally shoved her hair away from her face. "I don't know."

Something in the way Ally's eyes shifted clanged an alarm through Melody. "Ally, if you know something about what Daniel was involved in before his death you need to tell. Now."

The younger woman hesitated as if debating whether she should reveal whatever was on her mind.

Melody laid a hand on her arm. "Please, tell me."

"Daniel had gotten mixed up with some nasty people."

"Was he working for The Boss?"

Ally tilted her head. "I don't think so. Daniel was trying to go into business for himself."

A fist-size lump lodged in Melody's gut. "So he *was* dealing drugs."

Ally nodded.

"Why didn't you say anything before now?"

"I didn't want to get in trouble. I knew everyone would think I was involved, too. I wasn't." A fat tear rolled down her cheek. "And I didn't want people thinking any worse of Daniel."

"How was Daniel getting the drugs to sell?"

"He had a partner. I don't know who it was. He wouldn't tell. He wouldn't tell me a lot of things."

"Did he ever mention a code?"

"No." She held out her hand, her eyes on the paper in Melody's hand. "May I keep that?"

Melody laid the love letter into the young woman's palm. "Of course. Ally, it's very important you tell me anything else you know."

Ally stood. "I don't know anything else."

Melody wasn't so sure, but the stubborn jut of the girl's chin told Melody she wasn't getting anything else out of her right now.

Ally had confirmed the suspicion that Daniel had been dealing drugs. And added a new piece to the puzzle.

Daniel had had a business partner. Who? And had this person been the one to shoot and kill Daniel?

"You are not wearing that!"

Melody held open the door to her suite and stared at the women standing at the threshold.

Front and center was her friend, dog trainer Kaitlin Mathers, wearing a pretty emerald-green gown that heightened the green in her hazel eyes. Her honey-blond hair was loose about her shoulders and a sparkly necklace encircled her slender neck. Flanking Kaitlin on either side were dog trainer Francine Loomis, decked out in a black-and-white striped dress with more ruffles than Melody had ever seen on one person, and Officer Valerie Salgado in a flowing purple floor-length dress that accentuated her creamy skin and red hair.

When Melody had heard the knock on the hotel suite door, she'd expected to find Parker ready to escort her downstairs to the ball and her pulse had responded in a manner she'd come to accept. When she'd opened the door and saw these three women she didn't know what to do. "Excuse me?"

"Can we come in?" Kaitlin asked.

"Why not." Melody stepped back and allowed the trio to enter.

Francine gestured up and down with one pink-tipped finger. "What you have on is not appropriate for tonight."

Melody glanced down at the black tailored pantsuit that she considered her best outfit. It was designer and had cost her a pretty penny. "What's wrong with what I'm wearing?"

"This is a formal affair and you're going with a handsome date." Francine's tone suggested Melody should already know this.

"It's black. Black is formal. And it's not a date." Melody couldn't even believe they were having this conversation. "Where's Parker?"

"Rehearsing with his group," Valerie offered.

"So he asked Charlie's Angels to escort me?"

"Ohhh, Charlie's Angels." Francine pressed her hands together like she were holding a gun, cocked a knee and struck a pose. "I'm the Demi Moore character."

A smile tugged at Melody. "Uh, wasn't her character the villain?"

Francine's expression fell. "Oh. Right."

"If you're not dating Parker then what's going on?" Kaitlin asked.

"Our bosses assigned him the task of keeping me safe."

Worry wrinkled Francine's brow. "From what?"

Melody told them about the break-ins and the threatening note. "I think it has something to do with Daniel's murder and Rio's disappearance."

Anxiety darkened Kaitlin's green eyes. "You'll be careful, right?"

Touched by her concern, Melody squeezed her friend's hand. "Yes. Of course."

"Well, if you have to have someone watching your back, Parker's a good candidate. And cute, too," Francine remarked.

"Parker feels protective toward you," Kaitlin said.

Valerie's smile reminded Melody of the Cheshire Cat. "I don't think it's only his protective instincts."

Melody narrowed her gaze. "Why do you say that?"

"Woman's intuition."

Right. A nervous flutter hit her tummy. What had Parker said to give Valerie that impression?

Melody grabbed her purse from the sideboard table in the entryway. "Let's go."

The three women exchanged glances and didn't budge.

"What?" Melody arched an eyebrow.

Kaitlin smiled. "Honey, wouldn't you rather put on a dress?"

"I don't own a dress." Her closet was full of pantsuits and button-down poplin shirts. She did have a couple pairs of jeans and some T-shirts for her days off.

"We can remedy that." Kaitlin considered her for a moment before walking to the phone sitting on a table beside the leather couch. Kaitlin dialed the concierge and asked for the hotel's boutique. "How late are you open? Oh, good. I have an emergency. Do you have anything formal in a size…?" Kaitlin's hazel eyes grazed over Melody. "…six? And shoes?" Kaitlin cupped the receiver to say, "What size shoe do you wear?"

Bemusement prompted an answer. "Eight."

Kaitlin repeated that into the phone. "Good. Pull everything you have. We'll be right down."

Melody glanced at the clock. "The ball starts in a half hour."

Kaitlin waved away her concern. "That's plenty of time." She tucked her arm through Melody's. "Let's go, Cinderella. Time to get ready for the ball."

It wasn't Charlie's Angels who'd come to visit but three fairy godmothers. Melody laughed at the irony and followed them out the door. At least she would be well protected with her entourage.

Chapter Nine

"That is perfect," Valerie declared when Melody stepped out of the dressing room wearing one of the many dresses that Maggie, the manager of the hotel's chic boutique, had pulled out for her to try on.

Melody could hardly believe she was staring at herself in the mirror. The reflection looked more like a storybook princess than a cop. She fought the urge to twirl. The silky blue sleeveless dress clung to her curves, making her look sleek and svelte. And daring silver heels with peek-a-boo toe cutouts flashed from beneath the hem of the dress. The neckline was modest, yet she felt like she was exposing way more of herself than she was comfortable with. But how often did a girl get to be Cinderella?

Kaitlin came up behind her and unclipped the barrette at her nape, then fluffed her dark hair around her shoulders. "We'll run over to the hair salon and add a few curls with the hot iron and you'll be set."

"I don't know that we'll have time," Melody said. "Parker will be wondering where we are."

"The man will wait. Besides, once he sees you, he'll

think the extra few minutes worth it," Francine predicted.

A spurt of anticipation and anxiety made Melody's heart pound. "This is not me."

"It *is* you," Kaitlin insisted. "The blue in the dress makes your eyes almost translucent."

She couldn't argue with that. Even though blue eyes were a family trait, her eyes looked especially bright right now. It had to be the shop's lighting and not the excitement bubbling up from deep within. She smoothed a hand down the sleek lines of the dress. She felt sophisticated and feminine and pretty. What would Parker think? Why did she care?

Maggie stepped up with a mascara wand in one hand and a dark eyeliner pencil in the other. Nearing fifty, the fashionable woman looked like she could be in a magazine rather than tending shop in Sagebrush. "Let me darken your lashes."

Melody held still as Maggie applied the mascara and then the liner.

"A little lipstick," Maggie said as she stroked a tube of a velvety color over Melody's lips. "And a touch of gold." She snapped open a black case with a variety of eye shadows. Using the small brush she dusted a shimmering gold powder over her lids. When she stepped back, Melody was able to see the effect.

A nervous laugh escaped. The gold shadow and dark liner emphasized her eyes. The red lipstick stood out in stark contrast to her light skin.

She hardly recognized herself. "I don't know… I feel like I'm playing dress up in my mother's clothes." Though honestly, she couldn't remember her mother wearing anything as glamorous.

Valerie tsked. "You're just not used to it. You are absolutely beautiful and you're going to knock the socks off Parker Adams."

Melody couldn't deny the heady anticipation of seeing Parker's reaction. Not that what he thought mattered in the grand scheme of things. Tomorrow this sparkly version of herself would be tucked away as a nice memory. Nothing more.

But she planned to enjoy tonight.

When Melody walked sedately through the hotel's lobby, Parker did a double take. His core ignited in a burst of flames. He forgave her tardiness in a quick heartbeat. "Wow. You're…uh, hmm…"

He already thought she was a knockout. Now she'd transformed into a vibrant butterfly. Her dark hair curled around her shoulders. Her flawless skin provided the perfect backdrop for the carefully applied makeup that enhanced her features. The dress, well, the dress showed off her figure to perfection, leaving him tongue-tied.

The shy smile and the uncertainty in her vivid blue eyes touched something deep inside, making him want to pull her into his embrace and show her how gorgeous she really was, with or without the accoutrements.

He jammed his hands into the pockets of his tux. "You're beautiful."

"Thank you," she murmured, her gaze ducking slightly. "I feel a bit awkward. I'm not used to wearing…" She gestured toward herself.

"It suits you," he said and grimaced at the lame words.

She arched an eyebrow. "Better than my suits?"

He chuckled. "I think you're beautiful no matter what you're wearing."

Her eyes widened. "Really?"

"Yes, really." And the less he said on that subject, the better. Determined to keep his attraction to her on a short leash, he held out his arm. "Ready?"

She glided forward and took his arm. "As ready as Kaitlin, Valerie and Francine could make me."

"Ah, you had not one but three fairy godmothers. That's appropriate considering your penchant for all things Disney."

A rueful laugh escaped her ruby lips. "You noticed that?"

"Hard not to." He steered her toward the elevators. "I especially liked the huge Cheshire Cat." Belatedly, he remembered the cat had been ripped to shreds during the break-in.

Her smile faltered. "My father gave that to me when I was eight. He'd taken Sierra and me to Disneyland. Those were the best five days of my life." She bit her lower lip for a moment. Sudden tears glistened in her eyes. "Two weeks later, he left us."

A fist grabbed Parker's heart and squeezed. "I'm sorry for bringing it up."

"Nothing for you to be sorry about." She blinked rapidly. "It makes me so mad when I think about someone breaking into my apartment and ruining everything. And for what? Nothing."

He pulled her into an alcove and gathered her close. "You have your memories. Those can't be destroyed."

She laid her cheek against his tux and rested her arms lightly around his waist. "Thank you," she whispered.

The fresh clean scent of her hair teased his senses.

She felt warm and pliant in his embrace. His chest filled with tender emotions that both scared and thrilled him. Getting attached to her wasn't part of his assignment. He should let her go, should set her away, but he couldn't bring himself to break the contact. He liked holding her. More than he should, more than was wise.

She lifted her head and leaned back to look up at him. The fire in her eyes caught his breath. Blue fire. The hottest flame. Apparently, she wasn't immune to the attraction flaring between them. The intoxicating thought swirled through him. Her gaze searched his face, lingered on his mouth then lifted back to his eyes. Her lips parted. The yearning to lower his mouth to hers exploded within him. Pressure built in his blood. He tightened his hold as his resistance floundered.

"We should probably go," she said softly.

"Probably." But he didn't want to leave the privacy of the alcove. Or to let her go. He wanted to explore the look in her eyes, to feel her body pressed close, to lose himself in the wonder of Melody.

"Parker?"

The slight tremble in her voice slammed into him, forcing reality to the forefront of his mind. As attracted to Melody as he was, kissing her wasn't part of his plan. Or part of his job. He had let her sorrow and his attraction to her muddle his objective. He needed to stay professional, keep their relationship strictly business. For her sake. As well as his own.

Blowing out a condensed breath, he released her and stepped back. Parker reined in his emotions and vowed to keep a physical distance from his very beautiful and very tempting coworker.

As they left the alcove, Melody visibly tensed. She slowed and looked around.

Concern arced through him. "What is it?"

"I don't know." She tugged on her bottom lip with her even white teeth. "It felt like someone was watching us." She gave a shaky laugh. "Probably just my nerves."

Or her instincts.

Forget keeping a distance.

He couldn't forget someone out there had threatened Melody's life and trashed her apartment. Her life was in danger. And it was up to him to protect her. Even if he'd rather be kissing her.

Parker guided Melody toward the elevator. His hand, placed at the small of her back, created sparks of warmth to spread through her much like his words had. When he'd said she was beautiful, she'd believed him. And that made her feel...beautiful. She couldn't remember the last time she'd felt like this.

Several other elegantly dressed partygoers crowded inside the small compartment with them, forcing Melody to step back against Parker's broad chest. He slid an arm around her waist, making her a bit weak in the knees. Ever since that moment when she'd thought he was going to kiss her, her whole being hummed with anticipation.

The close quarters in the elevator only heightened the energy racing through her.

When they stepped out of the elevator, she expected Parker to move away from her, but to her surprise, he didn't. He kept his arm around her, molding her to his side, his hand resting lightly at her hip. The possessive gesture made her feel cherished. Something she could honestly say she'd never experienced. The crush of people forced them even closer. Heat coming off him made her head swim. Overwhelmed by his nearness, she had to concentrate to put one foot in front of the other.

They jostled their way into the grand ballroom and paused inside the entryway. The opulence of the elegant Victorian-inspired space stole Melody's breath. A large ornate brass chandelier hung from a high vaulted ceiling. Hardwood floors, polished to a radiant shine, stretched across the length of the long room. Grandiose gold-framed mirrors and exquisite artwork enhanced the solid walls to the left while to the right floor-to-ceiling windows allowed the fading evening sun to stream through like beacons from heaven. Above the main floor of the ballroom, suspended balconies provided perfect places for guests to observe those below. A stage set with a band sat at the far end, while long tables filled with appetizers and desserts lined the far wall.

"Wow, this is amazing," she breathed out, feeling like she was indeed Cinderella stepping into her first ball.

"It's lavish, that's for sure," Parker murmured. "I've heard that Dante Frears is part owner of this place."

"Didn't he and Captain McNeal serve in the military together?"

"Yes. They go way back. In fact, Dante put up the reward money of twenty-five thousand dollars for any information on Rio. Fat lot of good it did."

"You'd think a carrot like that would entice someone to come forward with information." Another missing piece to this already-puzzling case.

"Exactly. But I think people are more scared of The Boss than they are desperate for money."

"Which says a lot about the power and scope of this

crime lord." Melody suppressed a shiver. Somehow she'd drawn this mysterious criminal's attention even before she started asking questions about Rio.

Ally Jensen's words rose to the surface of her mind. Melody tugged Parker out of the throng of people into a more secluded spot. "I forgot to tell you something. Ally confessed to me today that Daniel was indeed selling drugs. And he had a partner."

Parker frowned, his fingers restless on her hip. "Who?"

"She didn't know. But I'm thinking this partner could be the one who killed Daniel. Maybe it was Zane."

"Doesn't seem likely. Whoever took that shot was a skilled marksman and highly trained."

That didn't sound like Zane.

Parker raised his free hand in greeting to someone walking by. "Come on, let's join the others."

She followed his gaze to a large round table near a window. She recognized several of the K-9 officers. Her three fairy godmothers were also at the table. Kaitlin arched an eyebrow. Heat infused Melody's cheeks for having been caught touching Parker in a very uncoworker way. *Great.*

Melody and Parker made their way through the swarm of people to join them.

Introductions were made around the table. Though Melody had seen most of the officers and had on occasion interacted with a few, she was glad to formally meet them.

"This is Nicki Johnson, uh, I mean Worth," Parker said as a blonde woman rose to shake her hand.

Melody had heard that K-9 officer and explosives expert Jackson Worth had recently married. Melody smiled at his new wife. The pretty blonde wore a red, empire-waist gown and had a lovely smile. Melody noted the evident roundness of her belly but was too polite to ask if she were expecting.

"Nice to meet you and yes," Nicki put a hand on her protruding tummy, obviously seeing the question in Melody's eyes. "I'm pregnant."

Melody appreciated the woman's directness. "Nice to meet you, too. And congratulations."

Nicki beamed as she looked at her new husband. "We're happy."

The dark-haired Jackson Worth looked at his new wife with tenderness and love. "Yes, we are."

Melody wondered what it would be like to feel that kind of love. To be cherished and protected, not only physically, but emotionally. To have someone put her welfare ahead of their own needs or wants.

A cynical voice in her head claimed that kind of self-less love didn't exist. That these people were kidding themselves. Melody had only to look at her dad and her ex-husband to see prime examples of selfishness at its worst. Both had left behind the people they'd professed to love, leaving her alone and abandoned.

But a small, gentle voice nudged her with the knowledge that God intended for humans to love sacrificially, unconditionally.

Melody sent a quick, silent prayer that Jackson and Nicki had found that kind of God-ordained love.

Yearning to find that sort of love swelled, but Melody quickly squelched the tide. She'd risked her heart once. And had it sliced to ribbons. Love wasn't a risk she was willing to take again.

The man at Valerie's side rose and extended his hand. "Special Agent Trevor Lewis."

Shifting her attention to the dark-haired man, she shook his hand. "Agent Lewis, nice to meet you. I'm surprised you're still in town. Has a new case come up?"

"He's with me," Valerie spoke up, placing her hand on his muscular arm.

Light glinted off the diamond solitaire on her ring finger.

"I see. Congratulations."

Valerie and Agent Lewis had recently worked together on a case to bring down a fugitive that turned out to be another cog in the Sagebrush crime syndicate. And obviously fell in love in the process. Melody was happy for the couple. She cut off the twinge of envy trying to take root.

"Where's Lee?" Parker asked as he held out a chair for Melody to take a seat.

Lee Calloway was another member of the K-9 unit.

"He and Lucy are in the buffet line," Valerie answered.

Melody remembered Lucy's story from the files she'd read relating to Rio's disappearance. Lucy had been found in the Lost Woods a few months back with no memory of who she was or how she'd come to be in the woods. At first the police had thought she was involved in Rio's kidnapping. But eventually they discovered she'd been running from her abusive ex-husband. The man had tried to hurt Lucy but Lee apprehended him before he could do her any harm.

Trevor held out his hand to his fiancée. "I'm ready for some food, too."

Taking his hand, Valerie rose and followed him to the buffet tables.

"Are you hungry yet?" Parker asked Melody.

They way he looked at her with such care made her stomach clench. She shook her head. "But I would love something cold to drink."

He smiled and then looked at the others. "Anyone else?"

"I would love lemonade," Kaitlin replied.

Francine held up her glass. "I'm good."

"I'll be right back," Parker said and strode toward the beverage table.

Melody watched him walking away, feeling suddenly bereft. Which really didn't make any sense.

Kaitlin scooted closer with a curious gleam in her pretty eyes. "You and Parker make an adorable couple."

A heated flush swept up her neck. The thought of them as a couple pleased her more than she'd care to admit. "I've already told you it's not like that."

"It looked just like that when you two were getting cozy in the alcove downstairs," Francine piped in.

"You're the envy of every single woman here tonight," Kaitlin teased.

Melody's gaze drifted to Parker. He stood talking now with Austin Black, another K-9 detective, and their captain, Slade McNeal.

"We're just friends."

"Really?"

The doubt in Kaitlin's voice set Melody's teeth on edge. She really didn't want to entertain the fantasy that there could be more between her and Parker but her friend's reluctance to believe her was making it harder to block. "Yes. Really."

"He's a good man," Kaitlin stated. "You could do a lot worse."

She had no doubt about that. "We work together."

"There's no law that says you can't find love in the workplace," Francine said.

Melody shook her head. "Give it a rest."

"Give what a rest?" Parker asked from behind her shoulder.

She twisted to see him. He held two tall glasses of lemonade, and she reached for one of the drinks. "Thank you."

"Kaitlin."

"Thank you." Kaitlin took the glass he offered.

Parker took his seat. "So what are we talking about?"

"Oh, this and that," Francine said with a big grin.

Kaitlin snickered.

Melody sipped from her lemonade, hoping the cool liquid would soothe her burning cheeks.

Trevor and Valerie returned, their plates piled with savory treats.

"Valerie tells me you run the youth center," Trevor said as he settled into his chair.

"I do, along with Jim Wheaton." Only too happy to discuss the center, Melody told them about their programs and services.

"Melody has done an awesome job of providing the kids a safe and healthy environment," Parker added.

Pleased by his words, Melody smiled at him with gratitude. He stretched his arm across the back of her chair. His fingers drew lazy circles over the bare skin of her shoulder, making her forget people surrounded them. She lost herself in the chocolate depths of his eyes.

"Mind if I join you all?" Slade McNeal asked, standing near Kaitlin's right shoulder.

Pulled from the magnetic draw of Parker's gaze, Melody noticed that Kaitlin straightened but didn't glance up at the newcomer. Instead, her friend studiously sipped from her glass. Interesting.

Melody rose. "Here, sir. You can have my seat."

Kaitlin's gaze snapped to hers then quickly lowered. Was that panic in her green eyes? Doubly interesting.

Parker pulled Melody's chair out so she could move away from the table. He gave her a quizzical look.

"How about those buffet tables…" she said airily.

Parker held out his arm. "This way."

As they walked away from the table, Melody glanced back over her shoulder. Slade slid into the seat next to Kaitlin. Melody wondered why Kaitlin had seemed so nervous about Slade joining their table. Was there something going on with those two?

Parker led her to the food line. As they waited, they chatted with the older couple in front of them. Melody introduced Parker to one of the youth center's donors.

"This is such a lovely venue," Mrs. Atherton gushed. The Athertons were one of Sagebrush's more affluent families. "I'm so glad the committee decided to have a formal ball rather than a picnic in the park."

"I've always enjoyed the community picnic each year," Melody said politely, thinking how the picnic involved not only the adults but the kids of the community, as well.

"Yes, they are fun and all. But sometimes change is good. There was much debate about the venue for this year's fund-raiser. But Mr. Frears offered this place free."

"Are you on the committee?" Parker asked.

"My wife is on all the committees," Mr. Atherton intoned with a good dose of humor.

"I like to be involved," Mrs. Atherton huffed.

"More like you want to be in control, dear," her husband teased with a light laugh as he took a plate from a high stack.

"Nonsense." Mrs. Atherton touched the string of pearls at her neck.

Mr. Atherton winked at them before turning his attention to the variety of dishes available.

Parker's eyes twinkled with mirth as he handed Melody a plate, their fingers brushing against each other. Sparks traveled up her arm and heated her cheeks. They made their way along the table and then rejoined the other K-9 officers. Captain McNeal had left the table. As had Kaitlin. Melody glanced around and found her friend standing near the beverage table alone. Melody excused herself and wound her way over to Kaitlin.

"Are you okay?" she asked, reaching for another glass of lemonade. The glass was cold in her hand.

Kaitlin gave her a small smile. "Yes, I'm fine. Thirsty."

"What's with you and Captain McNeal?"

Kaitlin sputtered. "What? Nothing."

"It didn't look like nothing," Melody mused.

"I don't know what you're talking about."

"Are you still working with his son?" Kaitlin had been doing some informal dog-therapy sessions with Caleb McNeal ever since the boy's mother had been killed in a car bomb.

"Yes, I am."

"And?"

"And Caleb was making some good progress until Rio was kidnapped. They were best friends."

"Rio missing must be hard on them all," Melody said.

Kaitlin nodded. "It is. Patrick McNeal, Slade's father, blames himself. Caleb blames everyone. And Slade, well, he's more focused on finding Rio than he is on connecting with his son."

"I'm sure he's trying. He's a good man from what I know of him."

Kaitlin eyed her. "There were rumors he was responsible for your nephew Daniel's death."

"He wasn't." Melody sipped from her lemonade.

"I'm sorry, I shouldn't have brought that up."

She cleared her throat. "It's okay."

"I don't know if I ever told you, but I'd met your sister a few times when she worked at Arianna's Diner," Kaitlin said.

"No, you hadn't mentioned that." Sadness spread through Melody. "I miss her so much."

Kaitlin laid a comforting hand on her arm. "She seemed like a sweet woman. You two have the same eyes."

As her chest ached with grief, images of her sister rose in Melody's mind. "I heard that a lot growing up."

"Did Daniel look like his mother?"

"He had the same dark hair but his eyes were different," Melody replied.

"Oh, how so?"

"His eyes were an unusual silver color and shaped—" Melody's gaze was drawn to a tall, distinguished couple coming toward them. Dante Frears and his pretty wife in the flesh. His expensive tux emphasized the width of his shoulders. His salted hair was shorn close to his head. His odd silvery-blue, almond-shaped eyes zeroed in on her…

"Melody, you okay?"

Kaitlin's concerned voice barely penetrated the sudden fog enveloping Melody. For a moment, the world seemed to swim as an image of Daniel superimposed itself over Dante's approaching face.

They had the same icy almond-shaped silvery-blue eyes.

Melody's breath caught, her hand loosened on the glass she held.

Could Dante be Daniel's father?

Chapter Ten

The sound of breaking glass pierced through the din of the ballroom. Parker's gaze whipped to the source of the sound along with the attention of everyone in the room. The strains of music coming from the jazz band drifted to a silence.

Melody.

Shards of glass littered the floor at her feet.

Fear punched Parker in the gut. He scrambled from his seat and rushed to her side. With a quick once-over, he assessed her for injury. "Are you hurt? What happened?"

Her gaze lifted from the mess on the floor, flicked briefly to Dante Frears and then met Parker's. "I—the glass was slippery."

Two men in waiter's uniforms approached with a mop and cleaning supplies.

"It's okay, folks, just a little mishap," Dante said and steered his wife away.

Kaitlin touched Melody's arm. "We should move out of the way and let them clean this up."

Melody nodded. She reached for Parker's arm, her

grip firm. He slid an arm around her waist. She trembled. Something had unnerved her. But he'd have to wait until they were alone to question her. They walked back to their table.

He pulled out her chair and guided her into the seat. "You're sure you're okay?"

Her intense gaze held his. He could see she wanted to say something. She glanced quickly around and then nodded. "Yes, I'm fine."

Unconvinced, he sat next to her. Conversations resumed around them. Parker tried to concentrate on what was being said, but his attention centered on the woman at his side. She was pale and silent, lost in her own thoughts.

He leaned toward her. "You're sure you're okay?"

"For now."

He tucked a dark curl behind her ear and trailed his finger down her cheek. Her skin felt petal smooth. "I wish you'd talk to me."

She touched his arm and leaned closer. "Later."

He laced his fingers through hers. "I'll hold you to that."

When it was time for him to step up on the stage to perform as part of a quartet, he wished he didn't have to leave her side.

"It's okay. Go," she said, obviously sensing his hesitation. "I can't wait to hear you sing."

He glanced around the table at his fellow K-9 officers, knowing each would protect her if needed. She'd be safe until he returned to her.

He leaned in close to whisper in her ear. "We'll leave as soon as we can. Then you'll tell me what really happened."

She turned her head. Their gazes met. Gratitude softened her gaze along with something else. Something that made his heart pound.

"Yes," she breathed out.

He touched her shoulder, the skin warm and silky, then made his way to the stage.

The deep, pleasing tone of Parker's baritone voice made Melody smile. He sang the lead melody for most of the songs while the tenors and bass backed him up. With each note she found herself falling a little more in like with him. Not love. She couldn't go there. But like. Oh, yeah. She liked him a whole lot.

She clapped loudly when the quartet finished.

When he returned to the table, his eyes glimmered. "What did you think?"

"You were wonderful," she gushed, and touched his arm. "I could listen to you sing nonstop."

The pleasure on his face sent her heart rate soaring.

He leaned closer to whisper in her ear. "I'll sing for you anytime."

She turned her head to face him. Their lips nearly touched. Her gaze dropped to his mouth then back to his eyes. It was too easy to lose herself in the way he looked at her as if she were the only person in the room. Swallowing hard, she fought the urge to close the distance and kiss him.

"Let's get out of here," he said, his voice low and coaxing.

She blinked. Attraction sizzled between them, threatening to consume her. "Can we go for a drive? Get some fresh air?"

And some much-needed space.

The knowing look on his face said he understood exactly what she was feeling. "Brilliant idea."

They said their goodbyes quickly and made their way to his car.

"Where to?" He started the engine.

"Just drive." She sat back, trying to regain her equilibrium. What was it about Parker that made her forget herself? She nearly laughed aloud at the absurdity of the question. The answer was obvious. Everything.

"You gonna tell me what had you so freaked earlier?" Parker asked, breaking the silence. They were passing through town now. The shops were closing up for the night. A few pedestrians strolled down the sidewalks.

Jolted out of her musings, she thought back to the moment she'd met Dante Frears's gaze. Melody certainly didn't run in his circles, so she'd never seen the man up close before. He always sent his donation checks to the youth center through the mail.

So seeing him, seeing his almond-shaped silvery-blue eyes had sparked a sense of recognition so strong she'd been unable to function for a moment.

She shifted in the seat to face Parker. "I think Dante Frears may be Daniel's father."

Surprise flashed across Parker's features. "Why do you think that?"

"They have the same eyes."

He was quiet as he turned off the main road. "How can you be sure? You haven't seen your nephew in five years."

Gazing out at the looming trees of the Lost Woods ahead of them, she said, "Daniel's eyes were a different blue than Sierra's. They were almost silver just like Frears's."

"A lot of people have light blue eyes. Even Captain McNeal has them."

She shook her head. "The captain's eyes are more robin's egg blue than silver."

"For real?" he scoffed. "How do you even notice the difference?"

She rolled her eyes. "You are *such* a guy. But it's not only their eye color that is similar. The shape. The tilt. The *look*. Daniel's eyes are exactly like Frears's."

"It could be coincidence," he stated, bringing the car to a halt in the parking lot of the entrance to the Lost Woods. Up ahead, the trailhead marker could be seen in the beam of the Mustang's headlights.

"I don't believe in coincidence."

He cut the engine. "But eye color and shape are not enough to prove anything. Certainly not to prove Dante Frears is Daniel's father."

She leaned her head back against the headrest. "That's true. And I guess it wouldn't be a good idea to go up to him and ask if he'd had a relationship with my sister."

Parker undid his seat belt. "No, that would probably be a huge mistake. He and Slade are good friends. Offending Dante Frears could damage your career."

"I suppose you're right." Still, she couldn't shake the idea that Daniel was Dante Frears's son.

"Do you hear that?" Parker rolled down his window.

Melody tilted her head to listen, trying to discern the origins of the various noises of the woods. In the distance, she distinctly heard a dog barking. "Do you think that's Rio?"

"I don't know." He opened the driver's side door. He reached inside his jacket and withdrew his service weapon from the shoulder holster he wore. "Let's go find out."

Melody undid her seat belt, grabbed her weapon from her purse and climbed out of the car. Following behind Parker, she picked her way through the gravel parking lot as best she could, given her high-heeled sandals. When she stepped onto the trail, her heels sank into the soft dirt. She wasn't exactly dressed for a chase through the woods.

Parker paused to wait for her. She waved him on. "Go ahead. I'm right behind you."

The barking faded. The darkness swallowed them up. Light from the moon barely penetrated the canopy of tree branches. Pungent, earthy smells teased Melody's senses. She quickly lost sight of Parker on the trail ahead. Shadows shifted and swayed all around her, disorienting her.

She proceeded a little farther down the path then halted. "Parker?"

No answer.

A rustling from her left jackknifed her heart like an injection of epinephrine. She tensed. Darting for the cover of a tree, her breathing turned shallow and loud in her ears. Her finger hovering over the trigger of her gun.

A man stepped into view and her breath caught in her throat.

All around him the black forest created a dense barrier between him and his quarry. Parker stopped to listen. Silence, except for a chirping cricket or two. He could no longer hear the dog barking. He ground his teeth in frustration.

Doubling back the way he'd come, he expected

to find Melody close by. But darkness hid her. Trees loomed to his right and his left. A spear of concern skewered him. "Melody?"

She stepped out from behind a tree trunk. "Here. I wasn't sure it was you."

A shaft of moonlight streaming through the branches touched on her like a beacon. Her blue eyes and dress reflected the light, making her appear ethereal.

The anxious tension in his shoulders released but a different sort of tension filled him. Longing to take her into his arms spread through him, making his pulse pound. He strode toward her, willing his heart rate to slow and pushing the longing back to the edges where he wouldn't be tempted to give in to it.

She held her weapon at her side. "Could you tell which direction the dog went?"

"North. If I had Sherlock with me, I'd have followed." But Sherlock was kenneled at the training center so Parker could attend the party. And he couldn't forget about Melody. No way was he leaving her alone out here even if she was capable of taking care of herself.

"Do you think it was your captain's dog?"

"Could be. Like I mentioned before, a shepherd matching Rio's description has been spotted in the woods since his disappearance. And let's not forget about that informant fessing up that Rio was taken by The Boss to find something in these woods."

She nodded thoughtfully. "Daniel died in the north part of these woods. Whatever The Boss is looking for is most likely tied up with Daniel and his death."

"But that was five years ago. Rio was taken only four months ago. I don't see the connection."

"The connection is these woods. They hold secrets." Her voice trembled.

He wasn't sure if he heard distress or just the effects of the cool night air. He doubted she'd admit to any fear so he went with the latter. "You're cold."

He shrugged off his jacket and laid it over her shoulders. "Come on, let's get you back to the hotel."

When they arrived at the hotel, he parked in the hotel's underground parking garage and they took the elevator straight to the tenth floor. Officer Truman was already there waiting for Melody.

"I'll say good-night," Parker said at the door.

She slipped off his jacket and handed it to him. A soft smile played at the corners of her mouth. "Thank you."

Feeling her smile all the way to his toes, he folded the jacket over his arm to keep from reaching for her. *Get back on track, Adams.* "Tomorrow I plan to take Sherlock back to the woods and see if he can pick up Rio's scent."

She glanced back through the open suite door to where Officer Truman sat in a chair reading a magazine, then gazed back at Parker. "That's a good idea. It's too bad we didn't have him with us tonight."

He smiled as her words echoed the thought he'd had earlier. They were so in sync with each other. It was a bit disconcerting and yet…he found he liked it. He wished they could be alone for a few more minutes. "Yes. Though we are hardly dressed for traipsing in the woods tonight."

Her eyes sparkled. "Too true. You look handsome in your tux, by the way."

He sucked in a quick breath at the compliment. Though he'd already told her she looked stunning, he felt compelled to tell her again, just in case she forgot. "You are beautiful."

In the dim light of the hall, he could see her cheeks flushing. Their gazes locked, held. His nerve endings came alive with the velocity of an electric current. The impulse to kiss her overwhelmed him.

With a control he hadn't had to employ in a long time, he forced himself to remain still. Kissing her would be a bad idea. He'd been asked to keep her safe. And she was. The hotel was secure. She had a female officer in residence. There was no reason for him not to back away and say good-night.

Yet he didn't want to leave her. But staying was out of the question. Seeing her tomorrow was a given. "Would you want to come with Sherlock and me to search the woods in the morning?"

She blinked, a slow sweep of long lashes. "Yes. Yes, I would."

Her voice sounded a bit breathless as if she, too, were struggling with the attraction arcing between them.

He was relieved to know he wasn't the only one feeling the magnetic draw. All the more reason for him to be professional and rein in his longings. Tomorrow in the light of day, he'd have better control of himself. "Okay. I'll swing by tomorrow around eight."

"I'll be ready."

After a heartbeat, he turned to go.

"Parker?"

He braced himself and turned to face her. If he didn't retreat soon, his control would slip and he'd kiss her for sure. He wondered what she'd do if he did. The question had him stepping toward her.

"I know I'm right about Dante Frears being Daniel's father."

He silently groaned. A reality check if ever there was one. He'd hoped she'd let that theory go. He understood how important figuring out what happened to her nephew was, but he was worried about her. "Melody—"

She held up a hand. "I know. The only way to prove it would be DNA. And getting Dante Frears's DNA would be difficult unless he freely gave it."

"Approaching him about it would cause problems for you and the department." Needing to touch her, to show that he cared for her, he tucked a curl behind her ear. "Don't torture yourself with this. Daniel is gone. Whoever his father was doesn't matter anymore. He can't be doing anything for the boy."

A flash of pain crossed her face.

An answering ache throbbed through Parker. "I'm sorry. I don't want to hurt you, but it's not healthy for you to continue down this path. Your memory of your nephew's eyes isn't grounds to start an investigation into one of the town's most prominent citizens."

Her mouth twisted, and disappointment lingered in her gaze. "I suppose you're right."

Although she'd acquiesced, unease slithered down his spine. He knew her too well to believe she'd drop the subject so easily. "I know you want to find answers. I want to help you. We'll keep digging, I promise. We'll find out who killed your nephew and why."

"You're a good man, Parker." She leaned in to kiss his cheek.

Her words wrapped around his heart. Tender affection bloomed as her soft lips branded his cheek. He had to dig deep down for another ounce of control to not reach for her, to pull her closer and brand her as thoroughly. He couldn't forget they had an audience. But Officer Truman wasn't as big a concern as Parker's pounding heart.

He was in trouble. Big, big trouble. And he hadn't a clue how to get out of it.

Or if he even wanted to…

"Well, that was unproductive," Melody groused.

She was tired and her feet hurt. But at least today she was prepared for a romp through the forest. Last night she'd been dressed in heels and a form-fitting dress that had not only restricted her movements but had made her feel as pretty as Parker had said.

She still had to pinch herself every time she replayed his words in her head.

Which happened several times throughout the night and this morning while they'd searched the woods with Sherlock for two solid hours hoping to find Rio's scent. The beagle had tracked a rabbit to its burrow, found a baby bird that had fallen from its nest and led them on a merry chase through the trees only to halt at a fire access road.

"Not necessarily," Parker countered. "I'm betting that access road has more traffic on it than it should. I sent the CSU team to take imprints of the tire tracks we saw. They'll compare them to the forest-service vehicles."

He held the door to the youth center open for her. She walked past Sherlock, the cord of his leash rubbing against her pant leg.

"And if they don't match, we'll know for certain someone has been using that road unauthorized." That was sound logic. And hopefully, from the impressions, they'd discover what type of vehicle had been there recently. At least it would give them something to go on. Melody hoped Rio was still alive and well. She sent up a silent prayer for Rio's safe return. So many people were waiting for the dog to come home. Most important, Captain McNeal's son.

"I'll be back at five to escort you to the hotel," Parker said after she'd unlocked her office door and pushed it open. "How about we grab dinner together?"

An excited flutter hit her tummy. Another social outing? As a protective measure...or because he had feelings for her? Did she for him? Yes. Yes, she did. Friendship, caring, affection. Nothing too scary. Nothing she couldn't handle. Or voice out loud. "Okay. Sounds good."

With a salute, he and Sherlock left. Melody entered her office and sat at her desk. There was plenty to keep her busy for the next several hours, and the time flew.

A knock drew her attention. Ally stood at the threshold of the office.

"So everything is all set for tonight's movie night."

Melody waved her in. "Good," she said. "You did a great job with the last one. I'm sure this one will be a success, as well."

Ally smiled. "I don't think I've told you how much I appreciate you giving me the opportunity to help here. Being a part of the youth center has changed my life."

Melody remembered the angry and defensive girl she'd once been. "You're welcome."

"I'm sorry I didn't tell you about Daniel before."

A shaft of grief speared Melody. "I understand. Is there anything else you want to tell me now?"

The young woman shook her head. She walked to the framed photo sitting on top of the filing cabinet, and picked up the picture of Daniel and Sierra taken a year before they died.

"I miss him," Ally whispered.

Melody's heart squeezed tight. "Me, too." And Sierra. "Can you hand me that photo?"

Ally brought it to the desk. Melody stared at the picture of Daniel, studied his eyes. The photo was taken outside of Sierra's apartment building. Sunlight reflected in Daniel's silvery-blue eyes. Eyes eerily similar to Dante Frears's.

"I want you to look at something for me." Melody turned to her computer. Her fingers hit the keyboard and a few seconds later Dante Frears's image appeared on the screen. Almond-shaped silvery-blue eyes stared at the camera in a publicity head shot.

Melody held the photo of Daniel next to the computer. "What do you think?"

Confusion wrinkled Ally's brow. "About what?"

Melody didn't want to lead her to seeing the similarity. "Look at their faces. Tell me what you see."

Ally considered for a moment. Her eyes widened a fraction. "Their eyes. They have the same eyes. Who is that man?"

"Dante Frears."

Ally's mouth formed a stunned "oh."

Chapter Eleven

Elated that someone else saw the uncanny resemblance, Melody was more determined than ever to find out the truth.

Jim Wheaton stepped into the office. "What about Dante Frears?"

Melody motioned him over. If he saw it, too, then Parker would have to believe her and help her figure out how to confirm her suspicion. "Dante Frears might be Daniel's father."

Jim's steps faltered then he rushed the last few feet to her side. "You're joking. Dante Frears can't possibly be your nephew's father. That's ridiculous."

"Look closer. They have the same eyes," she insisted.

Jim's gaze bounced between the two images. "No. I don't see it."

"I do," Ally stated. "And that would make sense."

"How?" Jim barked. "How could Dante Frears, a well-respected and wealthy citizen of Sagebrush being the father of some drug-addicted punk make sense?"

Melody's temper flared. "Daniel wasn't a punk. He was a troubled kid. And my nephew."

"A kid dealing drugs," Jim shot back.

She narrowed her gaze on him. "That's only speculation." At least it had only been speculation until Ally had confessed to her yesterday that Daniel *had* been dealing. But Melody hadn't shared that information with Jim. And frankly didn't feel the need. Not with his surly attitude.

"Everyone knew it. You're the only one who wouldn't believe it," he countered.

Was that true? She searched her heart. Deep inside she knew what he said was true. She hadn't wanted to believe her nephew was dealing. "He had a partner."

Jim drew back. "He did? Who?"

Melody shook her head. "I don't know yet. But I intend to find out."

"You're like a dog with a bone. Let your nephew rest in peace. Stop trying to stir up trouble. Especially with Dante Frears. He's one of the center's top donors."

Beads of sweat rolled down Jim's temple. Overly hot or nervous? Why was everyone so afraid to upset Dante Frears? First Parker, now Jim. Just because the man had wealth enough to spare didn't mean everyone should walk on eggshells around him.

"I know that," Melody stated. "Which is why I won't say or do anything until I have proof."

"There's no proof to find." Jim's gaze narrowed. "You told me your sister wouldn't tell you who fathered Daniel. She obviously didn't want anyone to know. You should respect that and drop this whole thing."

"Daniel found out who his father was before he died," Melody informed him.

Jim pulled a face. "No way."

"I'm pretty sure he talked to the man," Ally interjected. "Daniel kept saying the guy would pay for not acknowledging him."

Jim whipped around to stare at Ally. "Did he say who this man was?"

She shook her head. "Only that the man lives here in Sagebrush."

Maybe he didn't want to acknowledge the similarities between Daniel and Dante but he saw it, Melody was sure. "Don't worry, Jim, I'm not going to do anything to jeopardize our funding."

He nodded stiffly. "I hope not. It's hard enough keeping the doors on the place open with all the rumors of drug trafficking."

Melody frowned. "We've put those rumors to rest."

He shrugged. "People have long memories."

Parker and Sherlock appeared in the doorway of the office. "Is this a private party or can we join in?"

Melody's heart did a little flip at the sight of him. He looked so good in his uniform. Though he'd been spectacular in his tux, as well. "Come in. We were discussing the rumors that the center is being used for drug trafficking."

"Sherlock and I haven't found any more, not even traces."

Satisfaction arched through Melody. "See, nothing to worry about."

Jim's mouth pressed into a thin line. "Just don't go starting any other rumors." With that he stalked out of the office, brushing past Parker and Sherlock without acknowledging them.

Parker shook his head. "Is he always so grouchy?"

"Yes!" Ally nodded in an exaggerated way.

Feeling the need to defend her partner, Melody said,

"He's not a bad person. I don't think he ever really got over the death of his wife. And the center has become his whole world. He's protective of it."

"What rumors are you going to start?" Parker asked, alluding to Jim's parting shot.

She turned her computer monitor toward him and held up Daniel's photo so the two images were side by side. "You tell me."

Parker studied the images. His gaze then zeroed on her. "You're not going to give this a rest, are you?"

She shook her head.

He glanced back at the photos. "There are similarities but…"

"But you still don't think it's enough to require checking Dante's DNA?"

"We don't have the authority to do that. Even if he is Daniel's father, that isn't a police matter. Besides, what point would there be to bringing it to light now? It would only embarrass Dante."

"But it could shed some light on why Daniel was so out of control that night." She couldn't keep the pleading tone out of her voice.

"You're tenacious, I'll give you that."

Hadn't Jim said that, as well? "It's what makes me a good cold-case detective."

"True." He let out a resigned breath. "I'll talk to McNeal. But don't get your hopes up."

Pleased, she beamed. Not only were some of her questions on the brink of being answered, but also Parker believed in her enough to put himself out there by taking her suspicions to his boss. Affection flooded her heart. She could easily find herself falling for the handsome detective if she weren't careful. But letting her guard down wasn't something she wanted to do again. No matter how much she cared about Parker Adams.

At dinner last night, Melody had agreed to accompany Parker to church again. So this morning Parker headed downtown to the Sagebrush Hotel to pick her up. As he drove, he realized how happy it made him that she'd let her faith show.

Her story about her grandfather had touched him, and he was thankful she'd had such a strong and positive influence in her life. Especially given that her father and her husband had both abandoned her.

He couldn't imagine what her ex-husband had been thinking. Melody was such a tremendous lady. Kind, smart, fun. Tough, yet vulnerable. Parker had to admit, to himself at least, that she was working her way into his heart. But caring for her was as far as he could allow himself to go. Anything more would only be a disaster. He'd end up disappointing her or hurting her. Neither of which he was willing to do.

He parked in the garage of the hotel. His phone rang before he climbed out of the car. An unfamiliar number displayed on the screen. "Parker Adams."

"There's been a hit put out on a cop."

The words sent a chill down Parker's spine. He knew that voice and trusted the caller. "Harry, you better have details."

His confidential informant cleared his throat. "I'm not 411, you know. I just pass on what I got."

"Who's the hit on?"

"A detective named Zachary."

Air swooshed from Parker's lungs. Melody. He couldn't let anything happen to her. "Who put out the hit?"

"Hey, man, if I tell you that I'm as good as dead. You do your thing and protect the cop and it'll be good."

Rage built in Parker's chest. No one was going to harm Melody. "I need to know who ordered the hit."

A moment of silence met his demand. "Get me a ticket out of this town and I'll tell you."

"Done."

"Meet me at the bus station in an hour."

Parker checked his watch. "An hour." He hung up and dialed Melody's suite, his fingers clumsy on the phone.

"Hello?"

Hearing her voice did funny things to his insides. Things he chose at the moment to put on the back burner. Her safety was the priority. And he'd do anything in his power to protect her. "It's me. Are you okay?"

"Yes, fine. Are you here? I'll be right down."

The happiness in her voice tugged at him in a way nothing else could. "No. Stay in the suite and away from the windows."

"Why?" Her voice sharpened. "What's happened?"

He swallowed past a lump of dread to say, "Someone's put a hit out on you."

Her soft gasp echoed in his head.

"I'm on my way to meet with an informant. I'll get the details. Until I return, stay safe. Fill Officer Truman in."

There was a slight pause before she said, "I will. You be careful, too."

"Count on it." He had to come back to protect her.

But first he needed to find out who wanted her dead.

* * *

The bus station at the edge of Sagebrush's main drag was busier than Parker would have guessed on a Sunday morning. People must want to start their journeys early. He spotted Harry huddled near the ticket booth. Parker casually made his way through the milling passengers waiting for the bus to open its door.

The attendant smiled a greeting when he stepped up to the ticket window.

"Where's that bus going?" Parker asked.

"Los Angeles," the attendant replied.

Parker glanced at Harry and received a subtle thumbs-up from the older man. Parker bought a one-way ticket, then walked into the restroom. He made a quick sweep, making sure there was no one inside. A moment later Harry shuffled in.

"It's clear," Parker assured him. "Who put the hit on Detective Zachary? Was it The Boss?"

Harry shook his head. "Naw. But he works for The Boss, so it's almost the same thing."

"A name," Parker ground out.

Harry held out his hand. "My ticket."

"Not until you give me what I want."

"Another cop. Jim Wheaton."

The name punched Parker under the ribs like an upper cut. "Are you sure?"

"Yeah. I'm sure. That cop has rousted me a couple times from sleeping in the youth center parking lot. So yeah, I recognized him when he came into the neighborhood last night."

"Did you hear him say the words? Actually say he wanted Detective Zachary dead?" Parker couldn't accuse Jim of hiring an assassin to take out Melody without being absolutely sure.

"With my own ears. I saw him down on Lost Woods Road. I knew he was up to no good. I followed him. Saw him meet with a couple of thugs. Real nasty dudes. Heard him say he wanted Detective Zachary off the streets by tomorrow. He paid them a bundle of cash. Told them they'd get more when the deed was done."

Parker's fist clenched around the ticket, crumpling the paper.

"Hey, don't ruin it. You'll have to buy another," Harry snapped.

Parker handed over the ticket. "Thank you, Harry. Take care of yourself."

Harry snatched the ticket. "I always do. See you later. Or not."

He shuffled out of the restroom. Parker gripped the sides of the sink. Fury like he'd never experienced detonated in his chest. Jim Wheaton. Melody's partner and friend had put a hit out on her. She would be crushed when Parker told her. His gut clenched.

Not a task he was looking forward to, no matter how necessary. He hated the thought of causing her more anguish, but it couldn't be helped. She had to know the truth. As did their bosses. But he owed it to Melody to tell her first.

He hightailed it back to the Sagebrush Hotel and prayed with each passing second for God to give him the words to tell the bad news.

"I don't believe you." Melody stalked away from Parker while his words echoed in her head. "There's no way Jim would do anything to harm me."

Parker spread his hands. "What can I say? I'm telling you what my informant told me."

"And you trust this informant over me?"

He frowned. "What? No! But I do trust my informant over Jim Wheaton."

"Why? Why would he want me dead?" It didn't make sense. But then nothing had made sense for a long time now. From Rio's disappearance to her nephew's grave being dug up to the drugs being found in the locker at the youth center. Not to mention the break-ins and the threatening note. What was she missing?

How was Jim involved? *If* he was involved. She thought about his nervousness yesterday. She'd thought it was due to his concern for the center. What else was going on?

"Have you reported this?" she asked.

"Not yet. I wanted you to know first. I hated the thought of you hearing this from someone else."

On some level his words pleased her, but she was so upset by his news that she couldn't take the time right now to analyze what she was feeling. "Look, I've known Jim for a long time. Worked with him closely. Can we give him the benefit of the doubt until we talk to him?"

A scowl deepened the lines between his brows. His eyes grew hard and implacable.

"Please," she implored before he could refuse her. "Let me talk to him. I'm sure there's some explanation. And if it comes to it, I'll arrest him myself." Though she couldn't fathom what that explanation could be. Her stomach roiled. For a moment she thought she might lose the breakfast she'd eaten an hour ago.

Parker's expression softened ever so slightly. "For you…we'll go to his house and talk to him. But we have to inform our captains and we're not taking any chances with your safety. I'm not going to let anything happen to you. We're taking a couple of uniforms with us and getting a search warrant, just in case."

Sudden tears pricked her eyes. She wasn't even sure why. Maybe because for the first time in a very long time, someone cared about her, really cared. "Thank you."

An hour later after arranging backup and securing the warrant they were on their way to Jim Wheaton's residence. He lived in a suburb on the east side of town in a single-level ranch on a quiet street. Parker pulled the Mustang to the curb. Sherlock had his paws up on the back of her seat. His hot breath ruffled the fine hairs at her nape, but she found she didn't mind. Having the canine with them made her feel even more protected.

A blue-and-white cruiser stopped behind them.

Trepidation churned through Melody. She walked next to Parker and Sherlock to the front door, and each step felt like a nail was being driven into her chest. Parker rapped his knuckles against the white painted door. Sherlock sniffed the crack of the door.

No one answered the knock.

Melody moved to the window and peered through the open blinds. The living room looked like a tornado had touched down. Tension tightened the muscles in her shoulders. Was this chaos a sign of a struggle or was this indicative of his housekeeping skills? The mess seemed out of character with the man who kept his woodworking tools neat and orderly. "I don't see him. But the place is a wreck."

"We'll have to come back," Parker stated.

"Let's check the back," Melody said, not willing to

give up so easily. The man's reputation was on the line, not to mention her life. And the odds of him waiting inside to blow her head off were how high?

Using caution, she stepped off the porch and across the brown grass toward the rear of the house.

The back patio had weathered furniture beneath a faded awning. The glass slider was locked. Melody cupped her hands to the glass and peered inside. The kitchen and dining rooms weren't any better than the living room.

Her heart hammered against her ribs.

"Parker!"

"Here," he whispered from right behind her. Sherlock nudged her foot.

"Something is wrong." Was Jim a victim of violence? Had the same person who'd ransacked Melody's office and apartment now targeted Jim?

Sherlock's sudden barking shattered the silence following Melody's announcement. The dog pawed frantically at the slider, his nails scraping on the glass, at the wooden frame.

Dismayed, she lifted her gaze to meet Parker's. She'd seen the small beagle behave like this once before. At the youth center. When he'd found the stash of drugs in the locker.

"Only one thing does this for him," Parker confirmed. "Contraband."

Chapter Twelve

The grim tone to Parker's voice slid through Melody, and she shuddered with dread. "Oh, Jim, what have you gotten yourself into?"

And what did it have to do with her? Why did he want her dead?

Parker turned to the uniformed officer who'd followed them around the house. "We need that search warrant."

A lump of apprehension stuck in her throat. Swallowing around it, she shook her head. She didn't want to believe this was happening. How had Jim become the bad guy? Worry chomped through her. "He could be inside hurt or possibly even…" A deep grief impaled her. "Dead."

Sympathy pooled in Parker's gaze. Her chest heaved as alarm reared. She'd say this qualified for exigent circumstances, which superseded a warrant. "We need to find a way in."

"Agreed." He tugged Sherlock from the door so he could work on the lock. "Not sure I can jimmy this open."

"How about a window?" She stepped off the patio and onto the soft dirt beneath what she assumed was a bedroom window.

She could just reach the edge of the screen. Using her fingernails, she pried the screen loose and popped it out, setting it to the side. Leveraging her hands against the glass pane, she pushed sideways and it slid soundlessly open. Triumph flared.

"Jim!"

Only silence met her call. She sent up an anxious prayer. *Please, God, don't let him be dead.*

She gripped the windowsill with both hands. "Give me a boost, please."

Parker's hand gripped her elbow and tugged at her. "I'm going in," he stated with a determined note to his voice.

"I can do it," she protested, unwilling to release her hold on the sill.

"You don't know what you'll face inside there."

"I can handle it," she said.

"This is someone you know and care about."

The truth of his words sliced into her. Horrible images came to mind. Images of Jim broken and bleeding. Whatever he'd done, she didn't want him to be hurt or worse. "I—"

"Do you really want to stand here and argue?" Parker pressed. "We're wasting time. If Jim is inside and hurt, we need to get to him now."

The unmovable expression on his face grated across her nerves. He was right of course; they needed to get in there. She released her hold on the sill and moved back.

He placed Sherlock's leash in her hand. "Hang on to him." Her hand closed over the nylon cord in a tight hold. To the remaining officer, he said, "Keep them safe."

The young cop nodded. "Yes, sir."

Melody couldn't work up any resentment at the implication that she couldn't take care of herself and Sherlock. Her only focus was on what Parker would find when he went inside.

Parker gripped the edge of the window and he easily lifted himself up, swung a leg over and disappeared into the house.

Sherlock strained at the leash, tugging her back toward the sliding glass door.

A few seconds later, Parker unlatched the door and stepped back. "He's not here."

A mixture of relief and concern raced over her. Where was Jim?

Sherlock lunged forward, ripping his leash from Melody's hands. The dog disappeared down the hall. Parker and Melody quickly followed. They found the beagle in a home office, scratching at a closed closet door. Melody's stomach clenched. Maybe Parker spoke too soon. Would they open that door and find Jim's body?

Parker took out two sets of latex gloves from the pack at his waist. He handed a set to Melody. Grimly, she accepted them. After they'd both donned the gloves, he reached for the handle. Melody braced herself. The door swung open. Sherlock darted forward. His loud triumphant barks echoed inside Melody's head. She stared at the shelves stacked with plastic-wrapped bricks of cocaine.

"Good dog," Parker said, reeling Sherlock away from the offending substance.

Her face flooded with shock and disappointment.

The implications of this find couldn't be denied. A deep, welling anger expanded through her, chasing away the horror of realizing the man she'd been working with for the past four plus years wasn't what he'd seemed. She'd been duped. Her trust once again abused.

The house hadn't been tossed like she'd first assumed, otherwise the drugs would have been found and taken. These drugs belonged to Jim. And he must have been the one to stash the baggies of the white powder they'd found in the locker at the youth center. And no doubt with the intent to sell.

Stomach roiling, Melody stumbled back.

Parker's strong arms steadied her, drawing her into his tight embrace. She turned in his arms and dropped her forehead to his chest. Tears pricked her eyes but wouldn't fall.

She remembered Jim's supposed shock at seeing the drugs in the center. His feigned suspicion of the kids and volunteers. His constant barrage of complaints. All of it was to cover his real activities. Part of her wanted to still give him the benefit of the doubt, to say there had to be a reasonable explanation. But the evidence staring at her in the face taunted that idea like a schoolyard bully.

Jim was dirty. No two ways about it.

She let out a bitter sigh of resignation. Jim was another man to let her down.

She lifted her head, her gaze meeting Parker's. The concern in his eyes drew her up short.

Show no weakness.

Stepping away from him, she regained control and ruthlessly cut off her emotions. "We have to call in CSU."

"I'll take care of it."

She spun away from him while he made the call. She studied the room they were standing in. An old, cheaply made desk butted up against one wall. A file cabinet stood in the corner, stuffed so full, the drawers didn't completely close. On one wall was a white board. Puzzled, she stared at the board trying to make sense of what was written there.

"That looks like some sort of schedule," she said, walking closer to scrutinize the times and dates. With each set of numbers was a set of letters.

Parker came to stand beside her. "It does look like some sort of timetable. And the initials? Recognize them?"

"I don't know. If I thought about it hard enough, I'm sure I could come up with several people with the same initials."

"Yeah, me, too." Parker moved to the desk. "Let's see what we have here." Systemically, he went through the contents, first the top, then the drawers.

For a moment, Melody watched him. Watched the way his powerful hands handled papers and files with gentle care, keeping his contact with each to a minimum so not to smudge any prints. She studied the lines of concentration on his face, memorized the slope of his nose, the angle of his strong jaw. She'd rather keep her focus on him than the fact she was now investigating her partner.

With a sharp shake of her head, she turned her attention to the filing cabinet. She started at the bottom rather than the top. She knew Jim well enough to know he'd think the bottom drawer safer than the one on top.

Most people would begin a search at the top and work their way down, maybe even giving up before reaching the last drawer.

Melody tugged the bottom drawer out. Papers crunched against the sides. She removed two handfuls of files from the front and set them aside. When she could slide the remaining files forward, she searched the contents, starting with the last file and working her way to the front. She had no idea what she was looking for.

When she reached the last of the second batch of files, a folder caught her attention. Her sister's name jumped out at her from the label. With her heart in her throat, she removed the folder and opened the file. An autopsy report. She frowned. Why would Jim have a copy of the ME's report from Sierra's suicide?

As she scanned the report, the reality of what she was reading crashed in on her. Bile churned in her gut, and she choked back a sob.

"Melody?"

Parker's voice sounded so far away. The file trembled in her hands. She fought to control her reaction but the shock was too great. The awful truth overwhelming. She lifted her eyes and stared into his worried brown gaze.

"My sister didn't commit suicide. She was murdered."

Parker rushed to Melody's side. She looked like she might faint. He wouldn't have blamed her. The revelation was staggering. He took the report from her shaking hand and scanned the contents. His gaze slid past the particulars straight to the important part of the matter.

Probable cause of death: asphyxiation

Though a large dose of the drug zolpidem was found in her system, along with enough alcohol that alone would have been over the legal limit, there was evidence of suffocation.

Under the heading of *Marks and Wounds* the ME had written: *Petechial hemorrhaging in both eyes. Faint bruises over the mouth and nose.*

Parker's gut flinched at the image those words provoked. Someone had held their hand over her mouth and nose, cutting off her air supply. The lethal combination of drugs and alcohol plus lack of oxygen had killed her.

Official ruling: Homicide.

There was no mistaking it. The box was checked.

The medical examiner who'd signed the report in Parker's hand was the retired ME, John Bale.

Parker needed to compare this signature with the one on the report that was filed with the county to know which report had been forged. If the signatures matched, then someone had paid off the ME to falsify a new report ruling Sierra's death a suicide.

"Did Jim know your sister?" he asked, wondering what the connection was between Wheaton and Sierra.

Melody shook her head. "Not that I know of." She gave a dry, humorless laugh. "But apparently there's a lot I don't know."

He tucked the folder under one arm and wrapped the other around her waist. "Come on. We'll wait for Rose and Clay outside. We'll let them do their job."

He guided her out of the office, down the hall and out the front door.

Within a few minutes the place was crawling with

uniformed law personnel. Rose and Clay climbed out of the CSU van and with curt nods headed inside. Captain Drexel arrived in a brown sedan.

Melody explained the situation. Her voice was robotic; her tone detached. She was doing a good job of hiding how horrific the situation was for her. And Parker admired her strength. He hoped she didn't let the hardness settle too deep. It was one thing to compartmentalize in order to function, and another to internalize. She'd been dealt a devastating blow by learning of her partner's betrayal. And knowing her background, Parker worried she'd let this incident heighten her distrust of relationships.

Parker's own captain arrived, as well. Parker drew Slade aside and gave him a verbal report.

Captain McNeal shook his head. Sadness filtered the blue of his eyes. "Hard to believe Jim Wheaton was a dirty cop."

Glancing over at Melody, Parker's heart twisted in his chest. "Yes. But we knew there was someone within the department who was working for The Boss. At least now we can plug the leak."

"We have to find Wheaton," Slade said, his voice fierce, his expression determined. "Get him to flip. I want this supposed boss."

As did Parker. "I'd like permission to follow up on the medical examiner."

Slade nodded. "Whatever you need to do."

They turned as Captain Drexel and Melody approached. Resolve set her features into grim lines. Her bright blue eyes were hard like gemstones set against her pale complexion. Parker resisted the urge to take her hand, to offer support. Better to keep up a professional front while their bosses were present. Better to keep a distance for his sake, as well.

"Detective Zachary tells me there's a hit put out on her by Wheaton," Drexel said.

"Yes, sir. I had credible intel which led us here," Parker confirmed.

"Glad you followed the lead." Drexel leveled him with a pointed look. "Next time I'd like to know if one of my officers is in danger."

Feeling the reprimand deserved, Parker nodded. "I take full responsibility for not reporting in right away."

"Hardly," Melody interjected as her gaze locked with Parker's. "It was my idea to come here first. My wish was to give Jim the benefit of the doubt. I owed him that." She met her captain's stare. "My fault. If there's to be any consequences, I should pay them."

She was trying to protect him. Deeply moved, Parker stepped closer to her.

"I think you both were blessed this time not to have this situation turn deadly. Next time it might not go as well. Keep that in mind," Drexel said.

"Yes, Captain," Melody replied.

"Yes, sir," Parker concurred.

"Parker has asked to follow up on the medical examiner," Slade informed Drexel.

"So has Detective Zachary," Drexel commented. "They can work that angle together."

Slade inclined his head in approval.

Glad that they would be allowed to continue working the case, and together no less, Parker glanced at Melody to see how she'd take the news. Her expression was shuttered, closing off her thoughts. And it hurt way more than it should to be shut out.

Yes, he was definitely wading in too far with Melody. If he weren't cautious, he would find himself in the deep end without a life preserver. Good thing he could swim. But he had a feeling he'd drown beneath the weight of his feelings for Melody. Best to start paddling now and keep a professional and emotional distance between them as best he could.

With their mandate in place, the two captains left the scene. Parker waited a moment for Melody to say something. She seemed lost in her thoughts, her gaze on the house. Likely trying to digest all that had happened. Her partner was dealing drugs and she'd found out her sister had been murdered. He curled his fingers to keep from reaching for her hand.

"Let's head to the county coroner's office," she finally said, breaking the silence.

Glad to see her ready to work, he nodded. The central clearinghouse for the county medical reports was housed in the Sagebrush coroner's office on the other side of town. When they arrived, they signed in at the front desk and then made their way to the records room in the basement. The place was warm from the day's heat and smelled musty. Parker explained their request to the attendant, an older man with a wide girth and a lined face that seemed to hold a perpetual frown.

"Sorry, all requests must be made in writing and go through the brass upstairs," the older man stated flatly, not deigning to rise from his chair.

More like the guy didn't want to be bothered. "We don't have time for reports. This is urgent."

The man shrugged. "Them the rules."

"I'm sure Mayor Hobbs would not agree," Melody said, her voice cold. "Let's call him and find out."

Frowning, the man held up his hand. "Hold on there, missy. I don't think we need to get the mayor involved." He hefted his considerable bulk up from the chair and lumbered over to a desk with a computer. "What file do you need?"

Parker repeated what they'd already told him.

"Five years ago?" He shook his head. "Hmm, that'd be before the city installed the new-fangled computers." He pointed toward the rows of boxes behind him. "You'll have to find the file manually since we've only scanned in reports for the last three years."

Without a word, Melody marched past the attendant and started searching for the box with the right date. Parker joined her. Patience, he realized, was one of Melody's many virtues; he, on the other hand, grew antsy as time ticked by. Three hours later they located a box with the correct year written on the outside in big bold letters.

Parker took the box from the shelf and set it on the floor. Melody immediately rifled through the many files inside.

"Here we go," she said, taking a file from the box.

"Let's take it to the station," he said. "We'll have Clay compare the signatures."

Taking their find with them, they hurried down the block to the Sagebrush Police Station. The one-story brick building was thankfully air-conditioned. They found Clay in the crime lab. He was bent over a microscope when they walked in.

"Hey, Clay, we have a favor we need from you," Parker said, halting beside the quiet man.

The CSU technician lifted his head and eyed them warily. "I'm pretty busy."

"This shouldn't take long." At least Parker hoped not. "We need you to analyze two signatures and tell us if they are the same signer."

"Do you have the originals of each document? Because photocopies won't hold up in court, cuz there's too much room for error in ink placement, light fractures—"

"We have them both," Melody interjected.

"Okay, good." Clay led them to a light board. "Place both copies here."

Parker opened the large manila envelope and slid the contents out. He placed the two versions of Sierra's coroner's report on the board.

Using a handheld magnifying glass, Clay studied the signatures at the bottom of the two reports.

"These are the same," he declared.

Anger tensed the muscles in Parker's shoulders.

Melody pressed closer. "Are you sure?"

"The *J* in the name John loops slightly at the bottom of the downward stroke. They're identical. And in the last name you can see how the signer double backs over the letter A before moving on to the *L*."

Melody stepped back. "Thank you, Clay. You're a gem."

The man moved away from the light board with a shy smile. Parker took the two reports and replaced them in the manila envelope.

Stalking out of the lab, Melody said, "We have to find John Bale."

"Back to the coroner's office. They should have an address for Bale."

This time they talked directly to the current medical examiner, Nolan Rader. The thirty-something coroner had the information they sought.

"It's so odd that you'd be asking about Dr. Bale," Nolan said as he handed over the address for the retired ME.

"How so?" Parker asked, glancing at the sheet of paper where Nolan had written out the address. Bale had retired to Corpus Christi. An hour's drive.

"Dr. Bale called last month. I hadn't heard from him since the day he left, then out of the blue…"

"What did he want?" Melody asked.

"He'd heard about the desecration of a grave. I guess it made headlines all over the state. Anyway, he wanted to know the identity of the person in the grave."

Parker and Melody exchanged a charged look. That *would* be odd if they hadn't already discovered the man had falsified Sierra Jones's autopsy report. Clearly, Melody's cold-case instincts were on high alert also.

"And you told him the person's identity?" Melody asked.

Nolan shrugged. "I didn't see any reason not to. He was the coroner of record for the boy's death."

Anger darkened her eyes. "He was probably relieved to know it wasn't Sierra's grave."

Confusion crossed Nolan's face. "Come again?"

Shooting her a warning glance, Parker cupped Melody's elbow and steered her toward the door. He didn't want to divulge what they knew. He wasn't sure who to trust. "Thank you, Doctor. You've been most helpful," he called over his shoulder.

When they were back in the station house, Parker

handed Melody the address for John Bale. "You up for a road trip?"

Purpose lit her expression. "Let's do it. Let's nail this creep to the wall and find out who killed my sister."

Chapter Thirteen

John Bale lived in a retirement community in a posh neighborhood near Corpus Christi Bay. A place that looked too costly even for a retired medical examiner. It was more in the realm of celebrities and former big-time business moguls. But then again, Melody thought bitterly, he'd most likely been paid handsomely for his duplicity. Enough to keep him in style through his golden years. Well, she wondered how he'd like prison life.

She marched up the walkway toward the front door with Parker and Sherlock at her side. Parker wore his Sagebrush uniform, making him appear intimidating and more handsome than a man had a right to be. Even Sherlock looked smart in his chest vest with the SPD emblem. They worked well together. Both professionally and personally. A team. On so many levels.

They entered the three-story facility, leaving the May heat behind. The almost frigid air-conditioned temperature made goose bumps break out on Melody's arms.

She felt like she'd walked into a library rather than a senior citizens' center. The bottom floor opened to a central space with balconies overlooking the ground floor, making the center more cavernous than the outside suggested. The entryway was lined with bookcases filled with all sorts of books, some old and leather bound and some paperbacks. Inviting cushy chairs were placed in several small groupings allowing for intimate conversations.

An oak desk sat in the middle, manned by a pretty woman in her forties. And behind her was a game room, complete with a Ping-Pong table and a television with an electronic gaming system being used by two white-haired gentlemen. Chess tables were set up near the windows, as well.

To the right, Melody could see a dining hall with red linen tablecloths covering various-size tables for groups of two to six. It was all very appealing in a way that she found disconcerting.

When the time came would she opt for a community like this where she'd be with others her own age? Or would she grow old alone and lonely?

The question left her feeling a bit melancholy.

And realization had her heart thumping. She'd always figured she'd be on her own like she'd been most of her life. But a solitary future didn't appeal the way it once had. She should make more of an effort to form connections. Healthy connections.

She slid a glance Parker's way.

One thing the last few days had made clear to her was she'd isolated herself too much.

The receptionist's eyes widened when they walked up. "Can I help you?"

Melody glanced at Parker. He gave a slight nod, letting her take the lead. She liked that because it made her feel respected. She would thank him later. He, at least, was dependable. Unlike the other men in her life.

But for how long? a cynical voice in her head asked.

She shut down the thought and focused on what she needed to do.

"I'm Detective Zachary and this is Detective Adams." Melody held out her badge for the woman's inspection. "We'd like to see one of your residents. John Bale?"

"Doctor Bale, you mean?" the woman said, her gaze raking over them warily. "You'll need to sign in." She gestured to a white binder on the counter.

Melody printed and signed her name. Parker did likewise.

The woman picked up her phone and spoke to someone on the other line. "Doctor Bale has guests. Would you be able to take them back?"

She hung up and gave them a polite, practiced smile. "One of the nurses will be up shortly to take you to see the doctor. If you'll wait over there, please." She pointed toward a grouping of chairs near a low table filled with promotional material.

Parker picked up a brochure. "Nice place. Housekeeping and meals are included." He gave her a crooked grin. "Wouldn't mind spending my golden years in a swanky place like this."

She could see Parker adapting easily to a community setting like this. As social as he was, he wouldn't grow old alone. Someday he'd marry, have a family. Be surrounded by people who loved him. People that he loved. A stab of jealousy made her look away from him.

Their lives were so different. Their futures were worlds apart. Her throat clogged.

A moment later a male nurse wearing white scrubs

approached. "Officers, I'm Terrance, Doc's nurse. This way, please."

Thankfully, she didn't have to respond.

They followed him toward a set of closed double doors. He waved a key card in front of a box on the wall and the doors opened soundlessly. This part of the facility looked more like a hospital with linoleum floors, beeping monitors and antiseptic smells.

"I thought this was an independent living retirement center," Melody said, confused by this additional wing.

"We're a full-service facility," Terrance answered. "Independent living, assisted care, memory care and hospice care. We allow our residents to transition gracefully through the latter stages of life."

Obviously, John Bale had transitioned to a different stage. She prayed he'd be coherent enough to tell them what they wanted to know.

Terrance led them to a common room. Residents sat at several lounge chairs scattered about. Some had IV drips attached to their arms. Others looked frail and weak. A few slept. A large-screen television broadcasted the afternoon news in the corner. Large picture windows provided stunning views of the Corpus Christi Bay and beyond that, the Gulf of Mexico. Her heart ached for the men and women here, cut off from the outside world by glass and pain.

Terrance stopped beside the wheelchair of a man with thin patches of silver hair. A brightly colored blanket was tucked around his legs. His gaunt cheekbones stood out in sharp angles. His eyes were closed, his body still. Sherlock ventured close to sniff his feet. Finding nothing of interest, the dog lay down, putting his head on his paw.

Melody glanced at Parker. He looked as stunned as she did. To Terrance, she said, "Is Dr. Bale ill?"

"Stage four colon cancer," Terrance replied.

Despite her anger at the man for filing a false autopsy report on her sister's death, sympathy tugged at Melody. She didn't have much experience with cancer, but she knew enough to know stage four wasn't good.

Terrance touched the older man's shoulder. "John, you have visitors."

Bale awakened and for a moment looked confused, then his dark-eyed gaze cleared as he took in Parker and Melody. "Sagebrush." He let out a raspy laugh. "I knew this day would come."

"Then you know why we're here," Parker stated drily.

Bale nodded. "Can we go outside? I'd rather not have my dirty laundry aired out for everyone to hear."

Terrance reached for the handles of the wheelchair, but Melody beat him to it. She wanted the privacy as much as Bale. Nervous anticipation of what she'd learn about her sister and nephew hummed in her veins. Her fingers gripped the handles tightly. "I'll do this."

The nurse stepped back and gestured to his right. "Through that door is a path that will take you to the gardens. Don't keep him out long. A little sun is fine, but we don't want to add heat stroke to his condition."

"We won't be long," Melody promised.

Parker held the door open while she wheeled Bale out into the sunshine. The sun's rays immediately chased away any traces of a chill from Melody. They moved along the path in silence through a green lawn, flowerbeds and benches until they'd moved far enough from the facility that there was no chance anyone would overhear them.

"I assume you're here about Sierra Jones?" Bale said, his voice flat.

Melody sucked in a bracing breath.

"Yes. We found your original report," Parker replied. "Her death was not suicide, but a murder. A murder you helped cover up."

Melody pressed the wheelchair's brakes with the toe of her boot and came to stand in front of Bale. She rocked on her heels, itching to get down to it.

Parker stepped back and a little off to the left, once again letting her take charge. When this was over she was going to owe him big-time, not only in gratitude but also in respect. Not many officers would willingly take a backseat on a case. Sherlock stretched his leash to sit at her feet.

"Sierra was my sister," she said to Bale, her voice shaking with equal parts fury and grief.

Bale shaded his eyes with his wavering hand and looked up at her. "I'm sorry for your loss."

Fisting her hands, Melody tried to stay calm. "I want to know why you did it and who you're covering for."

He considered her a moment. "I'm not proud of what I did. You have to understand, it was a difficult time for me. My wife had passed on the year before. I had just been diagnosed with cancer. I had used up all our resources on my wife." He sighed heavily. "There was nothing left for me. Even my pension wouldn't have provided enough. I wanted to spend my last few years on earth in comfort. Is that so bad?"

"Was it Jim Wheaton who paid you?" she pressed, her voice sharp. She needed to understand.

Sherlock growled. She glanced at the canine. He'd moved and was facing the parking lot.

"What is it, boy?" Parker asked quietly, bending down to pet the dog. Melody shifted her attention back to Bale.

"The sum was enough to keep me here until I pass and then some." Bale dropped his hand and looked out at the ocean in the distance.

"Why did Jim kill my sister and pay you to make it look like a suicide?"

"I—"

Sherlock erupted in frantic barks.

The sickening thud of metal penetrating flesh jarred through Melody. Bale jerked forward and tumbled out of the chair. Warm blood splattered her. Horrified, she gaped at the hole in the back of John Bale's head. The shot fatal. *"Sniper!"*

Before the word even left her mouth, Parker tackled her to the ground, his body falling hard against her, knocking the breath from her lungs. Another bullet hit close. Chunks of dirt spit at her in the face. Too close.

"Come on, we've got to get to cover," Parker yelled in her ear.

She wiggled out from under him. "There isn't any!"

The nearest tree was at least 50 feet away. They'd never make it.

Parker tugged Sherlock close then yanked on the wheelchair, maneuvering the chair to provide a meager barrier between them and the gunman.

She crouched low, her gaze searching for the threat, while her hand pulled her gun from its holster. "Do you see him?"

Holding Sherlock's leash to keep him from going after the shooter, Parker reached for his cell phone.

"Shots came from the parking lot. I don't have an exact position."

Heart hammering in her chest, she lay prone, aiming toward the parking lot between the wheels of the chair while Parker called for backup.

All she saw were cars. No, wait. There was a dark shadow on the opposite side of a Mercedes that elongated the rear tire into an abnormal shape. That had to be the shooter. She took a shot. The loud retort of her gun firing echoed across the garden and rang in her ears. Her bullet embedded itself on the side of the rear well of the Mercedes. The shadow jerked, then disappeared. The sound of a car engine turning over reached her and then tires peeled against the asphalt as the shooter got away.

Frustration ran a marathon in Melody's veins. She dropped her head to her arm. Only one person had reason to want John Bale dead so he couldn't testify against him. Jim Wheaton.

A cold wet nose nudged her. She lifted her face to find herself staring into Sherlock's big brown eyes. His tongue darted out and licked her face. Tears burned her eyes. Tentatively she petted the dog, appreciating his attempt at comfort. Over Sherlock's head, she met Parker's concerned and surprised gaze.

The welcome sound of sirens filled the air. Within minutes, Corpus Christi uniformed officers descended.

Parker helped her to her feet. "You okay?"

"No." It took every ounce of control not to sag against him. She retreated behind a numbness that kept her protected from the pain trying to claw its way to the surface. "I want to go home."

Wrapping an arm around her, she let him lead her

away from the terrible scene. She forced herself to put one foot in front of the other. She had to keep moving forward. *Show no weakness.*

Parker drove Melody to the hotel so she could shower and change her clothes. Though Melody's mind was foggy with shock and grief, she appreciated his thoughtfulness. However, no amount of hot water could wash away the horror of witnessing Bale's murder. Or the certainty that Jim was the one who'd killed the man and then tried to kill her. Had he killed her sister, too? She wouldn't know for sure until they found Jim and he answered the question.

Once dressed, she sat on the small sofa in the corner of the room. She needed time to gain some control of her emotions so she could function. Despite her efforts, grief filled her to bursting. Tears welled. Her chest ached. A sob built from deep within.

She'd loved Sierra. And Daniel.

Five years ago she hadn't cried. She'd buried her grief beneath the anger and let the rage fuel her forward, determined to find justice for her nephew. And redemption for herself for not being there for Sierra. But now...the hollow places inside of Melody opened wide, threatening to swallow her up until she was nothing more than an empty shell. She buried her face into her hands, hating this show of weakness, yet unable to do anything to stem the tide of anguish overtaking her.

The sound of a knock on the bedroom door barely penetrated through her despair. The door opened. She stiffened. Desperately, she tried to stifle her crying. She wiped at the tears cascading down her cheeks. Fought to catch her breath. She kept her gaze fastened on the

floor. She didn't need to look up to know it was Parker.
She felt his presence like a burst of sunlight on a cold
winter's day. His energy enveloped the room, making
her want to partake of his heat and strength even as
she despised herself for the longing. The sofa cushion
dipped as he sat next to her. Without a word, his arms
came around her.

A noise of distress escaped. She wasn't sure if in protest or submission. Another sob swelled. She wrestled
to keep it trapped within but when he tugged her closer
so that her back rested against his broad chest, she lost
the battle. The sob exploded out on a gushing wave.

Slowly, he turned her to face him. Her arms slid
around him, holding him tight like an anchor in a storm-
tossed sea. She buried her face within the warm crook
of his neck, giving herself a moment to accept the comfort he was offering.

His hand soothed over her back. His gently murmured words of comfort calmed her tears. His scent,
spicy and masculine, filled her head. Awareness shimmied past the misery. She lifted her head, needing
something more from him, needing to feel alive and
whole. Needing to know she wasn't alone.

Her mouth found his. She felt his surprise in the
tenseness of his lips, then they softened, and he kissed
her back. Delving into the kiss, she lost herself in the
sensations rocketing through her system, leaving a fiery
trail of longing to burn her mind, her heart, her soul.

She tore her mouth from his. He dropped his forehead to hers. His chest heaved on an intake of breath,
but he stayed silent for a moment.

Questions spun in her head like a whirlwind. What
was she doing kissing Parker like there was no tomor-

row? Kissing him as if her very life depended on it? Kissing him as if she had any right?

Where would this lead?

Nowhere.

They were colleagues. Friends, even. And no matter how much she wanted to risk trusting him with her heart, she couldn't. She wasn't that strong. She'd been down that road and found nothing but a dead end.

"I'm sorry," he finally said.

That was so like him to take responsibility that wasn't his to take. She laid a hand on his chest and eased back to look into his handsome face. "I kissed you. If anyone should apologize, it's me."

He grinned, knocking the air back into her lungs. "Okay. I take it back. I'm not sorry."

The look in his eyes sent her pulse jumping. Her lips tingled with want for more of his kisses. Obviously, the attraction wasn't one-sided but it would be foolhardy to let herself become carried away. She'd prided herself on not making imprudent choices. She thought things through, weighed the consequences, viewed her options. Kept her emotions in check.

But with him…with Parker she didn't want to be prudent. She didn't want to make the wise choice to walk away while she had the opportunity. She didn't want to withdraw her arms from around him.

No, what she wanted to do was release the impulsive side that had to be in her DNA if her sister's life was any indication.

And look where Sierra had ended up because of her impulsiveness.

The thought rocked Melody to the core, shaking up all the reasons why she'd held herself firmly apart from others. Even her ex-husband. Truth be told, she assumed some of the blame for her ex-husband's abandonment. She could have followed him, fought for the marriage. But that would have required losing too much emotional control. Control she couldn't give up now.

Slowly she extracted herself from Parker's embrace. "This can't happen."

"What can't?"

Was he deliberately being obtuse? "Us. I shouldn't have kissed you. It was a moment of insanity. I let my grief get the better of me."

He trailed a knuckle down her cheek. "Holding all that anguish in isn't healthy."

"Neither is kissing you," she retorted glumly. It didn't matter how much she enjoyed the kiss. It had been a mistake. A lapse in judgment and good sense.

"It was a kiss, Melody. You won't die from a kiss," he remarked wryly.

Maybe not physically. But emotionally? Oh, yeah. That was a slippery slope if ever there was one. And she had no intention of sliding into the abyss. She stood and glanced at the open bedroom door, using the excuse of the other woman in the living room of the hotel suite as a means to change the subject. "I'm sure Officer Truman must be wondering what's going on in here."

"I sent Patty to pick up takeout. I hope you like chow mein and chicken fried rice."

His kindness once again softened her, making her regret that this thing between them couldn't ever go anywhere. She couldn't let it. "You are a very thoughtful man."

He made a noise in his throat. "If I were that thoughtful I wouldn't have taken advantage of your misery and kissed you, especially if I'd known you'd regret it."

"I kissed you," she reminded him. "I don't regret the kiss." The admission heated her cheeks. "It's just… I'm not ready to be in a relationship. I don't know if I'll ever be."

His eyebrows plucked together. "Melody—"

The outer door to the suite opened. Officer Truman returning with their dinner. Melody wasn't sure she'd be able to eat, but she used the opportunity to escape.

What she'd said to Parker was true. She didn't know if she'd ever be ready or willing to give enough of herself, relinquish enough control, to be in a relationship again. Not even with someone as wonderful and charming as Parker Adams.

The thought left her feeling depressed.

But she had no choice. Not if she wanted to keep from being hurt again.

From this moment forward, she had to maintain a boundary to protect herself. But how, she didn't know. Especially when her heart wanted to be as close to him as possible.

Chapter Fourteen

With his fork, Parker pushed his noodles around on his plate. His appetite was nonexistent. He forced himself to eat to keep up his strength, because the last thing he needed was to be groggy from lack of food. Not with so much at stake. But he was having a hard enough time getting his brain to function with memories of Melody's kiss burning a hole through his head.

Saying he'd been surprised when she pressed her soft lips to his would be an understatement. She'd tasted like salty tears and sweetness. For a fraction of a second he'd thought to resist, but then his whole body responded. Kissing her back had sent his senses careening out of control like a racecar taking a turn without a skid block to keep the bottom from hitting the track.

A major violation if ever there was one.

He'd vowed to keep her safe. He hadn't realized he'd be the one needing protection from her. But when he'd heard her crying, he'd been unable to keep himself from going to her. He'd felt so powerless in the face of her anguish…and couldn't help but reach for her. Holding her had been the only thing he could think to do.

Kissing her had been pure pleasure. And pain, because the rational part of his brain told him he shouldn't. He shouldn't get involved. He shouldn't get attached. He'd only end up disappointing her in the end, just like he had his family. His brother's death was an emblem he wore as a reminder of his failure. He hadn't been there for him when he should have. The only way to make sure he never let anyone else down was to not get involved. Not get too close.

I don't regret the kiss. The statement pleased him more than he thought possible, more than was wise. He was hard-pressed to say given the same chance he'd do anything differently.

I'm not ready to be in a relationship. I don't know if I'll ever be.

This, he understood. Because he was right there with her. Her reasons were clear to him. She'd been hurt badly by her father, then her husband. Now Jim. Men who should have stuck by her through all of life's ups and downs. But they hadn't. They'd left her. Betrayed her. Making her feel somehow there was something wrong with her. He'd told her there wasn't. And he wished he could find a way to prove it to her once and for all. But he couldn't. Doing so would only set her—and himself up for more heartache.

Lord, what do I do here? How do I protect us both. Parker's cell phone rang. He answered. Shock siphoned the air from his lungs, and it took a moment for him to find his voice. "We're on our way."

He clicked the phone off and met Melody's anxious gaze. A knot of dread formed in his gut. Though it would cause her more pain, he had to tell her. He took her hand.

She gripped his arm, obviously sensing something was wrong. "What's happened?"

"The Sagebrush Police have Jim trapped in a stand-off."

Alarm filled her eyes. "What? Where?"

"The youth center."

"He's still holed up in the woodworking room," Captain McNeal informed them when they arrived at the makeshift command post—the back of a tactical van parked down the street from the center.

The only light showing in the brick building came from the room where Melody knew Jim spent most of his time. From the moment Parker had informed her, she'd felt like she was in a daze. Jim was in a standoff at the youth center. The youth center they'd built together. They'd done so much good there, helped so many kids and had made a difference in not only the teens' lives but the whole community's. And now he was destroying that. She tried not to tremble with the shock.

FBI Agent Trevor Lewis joined them. "We've tried negotiating. He's not cooperating. The state police are assembling and plan to breach the building in ten."

"Are there hostages?" Parker asked.

Panic trapped the air in Melody's lungs. Her gaze searched the darkness and picked out the men dressed in tactical gear, ready to initiate a full-on assault of the center. Her throat closed with alarm. Penetrating the center would be a last-resort move. She prayed it wouldn't come to that.

"Yes. There's at least one," came Slade's grim reply.

"Who?" Melody asked, and winced at the slight quiver in her voice.

"Ally Jensen."

Anguish stabbed her. *Oh, no. Poor Ally.*

She had to do something. The youth center was her responsibility. Determination burned through Melody. She had to reach Jim, make him see how futile his actions were. There was no way this could end well if he didn't cooperate. She squared her shoulders and lifted her chin. "Let me talk to him."

"Absolutely not!" Parker exclaimed.

Irritation set her teeth on edge. "It isn't your call."

Captain McNeal's eyebrows rose nearly to his hairline. Melody wasn't sure if it was in response to her request or to Parker's vehement refusal. She jerked her gaze to Parker.

Thunderclouds darkened his face. "You are too close to this. Too emotionally involved."

She couldn't deny his assertions and wouldn't even try. "I can stay in control." She turned back to Captain McNeal. "I've had hostage negotiation training through the Austin PD. I can do this."

Before McNeal could respond, Parker interjected, "It's too dangerous."

Wheeling to face Parker, she said, "You heard Special Agent Lewis. They're planning a breach in ten. Whatever Jim's done, it's not worth losing his or Ally's life over. Which could happen if this situation turns into a battle." Unconcerned by the fact they were surrounded by his captain, FBI agent Trevor Lewis and a multitude of other officers, she placed a hand over his heart. "He knows me. I'm the best shot we have."

"I don't want you to get hurt," he said, his voice dropping to a low timbre that worked its way down to her soul. "Jim wanted you dead."

For reasons she chose not to examine, she needed
him on her side. "Putting ourselves in danger is part
of the job."

"I don't care about the job at the moment." Worry lit
his brown eyes. "It's you I'm worried about."

Any annoyance melted in the face of his concern. It
was her turn to implore him to understand. "I know it's
a risk. But some risks are worth taking."

He closed his hand over hers, trapping her hand
firmly against his chest. "Is this one of them?"

His words reverberated through her. "I have to try."
She pulled out the one card she knew would work to
sway him. "If I don't attempt to talk him out, I'll regret it the rest of my life. Ally is just an innocent kid."

He closed his eyes as if pained. When he opened
them, the respect there shored up her confidence and
made her realize that her feelings for this man had gone
way beyond anything she could control. "You promise
me you'll be careful?"

"Of course."

Please, God, don't let anyone get hurt.

With her heart pounding and her breath threatening
to seize, Melody stepped closer to the speakerphone.
It had taken a good deal of persuasion on Parker's part
to convince Captain McNeal and Agent Lewis to let
Melody have a chance to coax Jim out.

Parker's belief in her touched her, yet made her wary
at the same time. She was placing too much trust in this
man, but that was an issue to be dealt with later. Right
now she had a job to do.

*Oh, Lord, give me strength and help me to know
the right words to say.* She sent up the silent request

and inhaled deeply, calming herself. Pursing her lips, she blew out a breath and found her center. FBI Agent Lewis gave her the nod to proceed.

"Jim, this is Melody."

The silence sent a wave of uncertainty crashing through her. Would her presence make the situation worse?

"You shouldn't be here," he finally said.

Because I should be dead? The thought streaked through her mind. She bit on her lip to keep the words in. "Jim, this isn't you. You're a great guy. You love the center. You've worked so hard to make it successful."

"You don't know me," he barked. "You don't know what I've done."

She closed her eyes, mustering her strength. She thought she knew him. She'd also thought she'd known her father and her ex-husband. "Okay, Jim. That's fair. I don't know you as well as I thought I did."

She did have an inkling of what he'd done, but saying so wouldn't be prudent. "I'd like to know you better, Jim. Let me be your friend like you've been mine."

She opened her eyes and met Parker's steady, encouraging gaze. "This is just a big misunderstanding, right, Jim? You haven't done anything that can't be undone."

"You couldn't leave it alone," he yelled. "I told you to leave it alone. This is your fault."

Drawing on the training she'd had at the Austin police department, she stayed calm, focused and refused to rise to the bait of his words. Instead, she redirected the conversation. "Jim, are you injured? Is everyone okay? Ally? I'm sure she's confused and scared. Who else is there?"

"We're fine in here as long as you all stay out there," Jim said.

"We'll stay put." She glanced at the men around her, willing them to do as Jim was asking. "No one's been hurt yet. It's not too late to make this right. You can make this right, Jim. Let Ally go. Let… I'm sorry. Who else is with you?"

Silence met her question. Each passing second tightened the knot of anxiety squeezing her chest.

"Joy," he finally answered.

An image of the teen ran through Melody's mind. Her heart ached. The fifteen-year-old must be terrified. "Joy Haversham is with you. Okay, I'm sure she and Ally would like to go home. They deserve to go home, don't they, Jim? You can make that happen for them."

"Then what? I don't have any leverage," he rasped out.

The strain in his voice worried Melody. She knew from her training that when a hostage taker felt cornered, they tended to react violently. "What can we—I—do to make this right? I want to help. Please let me help you."

"You can't. Not now."

The harsh sound of the phone slamming down echoed in Melody's head. Disappointment and anxiety spiraled through her, and she struggled to remain calm.

Parker wrapped an arm around her. "You did good."

Leaning into him, she shook her head. "He hung up. I failed."

"No, you haven't," Trevor stated, his dark eyes sincere. "We know he has two hostages. That's more than we knew ten minutes ago. We'll call him back in a few minutes."

The waiting stretched Melody's nerves until she

thought she'd scream. Thoughts of what could go wrong ran through her head, making her incredibly antsy. Only Parker's comforting arm around her held her together. His calming presence was a Godsend on so many levels.

She'd be crawling out of her skin with worry if not for him. She hadn't realized how much she needed Parker's backing. Knowing he believed in her gave her the confidence to see this ordeal through. She didn't know what her life would be like when they no longer were working so closely together.

At the moment thinking about that was more than she could bear.

Four minutes later, she was given the go-ahead to try again. Her heart bumped against her ribs.

"You can do this," Parker whispered close to her ear as Agent Lewis dialed the center's landline again.

She laid a hand on Parker's arm in gratitude.

When Jim came back on the line, she said, "Jim, you said this is my fault. I take responsibility. I'll make it right. Tell me how I can make it right."

"All your questions. All your snooping. It has to stop."

Steeling herself against taking offense, she kept her voice steady. "You're right. I do ask a lot of questions. We've worked together for a long time, Jim. I didn't realize my curiosity bugged you. I can change. Come out so we can talk about that. You can help change my ways," she said, hoping the carrot would be taken.

He scoffed. "Why did you bring him in? *I'm* your partner. And that dog! I hate dogs!"

Mind reeling, she glanced at Parker. His eyes narrowed in speculation.

Jim was jealous of Parker. She wasn't sure how to respond to that.

Agent Lewis made a motion with his hand, wanting her to keep talking. "I can see how that would upset you. I had no idea it would. But now that I do, we can remedy that. Parker and Sherlock don't need to come to the center again. It can go back to being you and me. A team."

Parker tucked in his chin. She shook her head, hoping he'd realize she was trying to appease Jim. That she had no intention of barring Parker and Sherlock from the center. They'd added so much. The kids had grown used to seeing Parker and they all loved Sherlock.

"The damage is done." The resignation in his tone sent a chill of dread gliding over her skin. "I'm a dead man no matter what I do."

His words sent alarm surging through her. She had to dispel that thought. "It may seem hopeless right now, but it's not. Jim—"

The gentle click of the receiver as he hung up was worse than when he'd slammed the phone down. Panic gripped her. "Get him back."

Lewis redialed. Nothing. They tried for several minutes before Lewis shook his head. "He's left us no choice." He turned to the tactical teams leader. "You have permission to go in."

"No!" Melody's legs trembled. She nearly toppled over, but Parker held her upright.

"Can we get a chair?" he asked.

Someone brought over a small stool.

"Sit," Parker instructed.

"I can't." Sharp talons of torment clawed at her. "This is my fault. I couldn't talk him out of it."

Parker took her hands in his. "No. This isn't your

fault. He brought this on himself. You did your best. All we can do now is pray for a good outcome."

She tightened her fingers around his. Grateful for his steady presence, for his faith. "Would you?"

"Of course." He drew her away from the command post to a secluded spot where they could have a moment of peace. "Lord, we ask for Your presence here. You know the situation. You know how dire it is. We ask for protection over Ally and Joy and the men going in after them…and Jim. Please bring them all out safely. Amen."

"Amen." She tugged on Parker, drawing him toward the action. "I want to get closer. I need to see what's happening."

They made their way to where Captain McNeal and Agent Lewis had taken a position with a clear view of the front of the building. A dozen or so men, dressed from head to toe in black tactical gear, prepared to enter the building. Melody's heart pounded so hard she thought she might break a rib.

The leader motioned with his hand, signaling it was time to breach the center. Melody braced herself. Just as the men stepped forward in a unified movement that spoke to the intense training and harmony of their division, the front door to the center opened. Melody's breath hitched. Was Jim giving up?

With a raised hand, the leader halted the men.

Ally and Joy came out, their hands held up in the air.

Behind them, Melody could make out Jim's balding head. She let out a small sigh of relief. He was coming out. "Thank you, God."

Then Jim shoved Ally and Joy. They stumbled forward. Two tactical team members grabbed them and pushed them out of harm's way. Jim was left exposed in the center of the doorway, a sniper rifle in his hands, the barrel pointed skyward in his outstretched hand. A dozen red dots glowed bright dead center on Jim's chest.

A small gasp escaped Melody. *No. No. No.* She didn't want to believe this was happening. She clutched Parker's hand.

The tactical team had Jim in their sights. She was sure he'd surrender now. Prayed he'd surrender. He had to. If he didn't…she couldn't let herself go there. God would protect him just like He had Ally and Joy.

"Come on, Jim," she said beneath her breath, willing him to do the right thing, the only thing, and turn himself in.

"Drop your weapon," a harsh voice rang out, commanding Jim to relinquish his hold on the rifle.

For a breath-stealing moment, Jim didn't move. His gaze roamed the crowd of law enforcement circling the front of the building. He zeroed in on Melody.

She released Parker's hand. The sadness on Jim's face made her step toward him, wanting him to know she was here to help him. She would stand by him, help him the way she hadn't been able to help Sierra and Daniel.

Jim's gaze drifted to Parker beside her and twisted with anger and jealousy.

In one swift move, Jim raised the rifle and sighted down the barrel, his aim directed at Parker.

Chaos exploded around her. Shouts for Jim to drop his weapon rang in the night.

Parker yanked her behind him, turning so his broad back acted as a shield.

A single shot rang out.

Melody winced.

Parker's body stiffened. His arms tightened around her. For a panicked moment the horrible thought that he'd been hit stormed through her mind.

"Melody?"

Parker's voice splintered her terror. She leaned back to look into his dear face. "You're okay?"

His grim nod didn't reassure her. Something was wrong. Then her mind kicked into gear and processed what she'd heard.

One shot.

Parker hadn't taken the hit. That meant...

With a certainty she wanted to refute, she knew Jim hadn't fired his weapon. A police sharpshooter had taken the shot.

Jim was dead.

A cold numbness swept through her like an eerie fog. A weight pressed down on her chest.

Her partner.

Her friend.

She extracted herself from Parker's arms. With slow, deliberate steps she walked to where Jim's body lay on the center's steps. Blood pooled on the cement.

Tears rolled down her cheeks. Anger choked her. God hadn't answered her prayer. At least not all of it.

Her gaze sought Ally and Joy. They huddled together. A female officer comforted them. The young women were safe. And Melody was grateful for that blessing.

But Jim...

Her attention returned to the prone body of the man at her feet. The man who had wanted her dead.

One of the tactical team members had pushed Jim's rifle aside. She stared at the long, deadly weapon. Her pulse spiked. "Parker!"

"Here," he said from close behind her.

She reached for his hand and swallowed back the bile rising to burn her throat. "Is that—?"

He drew in an audible breath. "Looks like a FN SPR. 308."

Her heart thudded. "Like the one that killed Daniel?"

"Exactly like. Only ballistics can confirm it."

She staggered backward, nearly missing a step. Parker caught her. His strong, safe arms held her steady, keeping her from disintegrating into a glob of anguish and despair.

Any chance she had of learning the truth behind her nephew and sister's deaths had died with Jim. Now she would never know what had really happened. Now she would never be able to make things…right.

Chapter Fifteen

"Why did he do it?" Melody's tortured whisper echoed inside Parker's car.

He hated seeing her so distraught. When she'd almost fainted on the steps after realizing the rifle Jim carried matched what they believed to be the weapon that killed Daniel, he'd propelled her away from the scene. She needed to process what had happened.

Better to do it in a safe, familiar environment. It would take time to heal from this wound and the quicker she put it behind her, the better. This ordeal had taken a devastating toll.

At a stoplight, he reached to take her cold hand in his. "I'm so sorry."

"I should have seen that something was wrong." Self-recrimination echoed in her voice. "All the signs were there. His nervousness, his furtive activities." She let out a tortured laugh. "His seeming dedication to the center was all a sham. How could I have missed that?"

"You were too close to it. You trusted him. There was no reason not to. We all did." Okay, Parker hadn't fully trusted him, not after the way he'd treated Sherlock. The light turned green. He stepped on the gas but kept his hand on hers.

A half scoff, and half sob escaped her throat. She extracted her hand from his. "You'd think I'd know better than to trust. Even God let me down tonight."

Appalled that she'd think that way, he said, "No, He didn't. We prayed for protection for Ally and Joy, as well as Jim. He came through for us. Ally and Joy are safe now."

"And Jim is dead."

Parker touched her arm. "But he had a chance to save himself. He's dead by his own choice."

There was no doubt in Parker's mind Jim Wheaton had chosen to end his life on the steps of the center by forcing the tactical team's hand to avoid facing a prison sentence.

"You can't blame God for that. He gives each of us free will to choose for ourselves how we'll act, whether we'll choose good or evil."

"Right. You're right." She shifted away, out of his reach. "Jim was stuck between the police, prison and The Boss. I guess he didn't like his options."

"Did he admit to working for the crime syndicate?"

"Not in so many words." She rubbed at her forehead. "He said he was a dead man either way. I can only assume he meant he feared The Boss would get to him."

Parker's hands flexed on the steering wheel. "He probably could have identified the crime lord."

"Yep. But we'll never know what secrets he harbored, will we?"

His gut clenched at the bitter tone to her voice. "You'll have some closure in Daniel's death if the ballistics come back a match to Jim's rifle."

"Closure? Hardly. All that report will tell me is Jim fired the shot that killed Daniel, but it won't tell me why. Or why he killed Sierra. The *why* is going to haunt me the rest of my life."

Parker wished he could refute her words, but there was too much truth there. They would never know why. But at least she was safe from Jim now.

However, a niggling feeling of disquiet tugged at Parker. "Could Jim have been the guy dressed all in black that ransacked your office?"

She shifted in the passenger seat to stare at him. "Maybe. It all happened so fast... The man seemed bigger to me, but it could have been the shock of interrupting the intruder that made him appear so large and scary."

An uneasy tension settled between them. "But you can't be certain, which means you could still be in danger."

She shrugged and turned to face the front window. "I suppose. But once again, why?"

Frustration echoed in her words and reverberated through him. They still didn't know what the masked man had been looking for in her office and her apartment. They suspected it was the code. If only they knew what that was. Jim probably had known. Though their search of his house revealed nothing helpful on that score.

As he pulled into the hotel's parking garage, Parker's cell phone rang. The caller ID showed the police station's number.

"Adams," he answered.

"Parker, Slade here. How is she?"

Sliding a glance at Melody slumped in the seat next to him, he said, "Holding it together."

"Good. She's strong. She'll get through this."

"Yes." And Parker would be there to make sure she made it through this ordeal in one piece. She'd come to mean a great deal to him, more than he'd thought possible. No matter how much he wanted to remain emotionally detached from the pretty detective, she had worked her way beneath the protective barrier around his heart.

He loved her.

The thought rocketed through him, leaving behind a white-hot trail of shock. He leaned his head back against the headrest. He loved Melody. He wasn't sure how to deal with the realization. He certainly couldn't declare his feelings to her. Not now while she was grieving and full of anger.

"I need you and Sherlock to meet me at the Lost Woods," Slade said, drawing Parker back to the conversation.

"When?"

"As soon as you can. I want to have Sherlock try to find Rio."

"We were there this morning, Slade. Sherlock didn't pick up on his scent."

"I know, I read your report. All the sightings of Rio in the woods have been at night. I have a feeling that with Jim's death The Boss might get overconfident and show up more often. I want us to be out there waiting for him when he does."

Parker was tempted to tell Slade no. Parker didn't want to leave Melody. She was hurting and he wanted to be the one she turned to for help.

If they caught the crime lord and brought him to justice, Parker would have no legitimate reason to stick close to her. Unless…he admitted his feelings.

And risked her rejecting him because she couldn't trust anyone.

Was he ready to take that risk?

No. He needed time to absorb this shocking truth and make a plan on how to proceed.

"We'll be there in twenty," he told Slade, and hung up.

"Be where?" Melody asked, her blue eyes luminous in her lovely face.

"My captain wants Sherlock to try to track Rio again."

"Tonight?"

He nodded. "I'll walk you up. Officer Truman should be there waiting for you."

"I want to go home, back to my apartment."

He understood her need to go home, but couldn't allow it. "I'm sure you do. But you know you can't. Not yet. We don't know if you're out of danger."

"I can't live in a hotel forever," she stated, her voice flat.

"It won't be forever."

"You can't make that promise," she said. "You can't promise you'll bring down the crime syndicate or predict when. At some point, I have to return to my life. I can't keep living like this. I need to get back to normal." Her voice caught on the last word.

His heart twisted. She was grieving and not taking into account the possibilities that her life could still be in danger. "You're safer at the hotel. Jim put a hit out on you, remember?"

"But with Jim dead, there's no one to pay for the deed, right? That's no longer an issue."

"We can't be certain that's true."

Her fingers curled into fists. "I wonder what my life is worth?"

"Don't go there," he said, worried that self-pity would take a hold of her. "You're worth more than any amount of money there is."

"Careful, Parker, I might think you care," she shot back.

"I do, Melody. I love you." The words were out before he could call them back. His breath caught and held.

In the dim glow coming from the overhead parking lights, her eyes widened with what he hoped was joy, but she remained mute.

A charged silence filled the car. Parker's heart hammered so hard in his chest he was surprised the whole car wasn't rocking from the vibrations.

Melody closed her eyes. A spasm of pain crossed her face.

An unnerving dread choked Parker.

She pressed her lips together. Then she took a breath, her shoulders rising and lowering as she exhaled. When she finally opened her eyes, the total lack of emotion shining in the swirling blue depths sent his stomach plummeting.

"I'm sorry, Parker. I can't. I can't do this." She turned away from him to climb out of the car.

A deep, welling pain carved out a hole in his heart. He dropped his head to the steering wheel. It was better this way, he told himself. He'd known surrendering to his feelings would put himself at risk of disappointing her, failing to live up to her expectations. Yet, he'd hoped with Melody he could be the man she needed.

He'd known she wasn't interested in romance. Too many men had hurt her in her life to trust again.

It had been wrong to profess his love and expect her to feel the same back.

Forcing himself to move, he climbed out and escorted her to her hotel suite, careful to keep a distance. A distance he should have maintained all along.

After Parker left her hotel suite, Melody placed her holster and weapon on the dresser with care, double-checking the safety. Her insides quivered with a strange mix of regret and sorrow and possibility. Flipping off the light switch, she collapsed face-first on the bed in a weepy mess.

The darkness, broken only by the faint glow of the living-room light seeping in from beneath the bedroom door, allowed her a sense of privacy. Truman was out in the living room. But here alone, in the suite's bedroom, Melody could break down.

Her mind reeled. Pain throbbed in every fiber of her being.

I do, Melody. I love you.

Parker's words played over and over in her head like a CD stuck on a scratch.

Part of her wanted to shout with joy. Hearing those words from him was a dream come true. He made her feel special, cared for, loved. Every act, every gesture had pointed to his growing feelings. She saw that now. She should have realized long before that she'd let her guard down around him.

Who was she kidding? She'd fallen for him almost

from the moment he had strode into the youth center all swagger and charm.

Yet her self-preservation was too strong. Her trust broken and abused too often to think she could really risk finding lasting happiness with Parker.

With anyone.

Parker had said God gave her free will to choose. She was choosing life without love. Life without the risk of betrayal and hurt.

That's what she wanted. What she needed. She would learn to live with this throbbing pain in her heart. It would scab over like the other wounds and she would be fine. Okay, not fine exactly, but she'd survive.

But just barely.

And really, what more could she hope for?

Spent, her tears dried and her heart aching, she flopped onto her back. Her backpack-style purse dug into her flesh. She hadn't realized she still wore the bag. She shrugged the straps off her shoulders and dropped the purse on the floor. Lying prone, she stared at the shadowed ceiling, praying for the abyss of sleep to take her away from the thoughts marching through her head.

The youth center wouldn't be the same without Jim. He'd been such a big part of its conception and implementation. A fixture.

But she had to believe the center would survive. It would take some adjustment and time. Lots and lots of time.

Just as it would take her time to figure out how to live without Parker.

Oh, they'd still see each other on occasion. But that was all she dared. Life would somehow go back to the way it was before he stormed into her world, upsetting all her carefully constructed ideas of keeping her heart safe.

But any contact would be torture. Seeing him, being near him but knowing she had to refrain from confiding in him, from depending on him. From loving him.

She wanted to do all of that and more, but she was too afraid. Too afraid to give herself over to the uncertainty, always wondering when the day would come that he, too, would leave her or betray her, when he would destroy her trust.

A thump from the outer room of the suite raised the hairs on her arm. She bolted upright.

Officer Truman had probably bumped into a table.

Still, Melody strained to listen.

The slight squeak of the bedroom doorknob turning knifed through her. She rolled off the bed and crouched on the floor, reaching for her sidearm. She grimaced with frustration. She'd left her weapon on the top of the dresser.

The door swung open. Light flooded the room. The dark silhouette of a man filled the space.

A man wearing a ski mask. His eyes blacked out. He held a gun.

Her heart hammered against her ribs. She wedged herself under the bed. On her belly, she inched herself toward the other side. If she could reach her purse, she could call for help.

A hand closed over her ankle. She kicked for all she was worth.

Please, dear God, save me.

Chapter Sixteen

Parker allowed Sherlock a long lead as he and Slade cut a path through the underbrush of the Lost Woods. The dog led Parker and Slade deeper into the woods, away from the trail, the earthy scents of the woods filling Parker's nostrils. He could only imagine how much more intense the smells were for Sherlock.

The bobbing glow from his flashlight bounced off tree trunks and thick tangles of leaves and branches. So far they hadn't seen any sign of Rio or the masked man. Patience, he told himself. Catching the guy might not happen tonight. But it would happen. The Boss couldn't stay hidden forever.

The woods were quiet.

Unlike Parker's thoughts.

He couldn't believe he'd blurted his feelings to Melody like that. He knew better. He had already told himself to wait because she was in shock and grieving. He didn't blame her for withdrawing and putting up a wall between them. He'd ambushed her with his declaration without a thought of the consequences.

Had his subconscious somehow known that admitting his love would send her running?

The realization slammed into him.

Had he sabotaged their relationship only subconsciously? Or was he counting on her rejection so he wouldn't have to risk disappointing her? Perhaps, deep down, he didn't trust her enough to love him despite his flaws.

Suddenly the landscape of his life spread before him, and he saw that he'd run from every relationship for this very reason. He didn't trust anyone to love him enough.

Wow, he'd thought Melody was the only one with trust issues. He sucked in a sharp breath.

"You okay?" Slade asked.

"A root in my way." A deep one.

I know it's a risk. But some risks are worth taking.

Melody's words rushed back to him. She'd been talking about the situation with Jim, but she could have easily been referring to herself and Parker. They both were so afraid to trust. How could they overcome their fears?

Certainly not by being apart.

He remembered the way his parents had fought for their marriage after his brother died. They could have easily separated, each one dealing with their grief and pain alone. But they hadn't. They'd forged ahead together, as a team, a couple. Their love was stronger for it now. Parker wanted what they had, to follow their example.

He'd have to make Melody see they were stronger together than apart. They were meant to be a team, a couple. He loved her and would have to convince her he could be trusted. And he'd do everything in his power not to disappoint her, but he would have to trust that their love would be deep enough that she would love him no matter what.

There were no guarantees in life. However, Parker had faith that God would see them through.

He pulled out his phone, intending to call her.

"Problem?" Slade asked in a low tone, reminding Parker where they were and why they were out in the woods.

Parker pocketed the phone. "No. I was just thinking about Melody."

"It was a rough night for her."

"Yes." A rough night, day, week. Actually she'd had a rough five years of grieving for her sister and nephew.

Though Parker didn't know how they'd ever discover why Jim had done what he had, he could at least help Melody discover if Dante Frears was Daniel's father or not and put that question to rest. "Slade, Melody and I have something to discuss with you."

"My door is always open," Slade replied in a low tone. "You've become close to Detective Zachary."

Parker was glad for the shadows to hide the heat creeping up his neck. "Yes. Though I blew it tonight."

"How?"

"I told her I loved her."

Slade whistled through his teeth. "That's big. I take it she wasn't thrilled to hear this."

"Not really." The image of her face when he'd told her rose in his mind. For the briefest of moments he'd seen a flash of joy. And that one moment gave him hope. Hope he would cling to. "But I'm not going to give up."

"Good. She deserves happiness. You both do."

Sherlock erupted in a frenzy of barking. Parker and Slade hurried to where the dog pawed at the ground beneath a bush at the base of a tall cottonwood.

"What is it, boy?" Parker knelt down beside the dog. The beagle dug his nails into the ground, grinding up fallen leaves and spraying dirt. His barks echoed through the trees.

Slade removed a small trowel from his utility belt and handed it to Parker. "Here."

While Slade shone the flashlight on the spot, Parker scraped away decomposing leaves and dug the sharp tip of the trowel into the dirt. He dug for several minutes before the trowel hit something hard. Sherlock howled.

"Sit," Parker commanded.

The dog obeyed with another mournful bay.

Slade slid on gloves and then dug around the embedded item. They managed to wrench the square plastic container out of the ground. Parker pried the lid open, releasing a rancid odor. His stomach heaved. His eyes watered.

Sherlock let out another long howl. The inside of the container was rimmed in a yellow film that also coated the sides of a brick of cocaine wrapped in plastic, tinfoil and duct tape. One corner of the brick had been eaten away allowing the white substance to leak out. A dead beetle lay on his back next to the hole.

Grimacing, Slade asked, "What is that smell?"

"Not sure. Something meant to disguise the scent of cocaine. Best guess is urine. But thanks to our dead friend, here, for having eaten away the wrappings, Sherlock detected the drugs."

"This is close to where the Jones boy was killed," Slade stated, his tone grim. "Makes me wonder if this stash belonged to him."

"Clay in CSU will give us an accurate time frame for how long this has been buried." Parker inspected the container. "The plastic's pretty eroded. Whatever was in here was very acidic."

"Bag this up."

Parker closed the lid to the box and put it inside a large plastic bag he'd pulled from his waist pack.

"I hope this isn't what the code leads to," Slade said. "There has to be more than one brick of cocaine at stake." Picking up the trowel, Slade started to dig. "Let's see if there is anything else here."

Parker's cell phone chirped. A quick glance at the caller ID sent his heart rate into triple time. He hit the answer button. "Melody?"

"Help."

The barely audible whisper came through the line and grabbed him by the throat, cutting off his air supply.

She was in trouble. Everything inside of him twisted with terror. He couldn't let her down.

"I'm coming!" he ground out.

Melody closed her hand over the phone with equal parts relief and terror. Parker was on his way. He would defeat this monster. But would he arrive in time?

She wasn't sure how much longer she would be able to avoid capture. She was trapped under the bed, her legs tucked up as much as the shallow space would allow. She'd managed to kick her attacker hard enough to make him release her ankle.

Each time he stretched his arm under the bed, trying to grab her, she scooted out of reach. As long as she stayed in the center and remained aware of where he was so she could move, she'd be able to keep from harm until Parker arrived.

Her attacker's growl of frustration echoed through

her. The primal rage in that deep roar sent a shiver of dread racing down her spine.

For whatever reason, this man wanted her dead. If he caught her...the future flashed in her mind. A future with Parker, something she'd never imagined before, something she couldn't imagine living without now.

Lord, I beg You, please...

She heard his footsteps retreating to the living room.

She scooted to the head of the bed, her knees and elbows scraping on the rug. Her gun was on the dresser. That was her only hope if Parker didn't show up soon. She inched to the edge of the bed frame.

The sound of something dragging on the carpet sent a fresh wave of fear through her. What was he doing?

"Come out or I'll kill this officer," the harsh voice jolted through the room.

Oh, no. Officer Truman. Melody couldn't let anything happen to her. Without hesitation, she scrambled out from beneath the bed. The intruder held a gun to Officer Truman's head.

"Let her go," Melody demanded.

"Not until you give me it!"

She spread her hands out. "What do you want?"

"Your nephew's watch. Where is it?"

So not what she was expecting. Not that she'd ever been in a situation like this. Not even during training at the police academy. But she knew she needed to remain in control. Unemotional. She took a calming breath. "Daniel's watch? It's a cheap knockoff. Worthless. I don't understand why anyone would want that."

"You don't have to understand. Where is it?"

She needed to buy time for Parker to arrive. "In my purse. Under the bed."

"Get it!"

Dropping back down she wiggled under the bed-frame and stretched her arm for her bag. *Slow down,* her mind screamed.

Though her fingers closed around the strap of her purse, she made a show of trying to reach farther.

"Hurry up!"

"I'm trying."

A thump echoed in the room. Thundering steps shook the floor. He yanked her out from under the bed. Officer Truman lay in an unconscious heap near the door.

Jumping to her feet, Melody faced the masked man. A plan formed. It was now or never.

She threw the bag at his face.

He ducked.

She scrambled over the bed, trying to get around him. She needed to get out of the suite. Get help for Truman.

His big hand closed over her arm, jerking her backward.

She tumbled off the bed and landed on her back with a thud on the floor, her head snapping with the impact. Bells rang in her ears. Stars exploded behind her eyes. For a split second, the world dimmed.

She fought to stay conscious. She forced herself upright.

The masked gunman blocked her way to the door. He ripped open her purse and dumped the contents on the bed. He snatched the watch and quickly dissembled the timepiece, pulling the back off. A small, folded piece of paper fell out. He gently undid the folds and held the paper up so the overhead light could shine across it.

Melody squinted to see what was written on the tiny scrap of paper. She could make out a set of numbers. She had no idea what they meant.

"Finally, the code," the masked gunman exclaimed.

Surprise washed through her. This man must be The Boss. And she'd unknowingly had the code all along. Her nephew must have been the one to steal it. But why? What had he planned to do with the code? Why hide it in his watch? What did it lead to?

The Boss pocketed the paper and raised his weapon, aiming at her head. "Thank you. You've served your purpose."

Melody's heart pitched. Parker. She didn't want to die and leave him. She loved him. But now it was too late. She flinched, bracing herself for the deadly shot that would take her life.

Lord, spare me.

An eruption of barking splintered the air. Sherlock raced into the room, positioning himself between her and the gunman.

Parker blasted through the doorway, his weapon drawn. "Drop your weapon."

Melody's heart leaped.

The Boss spun around. His weapon discharged. The loud bang rocked the room. Parker jerked backward, a red stain spreading from his shoulder and across his chest. He crumpled to the ground.

Horror filled Melody. The bullet missed his vest.

Sherlock barked and snarled.

The gunman vaulted over Parker and raced out of the suite. Sherlock chased after him.

Choked with fear, Melody crawled to Parker's side. He lay still. His eyes closed.

Tears ran down her face. Anguish seared her heart.

"Halt!" Melody heard Slade's voice. Another shot

rang out. She could only pray the K-9 captain had stopped the crime lord.

Hands shaking, she gingerly lifted Parker's head to her lap. She smoothed his hair back from his dear face. "Please don't die," she whispered. "I need you."

Sherlock raced back into the room. He nudged his way under her arm and licked Parker's face.

"I love you, Parker." The words broke on a sob. She buried her face against Sherlock's velvety coat.

Within minutes, law enforcement and paramedics filled the hotel suite. Officer Truman was taken out on a gurney. Slade drew her away from Parker to allow the paramedics to tend to him.

"Did you get him?" she asked.

Grim faced, Slade shook his head. "No. He got away. But I'll take him down if it's the last thing I do."

"He—" she broke off when the paramedics lifted Parker onto a gurney. She stepped forward to follow but Slade captured her elbow.

"Melody, I need you here," Slade insisted. "You have to tell me everything that happened."

She knew it was standard procedure for her to give a statement now while the events were fresh in her memory, but her heart didn't want to follow protocol. "Please, let me go with him. This can wait."

For a strained moment she thought he'd refuse. Then he nodded. "Go. I'll take care of Sherlock then come to the hospital and talk to you there."

She hurried to catch up to the paramedics. She held Parker's hand the whole way to the hospital. When they arrived at the E.R. entrance, she was brushed aside by doctors and nurses intent on saving his life. She was too anxious, too upset to sit. She paced the waiting room, praying the whole time beneath her breath.

"Please, Lord, let him live. I'm trusting You to let him live."

"Melody!" Kaitlin rushed to her side and enveloped her in a hug.

More tears pooled in Melody's eyes. She clung to her friend. Soon Melody became aware that others joined them. The whole K-9 unit showed up.

"We're here for you and Parker," Val whispered into her ear as she pulled her into a hug.

Melody managed to croak out a "thank you." These people loved Parker, too. They were a family in a way that she'd never experienced. But today she was one of them.

She belonged. Because of Parker.

A fresh wave of love washed through her. Unknowingly, he'd fulfilled her heart's desire.

Slade arrived and pulled Melody to the side. She told him everything she remembered about the attack and The Boss.

"The code was in Daniel's watch all this time?"

"Yes, sir." She grimaced. "I had no idea."

"None of us did."

"I caught a glimpse of the numbers and letters on the paper," Melody told him. She quickly recited them while Slade wrote them down on a notepad.

"I'll give this to the forensics team and see if they can decode it."

"Sir, I'm sure this has something to do with the Lost Woods."

He nodded. "You're right. Everything keeps coming back to the Lost Woods."

Finally, a doctor in green scrubs entered the waiting room. "You all are here about Detective Adams?"

"Yes," came a resounding chorus of male and female voices.

The doctor broke out in a smile. "I'm happy to say your friend will be fine. The bullet went through his shoulder and didn't hit any vital organs. He'll recover nicely."

Melody sagged with relief. "When can I—we—see him?"

"He's awake now, but a bit groggy. You can go in one at a time. But limit your visit to a minute or two."

"Melody, you go first," Slade said.

Grateful to the captain, she hurried to Parker's room with every intention of telling him she loved him and wanted nothing more in life than to be with him.

She only hoped he'd give her a second chance.

Parker blinked. He was sure the medication was making him hallucinate. He blinked again.

Nope. Melody stood beside his bed, looking disheveled yet remarkably pretty. Tears streaked down her pale cheeks. Her big blue eyes held so much emotion in their swirling depths, he found himself happily growing dizzy staring into her gaze.

"You're safe," he said as his chest expanded with love for her. When he'd walked in and saw that monster aiming at her, it had taken all his self-control not to drop the masked gunman on the spot. His hesitation cost him, but it had saved Melody. No regrets. The price had been well worth paying.

She clutched his hand, her fingers entwining with his. "I'm safe. Thanks to you." She gave him a watery smile. "And Sherlock."

His face darkened with concern. When he tried to sit up, pain shot through him. "Where is he?" he asked between gritted teeth.

She laid a gentle hand on his chest. "Slade took him to the training yard."

Relieved, he sagged back against the pillows. "That's good."

Her gaze caressed him. "I was so scared we'd lose you."

"Not half as much as I was," he countered and suppressed a shudder at the horror of thinking the worst had happened to her. The thought of losing her... "I was afraid I wouldn't make it in time."

"You did." She lifted his hand to her cheek. "I owe you so much."

He winced. He didn't want her here out of gratitude. He wanted her love. "You don't owe me anything."

"I owe you an apology."

"Why?" he asked gruffly.

"Because I was a coward."

"Not true," he said. "You were brave and found a way to call for help. That's not the actions of a coward."

"I trusted God to save me. He sent you."

It made his heart glad to know she'd clung to her faith. "God will never let you down."

"Neither will you. I trust you, Parker. You'll never let me down."

He looked away. "You can't be sure."

She brushed her hand over his forehead. "I'm sure."

Her touch seared him, made him ache in a peculiar way. He met her eyes. "I'm very flawed."

She arched an eyebrow. "What flaws?"

Her trust meant the world to him. But he wanted her love. "But you don't love me."

Dropping her gaze, she tugged at her bottom lip with her teeth. "That's why I owe you the apology."

"I don't understand?"

Lifting her eyes to his, she said, "I wasn't honest with you about how I felt."

"Oh?"

Her expression turned sheepish. "I was too afraid to admit that I love you, too."

Hope ballooned in his chest. "You do?"

She nodded. "I do. And I can't imagine my life without you. I don't want to imagine it."

Her words sent his heart spinning. Fierce emotion pushed any physical pain he felt aside until he was filled with a deep abiding happiness. "I can't imagine my life without *you*. You've become my whole world."

Delight lit up her face. "Me and Sherlock, you mean."

He laughed. "You and Sherlock and maybe one day a couple of kids?"

Her eyes widened, then a soft joyous smile spread across her face. "That sounds like the perfect plan."

He tugged her closer until her lips hovered over his. "Kiss me then and show me you mean it."

"Gladly."

Their lips met. And Parker felt like he was flying on the wings of her love guided by God's hand. And he never wanted to land.

* * * * *

With over seventy books published and millions in print, **Lenora Worth** writes award-winning romance and romantic suspense. Three of her books finaled in the ACFW Carol Awards, and her Love Inspired Suspense novel *Body of Evidence* became a *New York Times* bestseller. Her novella in *Mistletoe Kisses* made her a *USA TODAY* bestselling author. Lenora goes on adventures with her retired husband, Don, and enjoys reading, baking and shopping...especially shoe shopping.

Books by Lenora Worth

Love Inspired Suspense

Military K-9 Unit
Rescue Operation

Classified K-9 Unit
Tracker
Classified K-9 Unit Christmas
"A Killer Christmas"

Rookie K-9 Unit
Truth and Consequences
Rookie K-9 Unit Christmas
"Holiday High Alert"

Capitol K-9 Unit
Proof of Innocence
Capitol K-9 Unit Christmas
"Guarding Abigail"

Visit the Author Profile page
at Harlequin.com for more titles.

LONE STAR PROTECTOR

Lenora Worth

Cursed be he that smiteth his neighbor in secret.
And all the people shall say, Amen.
—*Deuteronomy 27:24*

To K-9 officers and their canine partners. Thanks for your hard work and willingness to serve. It was a joy to learn more about what you do every day.

Chapter One

"Don't make a sound."

K-9 trainer Kaitlin Mathers felt the cold nozzle of the gun sticking into her rib cage, shock and fear pouring through her system like a hot, blowing wind. The man holding her had a raspy voice and wore silky black coveralls and a black ski mask, even though it was June in Southwest Texas. She could feel his sweat breaking through the lightweight material of his clothes, could smell a musky scent that probably came from the heat and high adrenaline. When she tried to squirm away, something cold and metal pressed against her backbone. A zipper, maybe? Determined to keep it together, Kaitlin didn't move or try to speak. She had to stay calm so she wouldn't be killed. So she could get away.

Across the K-9 training yard, Warrior barked and snarled from his vantage point inside his mesh kennel porch. Thankfully, she hadn't put the young trainee inside for the night yet. Someone would hear the barking and come around the corner, wouldn't they? *Please, Lord, give me courage,* she prayed, memories of her mother's death playing through her head.

*That's what you get for working late all by yourself.
You're more like your mother than you realized.* But
it had never occurred to Kaitlin that someone would
be hiding in the bushes right outside the doors of the
Sagebrush K-9 Training Facility. Especially since the
building and training yard were located inside a locked
fence directly behind the Sagebrush Police Department.

The man holding her must have known the risks, but
he'd somehow managed to get through that gate. He hurriedly shoved her toward a waiting van, the same dark
van she'd only minutes before noticed parked underneath an old oak near the back parking lot.

"I need you to come with me," he said, his whisper
like a knife slicing through her nerve endings.

"Why?" She had a right to ask.

"I'll explain that later, sweetheart."

Kaitlin looked at the van, then tried to look back at
her attacker. She caught a glimpse of strange, black
eyes, another shock wave jolting through her system.
Before she could see anything else, he jerked her back
around and pushed the gun hard against her side. "Let's
go."

Kaitlin didn't think about being silent anymore. If
she got in that van, the chances were very good that
she'd be dead by nightfall. *Just like Mom.* But unlike
her too-trusting mother, Kaitlin didn't intend to become
a victim. She screamed and started fighting for her life.

K-9 captain Slade McNeal was halfway to his vehicle when he heard barking. Excited barking. Whirling
toward the kennels, he wondered which dog had been
left inside them.

Warrior.

He'd just watched trainer Kaitlin Mathers putting the newbie, a strong Belgian Malinois that reminded him of his own missing German shepherd, Rio, through his paces. They'd spoken briefly, and he'd gone back to his office.

But where was Kaitlin now? It wasn't like her to leave a dog unattended, even kenneled. Warrior was sure upset about something.

The dog kept on barking, the sounds growing more urgent. Something was up. Slade hurried toward the building, his weapon drawn. He passed the kennels but didn't see anyone. Since Warrior would have a close bond with Kaitlin, it made sense that the dog was trying to warn her about something. Or alert someone else.

"Good job," Slade said when he passed the pacing, snarling animal. He didn't try to stop Warrior's barking.

Then he heard a scream, followed by grunts and shouts.

Slade stood at the corner of the building, then pivoted around the side, his weapon still drawn. About twenty yards away, a man in a dark mask had Kaitlin by the arm, trying to drag her across the asphalt toward an open black van. And he had a gun pointed at her head.

Slade's heart rushed ahead, pumping adrenaline right along with realization. He recognized this man. The Ski Mask Man, they'd labeled him around headquarters. Slade had been gunning for this guy for five long months. This criminal had some nerve, trying to kidnap a trainer right out of the training yard.

A multitude of angry memories raced through Slade's head, followed by the taste of victory. Could this case finally get a break? He glanced back at Warrior, then turned his attention back to the scene in front of him. He'd never make it to the locked cage to let the dog out, and he didn't have time to dig for his keys or call for backup. He could shoot the lock, but what if he hit the dog?

He'd have to do this on his own. "Drop the weapon!" Slade shouted. "Now!"

Kaitlin gulped a breath of relief. Slade was here. She kept telling herself that over and over. She also kept telling herself that she could handle this because she'd been trained as a police officer. She might be a little rusty since becoming a full-time trainer, but she'd find a way out of this. Somehow. She wouldn't end up like her mother.

Surprised at Slade's command, the man holding her pivoted toward Slade, his gun still aimed at Kaitlin. She pulled away, but he held her tight against him, his low whisper a warning. "Do you want to live?"

She did want to live, but Kaitlin wasn't going without a fight. She'd rather take her chances right here in the training yard with Slade McNeal than go anywhere with this man. Captain McNeal knew his job, and he was good at that job. He'd get them both out of this, and she'd find a way to help him.

Slade advanced a few steps. "Drop the weapon and let her go."

The man tightened his hold, but Kaitlin could feel the apprehension and indecision in his actions. Did he know the captain? She used the brief distraction to dig in her heels, kicking and hitting and screaming. Taking a chance, she elbowed the man in his side, then wrapped her leg behind his to trip him, causing him to lose the grip on his weapon. The gun slipped out of his grasp and hit the hot pavement. He cursed and grabbed Kaitlin again, holding her like a shield in front of him, his strong grip twisting her shoulders back so hard she cried out in pain.

"I'm taking her with me," the man shouted.

Behind Slade, Warrior was going wild against the confines of his big wire-front cage, his barks frantic and snarling. Kaitlin watched, afraid for Slade. The K-9 captain held his gun on her attacker and kept advancing, inch by inch.

"Let her go," Slade shouted again over the barking dog, his finger on the trigger of his Glock 22 service revolver. "Don't make me shoot you!"

The man stopped tugging and glared at Slade. Holding Kaitlin with one hand, he tried to reach down and scoop up his gun with the other. He seemed to know Slade wouldn't take the shot with her shielding him.

Kaitlin glanced at Slade, then using all of her strength, kicked the weapon out of her abductor's reach and, with a grunt, yanked herself away. She fell, the concrete scraping through her khaki pants to tear at her knee. But she scrambled to her feet and did a quick run toward some shrubbery near the building. That left the culprit in full view and diving for his gun. Slade could take the shot and kill the man right where he stood. Kaitlin went on her knees behind the shrubbery, watching as Slade pulled off a round, hitting near where the gun lay, causing the perp to jump and roll.

"Don't move," Slade shouted as he starting walking. "I will hit the mark next time."

Kaitlin held her breath, praying Slade wouldn't get shot. She should have picked up the gun. But the attacker took his own chances. He grabbed for his weapon, then pivoted and rolled into a ragged hunched-over zigzag toward the van, firing behind himself as he ran.

Helpless, Kaitlin watched from the bushes, her heart caught in her throat. But while she watched, she tried to memorize everything she could about her attacker.

She held a hand to her mouth, watching as Slade dived to the ground to avoid being hit, but got off a couple of rounds before the man returned fire. One of Slade's shots hit the side of the van, but missed the moving target. The suspect did a nosedive into the open vehicle and the van spun around in Reverse and took off. Two of them. He'd had a getaway driver.

Slade took one more shot, but the van swerved and skidded out onto the side street, then the driver gunned it and disappeared into the burnt dusk. Slade squinted into the sunset, trying to see the tag numbers. All he saw was a temporary tag with smeared letters and numbers. He couldn't get a read on it.

Nothing to do there. He got on the radio and alerted the switchboard operator. "McNeal, K-9 Unit 601, 207-A averted, back parking lot behind the training yard. Suspect got away. All clear."

Holstering his weapon, he hurried to where Kaitlin still sat pressing her entire body in between the prickly shrubbery and the building bricks, her eyes bright with fear and relief. This whole event had lasted a couple of minutes, but it sure felt like a lifetime.

"Hey, you okay?" he asked, placing a hand on one of her arms. With a gentle tug, he pulled her out of the shrubbery.

She jerked away, then looked up at him. "Slade?"

"Yeah, it's me. They're gone. You're safe now."

She nodded and then plowed into his arms and held

on for dear life. "Thank you." Her voice was shaky but getting stronger with each inhale of breath. "Thank you."

Slade allowed her to hug him close, his fingers hovering in the air before he put his arms around her shoulders and patted her on the back. "You're all right now. It's over."

The woman in his arms clung to him for a while longer.

Slade didn't try to pry her away. Her whole body seemed to tremble against him. His own heart echoed that trembling, but maybe for an entirely different reason. It had been a long time since he'd held a woman so close. But it hadn't been so long that he could get past the image of his wife walking out the door and getting in that car.

He wanted to hold Kaitlin and comfort her, but bitter memories tinged with regret pulled him back.

Besides, he knew if anyone saw this, they'd both have some explaining to do. And with a K-9 dog barking and shots fired in the back of police headquarters, the entire department would be rushing around the building any moment now.

He backed up, took her by her arms and set her a few inches away. "Kaitlin, listen to me. You're okay. I need to ask you a few questions."

Her shock changed to embarrassment, her face blushing pink against the pale white of her skin. Shimmying out from under his grip, she bobbed her head. "Before I give a statement, I have to check on Warrior."

Slade stopped her from bolting by standing between her and the fussy dog. "Warrior will be fine for a few more minutes. Listen to me, okay?"

She exhaled, called a command to the animal, then glanced back at Slade. "You need a description?"

"Yes, but first what happened?" He scanned the perimeter of the practice yard and the parking lot. Nobody. But he heard doors opening in the distance and voices echoing out over the headquarters' parking lot. Maybe someone else had seen something.

Kaitlin glanced toward the sound of running feet. "I heard Warrior barking. He alerted me."

"I heard him, too," Slade said as he grasped her wrist. "Let's move toward the kennels so we don't get shot by one of our own."

She let him guide her until they were a few feet from Warrior's kennel. Then she pulled away and ran to the dog, her key ring jingling as she quickly opened the mesh-wire door.

Warrior bounded out, his frustrated whimpers echoing over the yard. The dog paced toward where Kaitlin had been snatched, then glanced up at his trainer.

"Sit. Stay."

The order wasn't as commanding as in the practice yard, but the dog did as Kaitlin said.

Slade saw two uniformed officers push around the building, guns drawn. He held up his hands. "Hey, over here. We had an intruder but…it's okay now."

As the officers gathered around, Slade explained what had gone down. "I exited my office and heard a K-9 officer barking. Someone tried to abduct Miss Mathers. He held a gun to her head, but she managed to get away. I pursued the attacker and called for him to halt. He refused and fired back. We both shot off a few rounds, but he managed to make it to the getaway car. Black, late-model van, old with a dent in the front passenger-side door. Temporary tag, smudged and un-readable. Vehicle headed west on Trapper Street. I got off a shot that hit the right back side of the van."

"We'll put out a BOLO."

Slade nodded on that.

"Get a good look at the attacker?" one of the offi-cers asked.

Kaitlin spoke up. "He was wearing a dark mask like a ski mask. His eyes looked…so black, an eerie black. He must have been wearing special contacts because even the whites of his eyes looked dark."

Slade saw the shudder moving down her body. And felt the hair on his neck rising. This wasn't the first time he'd had a run-in with a man fitting that descrip-tion. Last month, he'd glimpsed a masked gunman with blacked-out eyes fleeing Melody Zachary's hotel suite after a tense standoff that left K-9 detective Parker Adams with a gunshot wound. However, he didn't let on in front of Kaitlin that this suspect had to be the hooded man who'd been wreaking havoc on his en-tire department. The body count kept rising due to the heavy-handed work of a local crime syndicate run by a mastermind known as The Boss. And now someone within this criminal's organization had made a bold at-tempt right here on police grounds. Five months ago, his K-9 partner Rio had been stolen and now this. Someone was deliberately taunting him.

He wanted this case over and done with before some-one else got killed.

Turning to the officer, he said, "That's an apt de-scription. He was average height, maybe a hundred and seventy pounds, medium build. He wore black cov-eralls." Slade stopped, a shiver of familiarity moving down his spine. He shook it off, figuring things had happened so fast he still had a lot of images running through his head. Especially the one of Kaitlin being held a gunpoint.

"There was a wide silver zipper down the front," she added, her voice becoming stronger. "He had a... raspy voice. He kept telling me I had to go with him."

Kaitlin kept her hand on Warrior and petted the dog over and over. She was scared but was clearly putting on a brave front. Slade's heart still thumped against his chest. The image of that masked man holding her at gunpoint would stay with him for a long time.

After the officers took their statements and along with the crime scene unit, covered every inch of the area where the van had been idling, Slade finally told the others he needed to get Kaitlin home.

"I can drive myself," she insisted tersely, her pupils settling into a stubborn dark green. "Warrior always goes home with me. I'll be fine."

"I'm taking you home," Slade said in his best captain voice. "So don't argue with me."

She stared him down, then shrugged. "Then let's get out of here."

Chapter Two

Word of the attack spread quickly.

Kaitlin's cell rang the minute Slade pulled the car into her driveway. The first call came from fellow trainer Harry Markham. "Kait, are you all right? I got a call from Callie."

"I'm fine," Kaitlin said, her eyes on Slade. The man was so solid and sure she couldn't help but feel safe, yet she worried that he'd take this kidnapping attempt to heart since he didn't take down the culprit. "It wasn't any fun, but I'm okay, really. Tell Callie—"

Her phone beeped another call. "That's Callie right now. I'd better talk to her."

She quickly told her supervisor, Callie Peterson, what had happened.

Slade got out and looked around her yard, then opened the car door for her.

"I'm home and Captain McNeal is here with me. He insisted on giving me a ride. Yes, I have Warrior. He warned me but...the masked man...he grabbed me from behind."

As she tightened her grip on the phone, Slade tightened his glare on her. "I have to go, Callie. Captain Mc-Neal needs to get home to his family."

She hung up and let the next call, from her trainer friend Francine Loomis, go to voice mail. "They're all concerned," she told Slade. "We're all close. Like family."

"You left out the part where you tripped him up and jabbed him in the ribs. Or how you managed to kick that gun away like it was a soccer ball."

She blinked at the mention of her ordeal. "I went into automatic response, I think. Self-defense and officer training from years ago kicked in."

"You took a big risk. He could have killed you."

"He didn't. Because I knew you'd take him down before he ever reached that gun again."

His jaw hardened. "Yeah, well, I somehow managed to let him get away."

Was he implying that she had distracted him? Hard to say. The captain's expression was a study in frustration. But then, the man was hard to read on a good day. And this had not turned out to be a good day.

"You didn't let him get away. The perp was returning fire so you had to protect yourself."

He grunted, his silver-blue eyes doing an intimidating sweep of the neighborhood. When they reached her front door, he turned to her. "Give me your keys."

Kaitlin did as he asked, figuring it would save time and save her from arguing with him. The man was like a steamroller. He rolled right along doing his job without hesitation, but he sure didn't like to engage in chitchat. Slade McNeal was always focused and intent on getting the bad guys.

Except earlier, when he held me in his arms.

Or rather, when she'd clung to him like he was the last Kevlar vest and she had dibs. Looking at him now, seeing that coiled bundle of strength and determination in his body language, she tried to put the memory of his solid chest out of her mind. She'd think about Slade McNeal and his silvery eyes and quicksilver moods later when she was alone and couldn't sleep. It wasn't as if she hadn't thought of him before and often. Her heart went out to him and his little boy, Caleb.

Slade's wife had been killed two years ago in a car bomb that, according to word around the yard, had been intended for Slade. Then five months ago, his K-9 partner, a beautiful German shepherd named Rio, had been taken from his backyard. That attack had left his elderly father Patrick McNeal—a retired police officer—injured and in a coma for weeks. Top that with a five-year-old son who had withdrawn after his mother's horrible death.

No wonder the man was grumpy.

Slade opened the door and stepped through, one hand gesturing at her. "Stay behind me. We'll send Warrior in first."

She glanced back. "Good idea."

Kaitlin called the command and willed the still-green animal to do a good job. Since she was purposely training this particular canine officer to help find Rio, she wanted Warrior to impress Slade. The Belgian Malinois, eager to let go of some of his own pent-up energy, hurled past Slade and danced across the hardwood floors of the living room, his nose moving from the floor to the air.

"C'mon," Slade said, reaching behind to grab her hand. His touch shot through Kaitlin like a sizzling dynamite fuse. She'd always had a little thing for the captain, but she wasn't so needy that she'd play this for all it was worth. If the man ever had a lightbulb moment and turned interested, she wanted him to come to her on better terms than her playing a damsel in distress.

She'd never be that woman. Not since the day she'd watched her mother being put in the ground. Kaitlin had learned the hard way to take care of herself. And she needed to remember that Captain McNeal was as tightly wound as a ticking clock. The man lived and breathed his job, especially since whoever had taken Rio kept coming after people they both knew.

He let her go once they were in the living room. "Kitchen looks safe."

She glanced across the hallway to her tiny efficiency kitchen. "It is, except for my cooking."

He almost smiled. "I'll take that under consideration."

Warrior rushed back, eager for a treat and a good rubdown.

"Didn't find anything, boy?" Slade asked, his tone softening toward the dog. He looked down at a basket by the door and found a chew rag, then held it out for Warrior. "He might have saved your life today."

Kaitlin went to her knees on the floor and tugged Warrior close, giving him a gentle hug. "Good boy. What a hero. Your barks warned me."

The captain looked really tall from this angle. "Yep. And what did you do? You walked right into a trap."

She stood so he wouldn't seem so intimidating. "I went around the building to see why Warrior was barking. I saw the van and thought someone might be lost or hurt. That's when the attacker came up behind me."

Slade didn't move a muscle, but she could see the throbbing pulse in his clenched jawline. "You could have called me."

"I really didn't have time to call anyone. Besides, I thought you were gone." She shrugged, tossing her ponytail. "You know what... I didn't even think, okay? I just acted on impulse, and I wasn't expecting any kind of danger."

He stepped back, his cold, blue gaze freezing its way around her tiny house. "Well, you need to think about it now. Whoever that was will probably be back. I don't think this was a random kidnapping attempt. They waited for the right moment and managed to get through a controlled gate to get to you."

Seeing the concern etched on his face, she said, "You're not making me feel very safe."

"You're not safe." He walked to the bay window in her living room. "Your attacker fit the same description of the man who's been harassing my whole team for months now. I'm pretty sure he or someone working with him is behind the recent string of attempted kidnappings we've had. And the string of murders we've racked up since the first of the year."

Shocked, she pushed at her hair. "Are you sure?"

"Yes. You said he had strange eyes, right?"

"Yes. They were all blacked out. Honestly, they didn't look real."

Slade seemed to go on alert after that comment. "They probably aren't real. He's using a mask and other methods to disguise himself."

"Why?" she asked, worried now that the crime syndicate might be targeting her. "Why would he come after me?"

He didn't answer her questions. "You might need protection 24/7."

Kaitlin almost laughed out loud. "Are you willing to do that?"

"I have to work on this case." He kept right on staring out the window. "But it might be a good idea to keep Warrior by your side at all times. And maybe you have a friend who can come and stay with you?"

"I won't endanger any of my friends," she said, shaking her head. "Warrior will do his job. That's what he's trained for."

"But is he ready?" Slade asked, staring down at the resting dog.

"He seemed ready today. We'll have to hope so," Kaitlin replied. "I'm not the type to live in fear, Captain McNeal."

He came close then, his face inches from hers. "And I'm not the type to let a woman think she's safe when it's obvious she's not, Miss Mathers." He stepped back. "Get your stuff. You and Warrior are coming to my house tonight."

Kaitlin couldn't believe the man. "No, we're not."

His tone brooked no argument. "Yes, you are." Then he held up his hand. "Look, I have a young son and my recovering father there. And two shifts of around-the-clock nurses. You won't be alone. *We* won't be alone."

Kaitlin thought it over, still reeling. "I don't want to impose on you."

"You won't be imposing. Caleb will be glad to see you. He's been asking about you…since the last time you babysat him. And it's just for tonight. Just until I can figure out the next piece of this puzzle."

Five-year-old Caleb had been traumatized when his

mother had been killed in the car bomb. The quiet little boy suffered from nightmares and other issues. Kaitlin had worked a lot with Caleb, using her dogs to bring the boy out of his shell. But it had been a while since she'd seen him.

Wanting to understand what she'd be up against, she asked, "What do you know, Captain? About that man's creepy eyes?"

He hesitated, almost shut down. But she saw a flare of trust shifting through his expression. "I don't think they're his real eyes."

She let out a gasp. "Contacts? That's what I thought, too."

His nod was curt and quick. "I think so." His gaze moved over her, then he looked toward the big windows. "Call it a hunch, but I'd just feel a whole lot better if you'd come home with me."

"Isn't that highly unusual? I mean, do you always invite people in danger home with you?"

"No."

"Why start now?"

He took a step forward then stopped. "Because this case has me by the throat and… I'm almost certain your attempted kidnapping has something to do with this crime syndicate. I couldn't live with myself if… something happened to you." He inhaled, rubbed a hand down his face. "And…because you mean a lot to my son. He feels comfortable with you since you've babysat him a few times and allowed the trainee dogs to befriend him. Truth is, he's been through too much tragedy already…and he'd be devastated if something happened to you."

Kaitlin couldn't catch her next breath after that comment. "I can't stay at your house forever..."

"No, but I can keep you alive if you'll listen to me."

She couldn't argue with that. He'd scared her with his bold words and all this talk of a crime syndicate and a masked criminal. He'd scared her with that tormented need she'd seen hooding his eyes, too. He didn't want his little boy to suffer anymore.

However, going with Slade would be like stepping across that forbidden line she'd put up between them. She didn't like mixing emotions and business together. Things could get really messy.

But when she thought about that man's eyes, she got the shivers. And given the choice of staying here alone or being with Slade and his family...well, there wasn't a choice.

"I'll pack a bag," she said finally. Then she turned and hurried out of the room before she changed her mind.

Well, now he could add stupid to the list of traits he needed to refine. He had a feeling he'd regret bringing a woman home, kind of like sailors used to avoid having a female on their ship. Nothing good could come of it.

Slade looked around the big living room of the house he shared with his father and his son and a retired K-9 named Chief. The rambling craftsman home had plenty of room for one or two more. But it had been a long time since a woman, other than his father's team of home health care nurses and Caleb's after-school nanny, had stayed in this house for more than a few uncomfortable minutes—for what his daddy called a "casserole" visit. Single women and widows loved to bring them casseroles. The women all expected something in return, of course. A couple of them had even asked Slade to the monthly church social.

Slade couldn't oblige them. It made for awkward visits.

But hey, the food was good.

"She's pretty and nice," Patrick McNeal said. "Kind of different from most of the casserole girls."

Old Chief, retired and getting fat and sassy, lifted his head and sniffed the perfume in the air. Even the dog had noticed this feminine intrusion.

Slade turned from where he was making sandwiches and nodded at his father. "Pretty, nice and now…on some thug's hit list." He slapped ham between two slices of white bread. "Why would anyone go after Kaitlin Mathers?"

Papa, as Caleb liked to call him, ran a hand down his white-whiskered face. Still recovering from the injuries that had left him in a coma, he said, "Maybe they need a dog trainer."

Slade stopped the knife he'd aimed at the mayo jar. "Good point."

"You think this attack is connected to all the others? Whoever took Rio might need a qualified trainer, too."

"I'm betting it's related, for that reason and maybe something more. I haven't come up with anything else, though."

Patrick held tight to his walker and turned to go back through the arched opening to his favorite chair in the den. Chief automatically followed him. "You'll figure it out, son."

Slade wondered about that. He and his dad didn't do much chitchatting here in the house. Caleb seemed to get agitated whenever they talked police business. But Patrick had made a connection that shouted at Slade. Someone might need Kaitlin's expertise. Or any of the trainers' expertise, for that matter. That someone obviously had taken Rio right out of the backyard. He'd have to beef up security around the training center. Not to mention keep a close watch on his son and his daddy. And he'd need to protect Kaitlin, whether she liked it or not.

Rubbing his hand on the back of his neck, he grunted at the twisted knots tightening his head and shoulders. Maybe he needed to hit the gym a little more to work out some of these kinks.

No, he just needed to catch The Boss. The mysterious leader of the local crime syndicate kept slipping through their fingers, but one way or another he vowed to bring this criminal to justice. Since the day his dog Rio had been taken right out of his yard and his father had been injured, he'd made this case a top priority. And his entire unit felt the same way.

He wanted his frail father to understand what he was trying to do.

He wanted his best K-9 partner back. Rio was part of his family.

He wanted his son to be strong and well and happy.

Then why don't you spend more time with the boy?

That question hit him hard in his gut. Patrick asked him that at least twice a week. When he'd turned to Kaitlin in desperation after Rio's kidnapping, the dog trainer and his sometime-babysitter had hinted that it might help for him to take more time with Caleb. Maybe that was why he always got so befuddled and tongue-tied around the woman. Maybe that was why bringing her here wasn't such a good idea, after all. He didn't want the woman judging him.

She wasn't married and didn't have kids. But she sure had a way with animals and children. She was all honey and sweetness when she wasn't barking commands at K-9 dogs. Today, after things had settled down, her hair had shimmered like burnished gold in the light of early dusk, but her hazel eyes had remained cool and questioning each time her gaze landed on Slade. Except for that little bit of sympathy he'd seen there in shades of green and brown. The woman had been attacked and yet, she still felt sorry for him?

He didn't need anyone's pity.

Slade needed to be a better father, but…it was so hard to relate to his quiet, sad little boy. The boy missed his mother. And Slade felt the weight of guilt pressing like a two-ton chain on his shoulders. He and Angie had been fighting the day she'd died in that car bomb. His wife had been leaving him, probably for good, when she'd cranked the engine.

Slade endured the torment of causing her death each and every day. His daddy told him he should pray about his feelings, but Slade didn't think he was worthy of asking God to release him of this burden. That bomb had been meant for him. He shouldn't even be standing here. He couldn't look his own son in the eye.

And…he had the nagging suspicion that the bomb that had killed Angie was related to this current case. Especially since similar bomb threats had been found at Nicolette Johnson's former rental. Detective Jackson Worth and his K-9 partner, Titan, had found one bomb in the nick of time to save Nicolette. Her house had been damaged, but that only reinforced how much danger she'd been in to begin with.

Then Jackson had also been threatened with a bomb under his car. Titan, trained to detect explosives, had saved the day again.

They might not be so lucky next time. Too many killings and too many kidnapping attempts had everyone on edge. And after today's bold attempt, Slade was sure there would be a next time. His bones told him that something else was coming. He only wished he could figure out what.

Chapter Three

Kaitlin had thrown her duffel bag in the spare bedroom, then immediately asked Slade if she and Warrior could go visit with Caleb. The little boy was in his
room playing with his trains and trucks, according to
Papa McNeal. Slade had nodded curtly, then returned
to making some sort of dinner.

Now Kaitlin was watching closely while Warrior and
Caleb got reacquainted.

"He's dif-fer-ent from Rio," Caleb said, the big word
twisting up in his mind but sounding cute when he
squinted through it. "And he's skinnier than Chief."

"Yes, he is," Kaitlin said. If she had to be forced to
stay here tonight, at least she could visit with Caleb.
"He's still young like you. But he likes little boys. And
I've told him all about you."

Caleb's big blue eyes, so like his daddy's, widened.
"He knows about me?"

"Of course," she said, her expression animated. "I
told him he'd get to come and visit you soon. I'm still
training him and you can help with that. I told him how
smart you are and that you are very good with dogs. He

needs to be gentle with children so you are the perfect person to help him learn."

Caleb tilted his head and gave her an impish stare. "Am I gentle?"

The innocent question tugged at Kaitlin's heart strings.

"Yes, you sure are. But you're also very brave. That's why I brought Warrior to visit with you."

Well, that and the fact that your domineering father told me in no uncertain terms that I would come here tonight.

She had Caleb for a distraction, at least. A good distraction. And she'd mostly given in to Slade's demand so she could see how Caleb was doing. She adored this little boy. He took her mind off what had happened today. He took her mind off the big man in the kitchen making sandwiches, the man who'd gruffed out an introduction when he'd brought her into the house.

"Papa, this is Kaitlin Mathers and her newest trainee, Warrior. You might remember her. She's visited Caleb and she's watched him for me at her place a couple of times. We had a prowler near the training yard who tried to kidnap Kaitlin. She's staying here tonight."

His father, white-haired and holding on to a walker, had smiled and nodded while Chief had hopped up to inspect Warrior. After the dogs had sniffed each other to their mutual satisfaction, Patrick McNeal had said, "C'mon in, Kaitlin. You'll be safe here."

She supposed law officers had their own code of speaking, because she was pretty sure she missed some of the undercurrents of that brief, curt conversation. She'd also heard bits of a whispered conversation when she'd come out of the bathroom.

Caleb didn't speak a lot, either, but tonight he'd actually talked to her more than the last time she'd seen him. That had been a few weeks ago when Slade had brought Caleb to work for a couple of hours and she'd offered to take him out onto the training yard. She'd promised Caleb they'd find his friend, but Slade hadn't asked her to talk to Caleb since then. And she'd tried to respect Slade's decision by not nagging him too much. She always asked about Caleb, though. Now she had a chance to help him again. She intended to keep that promise she'd made to the little boy, somehow. After the incident today, Kaitlin was once again reminded of how life could change in a minute. Something she'd learned after her mother had died.

Taking a quiet minute to thank God that she was safe and here now with this little boy, Kaitlin rubbed Warrior's soft fur, her gaze on Caleb. "So do you think you two can be friends?"

Caleb bobbed his head, his dark curls bouncing against his forehead. Then he reached up and patted Warrior on the head. "I can show him my secret hiding place. I wuv him."

"I do, too," Kaitlin said. She was about to ask Caleb where his hiding place was, but she looked up to find Slade standing at the door with a look of longing and regret on his face. His gaze slammed into hers with lightning-bolt precision, leaving her drained and shaky.

"Dinner's ready," he said. Then he turned and hightailed it back to the kitchen.

Wondering what was wrong with the man, and what was wrong with her for caring, Kaitlin gently tugged Caleb to his feet. "Let's go see what your daddy whipped up for dinner."

* * *

Slade ladled the vegetable soup the day nurse had made earlier into bowls to go along with the sandwiches. "Hope you like soup. Terri is a great cook. She let this simmer all day."

Not one for sparkling conversation, he decided to just give Kaitlin the soup and let her eat. After that scene in Caleb's room, he felt overwrought and disoriented. Truth was, seeing his son smiling and laughing with a pretty woman tore at the hole in his heart. He really should take one of the casserole girls up on attending the church social. Just to get out of the house more. Papa was always telling him he'd never find a woman if he didn't ever bother to be around available women. Why his dad worried about such stuff was beyond Slade.

Well, they both wanted Caleb to find a mother figure he could trust and love again. Slade didn't think he needed to be concerned about a female companion for himself, however. His job kept him occupied.

"Smells great," Kaitlin said. "Makes me think of my grandmother's kitchen."

"Where'd you grow up?" Papa McNeal asked, his hands pressed together.

"In Mesquite, just outside Dallas." She glanced at Caleb, then lowered her voice. "Just my mom and I, but my grandmother lived close by. My father had to… uh…leave when I was a baby and…my mother…passed away when I was a teenager. Then it was just Grandmother and me. But Grandmother had a sister here in Sagebrush, so after I left for college, she moved here to be closer to Aunt Tina. They both passed away just years apart."

Slade nodded, understanding she had chosen her words carefully because of Caleb.

"You all alone?" his son asked, clearly deciphering what "passed away" meant.

Slade hoped the boy didn't start asking about his mother. It was hard to explain over and over that she'd never come back to them.

Kaitlin glanced at Slade before answering. "I don't have any family nearby, but… I have Warrior and I have people I work with and go to church with. So no, I'm not alone."

Caleb's gaze moved from Kaitlin to Slade. "And you have us. Right, Dad?"

Slade felt as helpless as a new puppy. He grunted a reluctant, "Yeah, sure."

Warrior, having heard his name, did a little "Yeah, sure" of his own. That dog was a lot braver than Slade right now.

Papa, looking amused, took his soup from Slade and waited for him to sit down. Then he reached for Kaitlin's hand on one side and Caleb's hand on the other. "We say grace before our meals," he explained.

Kaitlin took his hand, then realized she'd have to take Slade's on her other side. She shot him a look that shouted "Oh, no."

So she was afraid of him? Maybe disgusted with him? She probably thought he was the world's worst parent. Or maybe the world's worst law-enforcement officer since he couldn't settle a five-month-long case.

He stretched his hand toward her, all the while preparing himself for the current of awareness he always felt when he was around her. Did she feel it, too?

She took his hand, then quickly lowered her head and shut her eyes.

Slade remembered having her in his arms earlier, remembered seeing that gun pointed at her temple, too. The first memory warmed his soul while the last one stopped him like a cold bullet.

He jerked his hand away before his daddy said Amen.

When he ventured a glance at the woman sitting at his kitchen table, he saw confusion and hurt in her pretty eyes.

Well, that was the effect he had on most women.

The house was quiet now.

Kaitlin lay on the comfortable bed in the spare room and listened, unable to sleep. Every creak settling in the walls, every twig brushing against the house, caused her to wake with a start. She hadn't tasted this kind of fear in a long, long time.

She thought about the man who'd brought her here. She should feel safe with him in the house and she did. But she couldn't get that masked man out of her head.

After dinner, Slade told her he had to finish up some paperwork. Mr. McNeal went to bed when his night nurse, Jasper, arrived. The big male nurse apparently slept in Mr. McNeal's room. Kaitlin, left sitting, offered to get Caleb ready for bed.

No one argued with her. She enjoyed helping Caleb with his bath and putting on his superhero pajamas. Then he insisted on showing her his favorite hiding place—a big plastic toy box that looked like a miniature house centered underneath the bay window in the dining room. Slade told her it was where Caleb and Chief apparently played and sometimes fell asleep.

After demonstrating how he and Chief could both fit inside the little house, Caleb asked her to read to him. So she snuggled up against a Texas Rangers baseball pillow with Caleb and read several books. It wasn't long before Warrior joined them, content to curl up at Caleb's feet and stare with adoring eyes at his new friend.

A girl could sure get used to that.

But not this girl and not with this family. Slade Mc-Neal practically shouted "Off limits" each time he looked at her. The man had pulled away from her during the dinner blessing. Did he find her that distasteful to touch? Did he wish he hadn't brought her into his house? Kaitlin had no answers. None at all. She knew how he'd made her feel earlier today when he'd comforted her after that attack…but she'd never know how Slade felt, good or bad. That man wore a coat of armor like a true knight. And he was good at rescuing damsels, no doubt.

But he needed to work on the Prince Charming factor a little more. Not that it mattered to Kaitlin. She'd given up on men a long time ago, since her work took up most of her time. She poured all of her love on the animals she trained. Maybe she was a lot more like Slade McNeal than she realized.

Now, wide awake and restless, Kaitlin got up and tugged her terry cloth robe over her flowered pajamas. Her throat burned like a parched desert. She needed a glass of water.

Opening the door slowly, so she wouldn't wake the whole house, she sent Warrior a command to stay. The big dog gave her a reluctant look, then curled back into a ball of fur.

Moonlight guided her up the wide hallway toward

the kitchen. Remembering where Slade had put the glasses, Kaitlin found a juice glass in the cabinet and then ran some water from the sink. She quenched her thirst and turned to stare over at the big plastic storage box under the window.

And heard a definite clearing of someone's throat behind her.

Slade watched as Kaitlin pivoted, the glass in her hand, and stared out into the darkness. "Who's there?"

Hating the quiver in her voice, he pushed away from the rolltop desk in the corner of the den and stood. "It's me. Slade. I didn't mean to scare you."

He heard her inhale a breath. "You shouldn't sneak up on people like that."

"I didn't. I was sitting here in the quiet. I didn't know anyone else would be up."

She walked into the moonlight and his heart stopped.

Her hair was down and tumbling in a shimmering honey-colored ribbon. Her robe was white but her pajamas had some sort of flower sprigs all over them. She looked young and vulnerable and beautiful.

But he didn't come out of the darkness to tell her that.

He couldn't move. He didn't know how to begin to flirt with a woman. He was old and bitter and washed up.

"What are you doing?" she asked. Then she drained the glass of water.

"Well, I was sitting here at my desk in my house, minding my own business."

"Then I'll leave you to it."

He stood up and caught her before she shot back up the hall. "Hey, are you all right?"

She looked down at his hand holding her wrist. "I thought I was. But... I keep seeing that man's eyes. I keep remembering that gun at my head."

Slade didn't stop to think. He tugged her close. "You've been through a bad experience. It's just nerves. You know you can talk to a counselor, right?"

She backed up and stared at him. "Yes, I know that. And that's very good advice."

He let her go. "You mean for myself, too, right?"

"And for Caleb. It might help."

"We've been that route," he said. "But when he's with you, he seems better." He didn't dare move any closer. "I've always wondered how you two bonded so fast, but I think I understand now. You lost your mother, too. What happened?"

A deep sigh shuddered through her. "She was a veterinarian and she was working late one night, sitting with a sick animal. A drug addict managed to talk his way in the back door. He attacked her with a surgical instrument after she didn't give him the kind of drugs he wanted. She bled to death right there on the floor."

Slade let out his own wobbly sigh. "Goodness. I had no idea."

"I don't talk about it much."

And Slade had specifically asked her to help his son. "I would have found someone else if I'd known—to talk to Caleb. I mean, it has to be hard for you—"

She backed up, shook her head. "I like being around him, letting him get to know the animals. I don't mind at all. Talking to him makes me feel better, and I just want to help."

"I know you do. And you're very persistent about such things."

She pushed at her hair, tugged at her robe. "*I* should just mind *my* own business."

He didn't agree with her, but he didn't encourage her, either. She was right. But he was glad she pushed at him. Somebody needed to hold him accountable. "I don't mind you helping Caleb. It's not that—"

"I'm going back to bed now."

Slade felt the rush of air as she moved away from him.

"Hey, wait a minute."

"You seem to want to be alone," she said, her voice a sweet whisper.

"Not tonight," he replied. "C'mon and sit with me awhile."

She stood there, hesitating. He could almost feel the conflicting thoughts rushing through her head. He felt the same kind of warning each time he was around the woman.

But she moved, finally. She went to the kitchen and put the glass in the sink and stood there for a minute staring out the window. Then she let out a gasp. "Slade?"

"What?"

"I—I think there's someone out there."

Chapter Four

Slade leaped into action.

Grabbing Kaitlin, he shoved her away from the window. "Stay inside."

He had his weapon drawn and was out the front door before Kaitlin could inhale. She stood in the shadows, fear and uncertainty clouding her mind until she took a deep breath. Hurrying down the hall, she called out to Warrior. "Come."

The dog trotted to her side, his tail wagging and his ears lifting. "C'mon, boy," she said, heading to the front door. She was about to open it and let the dog take the lead when the handle turned.

Backing up, Kaitlin held Warrior by his fur and quieted him. If the kidnapper had come back, she'd let Warrior deal with him this time. The canine sensed her apprehension. He let out a long, low growl.

The door opened and Slade walked in.

Kaitlin let out a sigh of relief and commanded Warrior to stay. "You're okay?"

"Yes." He gave Warrior a quick pat. "Someone ran away when I came out the door."

"Maybe I just imagined I saw someone. Warrior didn't alert."

"You didn't imagine anything. I heard them running and I found footprints in the dirt by the back fence. I think whoever it was hopped the fence and came right into the yard. You probably saw them before Warrior had time to pick up a scent."

"They know I'm here, then."

Slade moved closer. "Look, it could have been a kid out for thrills."

"Or it could have been that man again."

She shuddered in spite of the warm night. "I can't live like this. I won't live like this."

He reached for her, but she moved away, everything she'd held in check since being attacked pouring through her. "I had to live without a father. Don't even know where he is. And then I had to live without my mother. After hearing all the details of how she was murdered, I was afraid but I got over my fears." Her eyes brimmed with emotion. "I made myself get over all of it when I decided to become a police officer. I might not be a patrol officer anymore, but I learned how to protect myself...and I can still protect myself now. I won't let them win. I won't be afraid."

But she was afraid. Her worst nightmare had always been a fear of ending up just like her mother. She hated the fresh terror coursing through her. How could she control this? What should she do now? Would her prayers save her?

Slade pulled her toward him, his hands on her elbows. "It's gonna be all right. You don't need to worry. I'll put an officer on your house 24/7, I promise."

She backed away again. She couldn't depend on this

man. She'd been independent for a long time now. "I have Warrior. I'm training him as an all-purpose so he can help you find Rio. And we'll find the man behind this, too."

Slade shook his head. "No, Kaitlin. There is no 'we' in this. You can't get involved. It's too dangerous."

"I'm already involved," she said, anger taking over her apprehension. "They're after me. I don't know why, but they want something from me."

"They need your expertise," Slade explained. "You know how to make Rio do his job. They don't. That means they want something or someone that they can't get to, and they need you and Rio to help them."

"So they'll just kidnap trainers and animals until they get what they want?"

She saw something there in his eyes, a flicker of uneasiness that surpassed the concern she'd already seen. "What are you thinking, Slade?"

"They're coming after *you* for a reason."

"You said because of my expertise."

"It's more than that, I think." He put his hands on his hips and exhaled slowly. "They must know that you and I are—that we're close. I mean, I came to you almost two years ago and asked you to help me with Caleb. You've been to our house before and you've had Caleb at your place when I needed a sitter. They've seen us together at the yard and…they've probably been watching you with Caleb at the park, walking down the block—"

Kaitlin gasped and put a hand to her mouth. "They wouldn't hurt *him*, would they? Slade?"

He hit his hand on the door frame. "I don't know. We have to consider every possibility."

A cold calm came over Kaitlin. She refused to give

in to the dread that shadowed her like tattered black threads. And she surely wouldn't allow anything to happen to Caleb. "We have to consider that. If I'm around you and Caleb, then you both could be in danger."

He looked over at her. "You can't avoid us. You can't isolate yourself. We have to work through this together."

"But you just said I shouldn't get involved. You can't have it both ways."

"You're right, I can't. You're in danger and I need to come up with a way to protect you. But you're also good at your job. I need you to go about your normal routine. If you keep working with Warrior, we might be able to do something about this."

"Will you let me do that? Will you keep me informed and let me train Warrior to help?" She lifted her chin. "Don't shut me out, Slade. This is too important and I'm way too involved for you to go all stoic and righteous on me now."

A frown deepened his laugh lines. "Stoic and righteous? Is that how you see me?"

Kaitlin didn't want to pull any punches. "You're kind of single-minded and intense when it comes to this case. And I get that. Your partner went missing, your dad almost died and now your son might be a target." She held back a shudder. "You have every right to be on alert, Slade, but you need me. I want to help. If I don't, this fear will overcome me and I can't handle that."

He stood, silent and brooding, doubt flickering in his eyes. "You're right. I have a lot riding on this. My entire unit, for one thing. My job, my son. And you."

And you.

Awareness flashed through Kaitlin, a spine-tingling feeling that she couldn't deny. Did he feel it, too? This thing they had going? She wondered if she was just fixating on the one man who'd taken the time to get to know her over the years and had now possibly saved her life. Or maybe because Caleb was so adorable, she considered his daddy to be the same? No, this was about more than that.

They'd worked around each other for a couple of years now, but they'd both been professional and polite but standoffish. Then he'd approached her about using dog therapy to help Caleb out of his shell. And she'd readily agreed because she did empathize with the little guy since she'd been through something similar. And now they'd been thrown together in an intense brush with death. Being aware of Slade McNeal had gone up a notch or two from admiring him to admitting she was attracted to him.

Did he feel the same way? She decided that didn't matter right now. She only wanted Slade and his family to be safe. Caleb didn't need yet another trauma to deal with.

Slade McNeal was as strong as steel and as solid as an oak tree. The strands of silver near his temples matched that steely ice blue of his eyes. He was the kind of man she should run from, and fast. She needed to remember that, no matter the tension between them.

He must have realized what he'd said. "You are a part of this, Kaitlin. I can't let anything bad happen to one of our best trainers."

She'd take that, for now.

"Then let me help you. I'm trained to teach K-9 dogs on how to be the best. I know all the rules and I know all the procedures and precautions. And even though I quit the force, I'm experienced in all kinds of self-defense courses."

He nodded, a curt, quick movement. "We'll need to put surveillance on your house and the training yard. You can't be alone. You'll need someone at work with you at all times and you might need to stay with someone for a while. I can put Melody on this. She's as caught up in this case as the rest of us."

"Melody Zachary?" Kaitlin knew Melody. She was a good cop and a great friend who'd recently helped solve her nephew Daniel's murder. "But she's engaged now. She's busy planning her wedding to Parker."

"Yep, that seems to be going around a lot these days, but she still has a job to do. You can help her with the wedding stuff. You women seem to love that kind of thing."

Figuring he wasn't the marrying type, she said, "We all have a job to do." Then her smile broke. "But it would be fun to help plan a wedding."

Slade nodded. "I guess that's a win-win." He took another breath. "Look, it's late. We've got a lot to contend with. Think you can get some sleep?"

"I don't know. I'm exhausted but wired. I'll try."

He motioned to Warrior. "Take him and go back to bed."

"What about you?"

"I don't sleep."

The next morning, Slade was back in his office bright and early. He'd dropped Kaitlin by her house to get a few things, then they'd driven in together. The other trainers had been briefed on what happened yesterday, so they knew to stay on high alert. Slade had reported to the chief and now he was about to brief his unit and bring everyone up-to-date. They'd have to retrace their steps yet again to see what they'd been missing.

But when he turned to stare at the big white board where he'd placed all the clues and details they'd managed to collect over the past few months, he couldn't help but scan the pieces of the puzzle one more time.

His father had been attacked and Rio had been kidnapped. Eva Billow's son Brady had then been taken because the kid had witnessed the attack. Austin Black and his bloodhound Justice had found the child. And Austin had found love with the boy's pretty mother Eva. At least they'd gotten one arrest out of that part of the case. Only that lowlife Don Frist wasn't talking. Nobody wanted to talk, not even Charles Ritter, the high-powered lawyer Don Frist had ratted out. Ritter was sitting in jail. Which meant The Boss was a very powerful and dangerous man.

Then two more thugs had been murdered, and two middle management members of the crime syndicate were also dead. He stared at the mug shots of Andrew Garry, aka Blood, and Adrianna Munson, aka Serpent. They were all snakes in the grass in Slade's mind. Next up, Gunther Lamont—the Businessman—allegedly the second in command, now dead. Shot by Ski Mask Man. And last but certainly not least, dirty cop Jim Wheaton—who'd been on the syndicate's payroll—had been taken down by the cops during a hostage crisis.

They were getting closer and closer to The Boss. Slade should thank the man for culling his own criminals to the point of having no one to trust. That made a man desperate and dangerous. The Boss would slip up and when he did, Slade planned to be there to catch him. Trying to kidnap Kaitlin in the training yard and sending a thug to his house last night made this even more personal for Slade. The Boss kept toying with all of them, but he would slip up soon and Slade would be ready and waiting.

As he stood there going over everything in his head, he realized this had always been personal. They'd taken Rio out of *his* yard and tried to kill *his* father. And come to think of it, each of his team members had come dangerously close to getting killed, too. But all roads always came back to Slade and his family. Starting with Angie dying in that car bomb two years ago.

As the entire Special Operations K-9 Unit filed in, one by one, Slade nodded and spoke to each. Austin Black and Lee Calloway talked to each other as they headed to the coffeepot.

Valerie Salgado, a rookie who'd more than earned her stripes, laughed at something Jackson Worth said. And one of Slade's best friends, Parker Adams, nodded to Slade.

"What's up?" Slade asked when Parker came up to him.

"Can we talk later?" Parker asked. "I need to run something by you."

"Sure," Slade replied, curious. "Lunch after the meeting?"

"That'll work," Parker said. "Melody might be able to make lunch." He nodded and took a seat.

Wondering what that was all about, Slade started the meeting. "I know you've all been briefed on what transpired yesterday behind the training yard. Trainer Kaitlin Mathers's attempted kidnapping is now considered part of this case. Ski Mask Man has struck again."

Everyone started mumbling and talking. Slade held up a hand. "We're gonna go over every inch of evidence we have and we're going to pursue every lead. We want Rio back, but more than that, we want our town back. So let's start at the beginning."

The team had interviewed a low-level snitch named Pauly Keevers and all he'd told them was that there was something buried in the Lost Woods, a heavily wooded forest on the edge of town that hid a multitude of crime and evil. Pauly was dead now, too, taken out by the syndicate. Then informant Ned Adams was found buried in the woods.

"It looks like The Boss is killing people so they won't talk."

Jackson Worth spoke up. "Not to mention the infamous code we've tried to break and Daniel Jones's grave being dug up. And we did find that brick of cocaine. But two or so pounds of cocaine wouldn't bring about this much crime."

Not long after setting up surveillance in the Lost Woods, Parker Adams and his K-9 partner Sherlock had helped Slade find a small amount of cocaine, heavily scented to disguise it, in the woods.

Slade went back over that find. "You're right about that, Worth. It wasn't enough to cause this amount of secrecy and criminal intent. I believe there must be something else buried out in those woods."

"A body, maybe?" someone suggested.

Slade nodded. "That…or something worth much more than that small amount of cocaine we found."

Jackson spoke again. "Makes sense that we need to keep searching. They dug up that kid's grave, but they're still looking, too."

"Agreed, but we have to be careful," Slade replied. "The chief has given us special permission to stay on top of this, but let's keep in mind we have to continue to follow procedure and the chain of command."

Everyone nodded on that.

Parker again reported on how Detective Melody Zachary had solved part of a cold case that involved her sister Sierra and her nephew Daniel Jones. She'd found evidence that proved Jim Wheaton had killed Daniel and that her sister had not committed suicide. She'd been murdered. Did it all tie back to this case?

"No answers there. Dead men—and women—tell no tales," Parker said.

The body count kept rising. And so did Slade's blood pressure.

"Let's go back to that cocaine find," Slade said, a nagging feeling centered in his gut. "It wasn't enough to create this kind of violence."

"More like a smoke screen," Jackson said. "There has to be something else, something bigger out there."

"We'll have to find a reason to have another look," Slade replied, jotting notes on the board. "We'll set up more surveillance, too."

He believed the answers to this case were buried somewhere in those woods. He also believed that one of their highly trained K-9 officers would help him find whatever or whoever was out there. Now Kaitlin was training Warrior as just such a K-9.

"This brings us to Kaitlin Mathers. We're pretty sure they have Rio, but why try to kidnap a trainer?"

Valerie Salgado raised her hand. "Because they know she's smart and capable of handling a dog and they know she's been involved with you and your son. Hit us where it'll hurt."

Slade nodded. "I'm afraid that's it. Which means we have to put a tail on Kaitlin 24/7, for her own protection. And hopefully to find a pattern—someone following her, watching her. She'll go about her business and continue to train Warrior."

"I'll be glad to help with surveillance," Valerie offered. "And I don't mind hanging with Kaitlin."

They talked some more about recent events.

Then Slade stated the obvious. "I think Ski Mask Man might be more than your basic low-level thug." He glanced around the room then wrote on the board. "The Boss? Is he Ski Mask Man?"

While everyone chewed on that, Slade took one more sweeping look at the pictures and notes on the board.

"I'm pretty sure this whole setup has been aimed at me." He went back over the facts again, starting with the car bomb. "The Boss wants something that's buried in those woods, but he wants to make me suffer until he finds it. He's getting desperate, and that means we're all in jeopardy. So be on the alert at all times. We can't rest right now. It's too dangerous."

After everyone filed out, Slade turned to stare at the board again. Who was The Boss? And when would he make his next move?

Chapter Five

Slade went into the diner on the outskirts of town, still wondering why Parker and Melody couldn't talk to him at the office. Maybe Parker had a lead but was afraid to share it with the whole class. After the Jim Wheaton incident, Slade could certainly understand that. It was hard to trust anyone these days, but his gut told him he could trust all the members of his unit, especially Parker Adams. If Parker had something he only wanted to share with Slade, then that was all right by Slade.

He checked on Kaitlin before leaving for the lunch meeting. He found her hard at work out in the noonday heat, sending Warrior through all the obstacle courses and training runs.

Slade made a point to make sure she wasn't alone. Francine Loomis waved at him, her short dreadlocks lifting around her face, her smile always positive and uplifting. She'd watch out for her friend Kaitlin, no doubt there.

"Still putting him through his paces, I see."

Kaitlin turned at the sound of his voice, her expression cautious. "That's my job."

"How you feeling today?"

"I'm fine." When he didn't respond, she added, "I'm okay, Slade. Back to work. Work always helps calm me."

"You'll have an escort home and you'll have a car out front all night."

She nodded and sent Warrior for another practice run. "And I have Warrior. I think he gained more experience yesterday than he could have in a week."

"He wasn't practicing yesterday. He alerted us to you being in danger. That's the sign of a good officer."

"I want him to be good. Like everyone around here, I want this case solved. Warrior can help with that, I hope."

"We'll stay on it." He turned to leave. "I'm headed to lunch." Then he pivoted. "Oh, Kaitlin, I thought maybe you could come by and visit again with Caleb, maybe bring Warrior, too. He really took a shine to that dog."

She looked worried. "Do you think that's wise? I don't want to put Caleb in any danger."

"You'll be with me, too." He looked off into the distance. "Of course, these thugs did kidnap Rio right out of my yard."

"I guess we're not safe anywhere," she replied.

Frustrated, Slade nodded. "We'll stay close and keep an eye out, but yes, come to our house. Maybe have lunch with us?"

She hesitated, her expression guarded. "Okay. I'd like that. How 'bout Saturday? I don't have much planned then."

"We'll see you then. And in the meantime, be alert and stay safe."

He scanned the practice yard and the surrounding street before leaving. The back gate had been reinforced, too. Whoever had managed to slip in last time would find it hard to get in now. Everyone at headquarters had been alerted to be on the lookout for that black van, but Slade figured it was hidden in a warehouse somewhere. He wished he could find it. There were hundreds of black utility vans around the area. He could have the crime scene unit pull up makes and models. That might jar something loose.

Now he sat in the Sagebrush Diner wondering how he was supposed to keep his family and Kaitlin safe. When the door swung open, he waved to Parker and Melody, still wondering what they had to tell him. They'd already been through a lot together. Melody had been taken by Ski Mask Man and Parker had been shot by the thug when he came to Melody's rescue. Melody had matched up a cheap watch that had belonged to Daniel as containing the mysterious code the bad guy wanted. Ski Mask Man had taken the watch and while he'd gotten away yet again, thankfully Parker had saved Melody from a worse fate. The pretty, focused detective would make a good match for Parker.

Slade figured a man needed that kind of woman in his life. He thought about Kaitlin and wondered about the rest of her story. She'd obviously lost out on some things. They had that in common.

"Thanks for meeting with us," Parker said.

"No problem." Slade stood and greeted Melody. "Good to see you."

A waitress materialized and told them the special of the day. After they'd ordered their food, Parker glanced around, then looked back at Slade. "Melody has a theory and…we need you to hear her out."

"I'm listening," Slade replied.

Melody took a sip of her water, then let out a sigh. "I think I might know who Daniel's father is, and I wanted to meet with you to ask you about obtaining some DNA to prove it."

Now Slade was really listening. "Okay, but who and why me?"

Parker took Melody's hand. "We think it's your friend Dante Frears."

Slade put down his coffee cup. "What? He's happily married with a toddler. I must be missing something."

Parker nodded. "He wasn't always married. We think he had an affair with Melody's sister Sierra. When you get back to work, take a long look at Daniel's picture."

Melody gave Slade a beseeching glance. "I have one right here." She took the wallet-size print out of her purse and handed it to Slade. "I saw it right away when I encountered Frears at the Founders Ball last month. Their eyes—that pale silvery-blue color is distinctive, and they both have almond-shaped eyes, too."

While the kid did bear a resemblance to Dante, that didn't mean they were father and son. "Is this all you've got?"

Melody put the picture away and continued. "I've thought about it a lot. Frears is wealthy and more than able to support a child. My sister had someone taking care of her but she wouldn't tell anyone who—not even me. Daniel's girlfriend, Allie, says she thinks a rich man had an affair with my sister. She said Daniel knew his father but wouldn't talk about it. She thinks they had some sort of falling out…right before Daniel was shot."

Slade didn't want to buy into this, but Parker and Melody were both savvy police officers. He owed it to them to listen, at least. "But why Dante? He's a pillar of the community, a decorated veteran. He gave that huge donation to help us find Rio. He's always been behind the Sagebrush K-9 division."

"And all of that is good and fine," Parker said. "We just need you to get some of his DNA and let us test it—just so Melody can know the truth. If it was your son or nephew, you'd want to know, right?"

Slade couldn't argue with that. "Yes, I would. But I can't just march up to my best friend and ask him to hand over his DNA."

Parker glanced at Melody. She took a breath and said, "No, but you get invited to a lot of his fancy parties. It'd be easy for you to find a way to get his DNA."

Slade couldn't believe what they were asking him to do. "So you want me to go to his home and sneak around and do this? Without a warrant? Without probable cause? What if you're wrong?"

"Then I'll drop it," Melody promised. She motioned to Parker.

He leaned close. "Captain McNeal, if you consider what this means, you might be able to solve this case."

Slade's head shot up. "Come again?"

Parker tapped a finger on the table. "If Dante was Daniel's father, could he be retaliating for Daniel's death? You got blamed for it, but we now know Jim Wheaton made the kill shot. Frears might not know that or care. But if he does, then that's motive to come after our unit and especially you. It makes sense that someone with a lot of money is behind all of this."

"Someone who is also desperate and determined," Slade added, thinking Dante had no reason to be desperate. The man ran a legitimate corporation that involved several different investments—real estate and financing being at the top. He owned a lot of companies around town, too. Would his friend use one of those corporations or one of his businesses to hide a criminal empire? Could one of those companies have a fleet of black vans?

Slade couldn't see it. Or maybe he didn't want to see it. He sat silent while the waitress brought their blue-plate specials. Outside, the June sunshine sizzled in heat waves while Slade's mind hissed a warning that he couldn't voice. They couldn't be right. Dante was a decorated soldier. He'd saved Slade's life more than once when they'd served together. But he was also a demolition expert. The man knew all about explosives—how to make them and how to detonate them. Dante handled C-4 the way a toddler handled Play-Doh. Slade had certainly seen that with his own eyes on the battlefield. But that didn't mean Dante had planted that bomb in Slade's car, did it?

He stared at Parker. "This is a bit far-fetched, don't you think?"

"You got any better ideas?" the detective asked.

Slade chewed on that while he tried to enjoy his chicken-fried steak. "No, I don't." He stared at his plate for a minute then said, "I'll see what I can do. But not a word to anyone until I can prove or disprove your theory. And even if I do, we can't use it in court."

Melody gave her fiancé a quick glance full of relief. "We haven't said anything about this. We wanted to talk to you first. The man's your best friend. I'd like to be wrong on this, but I don't think I am." She cleared her throat. "I don't want to press charges or anything like that so we won't need to use the DNA as evidence right now. I just need answers as to why Daniel was shot and why my sister died."

Slade lifted his head again. "You've already established she didn't commit suicide. You don't think Dante had anything to do with her death, too, do you?"

When Melody didn't answer, Slade dropped his fork. "I can't see Dante killing a woman in cold blood, especially the possible mother of his son. I'm sorry, but I can't go for that scenario."

Parker lowered his voice. "If he's The Boss, he'd be willing to kill anybody who stands in his way, don't you think?"

Images of the man holding Kaitlin at gunpoint yesterday hissed through Slade's mind. Someone was sure willing to do desperate things. But Dante? It didn't make sense.

But Slade remembered one thing about yesterday's attempted kidnapping. That man had every opportunity to put a bullet through Slade and Kaitlin. What had stopped him?

I could have shot him easily, too, Slade thought. He'd hesitated because of Kaitlin. And because he wanted to bring the man in alive so he could get some answers. Now he only had more questions.

Slade had lost his appetite. "I'll have to think long and hard on this." He glanced from Parker to Melody. "I'll go back over everything and I'll consider what you've told me here today. I'll let y'all know if I get any leads on this."

"We know he's your friend," Melody said, "but…we also figure that gives him an almost perfect cover, too."

Slade inclined his head. "Because he'd have an in

to our department. No one would suspect our biggest benefactor of double-crossing us."

"Exactly," Parker said. "I'm sorry, Captain, but this could be the missing part of the puzzle."

Slade paid for their meal, then turned back to the two detectives sitting with him. "If what you're telling me is correct, then I've been the biggest fool of all time."

"It's not your fault," Melody said, her tone sympathetic. "He fooled all of us. Especially my sister."

"Allegedly," Parker whispered. "We don't have any proof yet."

"You will," Slade replied, making his decision. "I intend to get that DNA, one way or another, and I'm hoping to be able to prove you wrong."

Kaitlin hated this. She'd turned around a hundred times today, wondering if someone was out there watching her. Someone who might spring on her again and try to kidnap her.

And why? So she could bark orders at Rio? So whoever had the K-9 officer and the trainer would be able to use both of them for something illegal? It didn't make any sense to her at all. Rio had been missing for five long months now. Would he remember the commands they'd taught him? Would he remember her or Captain McNeal?

She thought back over her earlier conversation with Slade. Good thing she'd learned captain-speak over the years. The man mostly grunted out orders and commands, but rarely just came out and asked for help. She was touched as well as confused about his request that she come back to his house this weekend and visit with Caleb. But then, the captain loved his little boy even if he didn't have a clue as to how to deal with Caleb's silent moods and nightmares. Plus, she knew the other reason McNeal wanted her close. He felt responsible for her. The man took the world onto his broad shoulders and now she was one more thing to add to his list of concerns.

"What are you thinking about so hard?" Francine asked, her finger poking at Kaitlin's rib.

Kaitlin shook her head. "Life in general. I don't like this feeling of being unsafe. I'm beginning to doubt everyone around here."

The other trainer slanted her head and stared at Kaitlin with big brown eyes. "You know you can trust me, don't you?"

"Of course."

"Good then, 'cause I'm on you like white on rice." She giggled and winked at Kaitlin.

Kaitlin smiled at her always optimistic friend. "I happen to love rice and I happen to consider you my best friend, so I'm good with that."

"And I get to be your roomie for a few days. My mama is so thrilled that you and Warrior are gonna be staying with us this weekend."

"Could be a lot of weekends between staying with you and having Valerie or Melody staying with me on some weekdays," Kaitlin retorted. "Your mom might decide she's tired of us by then."

"Nah, she loves you. And besides, I think Captain McNeal is gonna crack this case soon. Whoever tried to take you made one fatal mistake. They came onto our territory. No one around here will stand for that."

"I hope you're right," Kaitlin said. "And I hope Mc-

Neal does find the culprit. I don't intend to live like this the rest of my life."

She'd only agreed to go to Francine's house later this week so they could both work on training Warrior. It would be good to put him in a different environment and see how he operated. And she always had fun when she was with Francine. Her friend had a big, loving family that had embraced Kaitlin the first time she'd gone with Francine to Sunday dinner. She loved being with them.

"I'm blessed to have you watching my back," she said.

Francine lifted a dark eyebrow. "You got the captain looking out for you now, girl. The way he looked at you this morning, I'd say you got more than that."

Kaitlin slanted her head. "Excuse me?"

Francine twirled one of her tiny braids. "I think Captain has his eye on you. In a good way."

Kaitlin ignored the thread of awareness that moved down her spine. "You're crazy, you know?"

"I've been told that. But I'm also very observant. I see what I see and I see a lot."

"You also talk in riddles."

"But I speak the truth."

Kaitlin laughed at her friend's antics. She could always depend on Francine to be the comic relief, even when she was brutally honest.

"We'll see about that," Kaitlin said. "I'm going over to his house on Saturday."

"Uh-huh."

"To spend some time with Caleb."

"Uh-huh."

She shook her head. "Don't go getting any ideas."

"Whatever you say." Francine grinned, then went back to her paperwork.

Kaitlin didn't tell her friend she was beginning to get some ideas of her own. Captain McNeal was good-looking and intense. Hard not to notice that. Hard not to be attracted to that. But…she didn't want to go down that road. The man lived for his work and from what she'd heard around the precinct, he didn't have time for any kind of personal relationship.

And neither did she. Kaitlin had learned a long time ago that she could only depend on herself. Even when someone was threatening her. When it came right down to it, she might have to take matters into her own hands. In order to survive.

Chapter Six

Kaitlin checked all the windows and doors one more time. Locked tight. Then she lifted a panel on one of the wooden blinds in her living room and saw the patrol car parked out past the streetlight. Someone was watching over her out there and Valerie was asleep in the guest room.

Warrior was nearby, too. The dog would alert at the least bit of noise. She could rest easy for now.

Her cell rang, making her jump. Hating this skittishness, she took a deep breath and answered. "Hello."

"Kaitlin, it's Slade McNeal."

As if she didn't recognize that curt, gravelly voice.

"Hello, Captain. Yes, I've checked the windows. Yes, the cruiser is parked outside and Valerie is sleeping here tonight. And yes, Warrior is right beside me."

"Can I speak now?" Slade asked, waiting.

She swallowed hard. "I guess so. What did you need to say?"

"Well, now that I think about it, you did answer all my questions. Are you sure you're okay, though?"

"I just told you, yes." She didn't want to sound ungrateful. "I'm okay, Slade, really. A little jittery, but then I've never come close to being abducted before so my new normal is a bit shaky right now."

"I could come over, sit with you until you get sleepy."

Kaitlin considered that offer and thought about having him here in her house, sitting on her couch. Tempting, mighty tempting. "I'm a big girl. I can take care of myself."

"These people are dangerous, Kaitlin."

"I know that. I'm the one who had a gun pressed to her temple, remember?" And now she had her own pistol loaded and nearby.

"I can't forget," he rasped out. "Okay, do it your way but be cautious. Put my number on speed dial."

She could do that, but she wouldn't need to. "I will, I promise. Now you try to get some sleep, too."

"I don't sleep," he said, probably to remind her again.

"Right." She wished him a good night and ended the call. Then she looked down at Warrior. "Neither will I, but he doesn't need to know that, does he?"

Slade put down the book he'd finished reading to his son. "Time to get some shut-eye, okay?"

Caleb looked up at him with big blue eyes. "I like Warrior."

Slade leaned forward in his chair. "I like Warrior, too. He's a loyal officer."

Caleb's eyelids became droopy. "Want Rio back."

"Me, too," Slade replied. He leaned forward and stood, his hand touching on his son's dark curls. "Sleep tight."

"No bed bugs bite," Caleb said in a sleepy whisper.

"No bed bugs bite," Slade repeated, wishing he could keep all the bad things in life away from his son.

But...that wasn't possible. Caleb had lost his mom in a horrible way and even though the little boy didn't witness the explosion, he'd certainly heard and seen enough to realize that his mother wasn't coming back. The same with Rio. How many hits could one kid take before he shut down completely?

Thinking about Kaitlin and how good she was with Caleb, Slade walked into his little corner office in the big den and sank down in the worn leather chair behind the battered desk.

What was it about this woman that always had him on edge?

She wasn't a classic beauty but she had nice honey-colored hair and those pretty, catlike hazel eyes. She was what his deceased mom would have called fresh-faced and earthy. Not a lot of fancy makeup or jewelry. Kaitlin's beauty shined from within. Maybe because she was a devout Christian.

Slade shook his head at that, thinking he was more of a doubting Christian. He certainly didn't shine very much. He shuffled through the papers on his desk, and wondered for the hundredth time how he could protect all the people he cared about.

Including Kaitlin Mathers.

Of course he cared about the woman. He cared about all the K-9 trainers. They were a vital part of his department. But Kaitlin, well, she'd always been there, willing to help with Caleb, willing to go the extra mile to make the animals do the best job possible. Now she was hard at work training Warrior. He'd be a good all-purpose officer. The best.

Slade sat up, his mind whirling. What if the syndicate came after Warrior, too? How long could he fight off these people? Then he thought about Melody's accusations against Dante Frears.

That put a whole new wrinkle on this troubling case.

And gave Slade a whole new set of worries to mull over.

Maybe he did need to turn back to God. Because he prayed he wouldn't have to take down a man who'd been his friend for most of his life. He prayed that Melody and Parker were wrong.

But in his heart, in his gut, he had that feeling of aching emptiness and nagging irritation. What if they were right?

Kaitlin woke up and stared at the clock. Three in the morning. Her mother used to call this the loneliest hour. A shudder moved down Kaitlin's spine. Had she dreamed about her mother? She thought so, but her mind refused to go back into that dream. She had a vague flash of her mother, smiling at her, laughing, reaching out a hand.

"Are you trying to warn me, Mama?"

Warrior heard her speak and stirred from his doggie bed at the foot of her bed. The big dog whimpered a greeting and waited for her to pat him.

Kaitlin rolled off the bed and grabbed her robe. "Let's make rounds," she said, giving Warrior a command.

Together, they moved up the hallway, the night-light she kept there glowing enough to show the way to the kitchen and living room at the front of the small house. After passing Valerie's closed door, Kaitlin automatically went to a window to check for the cruiser. It was still there, parked in front of her house.

"Good. We're safe for now."

She refreshed Warrior's water and set the big bowl down, then went to the sink to get herself a drink. Sipping her water, she thought about last night while she'd been in Slade's house. If she hadn't seen that shadow out the window, they might have sat and talked well into the night.

And she might have gained some insight into the man's head and heart. Did she really want to go there? Warnings sparked through her mind like a fuse sparking toward dynamite. She'd worked with men like Slade McNeal for most of her adult life.

No, that wasn't exactly true. She'd worked with a lot of uptight, hardheaded police officers, but she'd never been around a man like Slade before. He was uptight and hardheaded and most people considered him hard-hearted, too. But she'd seen the good side of the man. He loved his son, but he was afraid of what his work had done to Caleb. Slade had swallowed his pride by reaching out to her for help. That gesture showed Kaitlin a lot of things about him. He cared enough to put his own feelings aside. He had a heart, but he'd built that proverbial wall around it to protect himself in the same way he tried to protect everyone else.

Including her, now.

"I can't do this," she whispered to herself. "I can't let my feelings go beyond helping Caleb." If she got all caught up in trying to save Slade McNeal, she'd be the one who wound up hurt. Not to mention how awkward that would make things around the training yard.

"Not a good idea," she said, looking down at Warrior. The dog woofed a reply, then looked around for something to sniff.

And found it by her front door.

Kaitlin's gaze followed Warrior. The dog stopped and ran his nose along something shining white lying on her hardwood floor. Her pulse skittering, Kaitlin hurried toward Warrior. "What you got there, boy?"

Warrior looked up at her with eager eyes, then sniffed the piece of paper again.

Kaitlin went back to the kitchen and grabbed a set of tongs from the big container of utensils she kept on the counter. "Let's see what that is." She carefully lifted the paper, holding it tight with the tongs until she got it over to the counter where the stove light cast out enough light for her to see.

The words printed on the paper caused her to gasp and step back shivering.

I'm watching you.

Kaitlin turned, her back pressed against the counter, her heart pumping so loudly she could hear it over her erratic breathing. The house was dark and quiet, but she strained to hear anything else that might signal danger. Should she go to the window and check for the cruiser? Should she go back to her bedroom and get her gun and her phone? Or maybe let Warrior out to do a search around her house?

"No," she whispered, swallowing her fear as she hurried to Valerie's room. "That's what they want me to do."

She stood at the door, her eyes adjusting to the shadows as she strained to hear the sounds of the creaking house, the wind causing a branch to tap against the window.

Slowly, she calmed herself enough to think straight. Someone had managed to get to her porch and slip this note underneath her door. Even with a cruiser parked outside. Even with a trained K-9 officer present in her house.

"Who are you?" she asked out loud. Then she knocked on Valerie's door.

Valerie was up and at the door, her weapon held down by her side. "What's wrong?"

Warrior whimpered and woofed, probably sensing Kaitlin's anxiety. The dog badly wanted to get on with things.

"Someone slid a warning note under my front door." She motioned to Valerie to come up the hall and then showed her the note.

Warrior went to the door and sniffed again, then whimpered.

"Not now, Warrior," she said, calling him over. She put her hand on a tuft of his fur. "Not tonight, boy. They want me to let you out there. But I'm not going to let them win tonight."

Valerie readied her weapon, her green eyes flaring bright. "They don't know I'm here. I'm going out there."

"You need backup," Kaitlin said, following the female officer around the windows. Valerie had left her K-9 partner Lexi kenneled with another handler, but now Kaitlin wondered if the apprehension-trained dog should have come along, too. "Don't go until I call someone."

Valerie kept moving. "Hurry, then."

Kaitlin rushed back to her room and got her cell and her pistol. She could alert the cruiser at least. The officer had given her his cell number earlier in the evening.

Kaitlin punched in the numbers and waited.

But no one answered.

Slade heard the buzzing of his phone and came wide awake to grab it off the nightstand. "McNeal."

"Sir, it's Pete Ross."

The patrolman assigned to watch Kaitlin.

Slade was up and searching for his clothes. "What is it?"

"I saw someone up on Miss Mathers's porch. I'm doing a walk around the perimeter of the yard. I think he came through the back gate."

Slade closed his eyes and let out a grunt. "I'm on my way."

Dressing quickly, he alerted his dad's night nurse that he'd been called to work. The male nurse was used to this so he replied okay and went back to his recliner in Papa's room. He was good at listening for Caleb, too.

Slade was out the door and in his car in minutes. He was turning the corner to Kaitlin's street when his cell rang. It was Kaitlin.

"I hate to bother you, but Officer Ross isn't responding to my calls."

Slade turned into her driveway. "He called me. I'm in your driveway now."

"Oh, what a relief."

Slade wasn't sure if she meant him being here or if she was just glad the officer guarding her was alive and well.

He took the steps and was knocking at her door in seconds.

Kaitlin opened the door and looked past him, Valerie behind her. "Where is Officer Ross?"

"He's making rounds in your backyard. He saw a prowler."

Valerie pushed past them. "I didn't see him anywhere. I'll go check it out."

Kaitlin shut the door and turned to Slade. "That must be why he didn't answer my calls."

"How many times did you try to call him?"

Sighing, she held her hands against her robe. "Several times, and so did Valerie. He didn't answer so I got worried."

"Maybe he put his phone on silent to do a search," Slade replied. "That's probably why he called me."

"I'm glad he did." She pushed at her long hair. "I mean, I thought maybe I was imagining things but… whoever was out there left me a message under my door."

"What?" Anger and frustration snaked through Slade. "Let me see."

She took him to the counter and pointed to the note. *I'm watching you.*

Slade stared at the scrawled black words that stood out from the crisp white paper, a chill hardening his spine.

Kaitlin's voice was low and gravelly. "I think they expected me to send Warrior out to investigate. I didn't. I figure if I had, he wouldn't have come back."

"You're probably right, there," Slade replied. "We'll get this into the station, see if we can trace any prints."

"You won't find prints on that," she replied. "Not even mine. I used tongs to get it to the counter."

"Good thinking. But you never know. People slip up and that's when we nab 'em."

"This intruder managed to get this into my house

with an officer out there watching and another one sleeping in my guest room."

A knock at the door caused Warrior to bark.

"Stay back but ask who it is."

Kaitlin called out, "Who's there?"

"Officer Ross" came the reply.

Slade kept his gun at the ready but opened the door to let the officer inside.

Valerie came up the steps and entered before Slade could shut the door. "Nothing," she said, shaking her head.

"I didn't find anything, either," the young man said. "But someone wanted me to look. They threw a small limb right up on the hood of my vehicle, then ran away."

"You saw someone?" Slade asked, his stomach churning.

"Just a shadow. A man wearing a black mask."

"Like a ski mask?" Slade asked.

"Yes, sir. That's what it looked like."

"He lured you away while someone went onto the porch to leave a message." He pointed to the note on the counter. Then he looked at Kaitlin. "We'd better check the entire house."

Valerie eased into the kitchen and headed toward the back porch.

"Don't you think they're long gone?" the officer asked.

Slade's gaze settled on Kaitlin. "Yep. But...they might have left behind something even worse than a threatening note."

Chapter Seven

"Nothing."

Valerie held her gun down and shook her head. "I can't find anything, not even a shoe print."

Slade wiped a hand down his face. It had been a long night and now dawn was creeping through the trees to the east. "We'll go over it again in the light of day." He glanced toward where Kaitlin sat staring, Warrior by her side. "Maybe she should have let Warrior have a go at things earlier."

Valerie shot a sympathetic glimpse at Kaitlin. "She didn't want anything to happen to Warrior. I think she's right. If she had let him out, they could have killed him or nabbed him and possibly her, too. They set this up to distract us, and it almost worked."

Slade had to agree. If Warrior had gone after the prowler who'd hit the cruiser with that limb, the dog might be gone forever. And Kaitlin would have gone after the animal if he hadn't returned. An easy way for her to go missing, too.

"I guess you're right. But we have to search the perimeter of her yard again and take this note in to be analyzed."

Valerie glared at the white sheet of paper that lay on the counter. "I'll make sure the crime scene techs handle it with care."

Slade didn't worry on that matter. But he was worried about the woman sitting on the couch. He walked over to Kaitlin and settled down on the storage bench in front of the bright green sofa. "How you doing?"

She shrugged, wrapped her arms across her stomach. "I just need a good night's sleep."

"You'll get one," he assured her. "I'll be your patrol tonight."

She gave him a soul-searching stare. "You don't have to do that."

"I can't keep you safe if I depend on other people. Both of these officers did their jobs and yet, you were threatened again."

"So you intend to do it yourself, right?"

He set his jaw. "I feel better doing things myself."

"You need to sleep, too."

"I don't sleep."

He didn't dare tell her that he was bone weary and dead on his feet. He'd find some shut-eye here and there. He always did.

"What do we do now?" she asked, her hand on Warrior's stubby dark gold fur. "I don't like sitting around like a target."

He blinked and then rubbed his eyes. "I'll be here tonight. Then, unless something else happens, Melody will take over. You'll be with Francine and her family this weekend."

Kaitlin shot off the couch, causing Warrior to woof

out in surprise. She went to the window and paced around. "I can't be comfortable in my own home or anywhere else. Two nights in a row, this person has taunted me. At your house and, if that wasn't bold enough, now at my own home with two officers and a police dog watching over me. Who is this man?"

Slade wondered that same thing back at his office.

After briefing the entire unit on this latest development, he felt even more sure now that The Boss was not only targeting Kaitlin, but had to be after Slade, too. This was becoming way too personal. Now the culprit was leaving threatening messages. What next?

He didn't want to think about that.

But he did think about what Melody and Parker had suggested to him the day before. Picking up his phone, he scrolled through the numbers until he found Dante's cell number. Should he call his friend to say hello and see how he was doing, maybe thank him for the contribution?

It was a start. He hit the call button and waited.

"Dante Frears." His friend's smooth, confident voice echoed through the airwaves.

"Dante, it's Slade. How ya doing?"

"Good. Great. Hey, I'm glad you called. I'm having a get-together next weekend and wanted to invite you over. Bring a date if you want. It's just a casual thing by the pool."

Slade sat up in his seat. Coincidence or a carefully planned event? "What's the occasion?"

"It's Yvette's birthday. She wanted a pool party with just a few friends. Can you come by?"

"I'll certainly try," Slade replied. "And I might actually bring a date."

Dante chuckled. "Are you finally dating again?"

"No, not really." He thought about Kaitlin. "Just hanging around with a friend in need." He'd like to date her.

"Well, bring that lady friend over, man. It's been ages since we've gotten together."

"I was at that fund-raiser soiree you had last month, remember?" Slade hoped he didn't sound harsh, but Dante should at least acknowledge that he had been there since they'd talked a lot that night and Slade had thanked him several times for his contribution to the K-9 Unit.

"Oh, yeah. Of course I remember. That was a great shindig, huh?"

"The best," Slade replied. "By the way, you should see the new K-9 we're training. An all-purpose officer." He didn't mention Warrior by name. "He'll be able to sniff out anything from dead bodies to drugs to what kind of shampoo you use."

"Impressive," Dante replied, his tone not so cheery now. "I'm glad my money could help you obtain another K-9. We want to keep the streets of Sagebrush safe, don't we?"

"Of course we do," Slade said. He wanted to ask his friend if he really meant that. But he didn't. He couldn't tip his hand right now. Slade would have to play this light, stay cool and pretend nothing major was going on. "Okay, well, just called to thank you again and tell you about the new trainee. We appreciate all your support."

Dante laughed again. "Sure, man. Hope you can make it to the birthday get-together. I'll send someone by with an official invite just to remind you." Then he said, "Hey, Slade, why don't you come by soon and bring that new trainee, too. I'd love to see the dog in action."

"I might be able to swing that," Slade replied, wondering why Dante wanted to see Warrior. But then, if he was the Ski Mask Man and The Boss, he'd want to see the dog that his money had paid for—and maybe get a kick out of knowing that he was the one behind Rio's kidnapping at the same time.

Could his old friend really be that sick and twisted?

Slade thought back over the last two years since his wife had died. Dante had been the first person in the door to comfort him, bring him food and offer him anything that money could buy. Why would his best friend cause him that much heartache and pain? What had Angie ever done to Dante?

Slade thought back over the fight they'd had that day, about Angie's accusations that Slade loved his job more than he loved her and their son. She'd being angry at him for being out late at night, and being in dangerous situations.

Slade stopped, got up to wander around his office.

"You're in on drug busts. You shot a teenager a few years back, Slade. What if that kid had fired back? What if you're the one who gets the bullet next time?" Angie had said.

Why would Angie purposely remind him of that—to hurt him, to make him feel guilty all over again? Had she been talking to someone close to the situation? Or someone who was concerned about the boy being shot?

Dante?

Angie and Dante had always been close. But then,

most red-blooded women were drawn to Dante's good looks and quicksilver eyes. Strange, unusual eyes. Even more silver than Slade's own blue eyes.

Eyes that were so recognizable, they'd have to be disguised in order for Dante to hide. Slade looked at the calendar. He had a few days before Dante's party. He was going to do some checking with the crime lab about black vans. Maybe they could establish some sort of connection there.

And then next week, he could also take Warrior to the house and just see the K-9's reaction. But what if the dog alerted to Dante? Slade would make some excuse. Warrior was a trainee, after all. Or better yet, he could invite Dante to the training yard. That might be the best plan since he'd mentioned showing off Warrior to Dante, anyway.

That would keep both Kaitlin and Warrior in a controlled situation that could protect them. It would also give Slade a chance to observe Dante and Warrior together.

Valerie walked into his office, tapping on the open door to alert him. Slade turned. "Yeah, what's up?"

"The crime scene team seems to think we ought to be able to track that paper back to two shops here in town."

"Really?" Since they did live in a medium-sized city, it might be possible to trace certain papers to certain stores. "But we have several office supply stores all over town."

Valerie sat down across from him. "But one of the techs says his mother-in-law buys fancy paper at a certain store in the antique district. Parchment, crisp and almond colored. He remembers it because she made such a fuss over using it for her annual Christmas letters. You know the kind where the sender goes on and on about the wonderful year they've had?"

"I know the kind," Slade said with a cynical smile. "Is this that kind of paper?"

Valerie nodded. "We don't have the high-tech means to prove it, but some good old-fashioned footwork just might."

"Good enough for now," Slade replied. "Even if we can't prove it, we might at least be able to compare this paper to that and find out who in town might keep a supply of it."

"Exactly, and who in town might have ordered that particular weight and texture recently," Valerie added. "It's just a hunch, a guessing game."

"We'll put Melody on that one if she can be spared," Slade said. "Thanks."

Valerie left smiling. Everyone would be smiling if they got a break in this case. Just a tiny break could bring about some new action.

That or…something else unthinkable might happen to someone he cared about.

Kaitlin pulled her small SUV into the driveway of her house and let Warrior out. The dog immediately headed toward the front door, his nose moving from the floor to the air.

He turned at the door, waiting for her, then ran back to her, still sniffing.

"What do you detect, Warrior?" she asked, wishing the dog could tell her his thoughts. She knew that wasn't possible, but trained K-9 dogs could communicate with body language. And Warrior's body language spoke volumes. He'd probably picked up on the scent of the intruder who'd been here last night. Could it have been someone the dog knew already, someone Warrior was so comfortable with he hadn't alerted?

That sent a chilling tickle of dread down her spine.

"It's okay," she said, looking back toward the street. A cruiser had pulled up right behind her. Slade had called her earlier and said he'd bring home dinner.

Bring home dinner.

The words had a nice ring. What would it be like to have him with her at dinner every night? To watch Caleb play with Warrior and old Chief and hopefully Rio, Mr. McNeal hovering nearby while she and Slade put together a meal? Memories of her own childhood shot like bright sparks of light inside her brain. Her mother had always made things special, probably to overcompensate for the lack of a father in the house. Then her grandmother and her aunt had done the same after she'd moved here.

It would be nice to have someone to come home to, people around who loved her and wanted to ask her about her day.

Just a dream, she told herself as she gave Warrior the hand signal to search and stood back before she entered the house. When Warrior returned, looking both disappointed and hopeful, she figured her house was safe for now.

She went in and found Warrior's favorite toy and rewarded him with some toss and fetch. After Warrior had tired of the game, she sorted through the mail she'd taken out of the box beside the front door. A water bill, a bank statement, two catalogues, but nothing ominous. No one had left her any cryptic notes today. But the day was still young.

A shiver ran down her spine. Kaitlin had never been afraid in her own house but now, even with Warrior prowling around, she couldn't help but feel the claws of apprehension ripping at her skin. She didn't like being so vulnerable, so exposed. She didn't like being a target for someone's greed and revenge. The person behind that black mask was a cruel, misguided soul, an evil person.

She closed her eyes and asked God to protect her and those she loved, a verse from Thessalonians popping in her mind: *But the Lord is faithful, and He will strengthen you and protect you from the evil one.*

Where had she heard that? Oh, at her mother's funeral, of course. The verse had made her angry back then but now it made her stop and think. And it calmed her jittery nerves.

Thinking back over last night, she remembered Slade telling her he was going to have dinner with her tonight. *That* was both a comfort and a distraction. She could handle having a girlfriend helping her to stay safe, but Slade McNeal in the flesh? Dinner with the captain. She'd probably forget all about the pizza.

What would they do? Sit there staring at each other until Valerie got here?

Okay, you'll also have Officer Ross out in the cruiser. He'll be on alert and he works the night shift so he doesn't fall asleep on the job—ever.

She should be glad she had so many protectors, but she also wanted her life back to normal. If this went on much longer…

A car pulling into the driveway curtailed her thoughts. Slade was here and she hadn't even freshened up yet. Quickly running a hand down her ponytail, she grabbed her purse and slapped on some lip gloss then found a mint to pop into her mouth.

Silly measures since she had no intention of flirting with the man who'd vowed to save her. She didn't need saving. She just needed this stalker off the streets. She intended to work with the K-9 unit and the entire police department to make that happen. And she intended to keep training Warrior with every ounce of energy she had, so the dog would be ready for duty soon enough. That's really all she wanted or needed.

But when she looked out the window and saw Slade carrying a pizza box, his dark uniform making him look official and formidable, she wondered what else she needed.

A good man would sure be nice.

Especially a good man who'd brought home her favorite pizza.

Chapter Eight

"I wish you could have brought Caleb with you."

Slade glanced up at Kaitlin, the longing of her comment hitting him in the gut. "Me, too. But he's safe with Papa and Nanny Blanche. Not to mention the night nurse, Jasper. That man could split an oak with his bare hands."

She leaned across the table, her slice of pizza half-eaten. "But Caleb could be in danger, too. I'm not judging you for bringing me dinner. Just suggesting that I'm an adult and I can take care of myself. He can't."

"And he's surrounded by people who are aware of the situation," Slade retorted. "Do you think I'd leave him if I didn't believe that?"

"I know you," she replied. "I trust your judgment. But I can't help but worry, Slade. I'd never get over it if something happened to him while you're here with me."

Slade got up to get some more iced tea. "Are you trying to drive me nuts? I've thought of everything you just mentioned but I do this job every day. I've hired people trained to help my son and my father and I check on them all the time."

"I didn't mean to imply you don't care," she said, her eyes downcast. "I'm sorry."

Slade sat back down and stared at the pizza, his appetite gone for now. "Sorry I got so defensive, but that's a sore subject with me. I enjoy my job but the long hours and the midnight calls, plus me being a single dad takes its toll. I get a little hot under the collar when people ask me how I can leave my boy." He tapped his fingers on the wooden table, wondering if he hadn't jumped at an excuse to be with her tonight. Wondering and knowing he felt personally responsible for her attack the other day. "Let's just say it's not an easy decision and leave it at that."

"Good idea." She finished her meal, then sat staring out into the growing dusk. "I think I'm a little embarrassed, having all this security. I worked the beat for a little over a year, but then when the chance to become a trainer came up, I jumped at it. I sometimes wonder if I made the right decision."

"You don't like your job?"

"No, I mean, yes. I love my job. But did I change course because I wanted to work with animals...or did I do it because deep down inside, I'm a coward?"

"Did you like being a patrol officer?"

She glanced out the window. "I didn't hate it. But I always felt like there was something else for me. My instincts told me I'd be better suited to the K-9 division, working as a trainer."

"And you're good at that job."

She smiled at the compliment. "I do enjoy the work, but it also puts a filter between me and the hard stuff."

"Training an animal from the time he's a puppy till the time he makes his first find is nothing to sneeze at, Kaitlin. I think you're right where you're supposed to be."

"Me, too," she said, relief coloring her cute freckles. "That's why it's so odd, being someone's target."

"Yep. Odd and a pain for all of us. But we're gonna crack this case." He told her about what Valerie and the crime techs had decided regarding the paper. "If we can get a match, any match, we can narrow down how many people have purchased that particular paper recently. It's a long shot, but it's something."

"Amazing," she said. "And a good call. Valerie has moved from rookie to a good officer."

"Well, she does have a Rottweiler for a partner. And Lexi is a good, solid apprehension dog that you helped to train. Maybe we should have let her bring Lexi last night. She could bring her when she comes over later."

Kaitlin shrugged. "And let another officer dog get kidnapped or worse? I don't think so. I worry about Warrior getting caught in the cross-fire."

"I don't think they'll harm the animals unless they get frustrated and give up. They need them alive."

"And then, they'd just…get rid of the animals?"

"Or let them go. I hope every day that Rio will show up at my door."

She glanced over at where Warrior lay snoozing in his soft, square doggie bed. "I hope and pray for that, too. I won't give up."

Slade saw the determination in her eyes. She had something to prove, but he hoped she didn't try to use this episode to show the world she was capable of facing down the enemy on her own. "You stick with what you know best. Train Warrior and let the rest work itself out."

"I'll give you and the team one week, Slade," she replied. Getting up to clear away the empty pizza box, she pivoted at the counter. "After that, no more patrols or protection. I want my life back. I know the protocol, I know the rules. I know what to watch for now. And I mean what I say—you can't camp out here the rest of your life."

Slade let the thought of spending the rest of his life around her settle over him before he brushed it away. That would be nice, but that was just a silly dream. This was reality, and he had no doubt that this woman would bolt in exactly one week. She seemed determined to show the world she was more than capable of doing things her way. Why was she so stubborn about accepting help?

"You sure drive a hard bargain. I don't like working with a ticking clock over my head."

"The clock was already ticking," she retorted. "And time is running out."

"You don't pull any punches, do you?"

She shook her head. "I don't have time to be wishy-washy."

Slade understood that concept. "Neither do I. But I can't promise you I'll have this all wrapped up within a week."

"I didn't say that," she replied, already heading toward the hallway, Warrior right behind her. "I said I won't need any protection after a week." She turned at the arched opening between the kitchen and den and the hallway. "After that, I'll take matters into my own hands. I haven't forgotten how to use a weapon."

"Kaitlin?"

She waved off what she must have known would be a warning. "I'm going to take a shower."

Slade didn't call after her. But he didn't intend to let her take anything into her own hands. She was brave. Too brave. That could be a good trait or that could get her killed.

He wouldn't let that happen.

His cell buzzed. "McNeal."

"Sir, it's Valerie Salgado. I heard back about the stationery."

"And?"

"I recognized one of the names on the list of people who'd purchased that type of paper in the last month or so."

"What name?"

"Yvette Frears. I believe she's the wife of your friend Dante?"

"Yes. Correct." Slade rubbed his temple. "Thank you, Officer Salgado. Let's keep this quiet for now. I need to see the other names on the list before I do some investigating."

"I understand."

Slade ended the call and sat staring out into the dusk. Could be coincidence. Could be a big break in this case. Had Dante taken a piece of his wife's stationery? Or had Yvette herself left that note? But why would she?

He got up, then thought about the birthday party at Dante's place this weekend. Kaitlin had no idea Dante might be behind all of this and right now, Slade wanted to keep things that way. But he wanted to keep an eye on her, too. Would he put her in even more danger by taking her inside Dante's house?

Or would it be the perfect chance to see his friend's reaction to Kaitlin Mathers?

Kaitlin emerged about thirty minutes later, freshly showered and wearing her old cut-off jean shorts and a scoop-necked T-shirt with her old broken-in pink flip-flops.

She found Slade pacing in front of the slightly drawn blinds in the den, talking on his phone.

"Well, that's good that Nanny Blanche made you cupcakes. No, I won't be home to read to you tonight. Papa can read a little bit maybe. Or maybe Jasper will help Papa read, okay?" He turned when he heard Warrior's paws tapping against the wooden floors. "All right. Be good for Nanny Blanche, okay? I'll come by and see you before preschool in the morning."

Kaitlin smiled when he hung up. "How's Caleb?"

"He seems in a fairly good mood today. I never know. If he has a bad dream, it tends to ruin his whole day."

"And yours?" She shot him a sympathetic look. "I'm sorry I pushed you earlier. I know you're a good dad."

He gave her a skeptical glance. "I try, but I'm not sure it's ever enough." He put his phone away. "I know how it looks to some people, though, but I've got to work for a living."

Not sure if that comment was directed at her, Kaitlin began cleaning up the den. "I'm not usually this messy. Last night was tough so I didn't tidy up this morning."

"My house is much worse than this," he said, his gaze moving all around her. "I can't remember the last time I saw you out of your training uniform."

Kaitlin remembered, but she wouldn't tell him that. He'd dropped Caleb by on a rare Saturday, apologizing because his dad was sick and the babysitter was out of town. Kaitlin had been happy to help out, and she and Caleb had spent part of the day in the park and the other part at a kiddie restaurant. Slade had found them in the backyard, playing catch. She'd been tired, sweaty and without makeup. That hadn't mattered too much back then, and it burned her that it was beginning to matter now.

So she decided to be practical. "I was worn out from the heat. That shower helped." She pushed at her wet hair. "You're welcome to use the bathroom."

"I showered at the gym," he said. "I brought a change of clothes just in case." He pointed to a duffel bag by the door. "I try to prepare for anything."

"Okay."

The room went silent. Then she smiled to herself. He'd talked to her more during dinner than in all the times they'd been around each other in the past. Maybe the captain was warming up to her. Or maybe he was just doing his job.

He cleared his throat. "Kaitlin, you didn't mean what you said earlier, did you?"

"About taking matters into my own hands?"

"That would be it, yes."

"I need to brush up on my target practice," she said with a matter-of-fact shrug.

"So you were serious."

"I have to be, Slade. I won't live in fear. It took me too long to get over what happened to my mother."

She sank down in her favorite chair and motioned for him to join her. "Do you want something to drink?"

"I'm good." He settled on the couch, facing the door.

"And I'm sorry about your mom. But you don't have to be a hero."

"I'm no hero," she retorted, tired of this conversation. "But I'll do what I have to do to protect myself. Or anyone else those thugs try to hurt."

His brow furrowed in worry. "Let us handle this."

"I will, for now."

He stared at her, let out a sigh, then shook his head. "Okay. Enough for now." Then he leaned forward. "I have a better idea."

Her heart pumped a warning at the questioning look in his eyes. What did the man have in mind?

"Uh, I've been invited to a birthday party at my friend Dante Frears's house this weekend. I thought you might like to attend with me."

Shocked, Kaitlin didn't know what to say. "So you can keep an eye on me, Captain? Or as your date?"

He grinned, then rubbed a hand down his five o'clock shadow. "Well, I guess a little of both."

A bold step for him, she decided. "Killing two birds with one stone?"

He looked confused, then his expression changed to reserved, almost cautious. "I'd like you to go with me, yes. But I'd also like to keep my eye on you, even when you're there with me."

Kaitlin picked up on the intensity of his eyes. "Why is this so important?"

He shifted on the couch, but never took his eyes off her. "Because I can't be in two places at once. I promised Dante I'd be at his wife's birthday party and… I want to keep you safe, too."

She had to mess with him a little bit. "That does create a dilemma, doesn't it?"

Another shift, then he settled back, one leg bent over the other knee. "You're trying to make this way harder than it needs to be."

"Am I? It just seems out of character for you to be going to a party in the middle of this investigation, and it also seems strange that you'd want me to go along."

He leaned forward again. "I have my reasons, so I'd appreciate it if you'd cut me some slack and just say you'll go with me."

Kaitlin wondered what was behind this sudden need to have her with him at this particular party. Did he know something he wasn't telling her? Did she want to know?

Deciding she'd be wise to keep her eye on him, too, she finally nodded. "Sounds good to me. I can't turn down a party at the Frears penthouse. It's all swag and swank."

"It is that." He breathed what looked like a big sigh of relief. "It should be interesting. And fun."

"Fun? Do you actually ever have fun, Captain?"

He grinned at that. "I've been known to let my hair down, thank you very much."

She didn't see how his crisp, short hair could ever be let down, but it would be nice to see him in a relaxed atmosphere away from work and all the tension of this case.

"It'll be worth the trouble to see you out of uniform."

"Really?"

She put a hand to her mouth, realizing that hadn't come out the way she meant. "You know what I mean. I meant—you're always working." She stopped, laughed. "I'll stop digging that hole and agree to go."

"Good. Dante has the means to throw lavish parties, so it should be not only fun but interesting."

"Yes, it should be. I'll look forward to going with you."

But she had to wonder—if this was supposed to be such an enjoyable event, why wasn't the man smiling?

Chapter Nine

Kaitlin waved to Valerie as they parted ways the next morning in the parking lot. "Thanks again. I appreciate you spending the night. It was nice of your neighbor to stay with Bethany."

"No problem," Valerie replied, smiling at the mention of the toddler niece she was raising. "I enjoyed all our girl talk last night. We covered everything regarding my wedding plans."

"Me, too." Kaitlin yawned. "I think we stayed up too late."

Valerie nodded. "But…at least we didn't have any prowlers or notes underneath the door."

"Thanks again," Kaitlin said, lowering her voice since other workers were showing up.

Valerie gave her a big smile, then headed for the K-9 Unit's offices. Kaitlin went to her own cubbyhole of an office and got ready to start her day. Grabbing her equipment, play toys and water bottle, she headed out with an eager Warrior.

Slade was waiting for her in the yard. "So you had an uneventful night."

"We watched sappy movies and talked about weddings."

He lowered his gaze, clearly uncomfortable with that conversation. "Uh…that's good. No noises, no intruders, notes?"

Touched by his concern, she smiled at him. "Slade, we were fine. I told you everything would be okay, and it was. I don't think the intruder will be back now that the heat's on."

"Good. I intend to keep it that way, too." He turned to leave, then stopped to pet Warrior. "I'll see you later."

Kaitlin kept her smile intact, but inside she wondered how long any of them could keep this up. For most of this year, people on the team or involved with team members had been under siege. Slade couldn't keep carrying this burden much longer.

"Help us, Lord," she whispered as she grabbed some gear and started Warrior through his warm-up. "Help all of us to fight this attack."

She glanced up and looked around the yard. Just a normal summer day. The sun drew a path over the crusty, worn grass, promising more heat to come. A sneaky wind moved in and out of the big oaks, causing shadows to dapple and dance across the asphalt behind the yard. Cars revved to life, traffic honked and braked. A normal workday, except that each time Kaitlin glanced toward the back parking lot gate, she thought about being held at gunpoint by a man with blacked-out eyes.

In spite of the warm morning sun, a shiver wormed its way down her spine and a cold chill centered inside her heart.

* * *

Slade stared out into the bright sunshine, remembering how a few days ago he'd watched a masked man hold a gun to Kaitlin's head. Watched, fired and let the man get away.

He wouldn't miss next time. And his gut told him there would be a next time.

His phone rang. Dante.

"Captain McNeal," Slade answered.

"So formal. You must be in your office."

"You know me well," Slade replied, his gut burning again. "What's up?"

"Just checking to make sure you can make it this weekend. Yvette is excited that you're bringing a date."

Slade managed a passable chuckle. "Just a friend, nothing to get too excited about." He wouldn't tell Dante anything that might fuel the attack on Kaitlin. Reminding himself his buddy was innocent until proven guilty, he cleared his throat. "I talked to my friend last night. We'll be there."

"Good. Glad to hear it. I've been so busy this summer, it'll be nice to kick back and relax. How are things going on your end? You're still searching for Rio, right?"

An innocent question, or was Dante fishing for information? Slade decided to be careful with every word that came out of his mouth. "We're still on the case. We've eliminated some suspects, but we have our eye on others. That's about all I can say at this point."

"Vague as always," Dante retorted. Did Slade imagine the hint of sarcasm in that statement? "It goes with the job, as you always tell me."

"I'm afraid so," Slade replied. "That's the nature of my line of work."

"And you're good at your job." Dante chuckled into the phone. "It sure will be great to catch up and reminisce about the old days."

"Yeah, great. We'll see you Saturday night."

"Looking forward to it."

Slade hung up, his mind reeling with suspicion and anger. Last night, he'd done what he usually did every night when the house was quiet. He'd gone back over this case with an eagle eye, but this time he'd tried to place Dante in the middle of things. As much as he hated to see it, some things were beginning to add up.

Dante had the means to run a huge crime operation. With his money, he had the ability to hire people who'd be more than willing to keep silent and do the dirty work. And with his intimidating, commanding presence, he'd surely take care of anyone who crossed him. Someone within the organization had double-crossed The Boss, since the mysterious criminal had purposely taken out several of his own people. Dante had never liked being tricked or betrayed. Slade had seen him angry on more than one occasion for some small slight. Slade had even been on the receiving end of Dante's anger before, but they'd always worked things out.

But where was the motive? Dante was a smart man, a self-made man who'd come home after their Middle-Eastern tour of duty to become a real-estate mogul. That had led to other business venues and a lot of opportunities to make some serious money. Had he become so greedy that he'd forgotten what he'd been fighting for over there and decided to turn to the dark side?

The opportunities for such a career were certainly

staring all of them in the face. West Texas was known for being a corridor for illegal activities. Slade had been fighting those activities since the day he'd become a police officer.

He and Dante had served together, fought together and come home together. At times, they'd gone their separate ways and drifted apart. *But we always found our way back,* Slade thought.

Dante had never forsaken the camaraderie they'd built serving their country. And neither had Slade.

But what if his friend had forsaken his honor for greed? And what if Melody and Parker were right about Daniel being Dante's son? Slade had put a bullet in Daniel's leg, but someone else had killed the boy. Jim Wheaton, a cop gone bad. A cop who was now dead. Did Dante know Jim had made that shot?

When Slade looked at all the details of this case and placed Dante as The Boss, things began to make more sense. But he hated the idea that a man who'd been his friend for most of their adult lives might be behind all of these criminal activities. A man who could possibly be charged with multiple murders.

Could that man be Dante Frears?

What if Slade had to take down the comrade who'd saved his life on the battlefield?

Kaitlin heard the doorbell, her heart jumping ahead of her. Slade. Right on time.

"You look great," Francine told her, one finger putting the finishing touches on Kaitlin's upswept hair. "Now relax and have fun."

Kaitlin took one last look in her bedroom mirror. Her friend had helped her put her hair up in a loose chignon. It was elegant but not too fussy. She'd put on extra mascara and a deeper pink lipstick and a sweep of shadow and blush.

"I don't look overdone, do I?"

Francine shook her head. "You look good. So good that Captain McNeal is gonna pop an eyeball looking."

"I don't want that to happen," Kaitlin said as she grabbed her tiny white clutch purse and glanced at her dress one more time. "The dress?"

"Is to die for," Francine retorted, her gaze moving down the floral chiffon. "It looks summery but casual. Why you don't wear this thing more is beyond me."

"I've never had anywhere to wear it," Kaitlin reminded her. She'd bought it on a whim after finding it on a clearance rack at the local department store. "It does feel great against my legs."

"And you look great wearing it." Francine pushed her toward the front door. "Now go before the man breaks the door down."

"Thanks for helping me," Kaitlin said, her hand on Warrior's head. "So... I'll see you two back at your house after the party."

"Yes, ma'am." Francine winked, then stepped back. "Have fun, okay?"

Kaitlin opened the door and found Slade standing there wearing black slacks and a stark sky-blue polo shirt that brought out the deep blue of his eyes.

"Hi," she said, her suddenly dry throat making her tone gravelly.

Slade's gaze slid down her dress. "Hi. Wow. I mean, you look great."

Francine clapped her hands, causing Slade's gaze to shift to Kaitlin's. "Hello, Francine."

"Hi, Captain. She does look great, and I helped."

He laughed at Francine's antics. "You did a good job."

Kaitlin basked in his warm gaze. This was beginning to feel like a real date. That should make her nervous, but she felt elated and...safe. Slade made her feel safe. Not very romantic, but so vital on her list.

"Are you ready?" he asked, his smile tentative.

"I am." She turned back to Warrior and patted his head again. "Be good for Franny, okay, boy?"

Warrior barked and pranced, clearly confused at seeing his mistress in a dress. His dark brown eyes held a quizzical kind of adoration that made Kaitlin's heart melt.

"Go," Francine said, pushing her toward Slade.

Slade took her arm in his and chuckled after Francine shut the door. "She's a good friend."

"Yes. A little pushy, but the best."

"She's also a good trainer."

"Warrior sure thinks so. She's going to give him some play time at her house. I hope you don't mind dropping me off there after the party."

"No. I want to make sure you do go there. You can't be home alone yet."

"Yes, Captain," she said in a cheeky tone.

"Don't let that ruin our night," he replied.

Kaitlin wondered again why this night was so important to him. "Are you going to relax and enjoy this party?"

"I hope so. I'll try."

She hadn't missed the tension in him. Something was up with him, but then he was always edgy, even on a good day. She'd have to watch out for him tonight. Slade

McNeal was known for putting others first. Maybe it was time someone put him first.

But when he pulled his father's sedan up to the apartment complex where Dante Frears lived, she let out a giggle. "Wow, this building *is* so fancy."

"You seem surprised. You do know that Dante is a successful businessman."

"Everyone knows that and everyone knows about his penthouse. Of course, I rarely get this far downtown twice in a row."

Slade hit the steering wheel. "You were at the big fund-raiser last month at the Sagebrush Hotel."

"Nice of you to remember."

Slade found a spot in the parking garage. "I think the whole department was at that affair. But tonight, he promised just a few friends." He parked the vehicle and came around to help her out. "Did you speak to him that night?"

"Uh, no. The place was packed and Melody wasn't feeling good. We left early."

"Should be more relaxed tonight."

The undercurrent of tension filled the air. "You don't seem comfortable about this."

Slade put his hand on her back. "I'm *not* comfortable about this."

So he'd admitted that much, at least. Kaitlin knew not to push him. But his stoic words only reinforced her need to protect him in the same way he wanted to protect her. She didn't know why she suddenly felt this way. But her instincts told her that Slade being friends with such a powerful, pretentious man didn't ring true.

Did she dare ask him about that friendship?

She didn't get a chance. Some other people came up

and Slade started talking to them and then introduced her. They all rode the elevator up to the penthouse, the scent of expensive perfume and aftershave tickling Kaitlin's nostrils.

When the doors opened, Kaitlin had to gather her thoughts. So much glitter and glamour, so many of Sagebrush society's movers and shakers. She felt as out of place as a catfish at a lobster fest.

Dante and his wife, Yvette, were out by the rooftop pool, but the couple immediately came inside the thrown-open sliding doors that made up one wall to greet them.

"Slade!" Dante flashed his white teeth right along with his gold and diamond signet ring. "Man, it's so good to see you again."

"Same here," Slade said, his tone not quite so chipper and artificial. "Dante, this is Kaitlin Mathers. She's one of our top K-9 trainers."

Dante took Kaitlin's hand in his, his silver-blue eyes gleaming with interest. "So nice to see the woman who got Slade McNeal out of the house on a Saturday night. But I think we've met before, maybe."

"Possibly a few weeks ago when we all attended the fund-raiser gala." Kaitlin smiled and pulled her hand away. "It's nice to once again see the benefactor of such a generous donation. We really appreciate it, Mr. Frears. I'm sure Slade has mentioned I'm already training a very special dog, partly because of your funding."

Dante's beautiful dark-haired wife stepped forward, her arm possessively on her husband, her dangling golden earrings sparkling. "We totally support the K-9 Unit here in Sagebrush. Dante and I were honored to make the donation." She glanced at Slade. "I hope you find Rio soon, Slade. Dante keeps me up-to-date on the generalities."

"We're always on the case," Slade said, his tone firm but polite.

Kaitlin didn't miss the tension radiating off his body, though. She glanced around at the opulent room filled with gold-colored accessories and white leather. The penthouse was elegant and overdone, but that was just her opinion. The pool glistened in the late-day sun, floating candles taking over where the breathtaking sunset left off.

Kaitlin brought her gaze back to the moment and found Dante Frears staring at her with icy silver eyes that reminded her of a wolf. A shiver hit her neckline and worked down her arms.

Slade must have sensed her discomfort. He took her arm and smiled at his friend. "I think I'll show Kaitlin the pool and that view you paid too much money for."

"Enjoy it," Dante said, holding out his hand to entice them. "Yvette will have someone bring you two a drink." He moved on to the next guests coming in the door.

Yvette's smile seemed as forced as Dante's brittle laugh. "What can I get you?"

Slade asked for a soda and Kaitlin ordered water with lemon.

"Not heavy drinkers, I see," Yvette said with a soft smile. "I'll send your refreshments right over."

Kaitlin glanced over at Slade after Yvette left, but he'd turned his head toward where Dante stood with two other men. Kaitlin didn't miss the hint of a frown on Slade's face.

She didn't fit into this kind of world, but she held her

head high for the captain's sake. Maybe later, he would open up about his relationship with Dante Frears.

Until then, she'd do whatever Slade needed her to do while they were here. Because in her heart, she knew this visit was about a lot more than a birthday party.

Chapter Ten

As the evening wore on, Slade tried to memorize things that would give him clues to Dante's character. He noticed Frears never set his plate and utensils down anywhere. Yvette or one of the waiters was always there to take his dishes and wineglasses away. Odd, but then, Dante demanded efficiency, and he had some strange quirks regarding neatness and cleanliness. Slade did remember that about his old friend. Even in the middle of the desert, he had demanded neatness and order as often as possible.

Throughout the night, Yvette seemed relaxed and moved through the crowd with an easy elegance. But every now and then, Slade would catch her staring at her husband, a hint of worry in her eyes. Deciding to visit with her in hopes of hearing something that might give him a clue, Slade made his way to where she stood out by the pool. When she saw him coming, she smiled and disengaged herself from the group of women she'd been conversing with. Slade nodded at her, then turned to make sure Kaitlin was safe. She stood with another group who'd heard she was a K-9 trainer. They were asking her questions about the program. Right now, Kaitlin seemed to glow with pride while she discussed the subject near and dear to her heart.

Which made her even more near and dear to Slade.

"Are you having a good time?" Yvette asked, her arm on Slade's shoulder, her gaze following his.

"Yes. The food's great and it's good to see some friends."

"You don't come by enough these days," she replied, again sweeping the area behind Slade with a sharp eye.

Was she looking for her husband?

"I apologize for that," Slade said. "But I did tell Dante I wanted him to see the newest K-9 officer dog we've been training. The funds y'all donated helped to make that possible. Kaitlin is doing a great job on that."

Yvette's dark eyes seemed to brighten. "She's really lovely, Slade. Very girl-next-door. Seems perfect for you."

Slade didn't miss the hint of censure in that comment. Yvette had never liked Angie. The two used to spar and throw out catty remarks at each other. Pushing that particular memory away, he said, "Kaitlin is a good person. We're really just friends. But…we are both single. Who knows."

Yvette grinned at that. "I think I see a spark of interest in those blue eyes of yours."

He only laughed, but he couldn't deny it. He was interested in Kaitlin. Right now, however, he was interested in keeping her safe. Maybe when this case was solved—

Yvette waved to someone across the room. "Excuse me, Slade. I need to talk to Rachel about our meeting next week."

"Of course." Slade watched her go, then decided this might be a good time to go find a bathroom. If he ever wanted to get a sample of Dante's DNA, now was the time.

Kaitlin glanced around, looking for Slade. When she saw him heading toward the back of the house she figured he was searching for a bathroom. But when he glanced around, she noticed the covert expression she'd seen on the faces of many cops. Was Slade on the case? She'd wait for him beside the big, empty fireplace near the hallway door, guarding, just in case.

Making her way over there, Kaitlin looked up to see Dante staring down the hallway. Was he worried about Slade? Deciding to distract him in spite of being nervous around all of these people, Kaitlin waved a hand in his face. "Hi, Mr. Frears."

Dante tugged his gaze away from the hall and drew a smiling mask down over his frown. "Hello, there. Call me Dante, okay?"

"Okay." Kaitlin pushed at a curl dangling in her eye. "I wanted to thank you once again for helping us out. Our whole unit really wants to find Rio and get our operation back on track."

Dante's gaze turned to crystal but it melted away before Kaitlin could get rid of the goose bumps on her bare arms. "It was my pleasure. I'd do anything for Slade." He did a scan of the entire room. "Speaking of Slade, where did my buddy get off to, anyway?"

Kaitlin's heart did a warning beat. Whatever Slade was up to, she didn't think Dante needed to know about it. "I think he went to the bathroom. I'll watch for him."

Dante gave her a twisted smile. "You two seem chummy."

Kaitlin laughed, hoping it would hide the way this man made her feel. This creepy factor was odd and overwhelming, but she couldn't deny that something about Dante Frears made her feel edgy…and apprehensive. "We've been friends for a while now. He's a good man."

"Yes, of course he is." Dante gave her that cold stare again. "He loved his wife, you know. But…it wasn't enough. Men like Slade McNeal love their work more than they love the people around them. You might want to remember that, sweetheart."

Something familiar and frightening gnawed at Kaitlin's consciousness. "I'm not sure what you mean, but thank you for the advice."

"Yeah, you do know what I mean." Dante gave her another smile. "You're a big girl. You'll soon figure it out. Just consider yourself warned."

The look in his eyes seemed to say so much more. What kind of warning did he want her to hear? One about Slade? Or one about…him?

"Excuse me," he said, already moving toward the long, wide hallway. "I'm going to find Slade."

Kaitlin didn't know what to do or say, but a woman approached Dante and engaged him in conversation long enough for Kaitlin to leave her spot by the hallway and hurry outside. She'd seen another door out on the rooftop terrace. And she prayed that door would lead her to Slade so she could warn him that Dante was looking for him.

Slade slid into the shadows and worked his way toward the master bedroom on the far end of the big penthouse. He had a small paper envelope ready to take samples of Dante's hair. Hating the underhanded way he had to go about this, he rationalized that this was for his own purposes since this wouldn't hold up in court without a search warrant, anyway.

"Desperate men do desperate things."

Slade could hear his father's words of caution echoing inside his brain. How many times had Papa said that when trying to find a criminal? Slade believed it himself. Papa had been talking about criminals, but now Slade had to wonder.

Had he become desperate?

Maybe enough to risk this, at least.

He hurried across the plush, white shag carpet of the immaculate bedroom and treaded into the sprawling marble and chrome bath. After looking through a few drawers, he found a man's hairbrush and quickly donned a glove he'd tucked into his pocket so he could gather a few clumps. After he'd put the hair fibers into the small envelope and returned it and the glove to his pants pocket, he turned to leave and heard a door opening from the hallway.

Looking around, Slade realized he was trapped. A glass door at the end of the bathroom might lead to the terrace but he didn't have time to get to it. He glanced at the shower. Glass. Did he dare hide in the big closet?

To his surprise, even as he wondered who'd entered the bedroom, he also heard the door to the outside creaking open.

Whirling around, Slade awaited his fate.

And saw Kaitlin rushing toward him.

Before he could speak, she grabbed him to her and

planted a long, soft kiss on his lips. "Hold me," she whispered, her lips pressing against his again.

Shocked and still full of adrenaline, Slade sank into the kiss by taking her into his arms. Kaitlin held him tight, her lips clinging to his while a soft sigh sounded in her throat. A voice in Slade's head kept telling him to stop this, but his mind seemed to spin out of control.

He liked kissing Kaitlin.

So much so, that he didn't stop until she pulled away and gasped in shock.

Slade turned to find Dante standing there, grinning at them.

"So this is where you two got off to."

"Uh, yes," Slade replied, his gaze sweeping toward Kaitlin.

The warning look in her eyes told him that she'd just saved his bacon, big time. And made him even more aware of his growing attraction to her.

"It's my fault," Kaitlin said on a breathless giggle. "I told Slade I'd find him, so I kept opening doors until I did. Hope you don't mind, Dante. You know how it is when two people first discover each other."

She glanced back at Slade, her eyes going deep with meaning and what looked like true longing.

Slade shrugged and tugged her close. "Guess we're busted. Sorry, Dante. I don't usually plan clandestine meetings like this, but we rarely get a chance to see each other away from work."

Dante kept grinning. "I have to admit this is way out of character for you, my old friend. But…can't say that I blame you one bit."

His gaze moved over Kaitlin in a way that made Slade want to punch him out. But before that could happen, Dante waved a hand in the air. "Please, don't let me stop you. Carry on. Have fun."

"We're done," Kaitlin said, looking embarrassed. "I think it's time for us to head home, anyway."

Dante took her words in the wrong way, but Slade figured it worked to their advantage. Shaking his head, Dante laughed again. "Well, at least tell the birthday girl good-night. She's so glad you both came. And she loves the scarf you gave her, Slade."

Slade breathed a sigh of relief. "Kaitlin picked that out."

Dante gave her another probing appraisal. "You're a keeper, for sure." Then his crystallized gaze hit Slade. "You'd better take care of her, my friend."

Slade didn't miss the implications of that suggestion. Suggestion? More like a direct warning.

After Dante left, he turned to Kaitlin, his breathing ragged with relief and concern. "We just made a fatal mistake."

Kaitlin looked confused and hurt. "I had to do something to warn you. I'm sorry." She looked away. "I shouldn't have kissed you, but I couldn't think of anything else that would convince him."

Slade drew her close. "I didn't mind the kiss, Kaitlin. But...now Dante *knows* you're important to me."

"And that's a problem because?"

He put his lips to her ear. "Because he's just become the number one suspect in this case."

Kaitlin stared out the car window until Slade pulled off the road and parked underneath a streetlight.

"We need to talk," he said, shutting off the engine.

"I think so," she retorted, still in shock from what

he'd told her earlier. No wonder he'd seemed so tense. Maybe Dante was right. Maybe Slade really did put his work ahead of everything and everyone.

They were at a park near the police station. "Want to take a stroll?" he asked.

She looked around but didn't see anyone else in the beams of the security lights. "Sure."

He got out and came around to open her door. When she slid out of the car, he shut the door and held her there. "Kaitlin, what you did back there—"

"Was a huge mistake. I know."

"No, no. Listen to me." He pushed a hand down his face, his expression full of frustration.

"I make you mad," she said before he could berate her for being so foolish. "I was so worried that Dante would find you snooping, I didn't think straight. I didn't want—"

He stopped her words with a kiss of his own. A kiss that deepened and changed and caused her to sigh again. Somewhere in all the delightful joy of kissing him, Kaitlin realized that he'd been the one to do the deed this time.

Slade was kissing her out in the open, out in the park.

But...he still had something to say.

She pulled away. "Well. I... I don't know what to say to that."

"You don't need to say anything," he replied huskily, his finger grazing her thoroughly kissed lips. "I owe you a big thanks for saving me back there." Then he touched his forehead to hers. "And in such a very good way, too."

Surprised, Kaitlin let out a breath. "So you're not mad?"

"No, but I am concerned."

"Tell me what's going on."

He motioned to a bench. Once they were settled, he stared off toward the playground. "I think Dante might be The Boss."

Kaitlin's shocked gasp echoed out over the quiet park. But now the shadows and shapes seemed to loom closer and look darker. She thought about her talk with Dante earlier, shivers etching a path across her body.

"What makes you think that?"

Slade took her hand in his. "I can't give you all the details but... I *was* snooping tonight. I was collecting DNA."

"Dante's?"

"Yes. We think he might be Daniel Jones's father."

Kaitlin thought about that. "So you need the DNA to prove that?"

"Yes, but that's only for Melody's benefit. She needs to know the truth. Even if it's a match, I obtained it illegally. I'm not proud of that, but it will at least ease my mind. Besides, there's a lot more to this case."

"DNA doesn't make your friend a criminal," she reminded him. "I mean, if you're just trying to prove he fathered Daniel, I understand. But you said there's more."

"Yep. Dante has the means and the opportunity to run a criminal operation." He held her hand tight. "I always wondered how he'd made it big so quickly after we both came back here. It didn't make sense, but I got busy with my own job and kind of ignored it. I have to admit it's always bothered me." He went silent and still for a while, then said, "My wife, Angie, used to throw that in my face. She resented Dante's wealth, but she enjoyed dropping his name, too. She thought I should go to work for him."

Kaitlin turned to stare at him. "But your heart is in police work."

He looked up at Kaitlin, an appreciative curve in his smile. "You always did get that about me."

She rested her head on his shoulder. "Of course I do. I feel the same way." She thought about Dante's warning, but put that out of her mind for now. Then she nudged Slade to continue. "What else can you tell me about Dante?"

He lifted an arm across her shoulder to tug her close. "He could have possibly killed several people involved with this."

Kaitlin's heart did that warning stampede again and the food she'd eaten at the party seemed to harden in her stomach. "What else, Slade?"

He turned and stared into her eyes. "He might also be the Ski Mask Man."

Chapter Eleven

Kaitlin got up off the bench and twisted around, her mind in turmoil as she relived that day. "That's it," she said, putting a hand to her mouth. "That man, his voice—"

Slade stood to steady her. "What? Did you remember something?"

She bobbed her head. "Yes. That man called me 'sweetheart.' I didn't even remember it until just now, but today while you were in the back of the house, Dante called me that, too." She shivered, held her arms together. "When he said it, I felt something, a trickle of awareness, but I couldn't make the connection."

Slade grasped her arms, pulled her close. "He's taunting both of us."

She stepped back, nodding again. "He tried to warn me about you. He said men like you love their jobs more than they do people."

Slade brought her back into his arms. "I can't argue with that. At times, I've thought that same thing. But… I don't understand why he'd resent me for doing my job. Unless, of course, he's a criminal."

Kaitlin nodded again. "And…if he is Daniel's father and he blames you for his son's death, coupled with his need for control and respect, then that makes him desperate and dangerous."

Slade let out a short breath. "He came after Rio for a reason. He needs a trained canine to help him find something in those woods."

"Do you think he murdered someone else and buried the body out there and is afraid you'll find it before he can get back to hide it?"

"He could have easily moved a body," Slade replied. "I think someone within his organization double-crossed him, based on the recent body count. He didn't bother hiding those deaths. The Boss is involved in most of the murders we've had in the past few months. Maybe the double-crosser hid something important to him out there."

Her eyes lit with interest. "Keep going," she urged.

"He took Rio so he could find whatever he's after, but he hasn't been able to do that all these months. He got a code from Daniel's watch and used that to coordinate the spot in the Lost Woods. But he only found a small amount of cocaine. He had to realize that having a K-9 officer dog without knowing the commands presents a problem. So he's still trying to find something else out there."

"So now he's coming after us. Can he be that crazy, to think he could just grab me and that I'd give Rio the proper commands to search a dig site?"

"He's that desperate," Slade replied. "Or that stupid. He'd demand you give Rio the right commands so the dog can alert to whatever is out there."

"That kind of lunacy does make him both desperate

and dangerous," Kaitlin replied, a sliver of fear shooting through her system.

"We have to get back to those woods and find whatever is out there." He cupped her chin, his eyes holding hers. "We can't rush to judgment on this, though. I have to find proof that Dante's involved before I accuse him publicly."

"Is that what you were doing tonight?"

He nodded. "I collected his hair samples to match to Daniel's. It can't help this case, but...it will tell us if Dante is Daniel's father." He glanced around. "Forget I told you that. I've already done something I'm not proud of, but...finding out the truth will ease a lot of minds."

"I understand," Kaitlin said on a quick whisper. But when she thought of Dante, all of her antennas went up. She'd have to help Slade find that proof, and they'd have to do it by the book from here on out.

Slade pulled her close and she breathed a sigh of relief and said a silent prayer for being safe in his arms. "So what do we do next?"

He stood back, his expression as dark and shadowed as the trees dancing in the hot summer wind. "*You* don't do anything. Just be diligent and watchful and keep me posted on anything—and I mean anything—that seems out of the ordinary."

"And what are you going to do?" she asked, her heart stopping at the thought of him putting himself in danger.

"First, I'm going to let a friend have the DNA analyzed. Then, I'm going back out to that spot in the woods to look around one more time before I put in a request to have a team dig at the site again." He ran a hand down her back. "Meanwhile, I'm going to tail

Dante to find out his comings and goings. He'll slip up and when he does, I'll be there to take him down."

"This has to end, Slade," she whispered against his shoulder. "For all of us, this has to end."

"It will now. One way or another."

She didn't like the finality of that statement. "Even if you might have to go after a man you thought was your friend?"

His expression went dark. "I don't like it, but I don't have a choice."

Sensing the tightening in his muscles, Kaitlin put a hand to his face, their earlier intimacy making her bold. "Don't shut me out, and, Slade, don't shut down. You've been through a lot in the past couple of years, but your son needs you. Remember that." She kissed him, just a quick touch of her lips to hers. "And… I need you, too."

"I don't deserve you," he said, trying to move away. "We shouldn't be together." He put his hands on her elbows and looked down at her. "But when you kissed me—"

"No, don't go all captain on me now," Kaitlin replied, determined to stand her ground. "People will always disappoint you, or surprise you, or let you down, but that doesn't mean you have to just give up and shut yourself off from feeling anything."

"Kaitlin, I—"

"Please, Slade, let me continue. We both felt something wonderful with that kiss, no matter how it came about. You felt it, too. Or you wouldn't have kissed me again. God can see you through, Slade. God and me. And even though losing someone you love is hard, you can make it back to a good place." She took his face in her hands. "This, this is real. This is something we can both believe in and fight for."

He put one hand over hers and twisted their fingers together. "Are you talking about saving the world, Kaitlin? Or just me?"

She smiled then, her other hand tracing over his jawline. "If I save you, I do save *my* world. I'm in this with you now. Don't forget that."

"I won't." He leaned down and kissed her again.

And all around them, a dry, hot wind hissed and danced, as if to warn them that they were still being stalked by a sinister force that might overtake both of them.

Slade handed the tiny gold envelope to Melody Zachary late on Monday. He'd held it all day, wishing he could just throw it in the trash. But the curiosity of wanting answers surpassed his need to follow the rules. So he'd called the detective in. "I don't want to know how you decide to handle this, but it's the best I could do."

Melody quickly pocketed the package. "I'm sorry, Slade. But this is for my own benefit—nothing else. I just have to know. I'll get a friend in the state lab to do a comparison. If Daniel and Dante are related, this will show it."

"But you'd need some of Daniel's hair samples, too."

"I have some," Melody replied. "His room was pretty much the way he left it when I moved all their stuff. I found a comb with hair the color of Daniel's embedded in some of the teeth."

"It'll be a long shot, but worth it, I guess," Slade replied. He'd slept worse than usual this weekend. He couldn't get Frears off his mind. "If the comparison hairs were pulled out and still have a bulb, you'll have a chance."

"My friend is good at figuring out the Y chromosome," Melody said. "It has to work."

Slade rubbed his chin. "I hope it'll bring you some peace, at least."

"You look burned out," she remarked. "I hate putting you through this."

"I'll be fine." He sank down in his desk chair. "It's just a lot to take in. And for now, your theory on Dante Frears has to stay between us. If he is our man, we don't want to tip him off." He pointed to the envelope she'd tucked inside her vest. "That's the last time I risk my reputation. From here on out, we do things strictly by the book. If we don't, we might lose the most nefarious criminal this area has ever had."

He didn't tell Melody that Dante had already pushed him to his limit by taunting Kaitlin. And the worst of that, Dante had a point about Slade's workaholic nature, no matter how blatantly he'd tried to make it.

All the more reason for Slade to stick to the facts and stop thinking about how good it felt to have Kaitlin in his arms.

"I won't say anything," Melody promised. "I'll get this to my friend right away. Thanks, Slade."

He waved her away, then sat staring at the wall. Various pictures and award certificates and trophies showed off the K-9 Unit with pride of place. They'd won awards, fought the bad guys and worked hard to do their jobs. But why would one of their most fierce supporters decide to play them? Had Dante been playing them all along?

He got up to stare at the picture of Frears handing him a check for twenty-five thousand dollars. His friend smiled into the camera but when Slade looked closer, he was shocked to see that Dante's cold eyes held an icy stare. Had his friend lost his soul somewhere along the way?

"I should have been more vigilant," he whispered. He should have watched out for Dante more, should have visited and checked on him more than once or twice a month when they'd get together to watch a game and eat a good steak.

Maybe he could have stopped this.

But when Slade thought back over the years, he had to admit he'd always sensed a darkness in Dante. His friend had a need to be first—that had made him a strong soldier. But it had also made him ruthless and heartless.

"And I ignored it."

Slade had chalked it up to their war years, figuring they'd seen enough death and destruction to give any man nightmares. He'd come home determined to continue the good fight.

But Dante? He'd come home determined to have the all-American dream. Had he gone about achieving that dream through criminal activities?

Slade's cell phone chimed, jarring him out of his thoughts. "McNeal."

"Slade, it's Francine. I…my car broke down on the way home. I have Kaitlin and our canines with us."

"Where are you?"

She named a spot near the Lost Woods.

"On the way." Slade dropped his phone in its protective pocket on his utility belt and checked his equipment. After alerting the dispatcher, he headed out.

On a normal day, car trouble would be just that. Car trouble. But these days—it could be something else entirely.

Kaitlin stared down into the guts of Francine's late-model pickup. "I don't see any loose wires and the radiator seems to be intact. It's not running hot. Give it another try."

Francine turned over the key to test the motor.

Nothing.

"Slade's on his way," Francine called out. She reached back to calm the dogs. Warrior and Francine's trainee Bachelor were in the jump seat.

Kaitlin's gaze searched the empty highway. The sun slanted through the thick trees inside the woods, but soon it would disappear behind those trees and a dark blanket would cover this area. She didn't want to be here when that happened.

"We have the dogs," she told Francine. "We'll be okay."

Her nervous friend rubbed her hands down her arms. "Yep, but that doesn't help being out here where creepy things go on. People go missing in that thicket, you know."

"We'll be okay. Slade will be here any minute now."

Kaitlin prayed they'd be safe. She glanced at the truck's insides again. Everything looked normal. The brakes were working, at least. "What about gas?" she asked, running to the driver's side of the car.

"I just filled the tank two days ago," Francine said.

"And I haven't been anywhere much except to church and work today."

Kaitlin turned the key and watched for the gas gauge to move. "It's sitting on empty."

"Impossible," her friend said, getting in on the other side to stare at the unmoving needle.

Kaitlin pointed to the gauge. "Either you used a lot of gas somehow, or someone siphoned off every last drop."

Francine let out a gasp. "You mean, somebody came into my yard and stole the gas right outta my truck?"

"I think so," Kaitlin replied, turning the engine one more time. "And I don't think we're going anywhere until we get some fuel." Her gaze slammed into Francine's. "I don't like this. Especially if someone knew I'd be at your house this weekend."

"Me, either," Francine said, twisting to look up and down the road. "I don't like it one little bit."

"Warrior and Bachelor will watch out for us."

Francine turned to the two alert dogs. "It's okay, boys. We'll be fine." She petted Bachelor's brown head. "You're my good boy, right, Bachelor?"

The German shepherd woofed an answer.

Kaitlin could see the concern Francine was trying to hide. "We can call the attack command if anyone tries anything, Francine. Okay?"

"I'll call Slade back," Francine said, her finger tapping on her phone, her big brown eyes like chocolate orbs.

Kaitlin heard the roar of an approaching vehicle. "Wait, maybe that's him."

They both turned to stare out the back window.

A big black van was headed directly toward them.

Chapter Twelve

Kaitlin grabbed Warrior by the collar. "Francine, keep Bachelor in line. We might need them both."

The other woman moved her gaze from the approaching van to Kaitlin. "Why?"

Kaitlin took another look at the van. "I think that's the same van. The one my attacker was in the other day."

Francine swung around so fast her silver earrings danced against her cheeks. "The kidnapper?"

"I think so," Kaitlin replied, willing herself to stay focused. "Let's just sit here and see what happens. We can send out the dogs if we have to."

"Okay." Francine kept a tight hand on Bachelor's collar and then took a deep breath. "This is why we train canines," she kept saying. "They will protect us."

The van pulled up behind the truck. Kaitlin realized too late that the hood was still up, a sure sign that they couldn't get away.

Expecting a man dressed in all black and wearing a ski mask, Kaitlin waited with baited breath as the driver's side door opened. But a young man with shaggy, dirty-blond hair got out and ambled toward them.

"It's not my attacker," she managed to whisper before the man came up to the open window.

"Good afternoon, ladies," the man said, a grin on his face. "Got car trouble?"

"We do," Kaitlin replied. Behind her, Warrior let out a soft growl. "But we've called for help. Should be here any minute."

The man leaned close to stare into the truck, his brown eyes moving with radar precision over Francine and the dogs.

"Beautiful animals. Are they for sale?"

Thinking that was a strange and telling question, Kaitlin shook her head. "No. We use them as guard dogs. They go everywhere with us."

The guy backed up to stare at her. "Is that a warning, lady?"

"Yes, it is," Francine blurted out. "And our help just pulled behind your van."

Kaitlin glanced in the rearview mirror and sighed with relief. Slade was out of his vehicle and hotfooting it toward the car, one hand on his gun, his cell at his ear. He'd probably dispatched the tag numbers to get information on the van.

"Everything all right here?" he asked, glancing inside the black van as he walked by. He put his phone away, his eyes trained on the man standing by the truck.

The man whirled around, his hands palm out. "Just thought I'd offer my help. But I think these nice ladies have things under control."

Slade stared the man down. Dirty Blond shifted uncomfortably, sweat popping out on his pimply face. "Sir, can I see your license and registration, please?"

The man looked shocked. And scared. "What? What did I do?"

"Nothing that I know of," Slade said, his tone firm and calm. Kaitlin wondered if he'd already gotten a hit regarding the van. "But we recently had a near-kidnapping involving a van that matches yours. Mind if I verify that your vehicle wasn't involved?"

"I don't get why, man. I saw them broke down and just stopped to help. Can't I go now?"

Slade glanced around toward the van. "You have a broken taillight. I'd appreciate it if you could show me your license and registration."

"Whatever!" The skinny fellow pivoted to head back to the van.

Slade glanced in the truck.

"Go," Kaitlin said. "We're okay."

Slade went with the man to the van, but waited outside while the man leaned over to dig through the glove compartment.

Kaitlin watched in the driver's side mirror as Slade spoke into his radio. "He's doing a license check, I think. If that man's in the NCIC database, the captain will know soon."

"What if he finds something in the national database?" Francine asked. "What if that guy is crazy and pulls out a gun?"

"Slade knows what he's doing. He's going through his check list." She watched as he read over the registration papers.

Then he said something to the other man.

Dirty Blond's eyes widened and Kaitlin heard a string of expletives, but before anyone could blink, he pushed past Slade and took off running straight into the woods.

Slade immediately spoke into his radio, probably calling for backup. Then he shouted to Kaitlin. "Give me Warrior."

She did as he asked, commanding the animal to jump out of the truck. Slade took over from there and gave Warrior the attack command. Warrior sniffed the ground, already tracking the suspect.

"Don't move and don't let Bachelor out of your sight," Slade ordered. Then he dashed into the woods after Warrior.

Kaitlin sat staring at the trees. "I can't believe this."

Francine patted Bachelor and acknowledged the dog's alert growls. "It's okay, boy. You might get to go a round or two if anybody else shows up."

Kaitlin glanced in the rearview again. "I sure hope no one is hiding in that van."

Kaitlin thought about searching the vehicle, but Slade had told her to stay put. And yet, what if someone was holed up in there and they were too scared to get out now?

"Let me borrow Bachelor," she told Francine as she exited the truck.

"No, Kait." Francine held tight to her animal. "Slade said not to move. I'm not moving and neither is Bachelor."

Kaitlin couldn't sit still, waiting and wondering. She got out and paced by the side of the road.

When they heard Warrior's barks deep in the woods, Kaitlin turned to stare. "Maybe I should go after Slade."

"Like you said, the man knows his job and backup is

on the way," Francine replied. "Honey, just try to relax. I don't want something bad to happen to you."

Kaitlin nodded. "Okay, but only because I don't want to leave you alone."

"I appreciate that." Her friend kept searching the road. "I hear sirens."

By the time a backup K-9 patrol had arrived, Slade came stomping out of the woods, pushing the now-handcuffed runner along in front of him. The guy's shirt was torn and it looked like he had a bleeding bite mark on one of his arms. Warrior followed close by, trotting toward where Kaitlin stood by the truck.

"Good boy," Kaitlin said, reaching inside the truck to find an old chew toy. "Great job, Warrior-man." A tremendous shudder riveted her body, but she tried to give the illusion of calm.

Slade's eyes searched hers. "Y'all okay?"

"We're good." She eyed the young man being hauled to the patrol car. "What's his story?"

"He has an outstanding warrant. Deadbeat dad. Didn't pay child support. I ran a check and the warrant popped up. He split when I confronted him about it."

"Do you believe that?"

"The database has that information but not much else. I'll make sure he's telling the whole truth," Slade replied. "Let me go talk to Jackson and give him the scoop. I'll be right back." He turned around. "I saw some wrapper papers in a cup holder by his seat, so we'll search the van, too. Just in case."

Kaitlin sighed again. "Hey, Slade. The truck's gas tank is completely empty. That's why we broke down."

He came striding back. "Are you sure?"

"Yep," Francine said as she crawled out of the truck.

"I filled it up two days ago. No way I could have used that much fuel."

"We think someone deliberately siphoned it out," Kaitlin explained.

"Sit tight for a second." Slade hurried to the patrol car and said a few words to Jackson.

Jackson and his dog, Titan, did a quick search of the van, but after finding a baggie filled with what looked like a small amount of marijuana, Jackson shook his head. Then he headed back to the patrol car.

Slade turned back to Kaitlin. "Jackson's gonna call a gas station to bring you some fuel, Francine. I'll stay here until they get here."

"Thanks," Francine said. "I think I'll let Bachelor take a run while we wait. He's as hyped up as I am. Warrior can come, too."

Kaitlin lifted her chin. "Thanks, Francine."

That left Kaitlin and Slade standing alone.

"Are you sure you're okay?" he asked, his gaze lingering on her.

"I'm fine. Just another close call. Do you think that man is connected to The Boss?"

"I don't know. We've got him on the outstanding warrant, resisting an officer and a bag of weed. None of that can connect him to The Boss, though." He stared at the black van. "That sure looks a lot like the vehicle, but there aren't any bullet holes in the passenger door. "I ran the plates. It's not stolen and he has insurance and the title." He glanced back at the van. "We can haul it in and go over it again."

"Good idea. I'd feel better knowing for sure."

He took her by the arm. "C'mon. Let's talk."

Kaitlin waved to Francine and made sure she could

keep her friend and the dogs in her sights. And while she walked, she prayed this might at least give them a break in this case.

Because she couldn't take much more of this kind of upheaval.

"Everything checks out, but I still don't like it."

Slade's gaze moved over the unit officers he'd called into the conference room this morning.

Jackson Worth spoke up. "The van could have been cleaned and fixed up. Perhaps sold? Do we know how long that kid has owned it?"

"A few months," Slade replied. "That doesn't fit with what happened here last week, though."

Melody raised her hand. "Could the kid—Rudy Hampton—be lying?"

"A good possibility," Slade replied. "He's a jittery mess. I think he was almost relieved to be locked up." He tapped his fingers on the table. "Rudy has hit hard times and he got behind on his child support payments. Says he has a one-year-old."

"Being down and out can lead to all kinds of deals regarding money," Valerie said. "Maybe he's lying because he has to."

"To protect his child?" Slade mused.

Valerie nodded. "If someone offered him a way out from under that warrant or threatened him if he didn't cooperate, then maybe he might have to lie to us."

Slade appreciated Valerie's perspective since she had taken over raising her own orphaned niece, Bethany.

"How long can we hold him?" Parker Adams asked, his pen whirling through his fingers.

"Not long enough," Slade admitted. "If he lawyers up, he'll be out on bail in no time."

"I don't think he has the resources for that," Valerie replied.

The talk went on about trial dates and plea bargains.

Slade got up to scrutinize the picture he'd taken of Rudy's van. "Maybe I'll try one more time. If I can get him to bargain, we might get some information out of him."

"Couldn't hurt," Jackson said.

Later, Slade called Kaitlin to give her an update. "I'm going to question him now. That kid is hiding something besides an outstanding warrant. I'm gonna try to find out what it is."

Kaitlin was in the break room, drinking a soda. "Good luck with that. Most of the people you've taken in either won't talk or…they didn't live to tell anyone anything."

"Good point," Slade replied. "I'll call you later. Want me to bring by some dinner?"

"Would it be okay if I came to your house and brought Warrior with me? I'd like to see Caleb, but I don't want to put him in danger."

"Okay, but make sure the cruiser follows you to my front door."

"Yes, Captain," she said with a long suffering sigh.

He hung up with a grin in spite of the burning inside his gut. If he could get Rudy Hampton to talk maybe he could finally get a break in this investigation.

And that could lead to all sorts of possibilities.

Such as him finally bringing down The Boss and… him finally having the nerve to pursue Kaitlin Mathers without any regrets.

Chapter Thirteen

Slade was in an almost good mood.

Rudy Hampton had copped a plea. He still had to pay child support, but resisting an officer and possession of a controlled substance had been dropped. Since he'd had well under twenty grams of marijuana, dropping those two had been the easy part.

Getting Rudy to talk had been the hard part. He was deathly afraid of someone.

"If you so much as breathe in a fume from weed, you will be arrested, and next time, you won't get away so easily," Slade had told him.

Rudy only wanted to get out and get away. He'd be on probation for a few months, and Slade had even offered to help him find a job. But for now, Slade would settle for the information Rudy had given him.

"Somebody wanted to borrow my van," Rudy explained. "My friend offered me a lot of money to rent it out for a couple of days."

"Who was this friend?"

"I can't tell you that."

"Rudy, I can't agree to this plea if you don't give me the goods."

"Okay, okay, man. He went by the name D.J. And... he's really not a friend. Just some guy I met in a bar."

"D.J.? No last name?"

"I didn't ask, man. He told me—after I'd agreed to loan out my van for a couple of grand—that his boss would come looking for me if I told anyone."

"So you kept your mouth shut?"

"That's right, sir. I pocketed the money and rode a bike to work and back for about a week. I began to wonder if I'd ever see my van again. I'd just bought the thing a couple of months ago. Just now got the title and insurance all straightened out."

"Where'd you buy it?"

"One of those factory places. They were replacing all their old black vans with new green ones."

That got Slade's attention. He jotted down some notes. "What was the company?"

"Bug Busters. Over in that town near the border." He named the other town. "They said they'd sold several of the vans to one person."

Slade's pulse lurched. "Interesting."

"Not to me. I wish I'd never agreed to loan out my van to anyone. I needed the money, though."

"And then today they brought it back?"

"Yeah, today. But D.J. offered me an extra five hundred to do a little more work."

"And what was that?"

"Follow that truck I found today."

"You mean the Ford that was broken down on the road out of town—near the Lost Woods?"

"Yep."

"Did you do anything to the old Ford before you followed it?"

"Like what?"

"I don't know. Why don't you tell me?"

"I didn't do a thing. I just found the truck where D.J. said it would be."

"So you didn't happen to siphon any gas out of that truck?"

"Huh?"

Slade could almost understand someone hiring Rudy to do grunt work. The kid didn't have a clue.

"Did it ever occur to you to find out why you were being paid to let someone use your van or to follow that truck?"

"I know not to ask any questions. Like I said… I needed the money, man. I don't want to start selling drugs, so I thought this might work out okay. I figured D.J.'s boss wanted a big van to transport something and maybe he wanted me to follow the truck 'cause he was tracking a girlfriend or something."

"And you didn't have a problem just following orders?"

Rudy shook his head. "I thought what would it matter, you know? When I saw that same truck broken down, I figured I'd see who they'd wanted me to follow. Thought I might know the person, but I didn't know those two women. Besides, they had big dogs with 'em." He pointed to his bandaged arm. "I hope I don't get an infection from that bite."

"You'll be fine," Slade replied, wondering if Rudy had failed to figure out he'd been bitten by a K-9 officer dog.

"Did you wonder about the people who hired you?"

"No, I saw dollars and I took 'em. I thought maybe I could do whatever else they wanted, but...not now. Not anymore. I'm trying to go clean, so I can take care of my kid. I don't like this."

"And you have no knowledge of an alleged kidnapping last week?"

"No. Not with my van. If they did that, I wasn't a part of it. Am I in trouble for that, too?"

"Not if you're telling the truth." Rudy's body language shouted *scared and clueless*. "And when you got your van back today, notice anything different?"

"It was clean as a whistle. I think they even painted it and fixed some of the dents."

"You're sure about that?"

"Yeah, man. What's going on around here, anyway?"

"Nothing you need to worry about."

Rudy said he wanted to leave. Slade told him he had to stay in the state of Texas for a while since he'd be on probation. Rudy asked for protection. Slade agreed to put a cruiser on him for a few days.

Slade had gone over Rudy's statements in every which way, trying to shake the kid up and catch him lying. But he believed Rudy was telling the truth, as weird as that seemed.

And that meant that Rudy's old van had been the very van used to try and kidnap Kaitlin. Slade had put in a request to have the crime scene team go over the van with a fine-tooth comb to find anything—a stray hair, skin partials, a new scent. Or maybe, a new passenger-side door.

He also reported that someone had bought a whole fleet of used vans from Bug Busters. Was Dante hiding this fleet somewhere? Slade couldn't wait to find out.

He hadn't been able to put a tail on Dante today, but come tomorrow, he'd start watching and waiting. He'd have to be careful, do some of the surveillance on his own time, but the fire in his belly told him he was headed in the right direction. He had a prime suspect. And he was beginning to gather evidence. But it boggled his mind why the bad guys went to all the trouble of borrowing someone's vehicle to do a crime, only to send it back to that person all spick and span. Did The Boss think they'd pin the kidnapping on poor, misguided Rudy Hampton?

A foolish mistake. Now Slade could follow their M.O. He'd have to go back over the other attempted kidnappings and check on those vehicles, too. Stealing and ditching cars, buying old used vans to do dirty work and paying some poor sap to help. No wonder The Boss was so hard to track.

Now there was hope, he thought. Hope for a resolution.

Looking at the clock, Slade decided he'd relax a little tonight and spend some time with his son and Kaitlin.

And come tomorrow, he'd start watching his friend Dante Frears like a hawk.

"That was so good."

Kaitlin smiled over at Slade while they cleaned the kitchen. They'd enjoyed a delicious dinner of mixed beef and chicken fajitas from her favorite Mexican take-out, Roco Taco. Papa had already gone to his room, his night nurse, Jasper, helping him down the hallway. Caleb was coloring pictures in his room, Warrior right by his side.

She loved this. Loved being part of a family. It had

been so long since she'd had anyone other than friends and church members to shower with love.

Love?

Yes, love. In the way a friend loved a friend. In the way a mother would love a child. In the way a granddaughter enjoyed chatting with a grandfather.

I can't get attached to Slade's family, she told herself.

It was enough that she was becoming way too attached to the man. She needed to give that some time before she settled into a nice, comfortable routine with his family, in his home.

He's protecting you, she reminded herself.

Things could change once this investigation was over.

Her life would go back to the normal, routine workdays and the full but bland weekends. Up until now, that had been enough. She'd never thought past work and friends because she was so afraid to even harbor hope of finding someone to share her life with. Until now.

"What are you thinking about so hard?" Slade asked, one hand on the counter, his gaze fixed on her.

Kaitlin blinked, realized she'd been standing there drying the same dish for five minutes. Should she tell him the truth?

"I don't know. I... I really had a nice time tonight. I almost forgot why I'm really here."

"Because you're a target?"

"Yes. Hard to get that out of my mind, but those fajitas and your family managed to do just that."

"And me? Did I make you forget for a while?"

Surprised, she grinned. "Captain McNeal, are you flirting with me?"

"Maybe. I'm not sure I know how to flirt, but if it's working—"

"It is," she said on a low breath. "But—"

"I hate that word."

She slanted a gaze up at him. "But we both know that being forced together doesn't exactly seal a relationship."

"No, but kissing seals things a whole lot."

"Kissing is nice, but… I think we need to slow down a bit."

"You're not backing out on me, are you?" He leaned close, his words for her only. "Weren't you the one who told me not to shut down or shut you out?"

"I was the one," she admitted, giving him a direct stare. "And I mean that. I just want you to be sure. You've been dealing with a lot of things lately."

"I'm pretty sure I can handle this," he said. "But you're right about one thing. We need to wait until you're out of danger."

"And that means waiting until you find The Boss."

"I'm getting closer," he replied, a confidence in his tone. "Starting tomorrow, I'll be on Frears like a duck on a june bug."

"Rudy came through?"

"Rudy is a scared, down-on-his-luck man who got caught up with the wrong people, so yes, he came through. We've checked him out and other than missing child support payments, he has a pretty clean record. But he's the perfect candidate to be taken advantage of."

Kaitlin thought about her mother. "My mom was kind of like that. She was a very smart veterinarian and she loved her work. But she was so gullible at times. She thought wounded people were the same as wounded animals. They'd strike out because of the pain." She released a pensive sigh. "But animals can be soothed and treated. Humans, on the other hand, sometimes strike out because of evil, not pain. Or maybe their pain turns to something evil. I don't know."

He turned to lean against the counter so they were face-to-face. "And the drug addict who killed her? Was he in pain or was he evil?"

"He was a little of both, I think." She shut her eyes to the awful memories. "He didn't have anything to lose, so yes, that made him do something he might not have done if he could have been saved. But…the brutality of what he did made him evil in my mind."

"So you can't forgive him?"

"I have asked God to help me forgive him, but I won't forget. That's why I love training canines. I get to be around animals and that makes me feel close to my mother. But I also get to help put away the bad guys, so that helps me to forgive the criminal who killed her."

Slade touched a hand to her cheek. "You have an amazing perspective."

"Not so amazing. It's the only way I can cope."

"I'll get you out of this, Kaitlin," he said, his lips grazing hers. "I promise."

She believed him. He was the kind of man a woman could depend on. She needed to be the kind of woman he could depend on, as well. She needed to show Slade that he could turn to God to help him heal. And to help him find his way back to giving his son all the love he needed.

Slade tugged her close, deepening the kiss, showing her that he was in this for the long haul. He lifted his head and gazed down at her. "Who would have thought—"

"That we'd be here, kissing each other?"

"Yeah. I mean, I've known you for a while now but—"

"I hate that word."

He grinned at that. "But… I didn't act on any of the feelings you brought out in me. Until now."

"And that's why we need to take it slow and make sure we can work through this. I don't want crime and danger to be the only things holding us together."

He frowned at that remark. "I don't think those two things have anything to do with the way you make me feel."

"How do I make you feel?" she asked, too curious to stop herself.

"Safe," he murmured huskily. Then he kissed her again.

They might have stayed that way for a while, except his cell phone buzzed.

Slade pulled back and walked a couple of steps away. "McNeal."

Kaitlin watched as he listened, saw the deep frustration settling over his face.

"I'll be right there."

He put his phone away, glanced over at her, his eyes now full of shock and…regret. "Rudy Hampton is dead."

Kaitlin gasped. "What happened?"

"A neighbor found him on the back deck of his duplex apartment with a bullet hole in his forehead."

"Oh, Slade. I'm so sorry."

He hauled her into his arms. "I let that kid go. I promised him I'd have someone watch out for him."

"What about the cruiser?"

"I don't know. I don't know." He pulled back and scrubbed a weary hand across his face. "I have to go find out how this happened."

"I'll stay here with Caleb."

"Good. You can't go home alone. We told Melody you'd be home at eleven. I'll call her."

Kaitlin hated the torment in his eyes. "No. Let me stay here for a while. I have my car and Warrior is with us. I'll call her after I get Caleb settled."

He agreed, his tone reluctant. "All right. I have to go. Tell Melody to keep texting you every fifteen minutes or so."

"I'll do that right now."

Slade hurried toward the door. "I'll alert Parker, too. And we'll put a cruiser outside. Parker can check things out around the yard. If you need to, get Jasper to help, too."

"I'll be okay," she reassured him.

"Lock the door behind me and shut the blinds."

She nodded, a chill chasing away the warmth of his touch.

Slade turned at the door and gave her a quick kiss. "Maybe you're right. Maybe we can't plan a future until we bring down the criminal who's trying to destroy my whole department."

Kaitlin watched through the window until his truck pulled away and then dead-bolted the door and checked all the windows.

Another long, sleepless night. But at least she had

Warrior and she'd be able to keep an eye on Caleb for a little while.

She thought of Rudy Hampton and said a prayer for the little baby that was now without a father. Why did evil people prey on those who were too weak to run away?

"I know how that feels," she whispered. Then she hurried down the hall to Caleb's room. Hopefully, he'd fall asleep quickly and stay asleep right through this latest ordeal. If he asked, she'd have to find a way to explain to the little boy that his daddy had been called back out to work. And...she'd have to find a way to keep herself calm.

Just in case.

Chapter Fourteen

Kaitlin held Caleb close while she read to him from his favorite book. "You really love this little cowboy, don't you?" she asked when she was finished.

"He's a toy," Caleb explained. "But he gets to be a real boy, too."

"You're a real boy, aren't you?"

He bobbed his head and the scent of his lollipop bath soap drifted through the air. Warrior lifted his head, ever watchful.

"Can Warrior sleep with me tonight?"

Kaitlin wouldn't have it any other way. "Certainly. He might have to go home with me after you're asleep."

"Where's Chief?"

"He's sleeping in Papa's room tonight. He's tired."

Caleb looked up at her with big, wide eyes full of hope and longing. "I wish we could all live together. That'd be so much fun."

"It would," Kaitlin replied, her throat clogging with that same pain and longing. "But…sometimes people who are friends can't live with us all the time. Do you understand that?"

"Kinda. I don't like it, though." He did a little shoulder shrug. "Daddy says that's why Mommy can't come back. She has to live in heaven now."

Kaitlin's grip on his shoulder tightened. "Your daddy is telling you the truth. My mother is in heaven, too. I miss her every day but I know I'll see her again one day."

Caleb scrunched his nose. "I hope I see my mommy again."

"You will, I'm sure." Kaitlin stroked the top of his head.

"I don't like not seeing her. I wonder if she'll 'member me."

Swallowing again, Kaitlin nodded. "She will never forget you. How could she? You're a special little boy."

He stared up at her with those big blue eyes, and melted her heart. "I love Daddy, but I don't like not being in heaven with Mommy."

"Me, either." Kaitlin thought about her own mother and wished she could talk to her about… Slade. About life and love and hope and grace. "We have to love the people we have while we have them," she whispered, more to herself than Caleb.

When he grew quiet, she knew it was time to let him go to sleep. Kaitlin gently pulled away and settled Caleb on his pillows. "Nightie-night time, okay?"

"'Kay." His eyes fluttered then opened. "Warrior?"

The big dog jumped up on the bed. Kaitlin pointed to the foot of the twin-size mattress and Warrior obediently plopped down, his eyes on Caleb.

Caleb giggled, then gave Kaitlin a sleepy smile. "He's so silly."

"He is a silly dog," Kaitlin agreed. Then she leaned down to kiss Caleb's dark curls. "Night."

"Night. Love you."

Kaitlin stood there, her heart growing so big she thought it might burst through her chest. "Love you, too," she managed to squeak out. She patted Warrior on the head. "Stay."

Warrior gave her one last look, then laid his head on his paws, his focus on Caleb.

Caleb would be safe with the dog nearby, but she left his door cracked all the same. Passing quickly when she came to the big suite where Papa slept with Jasper on a nearby cot, she said a prayer for Slade and his family.

"Protect them, Lord. Hold them in Your grace. Help Slade to do his job. Stop the killings. Keep Caleb safe and let Your love pour over him."

And help me to figure out how to deal with the fact that I'm falling in love with Slade McNeal and his little boy.

Slade stood in the city morgue, staring down at the lifeless body of Rudy Hampton. He'd already heard the medical examiner's official report but he could see what had happened. Plain and simple. A single gunshot wound to the head. Close range. Instant death.

"This is my fault," he told Parker. "I should have watched out for him."

"You put a patrol car on him, Slade. We can't help that he went out on his back porch for a smoke and got a bullet in the head. What more could you have done?"

"I don't know. Brought him home with me?"

"Don't you already have a growing list of houseguests?"

Slade nodded tersely. "Yes. Guess I can't open up an inn for people who are in danger, huh?"

"No. You've gone way beyond your duty with Kaitlin. And I understand why. We've all had someone we care about involved in this investigation and endangered by it, too."

Overcome with emotion, Slade turned away from the kid he'd promised to help. "You're right. Maybe instead of trying to protect everyone against The Boss, I should just go out and find the man himself. I can end this thing if I do that."

He whirled and headed for the double doors, Parker on his heels. "What are you up to now?"

"I'm going back out to the Lost Woods and I'm gonna dig in that spot until I find something—anything—that I can use for evidence."

"The police chief won't like that."

"The chief doesn't need to know. I'll dig on my off-time."

"I'll go with you."

Slade shook his head. "No sense in both of us getting in trouble. Besides, I need you to check on things at my place."

"Sir—"

"Parker, I appreciate it but I need some time to think about this. The digging will help me get rid of my need to crack somebody's head."

Parker held up a hand. "I don't want that to be me, so be careful. Call me if you find anything."

Slade nodded and headed out into the night. If it took him working until his last breath, he'd find whoever did this. He'd find The Boss. Or die trying.

After checking in with Kaitlin, he told her to sit tight until he could get back home. But first, he had one stop to make.

"What's going on?"

"I can't talk about it right now. Just keep calm, Kaitlin."

"What are you going to do?" she demanded.

"My job."

He was headed out to the Lost Woods when he spotted Dante's sleek, black sedan turning on a side street on the edge of town. Most days, he'd see Dante riding through town and never think a thing about it.

But today was a different day. It was late at night, a time Frears should have been at home with his family.

Slade pulled back, slowed down and decided to follow Dante.

The car stopped at a big, rundown warehouse. A warehouse that looked vacant. He hid his truck down the block behind another building, then got out and hurried through a small thicket of overgrown saplings and weeds back to the warehouse. Hiding behind a fence, he watched as a garage door on the side of the old building swung open. He thought about going to check things out on foot, but decided that wouldn't be a smart move. And he couldn't call for backup—not yet. If Dante saw him, the investigation would get even more backlogged. So he waited, thinking at least now he had a location to connect to Frears.

But what he saw next made him sick to his stomach. A large, black van emerged from around the corner of the building. Then a man dressed in black from head to toe came out of the garage and hurried into the van.

Ski Mask Man.

The Boss?

Slade's heart thudded as adrenaline rushed like a frayed wire throughout his tired system, bringing him new life.

Dante Frears was the Ski Mask Man. The Boss. A criminal, a liar and a killer. His best friend was the man who'd tried to kidnap Kaitlin, a man who'd planted bombs and intimidated witnesses and...killed several people in the past few months.

His best friend.

Slade thought he might lose his supper right there in the bushes. He also thought about confronting Dante on the spot, losing his temper right along with his appetite. But he took several deep breaths and got it together. Where was Dante going?

Then it hit Slade. Dante might know that Kaitlin was at his house. He turned and headed back to his truck, his mind whirling. Cranking the motor, he waited until he saw the black van moving down the main road out of town, then he called Kaitlin.

"I just got a lead on a black van. Be aware and keep an eye out. I'm calling the patrol officer to warn him. Don't open the door for anyone except Parker. I'll be there in a few minutes. I'll explain when I get there."

"I know the drill," Kaitlin replied. "Slade, be careful. Call for backup."

"I will if it comes to that."

He hung up and waited until the van's taillights were about to disappear around a curve. The van wasn't going toward his house, thankfully. Slade intended to find out where Frears was going, though. He might not have a K-9 partner right now, but he had a fully loaded weapon and a new attitude.

Kaitlin paced from window to window, wondering if she should tell Jasper what was going on. Deciding the less he knew, the safer he and Patrick might be, she kept pacing. This could turn out to be a false alarm. No need to get the whole house up and out of bed.

Kaitlin checked the road and saw the patrol car parked underneath a large oak tree, her pulse echoing in a swift cadence inside her temple. She'd been around police enough to know that something was up and she might be in danger.

How much was she supposed to take? Only a week or so ago, she had a life. A life that she loved even if it was sometimes a solitary life. A lonely life. But a good, solid, secure life.

She wanted that life back now, and so much more.

"I'll check on Warrior and Caleb," she mumbled, turning to head down the hallway.

A door opened and she jumped back. "Jasper, you scared me."

"Sorry, ma'am," the big man said. "I wanted to get something to drink."

"Okay." Should she tell him what was going on? "Jasper, if you hear anything or see anyone outside, will you let me know?"

"Sure. Something up?"

What should she say? "A possible prowler. We're not sure. Just be careful. Watch for any alerts from Chief, too."

"I'll get my drink and hurry back to Mr. McNeal. Let me know if you need me, ma'am."

"Thanks." Kaitlin rushed toward Caleb's room. His door was shut.

Fear tightened her throat with the force of a hand around her neck. She'd left the door open last time she checked on him. All sorts of horrible images flashed through her mind as she pushed at the bedroom door.

When she swung it open, her heart melted in relief.

Caleb lay with Warrior, both of them curled up at the foot of the bed. Warrior lifted his head, his big brown eyes trusting and sleepy.

"Thank you, Lord," she said on a breathless prayer. They were safe. Caleb and Warrior were safe. Maybe Caleb had shut the door so he could sneak to the end of the bed and sleep near Warrior. Since she hadn't heard the canine's distinctive bark, that had to be it.

Warrior jumped off the bed and grunted a greeting.

"Hi, boy. You gave me a scare." She patted his head and hit a hand against her thigh. "Back on the bed. Stay."

After checking the window, Kaitlin backed out of the room, her pulse back to a normal pace now. When her cell buzzed, she let out a frightful breath. "Hello?"

"Kaitlin, it's Parker. Slade wanted me to do a sweep around the perimeter of his house. Sherlock and I walked the front and backyard and made sure the patrol officer was okay. You're safe for now."

"Thank you," she said, her heart still jittery.

But the closed door she found niggled at her fears. Had Jasper shut the door? Caleb, maybe? Or was someone else inside this house?

Slade slowed his truck on the outskirts of town. The black van had circled the city on every back road, some even Slade had never been down.

So what was Dante up to tonight and who was he, anyway? Family man by day and dark predator by night? Did he wait until late at night to wreak havoc on the city? Where was he going now?

Slade waited and watched as the van turned and

pulled into one of the many dirt lanes leading into the Lost Woods. Glancing around, he breathed a sigh of relief that Frears hadn't struck out toward his house, but the next breath was edged with worry and frustration. Did he dare follow Dante into those woods?

His cell buzzed. "McNeal."

"All clear," Parker said. "Sherlock and I have done a thorough sweep of your yard, and Kaitlin's got Warrior watching over Caleb. Everything's locked up tight. Everyone is safe."

"Thanks." Slade ran a hand down his face. "I've tailed Frears to the Lost Woods. I think he's going back in to dig but the van's just idling right now."

He watched the woods while Parker gave him an update on Kaitlin. "She's okay. Just aggravated. She wants to go home and get some sleep."

"Only if Melody can meet her there, but let's hold off on the swap right now."

"Not a problem. What about you? Don't you need to get some shut-eye, too?"

Slade lifted his head as one of the side doors to the van swung open. When a man dressed in black stepped out, Slade sat up straight.

Then the man turned and grabbed a leash, tugging it tight.

A big dark-colored dog jumped out of the van.

"Me, I never sleep." He disconnected and held his breath.

Could that big dog be Rio?

Chapter Fifteen

❧

"Where is Slade?"

Kaitlin waited with a tight-knuckled grip on the phone for Parker to explain things to her but after a cryptic silence, she decided she'd take matters into her own hands.

"Fine. I'm going to get Warrior and I'll find Slade myself."

Parker's stern voice halted her. "Hey, now, don't do anything rash. Slade knows what he's doing and right now he's on the case."

Kaitlin was done with being rational. "Yes, a case that involves me. He's out there chasing a man who might kill him because of me, Parker."

"He *is* doing this for you, but he's also doing this because he's the police captain and he has a lead. He can't drop that because you're worried about him. You know how this works." He took a long breath, the inhale scraping over the static on the phone. "Try to relax and stay calm. If you go out there now, even with Warrior, you might make things much worse."

Kaitlin's helplessness engulfed her with a heat that

rivaled the temperature outside. But Parker was right. If she showed up in the middle of a situation, she could endanger not only Slade, but other innocent people. "What can I do? I'm not good at sitting around."

"I'm sorry, but that's the only thing you *can* do right now," Parker replied. "I'll drive around and see if I can find him. He told me he'd call if he needed backup."

"Thank you," Kaitlin said, relief coloring her words. "I'll feel better as long as I know someone's watching his back."

"Good." Parker went silent for a second then said, "You know, Melody has this thing she does when she's worried about me."

Kaitlin listened and thought about how Melody must go through this a lot, even if she was a detective herself. "I guess you both have to deal with this, too. I'm sorry. What's her tactic for staying calm?"

Parker laughed. "Go to the freezer and look for the ice cream. I bet all the McNeal men love ice cream. And so does Melody. That's her coping mechanism."

"Ice cream?" Kaitlin shook her head and let out a chuckle that released some of the tension. "You're kidding, right?"

"No, ma'am. I'm serious. Find the ice cream and have a big bowl."

Nervous energy propelled Kaitlin to the refrigerator. "Oh, you're right. We've got caramel and chocolate chip. Someone in this house *is* serious about good ice cream."

"I know it's around one in the morning, but eat up," Parker said. "And call Melody to check in. She can have a bowl with you and keep you company over the phone. It'll make you feel better."

"Okay, I will," Kaitlin said, feeling better already.

In a few minutes, she was curled up on the couch with her ice cream, her cell to her ear. "Parker's a keeper, Melody."

"Don't I know it! He's as sweet as this ice cream."

"Speaking of that, this caramel pecan will add an inch to my waistline."

Melody paused, probably to dig into her scoop of rocky road. "It's either this or punching something."

Kaitlin took in a big spoonful, her brain freeze causing her to squint. "I might do that next."

They sat talking quietly for the next few minutes. They'd just finished up a nice girl chat and their ice cream when Kaitlin heard Warrior barking and growling. "I have to go, Melody. I'll check back in soon."

"No," Melody said tensely. "Stay on the line with me while you check."

Slade followed the man and dog through the moonlight, the hot night sizzling around him like a fired furnace. Sweat pooled between his shoulder blades, but he kept moving in a low crouch and prayed if that raggedy-looking dog was Rio, that he wouldn't alert to Slade's scent. *Not yet, Rio. Not yet, boy.*

After Ski Mask Man left the van, the vehicle rolled into a thicket of oak saplings, probably to hide and wait for instructions. Who was the driver? Slade wondered now, his breath coming in shallow wisps, his hands slippery with perspiration.

What was Dante searching for in these dark, lonely woods? Certainly not more drugs. Unless he had small amounts hidden all over the woods. That would explain why he'd snatched Rio. Did this have something to do with Daniel? The boy died here in these woods. Had Daniel left something behind that Dante needed to find?

Trying to keep up in the muted gray darkness, Slade didn't dare turn on his flashlight. When he heard a dog woof, he hid behind a tree and stilled himself, willing the dog to ignore whatever scent he'd picked up on the wind.

"Hush" came a sharp command. Slade recognized Dante's voice carrying through the trees.

"What you want me to do, Boss?"

Another man. Someone must have doubled back to meet Dante there.

"Since that imbecile Rudy messed up big time, we've gotta get this dog to do his job." Dante started ranting, profanity spewing out of his mouth like liquid fire. "Stupid animal. I need that woman here. She could make him do what he's trained to do. Rudy had her right there and panicked."

"Want me to make the call for action?"

"Not yet. That's a last resort. Things are too hot right now. Let's just dig."

Slade couldn't believe what he was hearing. Rudy was supposed to kidnap Kaitlin? The kid never confessed to that. And what was the last resort call about? Ski Mask Man—The Boss—had just confirmed what they'd all suspected. He needed Kaitlin to make Rio follow commands.

Rio.

Slade's heart pumped anew when he thought about the condition of his prized partner. Rough-looking didn't begin to describe the animal. Dull, ragged fur, a gaunt belly and eyes that looked defeated. From what Slade had seen in the growing dusk, Rio wasn't being treated humanely. He almost charged through the woods, gun blazing, to rescue Rio.

But he tempered that impulsive anger into a pledge. "I will end this." And he'd get Rio back.

Then he'd be able to tell Kaitlin that he wanted her in his life for a long, long time.

Right now, however, he needed to wait this out and see what he could find. Right now, he decided, might be a good time to start praying again, too.

So he waited and listened and prayed for guidance.

Dante ranted at Rio over and over, sometimes going into a rage while he jerked the leash against the dog's heavy collar. He was trying to walk off the coordinates of the code he'd found on Daniel's watch—R 23, L 34, R 12. Slade had to bite his tongue, tears burning his eyes, while he listened to Dante scolding and cursing at Rio. Did Dante think the dog could count, sniff out whatever Dante had in mind?

Slade held himself in check. He couldn't rush this. If he called for backup now, Dante might kill Rio. If that fiend did one more thing—

"We need to leave, Boss. Somebody's snooping up near the road."

"What?" Dante's growl matched Slade's frustration. "What is it with this town? Every time I come out here, somebody seems to be snooping. I thought we got rid of all the tattlers and moles."

"Sir, we need to hurry. It's a big place. Lots of people hang out around here."

More cursing. Then Dante gave a hard tug to Rio. "Get over here, you stupid mutt. I should just shoot you right now and dump you on Slade McNeal's porch."

Slade stood, ready to pack it all in and get his man.

But when he heard Rio's sharp bark, he realized the dog had recognized his scent. The bark had been high and light.

Happy. Rio was happy to find a familiar, comforting scent. The dog needed his help. But Dante obviously thought the bark was toward whoever was up by the road.

"Let's go. At least this mutt is good for alerting us that someone is coming."

Slade watched and listened as the two men scuttled in the opposite direction and hurried to leave the woods. In order to save his partner, Slade had to do this by the book. And that meant he needed to wait for backup and he needed to keep a tail on Dante Frears.

"Hang on, boy," he whispered to the hot, dry wind. "Hold on."

He radioed Parker and gave him an update. When the detective told him he was nearby, Slade suggested he get back to the house.

"They might be on the way there right now, but I'm hoping they got scared and called it a night. If they spot you, they'll know we're onto them."

"On my way back now with Sherlock. Are you okay?"

"I will be."

He waited until he heard the van crank and he prayed Dante wouldn't make good on his word to kill Rio. Or anyone else, for that matter.

After about thirty minutes of quiet, Slade made his way back to his truck and grabbed an old garden shovel out of his toolbox. In order to convince the higher-ups and this town that he wasn't going crazy, Slade knew he had to find proof. And that proof was buried in these woods.

* * *

"It's me—Jasper. I was just checking on you."

"You startled me," Kaitlin said, shaking her head after she'd spotted Jasper standing in the hall. "Warrior alerted."

Jasper did a quick scan behind him, then patted Warrior on the head. "Smart boy. He sure watches over us."

Kaitlin got a creepy feeling, standing there with the big-boned night nurse. "Yes, he's trained to do that. Where's old Chief?"

"In with Papa. He's about as old as his master, poor fellow."

"But still viable," Kaitlin replied, a sharp fear radiating up her back. She didn't really know this man, but Slade and Papa both vouched for him. So why did she suddenly feel insecure?

"Is everything okay? How's Papa?" She thought she'd crawl out of her skin if Slade didn't come home soon.

Jasper smiled. "Sleeping like a baby."

Kaitlin started to pass by Jasper. She needed to check on Caleb. "Good. He needs his rest." She forced a smile. "I'm okay, Jasper. I'll check on Caleb, then head back to the living room. Slade should be home soon."

"Of course." The night nurse whirled toward the kitchen. "I need a drink of water."

Kaitlin didn't realize she'd been holding her breath until she let out a sigh. "Excuse me." She waited until Jasper had gone into the kitchen before putting her phone to her ear. "All clear."

Melody's words sounded rushed. "Are you okay?"

"Yes, but I'll be glad when Slade gets here."

"Everything all right? Are you sure?"

Did she dare say anything? Jasper hadn't done anything to her after all. "Uh, I'm not sure but... I think so."

"I'm coming over," Melody replied. "And I'm calling Parker."

After making sure Caleb was still asleep, Kaitlin ordered Warrior back on the bed with the boy.

Then in a loud voice, she said, "So, Slade, you're on your way?"

Melody gasped. "Okay, you're scaring me. Yes."

Kaitlin stayed calm, ever watchful while Jasper made noises in the kitchen. "Yes, it has been a long night. I know you needed some thinking time, Slade, but I'm worried. I guess I keep on waiting, right?"

"Stay on the phone with me," Melody said. "I'll call Parker on the radio."

"Sounds good." Kaitlin hurried down to Caleb's room, Warrior trotting behind her. When she was out of earshot from Jasper, she whispered, "Night nurse. Suspicious."

And that's when she heard footsteps hitting the front porch.

Slade kept digging. He should call this in, but momentum kept him moving. He'd dug a wide square about two feet deep when the shovel hit on something metal. He tapped around, the moonlight guiding him, until he saw what looked like a rectangular metal box.

Now he'd have to call for backup. Now he had something that might provide proof. He touched the radio on his shoulder and called dispatch for assistance, then explained the situation. He'd just signed off when he heard a rustling in the woods. He wasn't about to let these crooks stumble on his find. Looking around, he started gathering some old limbs and bramble to hide the hole he'd dug, then he hurried and packed down the freshly dug dirt enough to hide the hole until he could get back. Crouching, he turned to go back the way he'd come, but gunfire sounded all around him and then he felt the whizz of a bullet ramming into his right shoulder.

Slade went down with a moan of pain, but recovered to quickly grab his own weapon. Crouching low, blood oozing down his dark sleeve, he managed to hide behind a thicket of tangled bushes and saplings. Glancing down at his shoulder, he gritted his teeth to the pain throbbing in a path down his arm. Best he could tell, the bullet had gone through and through. Just a lot of blood and a searing pain that threatened to knock him out.

Then he heard footsteps hitting the dry leaves and old branches, the snapping of brittle wood crushing against the crackling leaves. Someone was coming for him.

Slade heard shouting. Then barking. His backup or his enemy? With his right shoulder booming out a ripping pain, he managed to get up on one knee, then do a lightheaded stand against the old tree.

Searching for a place to hide, he saw a gnarled limb dangling from the ancient oak. The broken limb would serve as cover until help arrived. He worked his way over to the thick mass of dead leaves and tangled branches and sank down behind the big limb. Then he memorized his position to the path and the tree, praying he could stay conscious. Taking out his phone, he quickly took a picture, the small flash giving out an eerie light for a couple of seconds.

Then he got on the radio and gave his status and coordinates again. Assured someone would hear, Slade could only wait. He didn't have the strength to rush headlong into an ambush.

"Stay there. Help is on the way." Jackson. Maybe the barking Slade heard from a distance was from K-9 Titan.

Slade sank back against the tree limb, weak but still functioning. He heard barking again nearby and breathed a sigh of relief.

"Over here," he called, thinking the team was coming for him when he heard footfalls slapping against bramble.

But when he glanced up, a flashlight hit his face, blinding him. A dog growled, an ominous, dangerous sound. Slade glanced around for an escape route. The moonlight signaled a pale gray beacon on one of the many footpaths out of the woods. Could he make it? Slade lifted up and crouched again. When another gunshot rang out, he returned fire.

The barking intensified just a few yards away through the trees.

Rio?

And Dante Frears?

Slade stood straight, all fear and doubt gone now. He'd been waiting for this showdown for almost six months.

Then he heard more dogs barking up near the road and someone shouting a command.

His backup had arrived.

The flashlight went out, leaving a creeping darkness against the eerie moonlight shadowing the trees.

"Come back here, you coward," he called, his gun held in a grip of pain. "Show your face!"

Silence, except for running feet and a whimpering dog.

Slade sank to the ground and listened to the sound of footfalls, retreating this time. But this wasn't over. He knew the location of that buried metal box. And he intended to go back right now and find out what was in it.

Kaitlin had to get to Caleb. That thought made her turn and crouch low while Warrior snarled and barked.

Ordering Warrior to come, she sank down and started toward Caleb's room.

"What happened?" Melody said, shouting the words.

Kaitlin kept running, crawling down the hallway, the sound of shouts and gunshots echoing outside the house. "Someone's breaking into the house. I don't know where Jasper is but I'm going to Caleb's room. Warrior's right beside me."

"I'm almost there," Melody reassured her. "So is Parker."

"Slade," Kaitlin replied, now near Caleb's room. "Call Slade."

She burst through Caleb's open door, Warrior's sharp barking bringing her comfort. She called another command and Warrior went to work, guarding the door. He would attack anyone who tried to get near Caleb.

Caleb sat up and rubbed his eyes then called out. "Warrior!"

"It's okay, baby," Kaitlin said, diving for the bed and dragging Caleb and his cover down to the floor. "Hold on to me. You're okay. It's going to be all right."

Caleb clutched her shoulders, his stubby fingers grabbing tight. "I'm scared."

"It's okay."

Caleb shook his head violently. "No. No more bad guys." Then he started crying, his sobs starting in a huff and ending in a silent downpour that wet his chubby cheeks. "Where's my daddy?"

"He'll be here soon. Soon." Kaitlin prayed that God would be with them. "Just hang on to me, okay? Warrior will keep us safe."

Caleb burrowed closer to her robe, his little nose wet, his sobs echoing straight into her heart. Kaitlin held him there beside the bed, keeping his head down with a hand over it. Had Jasper been hit? Or was he a part of this?

Kaitlin gulped in short breaths, thoughts of what her mother must have gone through breaking through the terror inside her mind. She would not let this innocent little boy die.

A door opened and Warrior's barks matched another dog's frantic barking. Kaitlin gave Warrior the signal to guard. The dog waited, growling and snarling. She'd issue the attack signal if anyone tried to come through that door.

Kaitlin held Caleb close, protecting him, as footsteps tapped a slow, steady path toward the little bedroom at the back of the house.

Someone was coming for Caleb and her.

Chapter Sixteen

❧

"Kaitlin, it's me, Parker."

Kaitlin's pulse shifted down with each echo inside her head. "Coming," she shouted. She ordered Warrior to stay. The prancing, barking dog immediately became silent and still.

Lifting Caleb, she made eye contact with the frightened little boy. "It's okay, Caleb. It's only Officer Adams. The dog you heard is probably Sherlock. You know Sherlock, remember?"

Caleb sniffed and bobbed his head. Kaitlin stood, carrying Caleb in her arms. "Let's open the door. Will that be all right with you?"

He bobbed his head again. "'Kay."

Kaitlin took a deep breath and unlocked the door, glad to see Parker in one piece. "Hi," she said, feeling silly now that it was all over. "I'm sorry. I panicked."

"You have every right to panic," Parker said, eyeing Caleb. "Everything is okay." He gave her a warning look.

Realizing he didn't want to upset Caleb, she nodded. "Give me a few minutes. I'll be right there."

"Melody is here, too," Parker said. "And Sherlock is standing guard at the front door. All clear."

Kaitlin laid Caleb back down on his bed. "I need to step outside and talk to Detective Adams, okay?"

His big eyes widened in fear. "I want my daddy."

"He'll be here soon," she promised. "But Warrior will be here with you. He'll bark at me if he thinks you're afraid." She pointed to the door. "I'll be right out in the hallway. I'll stand where you can see me."

"'Kay." Caleb glanced around the room. "Can Warrior come close to me?"

"Yes, good idea." She signaled and Warrior hopped up on the bed. "Right here, boy." The canine scooted close to Caleb, his brown eyes centered on the little boy. "Stay."

Caleb immediately placed a hand on Warrior's head. The dog glanced at Kaitlin then laid his head down, nose to nose with Caleb.

"I'll be right outside," Kaitlin reminded him. Once she could see that Caleb was calm, she tiptoed to the hallway.

Parker and Melody stood huddled with Jasper. The night nurse looked as shaken as everyone else. Maybe she'd only imagined he was acting strange earlier. Jasper was as dedicated as they came and she knew that. She had to stop thinking everyone was a suspect.

"What happened?" Kaitlin asked, her nerves still jangled together like twisted vines.

"We almost had an intruder," Jasper replied in his slow, steady tone. But Kaitlin could see the fear in his eyes. "I heard someone outside so I hurried to the front."

Parker glanced from the burly nurse to Kaitlin. "I saw someone running away, but when I called for them to halt, they just kept running. I sent Sherlock to attack but they made it over the fence. He did manage to grab hold and tear some clothing."

Kaitlin noticed the torn black silk Melody had already bagged in a paper bag. "That looks like the jumpsuit that man who tried to kidnap me was wearing."

"We thought the same thing," Melody replied. "I think they were trying to get at you again." She shot a poker-face stare at the night nurse. "Jasper probably scared them away when he turned on the kitchen light, then ran to the front door."

Kaitlin saw the disbelief in Melody's eyes. Did she believe what Kaitlin had whispered over the phone? That Jasper was somehow involved. Did he run to the door to scare the intruder…or to warn him away? She'd have to explain to Melody later.

"I'm glad I happened to be in the kitchen," Jasper said, his brown eyes on Kaitlin. "I don't want nothing to happen to that little boy. I love that kid."

Kaitlin figured that at least was probably the truth. Maybe she'd been imagining things. Jasper had been with the McNeals for months—since Papa McNeal had been injured when Rio was taken.

"Then I showed up," Parker said, his tone full of restraint. "Another close call."

"Too close," Jasper said, shuffling around on his big feet. "I need to get back in with Papa McNeal."

"Go," Kaitlin said, her gaze moving from Melody back to Jasper. Had she been wrong about the gentle giant?

"Let us know how he's doing," Parker whispered after Jasper hurried up toward Papa McNeal's room.

"Yes, sir."

Melody moved close to Kaitlin. "Do you still suspect him?"

"I don't know. He just startled me and then everything happened after that. Maybe I'm just being paranoid."

"Or intuitive," Melody replied. "I'll run a check on him, but we all know Slade had him thoroughly vetted."

Kaitlin turned to check on Caleb. "He's asleep and Warrior is guarding him. Let's go to the den."

When they'd all settled down, she faced Parker. "Have you heard from Slade?"

The detective leaned forward on his chair. "I talked to him about a half hour ago. He was afraid something was up so I took off to the woods to help him, but he insisted I come here instead. He was supposed to call for backup. The chatter on the radio indicated help was on the way."

Kaitlin prayed Slade had received that help. "He always goes by the book. I hope he did that tonight."

Melody nodded and gave Kaitlin an encouraging smile. "And you did everything right by checking in with me. That's why I got here right behind Parker."

"Thank you both," Kaitlin said, too shaky to say much else.

"Parker, you have to find Slade. Caleb's asking for him."

Before Parker could respond, they heard a vehicle pulling into the driveway. Parker got up, his weapon drawn, and peeped through a blind slat. "It's Slade."

Kaitlin sank back on the couch, her head in her hands.

"Thank you, Lord."

* * *

Slade heard the front door of his house opening and looked up to find Kaitlin rushing down the steps and into his arms.

He grabbed her, holding tight with his good arm, her sweet warmth engulfing him. "Are you all right? Caleb? Is Caleb all right? And Papa?"

"We're all fine. A little shaken but okay." She stepped back, then gasped when she looked at the blood all over his shirt. "But you're not. What happened?"

"Gunshot. Through and through." He took her hand. "Let's get inside."

She held tight, her arm going around his waist as they hurried in the door. "He's hurt," she hissed to Parker.

Parker nodded. "I heard the dispatch call, but I didn't want to alarm you unless I heard more." He let out a breath, his gaze on Slade. "Glad to see you're still in one piece."

"I'm fine," Slade replied, shaking his head. "The paramedics took a look and wrapped it for me."

"You need a doctor," Kaitlin insisted, her hand touching on the gauze around his arm and shoulder. "You're still bleeding."

He chuckled at that. "I bled all over the woods so this is nothing. They gave me a shot and some pills to stop infection," he said, grimacing as he sank into a chair and handed Kaitlin the bottle from his pocket. "I've had worse."

Melody cast an uncertain look at Parker. Her fiancé shrugged. "The man's stubborn, what can I say? Slade, what happened?"

"You're taking a pill," Kaitlin said. Then she rushed to the kitchen and got him a glass of water.

Slade took the water Kaitlin handed him, figuring it would save time by not arguing. "I'm going to check on my son and then I'll come back and explain."

Kaitlin's gaze held his, but she moved out of the way.

Slade headed to Caleb's room, a great relief washing over him when he saw Warrior curled up with his little boy. Then he peeked in on Papa. Chief was ever present at the foot of the bed. Jasper lifted his head up. "It's been a bad night, Captain McNeal. But we're all safe and accounted for in here. Papa never heard a thing. He's sleeping pretty soundly tonight."

"Thank you, Jasper. Try to rest."

Slade came back into the den and sank down on the nearest chair. "Long night. I saw Frears cruising through town, so I followed him. Went to an abandoned warehouse on the west side of town, near some old factories. Black van pulled up, probably from around back, after Frears's car went into a garage in the warehouse. Guess who emerged and got in the van?"

"Frears?" Parker asked.

"Ski Mask Man, aka Dante Frears. I should have called for backup right then but I didn't want to tip 'em off. So I followed them to the Lost Woods. They had Rio." He stopped, gritted his teeth. "They were back at the dig site, trying to get Rio to alert to something."

"Did you go after them?" Kaitlin asked, clearly frightened for him.

"Got close, so close I'm pretty sure Rio caught my scent. Didn't have time to do much else after that. Frears got a call that someone was snooping up at the road."

"That could have been me," Parker said. "Sherlock and I were coming to find you."

"But I told you to come here instead." He looked

around, the tension in the room palpable. "What happened here, anyway?"

"Long story there, too," Parker retorted, his tone grim. "I got here in time to scare away another prowler. Jasper was in the kitchen and I think the prowler saw him and almost ran right into me when Jasper went to the door. Sent Sherlock after him and ordered him to halt, but he jumped the fence before Sherlock could get in a good bite. I fired a couple shots, but missed."

Kaitlin glanced from Slade to Parker. Slade thought he saw a warning in her eyes, but he was probably too tired to function. "Is there something else I need to know?"

Kaitlin shook her head. "No. I'm still kind of shaken." Another round of cryptic glances. She glanced over her shoulder, then whispered, "Jasper scared me when I found him in the hallway, but I'm glad he was in the kitchen when the intruder showed up. I overreacted toward him earlier. Just nerves."

Melody went to a table and picked up a bag. "Sherlock chased them over the fence, but nabbed a scrap of clothing." She handed Slade the paper bag with an evidence tag already on it. "Look familiar?"

Slade looked up, his gaze latching onto Kaitlin's. "Yeah. Black silk." Was this what she was so wired about?

"So if the intruder was here, wearing the black jumpsuit, how could Ski Mask Man be Dante Frears?"

Slade glared at Parker. "I saw someone come out of that warehouse wearing all black, mask and everything. Just as Kaitlin described it, exactly what I saw the day he tried to kidnap her."

Parker tapped the arm of his chair. "Can you be sure it was him? Or a decoy of some sort?"

Slade knew the answer to that. "I can't be sure, no. But I never saw Dante come back out. Could he have stayed behind, waiting for a report? Yeah, I guess so."

But he'd heard Dante's voice out in those woods. He was almost certain of that. Had Frears spotted him, too?

Kaitlin got up to pace by the empty fireplace. "Maybe they all wear black ski masks and jumpsuits when they go out at night to wreak havoc."

Slade held a hand to his aching head. "I heard him talking. I know his voice. He had time to leave the woods, but he could have sent someone after me. I heard someone traipsing through the woods with Rio. I know it was Rio by the way he snarled and whimpered." He hesitated. "I thought I had Frears on me. Someone shone a bright light in my face, but then we heard shouts and canines barking. They ran away."

"And you thought that was Frears?" Melody asked.

"I was sure it was him, coming to—" He stopped, lifted his gaze back to Kaitlin.

"Coming to kill you," she said, her hand going to her throat.

"I'll never know. They got away." He let out a tired breath. "But I did find one thing tonight. I dug all around where we found that cocaine and I hit on something metal."

"What was in it?" Parker asked.

"I don't know. I heard somebody coming, so I covered it up and tried to get out of sight. Then somebody started shooting and I got hit." He touched his injured arm. Almost got me good. I backtracked through the woods until reinforcements arrived."

Melody jotted her own notes. "Did you go back to the dig site?"

Slade let out another breath. "Took a whole team back to verify what I'd found. It's a small metal box—locked—and it's now safe with the crime scene team. We should know what they found first thing in the morning."

Kaitlin whirled to stare down at him. "Well, maybe they'll leave us alone now, at least."

Slade hated to disappoint her. "Frears won't ever leave me alone. This has become too personal for both of us. We have what they've been looking for now, but I don't know what that is yet." He gritted his teeth. "I have to confront him before he kills Rio and probably anyone who's crossed his path, including you."

"So you'll keep going after him, in spite of what almost happened tonight?" She pointed to his arm. "You got shot, Slade. Your son was crying for his daddy and I couldn't tell him where you were or what you were doing. I was so terrified, I almost let Warrior loose on Parker. Maybe you should let Dante Frears go. Let him take whatever he wanted so badly, and ask someone else to take over this case."

Slade saw the hurt in her eyes, saw the fear and the pain, but he wouldn't lie to her or paint her a pretty picture. "I'm sorry, but I can't do that. The man is a criminal. A sick, sadistic criminal who's supposed to be my friend. He made this personal, but I'll make him pay. I have to bring him in. It's my job, Kaitlin."

Parker and Melody glanced at each other and both hurriedly stood. "We'll...uh...go make some coffee and sandwiches," Melody said as she scooted past them.

Kaitlin barely acknowledged their friends. She stared

down at him, her hazel eyes bright with despair. "I know this is your job and...you're so close to bringing Frears in. But that's scaring me as badly as knowing the man's after me." She shrugged, folded her arms like a shield. "He's already tried to mess with my head. He told me you always put work first, but I understand that's your duty. It doesn't mean I have to like it."

Her words, spoken with such conviction, slapped him with a sharp hiss of reality, left him heartbroken.

His dead wife had said pretty much the same thing, but in a much harsher way.

And Dante, his so-called best friend, had warned Kaitlin about the same thing. "I think he's messing with both of us. If he spotted me tonight, then things have just gone up a notch."

Kaitlin folded her arms and blinked back tears. "I don't know how much more I can take." When she looked up at him, her heart was in her hand. "I can't lose you, too, Slade. Not when—"

"Not when we've just begun to know each other," he finished. "What am I supposed to do?" he ground out, hoping she'd think about what she'd just said. He was falling for Kaitlin but he'd always believed she understood how things were, regarding his job. Maybe she didn't, after all.

"You're supposed to do your job, of course. Just don't get so carried away with anger and bitterness that you forget what's important. Your son loves you and...other people care about you, too."

Slade tugged her arms apart and held her hands in his. "I'm going to finish this—for my son, and for everyone. Especially for you, so you can feel safe again." And yet, he couldn't plan a future when he didn't know how this would end. "Kaitlin? Please. Listen to me. I care about my family. I care about you, but—"

She bobbed her head, her eyes searching his. "You've gone beyond your duty in protecting me, but I need this to end so *we* can finish what *we've* started. Promise me you'll be careful."

Slade winced at the throbbing pulse in his arm. "I promise."

"I know you care, but don't go after him for revenge. Go after him for justice. Don't become like him, Slade."

Slade pulled her into his arms. "I'm not him."

"No, you've got a lot of reasons to live." She lifted up, gave him a gentle kiss on the lips, then turned and went back down the hallway toward Caleb's room.

Chapter Seventeen

Two days later, Slade walked out to the training yard to talk to Kaitlin. He'd been busy with the details of this case and what they'd discovered in the woods, plus surveillance on Dante Frears. He hoped he'd given her enough time to get past her fears and concerns. She'd been staying at Francine's house and only talked to him when he called to check on her. But even those sparse conversations consisted of him asking questions and Kaitlin answering with a yes or no.

He missed her already and he hated this protective wall she'd put between them. Kaitlin wasn't running away from him. She was running from the pain of her past. And the fear of a future with him. Slade couldn't blame her. He didn't have much to offer. He loved his work and after Angie's death, he'd given up on a personal life other than taking care of his son. Still, he wanted to clear the air with Kaitlin. And he needed a favor from her, anyway.

She couldn't run if they were face-to-face.

"Hey," he said as he approached her.

She was wearing her standard dark khaki training

uniform, but she still looked cute to Slade. Better than cute. He'd walked out here time after time over the years and chatted with all the handlers, but these days he was much more focused on only one. That sure was a big change in his life. His feelings for Kaitlin colored his every thought, but he couldn't tell her how he felt until he had Dante Frears behind bars.

"Hello." She glanced at his arm where he'd been shot, then went right on with her work. Warrior cleared a hurdle, then went through some wooden slates on an obstacle course. Kaitlin rewarded him with a play toy and some encouraging words after he'd cleared the obstacles in record time.

"He's improving every day," Slade said to break the ice.

The look she gave him was heated—even hotter than the near one-hundred-degree temperature. But even through that scorching heat, he saw a tenderness. "He's had a lot of extracurricular practice."

So she wanted to be all business and no forgiveness. Fine. He'd have to talk personal with her later. Maybe it was better if she stayed away until all of this was over.

"Look, I guess you've heard what we found in that metal box in the woods."

She watched the other dogs but her response was neutral. "I heard. And I also heard you haven't released that information to the public."

"No. That amount of diamonds—worth millions—would bring out all kinds of criminals. Explains why they needed Rio. Nobody knew where exactly they were buried and even after following that number code we found on Daniel's watch, they still didn't find anything.

We're keeping a lid on things so we can smoke out Frears."

She frowned at the trees. "Diamonds. No surprise that all the kidnappings and killing happened. No surprise that you're still trying to bring in your best friend. This is a big case."

She wasn't making this easy, but he needed her help. "Time to try a new tactic. I need Warrior for one more after-school operation, if you don't mind."

That got her attention. Ordering Warrior to stay, she tossed a chew bone at the big dog then pinned Slade with a gaze. "What kind of operation?"

Slade took off his cap and replaced it on his head. "I know you won't like this but... I need to take him to see Dante. I need to see if Warrior can sense if Rio has been in that penthouse and test Warrior for a reaction to Dante."

She rubbed one hand down the other arm as if to ward off the shivers. "You know he will. That's like asking the man to shoot both of you on the spot."

"Dante is too smart to make a move. He can't be sure what I know, and he has no idea we have the diamonds. He might have seen me in those woods the other night, but he can't admit that without revealing that he was there, too."

"Or that he sent someone there so he could come back to your house and kidnap me."

"True. Either way I need to put Warrior to the test, but I'll really be putting Frears to the test. I'm hoping to push him over the edge so he'll get careless with his next move."

Her cautious guard went down. "That's too dangerous."

Glad that she still cared, Slade remained neutral, too. "I'm tired of this standoff. I'm upping the stakes. I'm going after him instead of him terrorizing my team again."

"What are you going to do?"

Another wash of relief. She seemed to be warming up to the idea. "I'm going to take Warrior to Dante's house. If Rio is there or has been there recently, Warrior should alert. And if he recognizes Dante as the man who tried to take you, he should alert to that, too. But Frears won't recognize any of the signs that I can read."

She pushed at her bangs then tossed her ponytail. "And let's say Warrior alerts differently than you've planned. What if he shows hostility toward Dante? What are you going to do then?"

"I'll tell Dante he saw a squirrel outside or that he smells the cat. Warrior is still a trainee, after all. I can handle that."

She shifted back, then glanced out over the yard toward the spot where she'd been held captive. "Or you could get shot again."

Hearing the little catch of fear in her voice, Slade didn't dare make a move. Not here. But he couldn't help his next words. "Kaitlin, please look at me."

She raised her head, her gaze hitting him with a fierce emotion that mirrored his own. "My mother died because she wanted to help a drug addict, or would have, if the man had been in his right mind. She thought if she tried to reason with him, she could save both herself and him. Instead, he killed her without any qualms." Her lower lip trembled. "If Dante is behind all of this, then he's not in his right mind. He'll do what he has to do to survive. I can't watch you die trying to bring him in. I can't, Slade. It's not fair. We...we need more time."

Not caring who saw them, Slade took the two steps toward her. "I'm not going to die. I promise."

She pushed away when he reached out his hand. "You can't promise that. No one can."

"I'll do my best," he replied, his heart thudding in his chest. Hating the hurt in her words, he said, "For you, Kaitlin. For you and for Caleb, I will do my best to end this. I want so much, for us and for Caleb. You were right. I have a lot to live for."

"Do you, really?" Her expression hardened again. "Do you want that for us *more* than you want to bring in The Boss?"

He couldn't answer her question without being honest, but when he hesitated too long, she took it the wrong way.

"This is why we have to cool things until...after you bring him in."

"You're asking for the impossible," he said hoarsely. "You have no idea what I went through the day that madman tried to take you. No idea what I've been going through each time a new homicide report comes through on this case, each time someone else is threatened or abducted. The man probably killed my wife, too, because he wanted me dead."

Her frown softened, but her words were low and quiet. "My point exactly. I'm not asking you to give up. I only ask that you stay focused and careful."

"I am careful, for the reasons you've named." He held his hands on his hips, then shook his head. "I sat there in those woods the other night and prayed—yes, Kaitlin, prayed—that God would spare you and my son. I want the same things you want, believe me." He touched his hand to her face. "Right now, I have to do my job and as head of this department, I'm commandeering K-9 Officer Trainee Warrior to help me."

Tears sprang to her eyes, but she stood tall. Calling to Warrior, she signaled for the canine to go with Slade. After checking Warrior's protective vest, she said, "Take care of him. Remember, I did train him for exactly this purpose." She gave Warrior an encouraging pat on the head, then glanced back at Slade. "I understand your job, Slade. But no one ever trained me on how to stop my heart from breaking. And I'm a slow learner. I made a mistake—caring too much about you and Caleb when I can't be sure of our future."

Slade wanted to tell her it was no mistake, that he cared more for her than he had for any other woman, including his dead wife. But she marched back out toward the obstacle course while he stood there thinking about all the obstacles they had yet to overcome.

"Slade, come on in, brother."

Slade stood back, taking in the spacious, elegantly arranged penthouse, his mind wondering what secrets were hidden behind this glamorous facade. He knew Dante was alone since he'd had a uniform watching the building all week.

"I hope you don't mind. I promised I'd bring Warrior by and today seemed like a good time."

Dante stepped aside, his smile indulgent, his icy eyes turning crystal. Then he slapped Slade very near where Slade's shirt covered his bandaged wound. "As good a time as ever. Yvette is out shopping—what else? And the nanny took Emily to the park before dinner. We have the house to ourselves."

Invitation or warning? Slade had already commanded Warrior to stay and be quiet so the dog did exactly as he was told, but Slade had felt an immediate tension in the leash when Warrior spotted Dante. Warrior would show him the truth when all else failed. Trained K-9 dogs didn't know how to lie. They only knew to follow orders or pick up on different scents. But the big dog didn't sniff the air too much so that might mean Rio had never been inside the penthouse. If Slade knew Dante, his so-called friend was probably housing Rio somewhere else in a place that no one would connect to him. But even with surveillance at both the old warehouse and the Lost Woods, Slade still hadn't managed to pin anything on Dante yet.

He hoped this visit would at least verify his gut feeling—that his friend was a high-level drug lord. And he hoped Dante would see that the entire department was onto him now. Slade wanted to provoke him into becoming desperate. It was the only way to crack this case.

"Your trainee seems well behaved," Dante said. He stepped back into the room and casually stood behind a chair. "It's a hot day out there. C'mon in and we'll have a nice, cool drink."

Dante had yet to pet the animal, which Slade found odd, but then Dante was such a germaphobe, he might think Warrior was dirty or something. When Dante went around the kitchen counter, Slade saw that as putting another barrier between them, too.

Dante took his time slicing a lime for his drink. He poured Slade a mineral water then made himself a stronger drink. When he looked up, his face was a portrait of restraint and polite interest. "So this is your new superstar?"

"Yes," Slade said, glancing around, "this is Warrior. He's what we call an all-purpose officer. He's been trained to pick up on both air and ground scents. He can detect the scent of drugs, even if they are covered with another scent, and unearth bodies, as well, no matter how long they've been dead. If I give him a piece of material or an item, he can track that scent to the person those things belong to."

Dante remained impassive, studious, fascinated. But he stayed behind the big marble counter, his hands holding to the marble with a heavy, white-knuckled grip. "Impressive. Would you care for another drink? Something stronger, if you're not on the clock, of course."

"No. I don't have much time. Just thought you'd like to see where some of your funding went. Warrior is an excellent officer. He's already proven himself several times."

Dante sipped at his own drink. "In what way?"

Slade gave his friend-turned-nemesis a direct stare. "He's been on protection duty a lot lately. Involving a case that I can't seem to solve."

Dante drained his cocktail and immediately rinsed and dried the glass, his actions so methodical, Slade's stomach muscles clenched. He smiled over at Slade. "You'll figure things out. You always do."

Slade never took his eyes off Dante. "I intend to do exactly that." Then he patted Warrior on the head. "Would you like me to give you a quick demonstration on some of his skills?"

Dante glanced at the kitchen clock. "Sure. Why not? I have some time before Yvette and I go out to dinner." He came around the counter, then leaned down to reach a knuckle out to Warrior. "Show me what you've got, boy."

Warrior did a low growl and went for Dante's hand.

Anger colored Dante's face a pale red. Stepping back to stare at his hand where Warrior had nipped it, he glared at Slade with a white-hot coolness. "Hey, what was that? I thought you said he's a trained officer."

"Warrior, sit." Slade let the leash go slack and faked a puzzled frown. "Sorry about that. I'll give a report to his trainers. He's still got some issues with breaking behavior. We'll keep working on that."

Dante shrugged, then grinned. "Don't we all have issues? Why don't we try again? Let him loose, Slade. Go ahead."

What was this—truth or dare? Slade unleashed Warrior and told him to search, his gaze locked with Dante's. Not sure what would happen since he hadn't let Warrior sniff anything in particular, Slade waited in the hot silence. The big dog took off through the plush house, his paws hitting the marble hall tiles in a spin. After a few tense seconds, Warrior returned and sat at Slade's feet. Apparently, Dante's penthouse was so sparkling clean even Warrior hadn't picked up on anything suspicious. But he had almost bitten Dante even when he had been under an order to stay.

That told Slade everything he needed to know.

"Glad I'm not hiding anything here," Dante said on a chuckle. "Or maybe he's just not quite ready, huh?"

Slade forced out his own low laugh. "Maybe. But he's getting there. I have no doubt that he'll be at the top of his game when I finally apprehend the next criminal."

Dante leaned back against the counter, his eyes as

cold as the white marble behind him. "Well, you be sure to let me know when that happens. I'm all for fighting crime in Sagebrush."

"Thanks, guess we'll get out of your way." Slade reached out to shake Dante's hand. "I do appreciate the funding. Sorry about that little nip Warrior tried to give you."

"Not a problem. Maybe it was a love bite." Dante followed them to the door, always staying a few feet behind. "I hope you find what you're looking for, Slade."

Slade turned, his sunglasses in his hand. He put them on, adjusted them. "I intend to do just that, old friend."

After he was out of the building and down in his vehicle, Slade let out a breath of relief and frustration. He'd thought long and hard about letting Warrior smell that torn piece of black silk before they'd gone into the penthouse. But…that might have tipped his hand too much, so he hadn't let the K-9 sniff it. But it didn't take a lot of investigative sense to know that the conversation he'd just had with Dante Frears had held a whole lot of undercurrents.

They'd just upped the ante.

The next morning, Slade was reading over some reports when Melody knocked on his door. "Got a minute?"

"Sure." He closed the folder he'd been staring at, then rubbed his tired eyes. "What's up?"

"I got back the results for the DNA test," she said on a low whisper.

Slade got up and shut the door. "And?"

"They're a match. One of the hair samples you collected from Frears's brush had an intact root bulb. Same with the hair samples I found from Daniel's things. My friend at the state crime lab verified it this morning."

"Dante Frears is Daniel Jones's father." Slade released a sharp breath. "Wow. That sure puts a new wrinkle in this entire case. Jim Wheaton killed that boy and now he's dead. Did he turn on The Boss? Or did The Boss turn on everyone else?"

Melody nodded, then looked down at her hands. "I think they all double-crossed him—his son and his management team. One of them hid those diamonds and he's been scrambling to find them all this time."

Slade rubbed a hand down his face. "That tells me he had a lot of motive and opportunity for killing a lot of people, including your sister. I'm sorry for that."

Melody looked down at her hands. "I don't know why he killed Sierra, but I'm thinking she must have pushed him too far—maybe making demands or threatening to tell his wife. Who knows? I just know I've lost a sister and a nephew and while this verification doesn't change that, it gives me a reason to keep searching for the truth."

"And we'll get that truth," Slade vowed, getting up to come around the desk. "I'm close, Melody. Very close. In fact, I'm going back out to that dig site today with a team, to see if we can draw Frears out. It's a long shot, but he doesn't know we already have the diamonds." He shrugged. "For all he knows, his diamonds might still be in those woods. Whoever was out there the other night, they didn't have time to search. Frears will be back. He won't give up, even if he does think he got to me by shooting me."

"I hope you're right," Melody said, getting up to

shake Slade's hand. "I know you went to bat for me on this DNA thing. I won't forget that, Captain. Ever."

Slade accepted her gratitude in silence.

She turned to leave, then pivoted back. "Oh, by the way, I didn't find anything outstanding on the background check we did on Jasper. Kaitlin can be rest assured on that one. He doesn't have any sort of record."

"Kaitlin suspected Jasper?"

Melody came back to stand by his desk. "He startled her the other night. She said he was acting weird, but she told me to let it go. I didn't, of course. Never hurts to be sure. I think she might have overreacted, but better safe than sorry."

Confused, Slade put on a blank front. "Thanks. I'll let her know."

After Melody left, Slade sat back down, shock numbing him. He remembered Kaitlin saying Jasper had scared her, but... Jasper also scared away the intruder. That didn't add up. Now he could reassure her that they'd cleared Jasper.

But right now, back to this latest revelation. He'd hoped beyond hope that maybe Melody's assumptions about Dante were off base. But... DNA didn't lie. Once they arrested Frears, they could do another DNA test to use as evidence, this time by the book. With all the murder charges lined up against him, Frears could be put away for a very long time. Or worse.

As much as it disgusted him, that arrest couldn't come soon enough for Slade.

Chapter Eighteen

"Don't you think you're being a little unfair?"

Kaitlin checked for traffic, then pulled out onto the road before glancing over at Francine. "About Slade? No, I'm not being unfair. I can't take things any further until he solves this case."

Francine reached back to pat Warrior's head, then made a face at Kaitlin. "But you told me you understood about a police officer's life, that you could deal. It's hard work and it's a tough life."

"Yes, I did tell you that," Kaitlin replied, glad to be on the way back to Francine's house. After her friend had alerted Slade as to their whereabouts, they'd had a long practice session with Warrior at a busy nearby park with lots of open spaces and people all around, but now she was ready for a shower and a good Saturday night movie, with popcorn and chocolate. Francine had already rented the movie and they planned to order a pizza.

It beat sitting at her house alone.

"So you understand that Slade can't stop this now.

He's trying very hard to resolve this. You've never been judgmental before. I think there's more to this."

They'd discussed this most of the afternoon. "I only asked him to be careful and to consider his reasons for doing this. Technically, he's a K-9 officer. His only duty is when the situation calls for him and his partner to take action. This is an investigation. Melody Zachary is already involved in it. Most of the department is involved in it. But Slade has taken things to a whole new level and that scares me."

"A dangerous level," Francine replied. "And that's the part that bothers you, right?"

Kaitlin nodded. "Yes. I'm being selfish. I want Slade to be safe, for Caleb's sake."

"And for you, too." A statement this time, no question asked.

"Okay, yes, for me." Kaitlin slowed down as they neared the Lost Woods, memories hitting her like dry pine needles. Finally, she let out a sigh. "I think I'm in over my head."

"You've fallen for him."

"Yes."

She could admit that now that she'd pushed Slade away. "I tried not to fall in love, but...we were forced together so much because of this thing, because I was almost kidnapped by a lunatic. And the other night, Slade got shot and I was so afraid someone was coming after Caleb I almost let Warrior attack Parker. I've lost focus because I'm so worried."

"That kind of trauma brings out all sorts of emotions," Francine said, her tone gentle now. "Are you sure you're truly in love? Maybe once things settle down—"

"I'll still love him," Kaitlin said. "I can see that now.

And that's why I got so upset the other night. I realized I care too much, too fast. He got shot, Franny. I mean, he could have died."

Her friend stared over at her. "It's hard when you love someone, hard to let them go, hard to let go of control. You loved your mama and you couldn't save her. So you had to turn your pain over to God." She blew out a breath. "Don't you think you need to do that with your fears for Slade? Slade is close to busting this thing wide open from what I hear. And he's got the backing of the entire police force. Let him finish what he started and let God take over where you can't deal, okay?"

Kaitlin gripped the steering wheel. "I'm trying. I've prayed and hoped and waited. My life has been in turmoil for weeks now and it's the same as when I lost my mother. But this is Slade, a man I've always admired. I don't even know what it's like to have a normal date with the man."

"Then you have to hope for that day, a normal day where you and Slade can relax and really have some time together." She punched at Kaitlin's arm. "But you can't do that if you're kind of avoiding the man."

"I hate it when you're right," Kaitlin retorted. "I'll call him when we get home and maybe we can work this out."

As they neared Francine's house, Kaitlin's cell rang. Grabbing it with one hand while she slowed down, she said, "Kaitlin."

"Your dog is in the woods."

"Who is this?"

"A concerned citizen. You'll find him tied up on the Southside path, but you'd better hurry before they come back."

The connection went dead. Kaitlin slowed the van and stared straight ahead. The Lost Woods were about a mile up the road.

Francine gave her a questioning glance. "Well?"

"They said I'd find my dog in the woods. On the Southside path." Tossing her phone down, she said, "I'm going to look."

"No." Francine shook her head. "You know the protocol. You need to call someone. We need backup."

"I don't have time. I have to hurry."

A few minutes later, she looked over at the Lost Woods, a shiver moving down her spine. A movement on one of the paths caught her eye.

A dog.

"Rio!" Kaitlin pulled the van off the road in a skidding stop. "Rio, right there on the path. It's him."

Francine squinted and peered out the front windshield. "Are you sure? I mean, it could be a trap."

Kaitlin glanced to one of the trails leading into the woods, her blood pressure shooting up. "I don't know. The person said to hurry because they'd be back soon. But I'm going to look."

"I'm going with you," Francine replied, already opening her door.

Kaitlin scanned the road and woods. "No, stay here with the dogs. If it's him, I'll call out to you."

"I don't like this," Francine said nervously. "Take Warrior with you."

Kaitlin hopped out. "I don't want to scare him away. I'll be okay and I'll be quick." She started walking toward the path. "Rio? Rio, come. I'm here, boy. It's okay. Come on out where I can see you."

* * *

He had to try one more time. The woods had gone cold as far as criminals were concerned, but Slade felt a showdown coming.

In the Lost Woods.

Slade knew he was breaking a lot of rules, coming out here to these woods alone. But he was on his own time tonight and he'd waited until his shift was over, so it shouldn't affect anyone else. He'd gotten so close to Dante Frears and Rio the other night, he could have whistled and brought both of them running. He needed one more chance. Just one more.

No one outside of the department knew Slade and the crime scene team had found that box full of diamonds. Dante would come back here over and over and he'd get more and more desperate with each trip. Slade needed this to end or he'd never win Kaitlin back. His getting shot the other night had given her cold feet, relationship-wise. He couldn't blame her. He'd had surveillance on these woods and the warehouse since the night he'd been shot and no one had shown back up. Too much heat.

Tonight, he'd canceled the surveillance and told his team to stay away. He wanted to flush out Dante Frears. So he'd had a detective in an unmarked car drop him off up the road. He'd told the detective to wait for him by the car, just in case. Then he'd hiked through the woods, alone, with no K-9 backup. He had a hunch Frears would be here soon. He knew Dante better than anyone and patience had never been one of Dante's virtues.

He'd take his chances and try to lure Frears back to the woods.

And if that didn't work, he could very well be out

of options. So he waited till dusk and then hiked to the dig spot and stared into the turned earth. If Dante came back here with Rio, the dog would possibly alert to several familiar scents left by officers and the crime scene team. That would fool Frears into thinking he was onto something.

Slade wasn't sure what would happen after that. He'd either confront Frears or try to get evidence, anything, to prove the man was The Boss. He had the piece of black silk logged in as evidence. If they could match that scrap of material to anyone who came out here, they'd have the beginnings of a case.

So Slade waited and watched and prayed. He'd been praying a lot lately. Mostly for patience, but also for his son and for his father. He'd been caught between the two of them and he had to admit he had not been a happy father or a good son. Too late, he saw the bitterness that had driven him since Angie's death.

His son needed love, not bitterness.

"Time to change that, Lord." He nodded to himself. He had Kaitlin to thank for that. She'd shown him how her faith had helped her but…she still had a crippling fear of being hurt again. Now it was Slade's turn to help her.

"Help me to understand her, Lord. Help me to make her see that we can be good for each other."

Slade's stilted prayers ran a silent loop inside his head while he listened to the forest sounds settling into the night. He'd told the detective who'd agreed to wait for him to park underneath an old shed on the back side of the woods. Frears had come in on the other side last time he was here, but Slade had warned a couple of cruisers to be on the lookout, too. Frears was unpredictable and growing more and more desperate. Slade didn't intend to get shot again.

He wondered why it had to come down to this. Why had his life gone one way and Dante's the other? And why hadn't his friend come to him, instead of turning on him?

When he heard a car door slam shut and angry voices carrying through the trees, he knew the time had come for a showdown.

Kaitlin stood near the tree line, on a worn path into the woods. She could see Francine waiting in the van. When she heard a rustling, she called out again. "Rio, come."

She heard a yelp, then watched in amazement as the bramble parted and Rio slowly stumbled his way through the bushes. But when Kaitlin saw the K-9, her heart did a tumble. "Oh, Rio. Poor baby."

The animal's once shimmering coat was now a dull burnished brown, the color of old rust. He was gaunt and hollow-eyed, but when he lifted his nose and sniffed the air, Kaitlin saw the spark of recognition in his eyes. "Rio, it's me, boy. Come."

Rio was heading toward her when she heard footsteps crashing through the pine needles and bramble.

Kaitlin didn't want to leave the dog. "Rio, come."

Rio advanced another few steps but the pounding of footsteps didn't stop.

"C'mon, boy."

Then she saw why the K-9 couldn't make it out of the woods. Someone had tied him up with a very long rope. Whimpering, Rio strained at the rope, but couldn't get any farther.

Kaitlin took another look at the dog, thought about trying to untie him, but then decided she did need backup. She ran across the road and jumped back in the SUV.

"It's Rio, but he's tied up. I heard footsteps. I need to call Slade."

She had her phone in her lap and her finger on call when someone tapped on her window. Shocked, Kaitlin glanced up and saw the face from her nightmares.

A man wearing a black ski mask and a loose, silky black jumpsuit.

Francine screamed and Warrior started barking. Then Kaitlin's door flew open and before she could do anything but drop her phone, the man dragged her out of the vehicle, a glove-clad hand covering her mouth while her attacker kicked the door shut again. She smelled the leather she remembered from the first kidnapping attempt, her stomach roiling with fear and nausea. Had she hit Call before she'd dropped the phone? She couldn't remember.

Francine. What had they done with Francine? What about Warrior?

She could hear him barking and snarling inside the vehicle. Would he obey a hand signal? She could try. It was her only hope. But when she twisted toward the door, another man dressed in black pushed in front of her. Someone else stood at the back of the vehicle.

"Let the dog out when I tell you to," the man holding her shouted to the guy at the back of the van. "And hurry. I need that stupid animal."

Stunned, Kaitlin stopped fighting and relaxed. If she could make eye contact with Warrior and give him the signal to go, maybe he'd run away into the woods.

Ski Mask Man must have read her thoughts. "I'm going to remove my hand from your mouth, sweetheart. Tell the dog to back off, or I'll shoot him and your friend."

Kaitlin bobbed her head, then searched for Francine in the approaching dusk. The man standing by the van had a gun pressed to the glass and aimed at Francine. Kaitlin gave Francine a long stare, hoping the other trainer would follow orders. Francine's look of sheer terror trembled to a calm and she gave Kaitlin a slight nod.

Had she managed to get the call for help in?

"Tell the dog to calm down," the man growled into her ear, his breath hot on her neck. "And don't do anything you'll regret."

She nodded, already regretting a lot of things. When he removed his hand, Kaitlin took in a big gulp of clean air. "Stay," she called to the barking dog. "Stay, Warrior."

Warrior immediately stopped barking but stood at attention, staring out the back window of the SUV, his whole body quivering, his ears up.

"That's good. Nice." If she had any doubts as to who this man was, they all evaporated in the dry heat. She recognized Dante Frears's calm, cultured voice. "Now, I want you to get the dog out of the vehicle, okay? But I don't want him in attack mode, understand?"

She bobbed her head again, glancing at Francine. Her friend sat frozen to her seat but she didn't look as scared now. Maybe Francine would be able to keep her cool and get out of this alive.

He motioned to the man at the back of the vehicle. The other masked man opened the back hatch.

"Now."

"Warrior, come. Stay."

Warrior jumped out and came to sit by Kaitlin's feet, but she knew the dog well enough to recognize his tightly coiled position. Warrior was on go to attack. Just one word from her.

But then they'd kill Francine.

What should she do?

"We're going for a little walk into the woods, sweetheart."

"What about my friend?" she asked.

"I have other plans for her."

"Don't hurt her, please. She's not involved in this."

"But you are, right? Involved, I mean. You're in so thick with McNeal it makes me want to puke."

"Leave him out of this, too. I can help you find what you need in the woods. My dog and I can and then you can just go—"

He leaned in, his mouth close to her ear, his gloved hand stroking her damp hair. "Oh, I wish it were that simple. But it's not. Too bad, though. You're smart and pretty and you almost distracted McNeal enough to let me get on with things. But he's too stubborn to see what's right in front of him."

Hating that she'd practically accused Slade of the same thing, she whispered, "I can distract him again."

"Too late for deals, darlin'. He's waiting in those woods for me, and I intend to give him exactly what he wants."

Kaitlin's heart exploded inside her chest. Warrior was right there with her, but how could she order him to run away when her friend was sitting in the SUV with a gun to her head and Slade was somewhere out in the woods, about to be ambushed?

When Frears pushed her forward, she looked back once toward the SUV and saw the controlled smile on her friend's face as the sun began to set behind the big pines to the west. Kaitlin turned forward, searching for a way to escape. Rio was nowhere to be found now. An eerie wind stalked through the woods, its breeze tearing at the bent and twisted pines and dry-boned oaks, its touch rushing with a cackle through the saplings and sagebrush. She could almost hear the wind whispering a warning. Run, run, run.

If she did try to run, someone might die.

Kaitlin didn't intend to die in these dark woods.

And she didn't intend to get Slade or Francine killed, either, so she prayed that Slade would see them coming and stop this madness before it was too late for them all.

Chapter Nineteen

Too quiet.

After that echo of activity about thirty minutes ago,
Slade hadn't heard a thing except some night creature
foraging through the underbrush. Had he only imagined car doors slamming and voices carrying through
the trees?

No. His gut told him this was it. So he waited, his
mind scrutinizing the details of a case that had kept
him awake on too many lonely nights. He thought about
Kaitlin and how kissing her had made him feel whole
again. Then he remembered her angry words to him,
words full of an underlying fear for him. But her biggest fear was for herself. She was afraid to love again.

And so was he.

Or, he had been. Now he only wished he could tell
her what was in his heart. He loved her. Somehow, Slade
had to make her see that, had to find a way to mend her
heart and his own heart, too.

One more chance. He just needed one more chance
to make things right.

When he heard a definite rustling that sounded like

footfalls over the forest, Slade went into action. He lifted out from behind a tree and listened, the echo of the noises vibrating through the deep woods like a stalking animal. Someone was coming, but he couldn't tell who.

In the end, he didn't have to figure things out.

"Hey, McNeal, you out there?"

Dante Frears.

Slade let out a huff of breath. How had Frears found him?

"I know what you're thinking," Dante shouted, the words distorted and dangerous. "You're wondering how I always manage to stay one step ahead of you, right?"

Slade didn't respond. Let Dante come to him.

"I have watchers, McNeal. Watchers everywhere. It's amazing how easy it can be to bribe people and get them to do exactly what you want them to do." A chuckle, then, "If I can't bribe them, I just knock them out or kill 'em. I didn't kill your detective friend parked to the east, but he'll have a nice lump on his head when he wakes up."

Slade swallowed a lump of disgust and dread, but he didn't speak, didn't breathe.

"Come on, now, Slade. We've fought together enough for you to know I can see in the dark. I know you're here."

The footsteps came closer and Slade heard shuffling. The night creatures scurried away, the nocturnal birds lifted out of their roosts, wings flapping a warning. The wind stilled to a hot, silent blanket that suffocated Slade's senses. Sweat drenched his spine, ran down his face, tickled at his neck. But a cold, hard dread chilled his bones.

"For example," Dante called out, "your girlfriend here is willing to do just about anything I ask just to save your sorry hide."

Silence. Slade swallowed again and prayed, an image of Kaitlin in this madman's arms sickening him.

"Don't believe me, Slade? I have Kaitlin right here, a gun to her head. If you come out and play, I'll let you see her before I kill both of you."

Slade lifted up and stood tall, his weapon at his side, his mind whirling with different ways he could get Kaitlin out of this alive. "What do you want, Dante?"

A harsh cackling laugh filled the still night.

"I want what belongs to me, old friend."

Slade took a deep breath. "Why show your face now? You've managed to avoid this for a long time."

A ragged chuckle grated against the trees. "Frankly, I'm tired of searching. I know you're onto me since you made it a point to bring a search dog into my home, but I also realized I have some leverage now—I've got something you want, so let's just get on with it."

Slade knew what was coming but he bluffed anyway. "Okay, what's the plan?"

A flashlight shone a heavy beam into the night, temporarily blinding Slade. He blinked and searched the dig site. And saw Kaitlin's face shrouded in shadows and light, her eyes centered on him, her expression frozen in a silent scream.

"Kaitlin." He moved toward her, halted, moved again.

"Stay where you are," Dante said, his features shadowed with an eerie yellow light. Another man stood with him, a gun aimed at Kaitlin. "Stay right there and listen, McNeal."

"I'm listening," Slade said, his words shaky, his gaze holding Kaitlin's.

"First, put down the weapon."

Slade lifted the gun high then slowly lowered it to the ground, marking the spot. "Okay. Done."

"Good."

"Next, my friend here is going to throw you a shovel. You have some digging to do, don't you?"

Slade nodded. "If you say so."

Frears chuckled. "Always so agreeable, so consistent." He motioned to another man dressed in dark clothes.

The man brought Slade a shovel. Slade took it, thinking he'd like to bash it over Frears's head.

"Now, before you take that shovel and dig in the same spot you started a few nights ago, I need to let you know I brought you some help."

Dante stepped forward and Slade saw Warrior straining at a leash. The dog was so obedient, Slade hadn't even heard a whimper from him. But then, his trainer was with him and Warrior would do whatever Kaitlin commanded, even if the animal knew something wasn't right. Warrior lifted his head, his nose sniffing the air. He'd recognized Slade.

"I see you finally found a way to get a K-9 to respond to you," Slade replied, his gaze shifting from Kaitlin to Warrior. "What's the deal, Dante? Why have you gone to so much trouble?"

Instead of answering, Dante shoved Kaitlin toward the other man. "Your ace trainer is going to help me find what's mine. You're gonna dig where this dog tells you to dig, got it?"

"Got it." Slade nodded, but it was for Kaitlin's benefit. He'd get them out of this, one way or another.

"I sure hope you've got it," Dante said. "'Cause right about now, one of my guys is waiting in your house for me to say the word. If you try anything, McNeal, he'll get orders to kill everyone inside, understand? So don't send in the cavalry. Otherwise, your papa, your precious son and…that trainer Francine will all die."

Kaitlin gasped and struggled. "You can't do that. Let them go, please. Slade, tell him he can't do that."

"It's okay," he replied, a solid wall of terror slamming down on his nerves so hard he couldn't breathe. "Kaitlin, it'll be okay. Just do as he says."

"Smart man, wise words," Dante said, holding her in front of him. "Now, sweetheart, I want you to take your animal here and let him sniff this material."

He shoved what looked like a piece of clothing toward Kaitlin, then held it back. "This belonged to my son." He looked up at Slade. "My dead son. My dead son who double-crossed me, right along with my most trusted associates. My dead son, McNeal. You remember Daniel? You shot him during a bad raid. I know you were sniffing around my penthouse the other night, trying to find evidence. Well, now you have it."

"I didn't kill your son, Dante," Slade replied, a calm coming over him. "Jim Wheaton fired the kill shot. I saw the ballistics report. We matched the kill gun to him."

"Yeah, well, he's dead, too, isn't he?"

"Yes," Slade said, trying to stall. "You've destroyed everyone who did you wrong. What's left? What can you possibly gain by killing an innocent woman, by hurting an old man and…my son? By forcing a dedicated trainer to do your dirty work?"

Dante stepped closer, using Kaitlin as his shield. "I want to make you suffer the same way I've suffered." He leaned close to Kaitlin, sniffed at her neck. "You and your sanctimonious attitude, your do-good mentality. You could never get that being the good guy doesn't pay, Slade."

Slade inched closer. "So you'll make me pay for that? For doing what I think is right?"

Dante laughed, yanked Kaitlin back. "I'll make you suffer because I know you love this woman. You might not know how to show that love and you certainly never showed Angie any mercy, but…at least you'll feel the same torment I've felt since Daniel died. I've waited for the perfect moment and it's here, my friend."

Slade didn't know how to reason with such a man. "Dante, I didn't kill Daniel. I tried to save him. One of your own put that bullet in him. Don't you think it's time to let it go and end this vendetta?"

"No," Dante shouted, the sound lifting over the trees. "No. I came here for a reason. I want what's mine. I can't wait any longer. You're getting too nosy, too close. It's now or never, brother."

He shoved the material into Kaitlin's hand. "You take that dog and you make him earn his keep. You and Slade are going to find my diamonds or die trying."

He pushed Kaitlin toward Warrior. The big dog growled and let out a sharp bark. Apparently, Warrior recognized that Dante was dangerous, but like a true hero, he'd followed orders. But once Kaitlin had him away from Dante she could let go of the leash….

Slade prayed Kaitlin would make a run for it. He had to tell her, had to warn her. Somehow.

But first, he had to dig for diamonds that were no longer hidden in the ground.

Kaitlin held the old T-shirt to Warrior's nose, her pride in the dog's behavior giving her strength to survive. The rookie K-9 had gone beyond his duty, staying calm in a very adverse situation. She had to do the same. Somehow, she had to make Warrior attack once he'd alerted. Just long enough to either get away or call for help. Francine obviously hadn't been able to get through on the phone since Slade had been taken by surprise. So that left things up to Kaitlin, Warrior and Slade.

"Here, boy," she said, her hand on Warrior's neck. "Get a good whiff, okay? Do your job."

"He'd better do a good job," Dante warned. "I still have that mutt Rio to deal with, and I don't have any qualms about killing him, either."

"You've got nothing to lose, right?" Slade asked, the shovel in his hand, his gaze catching Kaitlin's.

"No, brother. Not much."

"What about your wife and child?"

Dante stomped forward. "You shut up about my family, McNeal."

"Oh, so it's okay for you to take my family hostage, but I can't talk about yours?"

"I said shut up," Dante shouted. "I mean it. I'll order the kill on your whole family right now."

Slade didn't speak, but he kept giving Kaitlin reassuring glances. Was he trying to warn her or get her to make a move?

"Let the dog go," Dante ordered Kaitlin. "I want this over with and done."

She whispered into Warrior's ear, hoping upon hope that she was making the right decision. When she lifted up, she shot Slade one last glance and prayed this would work. If it didn't, Slade's entire family and her friend Francine could all die.

She stood, her heart pumping, her gaze on Slade, the unspoken things between them disappearing in the flashlight's high beam.

I love you, her mind whispered. *Trust me.*

Slade lifted his chin a notch, his gaze holding hers. She could see the same message reflected in his beautiful eyes.

And for once, they were communicating.

"Attack," she screamed to Warrior. The big dog jumped into the air and sailed toward Dante, his growl feral, his teeth showing.

Slade turned with the shovel and hit the first man who came at him. Then he swooped down and grabbed his gun from the ground and rolled with Kaitlin, firing random shots behind him while they escaped into the darkness, Warrior's ferocious barks and angry growls filling the night.

Kaitlin heard a gunshot, a scream and then she heard hurried footsteps. Someone was running away. Warrior's barks filled the night, followed by foul language and angry shouts. Did Dante have a gun? His man had held a gun on her, but the other one had stayed with Francine.

"Get away from me!"

"Frears," Slade whispered as he pulled Kaitlin along the path. "Warrior's taking care of business."

Kaitlin wanted Warrior with them. "We have to go back. We can't leave him!"

"Hold tight," Slade said. He pulled out his phone and made an urgent dispatch call. A hostage situation at his house. After a quick explanation and a plea for the first responders to proceed with caution, he finished. "Get the SWAT team ready, but go in dark. My son and my daddy are in that house, along with my dad's male nurse and one of my trainers."

Then he turned to Kaitlin. "I have to get to Frears."

"I'll go with you."

Slade lifted her up and held her tight for a second. "No, run, Kaitlin. Run as fast as you can to the east. Follow the path out to where the unmarked car is parked. Go and get out of here."

"What about you? What about Warrior?"

"I'll find Warrior. And don't worry about me. Just go."

"I can't leave you, Slade."

"Yes, you can. Do this for me, please." He kissed her, then cupped her face in his hands. "It's just him and me now, Kaitlin. Just go."

"Slade, please?"

He turned back long enough to kiss her one more time. "Get help and get to my house. Take care of Caleb for me."

He took off before she had time to think about what he was really saying to her. Kaitlin stood there, staring into the moonlight, aggressive barking and angry shouts echoing through her mind.

Then she turned and ran into the darkness, the sound of the barking dog drifting toward her. The path wound through the brush but it was hard to see much in the darkness. Limbs and weeds slapped at her arms and legs, insects and spiderwebs hit her in the face, but she kept on going. She didn't stop running until she'd made it to the edge of the woods.

When she spotted a vehicle parked near an old shed, Kaitlin stopped to catch her breath. And looked up to find Dante Frears standing there, waiting for her.

Chapter Twenty

Frears grabbed Kaitlin, twisting her arm behind her back. "Stupid woman. Did you think you could trick me? Did you really think that dog would stop me?"

Kaitlin's breath caught in her throat. "Where's Slade? What have you done with Warrior?"

Already, she could hear sirens off in the distance. How much time did she have?

Dante started moving, pushing her along in front of him. "I don't care where McNeal is. And your faithful companion is gnawing at someone else's leg right now."

The other man. Frears had somehow managed to run away while Warrior went after the man Slade had struck with the shovel. Dante had probably used that man as a shield. But where was Slade?

Willing herself to stay calm, Kaitlin asked, "Did you kill Warrior?"

He laughed at that. "No. Stupid mutt's standing guard over my equally stupid now-ex-employee. Not a very good K-9 officer if you ask me. I knew this car was still here so I figured one of you would come running."

She closed her eyes, resisted him while he shoved her toward the road. "Did you kill Slade?"

Dante gripped her arm, his fingers digging into her flesh. "I told you I don't know where he is, but I intend to find out."

"And his family?"

"Don't worry, sweetheart. I can't pull that switch until I have my diamonds. After that…boom."

Did he mean a bomb? Kaitlin glanced around, frantic for some means of escape. If she could get away now, the backup team would be here in minutes. "What are you doing now?"

Dante jerked her close, his eyes a silvery gray in the moonlight. "I'm going to call your boyfriend, sweetheart. But first, we need to get you out of this heat. This kind of weather can kill a person. Lost in the woods at night, without water. Bugs, snakes, all kinds of sinister creatures."

"Stop it," Kaitlin shouted. "Stop it. You wouldn't be that cruel nor would you leave Slade out there. After all, he has something you need, right?"

He stopped, yanked her close again. "So you know where the diamonds are? You willing to barter on Mc-Neal's life?"

Realizing she'd slipped up, Kaitlin shook her head. "I don't know what you're talking about, I'm just quoting you. We never finished digging."

"Those diamonds aren't in these woods," he said on a winded hiss. "Like I'd fall for that."

"Then why did you try to make us dig?"

He pressed his face close, his eerie eyes shining white. "Once I'd forced Slade to tell me where the diamonds were—those were supposed to be your graves."

Kaitlin thought she'd never find her breath again. Had he killed Slade and dumped him in that spot? Had he already blown up Slade's house and murdered everyone in it?

The sound of approaching sirens screamed with a piercing wail through the night. "What are you going to do next?"

Dante pushed her forward toward the waiting black van. "I'm taking you to Slade's house so you can die with the rest of his family." With each push, his words gritted against her nerves. "I'm sick and tired of all of you."

He jerked open the van and shoved her inside. "Tie her up," he ordered the driver. "And hurry. McNeal has called the whole police department. Like that's gonna stop me."

A man got out and came around the van, then grabbed Kaitlin's hands and started tying them together. Struggling, she shifted on the seat, her right foot hitting on something soft and slinky. Kaitlin glanced down, startled to find yet another black jumpsuit tossed on the floor right by the open door. Did Dante have a whole closetful of these disguises? She sent a covert glance toward the man in the front. Dante was still wearing black and he was busy with his phone. Maybe all of his henchmen wore the same uniform.

"Be still," the man handling her said, his tone low and steady. But she could tell he wanted to hurry and get out of these woods before the authorities arrived.

She only wanted to get out alive. Should she stall and hope the police would find them? Or hurry and pray she could get to Caleb before Dante detonated that bomb?

Caleb needed her.

Kaitlin did as the man asked, sitting up straight and putting her hands up and over to the left so he could focus on tying them together. But while he struggled with the heavy ropes, she slowly shifted her right foot toward the wide, open door and gently pushed the black jumpsuit away and out the door. Maybe someone would find it and take the hint. It was her only chance.

"Hurry up!" Dante shouted. Then he twisted to stare into the back of the long van. "Where is the dog?"

Kaitlin glanced behind her and saw an empty cage. "Rio?"

The young man standing by her hung his head, his dark cap covering his face. "He...got away when I was trying to feed him. Wasn't my fault. He got all agitated and tried to bite me."

"Are you kidding me, really?" Dante lifted his hands in the air. "Get in and drive. I'll deal with you later."

The frazzled underling finished his feeble attempts then slammed the big door and ran around the front of the van. He never noticed the black material lying in a pool on the path out of the woods. Or if he had noticed, he was too afraid to stop and pick it up. The man's hands had trembled as much as Kaitlin's insides were trembling now. Rio had escaped!

Thank you, God, for one bright spot of hope.

Slade's head hurt and his mind moved in a long loop of doubt and worry. He'd at least warned the department about his family and Francine, but he had no way of knowing if Kaitlin had made it out of the woods. Sirens approaching gave him renewed energy.

But he couldn't find Dante Frears.

After spotting Warrior standing guard over the man

he'd hit with the shovel, Slade handcuffed the hurt, moaning man to a tree and called for more backup and the paramedics. Warrior had left several bite marks in the man's leg, but he'd live.

After praising Warrior, Slade turned to the man. "Where did your boss go?"

"Don't know. Got away."

Now what? Slade would have never sent Kaitlin off on her own if he'd thought Frears had escaped. Praying Kaitlin had made it to the detective's car, or that she was somewhere hiding, Slade called to Warrior and rushed through the woods, taking whatever trail he could find.

When he heard barking up ahead on the path, his heart thumped erratically. One of the other dogs? And reinforcements?

Slade took off at a run, his gun drawn. Warrior was already ahead of him. When the canine stopped and emitted a low growl, Slade slowed down. But what he saw there on the path shocked him.

"Rio?" he called in a light whisper. "Rio, come."

The big dog, looking scruffy and gaunt, came barreling up to Slade then danced around, facing the way he'd come. Warrior sniffed at Rio, a low growl showing he didn't like this new twist. "Warrior, stay," Slade said. He carefully held out his knuckles to Rio, his throat burning with a raw pain. "Hey, it's me, boy. Remember me?"

Rio nuzzled Slade's hand, his panting tongue indicating he was excited. After petting both dogs, Slade gently introduced Warrior and Rio to each other. When the big dog woofed and jumped up against him, Slade couldn't hold back the tears springing to his eyes. "Good boy. You're safe now, Rio." Warrior sniffed a bit but seemed to understand Rio was a friend.

Rio, however, pranced in a circle, looking back at Slade over and over. "What is it, boy? Do you have something?"

Warrior sniffed the air and looked at Slade. "Lead," he said, following Warrior and Rio along the path until they emerged on the east side of the big woods. Rio rushed onto a graveled path and stopped before a black blob.

Slade hurried to the dog, then stared down at the garment, relief washing over him. He'd imagined Kaitlin lying there, hurt or dead. With a nearby small limb, he lifted the garment up. Warrior ran up and started sniffing right along with Rio, both dogs on alert.

And no wonder. The black jumpsuit had a giant square missing off one of the wide legs. This had to be the same jumpsuit the prowler had been wearing when he'd tried to get into his house the other night. Had Dante changed out of it and dropped it here?

Or had someone else left it here for him to find?

Grabbing the garment, Slade rolled it under one arm and started off toward where he'd left Detective Lee Calloway. His backup should be there by now. If Lee was still alive, he would have radioed in, but Slade hadn't been able to contact him. Which meant Kaitlin might not have gotten away, either.

When he rounded a blanket of tall shrubs and saw the car sitting where they'd tried to hide it, then spotted officers and EMTs swarming around like bees, he knew something wasn't right.

Suddenly his phone buzzed. "McNeal."

"Hello, old friend."

Dante.

Slade swallowed the bile rising in his throat. "What do you want now?"

"I think that should be 'what do you want, bro?' And I think I have what you want."

Slade closed his eyes, prayed. "Dante—"

"No, you listen to me," Dante said, his words pebble hard and deadly. "I have your precious trainer, Ms. Mathers. I found her wandering around in the woods. She's here with me, inside your house. If you don't bring those diamonds to me in one hour, I will kill her and then I'll blow up the whole place—with everyone in it. Do you understand, McNeal?"

"Yes." Slade could only take one breath at a time, flashbacks of his car blowing up centermost in his mind. He couldn't let that happen to the people he loved. But he couldn't send the squad in with guns blazing, either. Relieved that he'd told them to stand down, he spoke one word. "Yes."

"Oh, and call off that SWAT team waiting in the dark. I mean it. If I see what looks like a cop, I'll take care of everything with one push of a button."

Slade held up a hand when Lee hurried toward him, a bandage on his head. Austin Black was right behind him. "Got it. Consider it done."

"Good. Now I have a helicopter waiting, so don't do anything stupid or I'll have to take the woman with me and drop her off somewhere else, if you get my drift."

"I understand. I'll get the diamonds to you."

"See that you do. I've had enough of you and your self-righteous, noble deeds. You just don't know when to quit, do you, Slade?"

"No, I don't," he concurred, steel behind each word.

"And I won't quit until you're either behind bars or dead."

"I wouldn't make threats like that, bro. Since I'm the one holding your woman and your family, you'd better do exactly as I say."

"I will," Slade said. And he'd deal with Dante Frears when he got there.

"One hour, McNeal."

The connection ended there. Slade was in a race for his life. He had to save his family and Kaitlin.

Kaitlin sat tied to a chair. She didn't speak or dare look over at Francine. They'd all been warned to stay quiet.

Frears had marched her into the house through the back, a gun to her head. The big van had barely by-passed the commotion of incoming police cars and an ambulance out on Lost Woods Road. Dante had directed the driver to take a backwoods route out of town that looped back around to the east side of the city. After hiding the van near a deserted house and telling the driver to get lost, Dante had grabbed Kaitlin and started out on foot.

"I'm taking you to be with the man you love."

"What have you done to him?"

Dante jerked her back so hard her head rattled against her shoulders. "I haven't done anything yet. But I will. He's going to make a trade—the diamonds for you and that houseful of people he neglects."

"He loves his father and his son," Kaitlin retorted, her gaze taking in the houses up ahead.

"Bingo. Give the trainer lady a prize." Dante tugged

her arm tight against her side, causing her to wince. "We're going to wait for him. One big, happy reunion."

When they came up on a narrow alley behind Slade's house, the whole place seemed shut tight. Not a light on, not a sound anywhere. Were they being watched even now? She didn't dare question Dante. Caleb was in that house and if she could get to him, she might have a chance to save him.

"Don't say a word," he commanded softly as he slowly pushed her in front of him. "Slide open the gate, right here. And remember, I'll have a gun pointed at you and I have the cell phone that will detonate the bomb."

"I understand." She bobbed her head and prayed that God would see her through, then slowly opened the back gate behind the small yard. Even if a team was surrounding the house, they couldn't make a move on Dante Frears because they didn't know where the bomb was or who could activate it. And he knew that.

"Looks like McNeal called a retreat. Good. That means he's finally taking me seriously."

So that's how he'd done it. He'd forced Slade to call for a stand-down. Or worse, no reinforcements at all.

"So we can walk right into the house?"

"Yep. Jasper knows what to do."

Jasper. Her instincts the other night had been right. But she'd never mentioned her concerns to Slade. If anything happened to Caleb, it would be her fault.

"You corrupted a night nurse?"

"Wasn't hard. Those folk don't get paid nearly enough if you ask me. I made him an offer and he took it."

Now Kaitlin's stomach muscles clenched as she thought about all the nights Jasper had been right there, sleeping in the house with Slade and Papa and Caleb. He'd even fooled Warrior, always petting the dog, talking to him with a calm voice.

When she thought of Caleb and how scared he must be, she wanted to slug Dante Frears. But she had to focus on protecting Caleb. If she only knew where the boy was. Afraid to ask, she feared the worst. Dante had hidden Caleb away somewhere.

"How's the happy household?" Dante asked Jasper now that he had Kaitlin tied up.

Jasper looked afraid, his eyes downcast. "Papa's sleeping away. I drugged him pretty heavy."

Kaitlin glared up at the man. "Are you crazy? You could kill him."

Dante's laugh was harsh and unforgiving. "Ah, and that would be such a shame." Then he frowned at her. "Shut up."

Jasper shuffled and stepped back. "I didn't give him enough to kill him."

Dante grunted at that. "Well, at least the gang's all here. And so we wait."

"Where's Caleb?" Kaitlin asked. "Jasper, what did you do with Caleb?"

Jasper shuffled again, cleared his throat. "I… I can't find him."

Dante slapped the gun across Jasper's face, drawing blood and knocking the big man back against a wall. "You stupid klutz. You lost the kid?"

Tears came to Jasper's eyes. "I didn't mean to. He got scared when they brought that other woman here. He saw them."

Dante didn't like that answer. He got in Jasper's face. "You were told to take care of that."

"I thought I did. He was supposed to be asleep."

"Did you drug the kid?"

Jasper wiped at his nose. "No, sir. I don't like drugging little children."

Kaitlin couldn't believe the evil surrounding Dante Frears. He'd obviously taken advantage of Jasper's teddy-bear nature and his need for more money. Maybe she could convince Jasper to help her and the others.

"Jasper, you really don't know where Caleb is?" she asked, not caring what Dante did at this point. She had to find Slade's son.

"No, ma'am." Jasper hung his head, his shaggy hair matted around his face. "I'm so sorry," he whispered.

Frears shoved Jasper away. "Get back to the old man. I don't have time to look for the kid right now. Maybe he'll just disappear and Slade can search for him for six months, too."

Kaitlin shouted a silent prayer to heaven. For help, for control and mostly, for justice to be served on this evil man.

And she prayed that Caleb was safe, wherever he was.

Chapter Twenty-One

Slade impatiently nodded while the SWAT team commander and the bomb squad team went over the plan. Jackson Worth stood by with Titan since the police dog was trained in sniffing out bombs.

"I got it," Slade said, glancing around the headquarters parking lot. He'd gone through the chain of command to secure the box of diamonds, signed them out of the evidence room and now held them in a small black satchel. "I get in, give him the diamonds and get him out before he blows up all of us."

The SWAT team commander held his cell, getting reports from the team surrounding Slade's house. He listened, then turned to Slade. "He's there. The team's spotted a man and woman entering the back gate to your house. He's armed."

Slade's heart seemed to burst. "Is it Kaitlin? Does he have Kaitlin?"

The other captain nodded. "Affirmative." He gave Slade an apologetic glance. "Gun to her head."

"Let's go," Slade shouted, his anxiety mounting.

Dante knew they wouldn't fire on him if he was using Kaitlin as a shield.

The SWAT commander held up a finger. "He sent two men dressed in black out the back door. Probably lookouts." He told his men to stand down, but to put eyes on the two henchmen.

Parker, Lee, Austin and Valerie all stood to the side, listening. And they'd each brought their K-9 partners. Justice, Lexi, Sherlock and Kip were all sitting at their partners' feet.

Slade had Rio and Warrior in his truck. He'd get veterinarian Connie Mills to check Rio later. Right now, he could only feed the dog and hope for the best. He had to get his family out of that house.

He glanced at his truck where Warrior and Rio were still buddying up to each other. "I'm ready to roll. I want this over with."

"My men will hold back as long as we can," the SWAT commander told him. "Slade, you give the go signal."

"Got it."

Slade got in his truck and started the short trek to his house, prayers stuck inside the lump of dread in his throat.

"It's now or never, boys," he told the two dogs who'd helped him tonight. "I need you both to be on your best behavior, okay?"

Warrior's big tongue hung out, but he looked official in his K-9 officer black Kevlar vest. Rio wasn't wearing a vest, but he'd stay in the truck anyway. Hopefully, Slade wouldn't need either of them. But they both had a stake in this, too.

He pulled up into the driveway and noticed the

house was dark except for a lamp silhouetted through the drawn blinds in the den. Taking a deep breath, he got out and called Dante's number.

"I see you came alone," Frears said. "Good man."

"Let's get this over with," Slade replied, his tone curt. Turning to Warrior and Rio, he ordered them to stay. He'd left the windows open so they could get some air.

"I'll be waiting at the door."

Slade carefully walked up to the porch. The neighborhood shined in an inky, wee-hours darkness, the sounds of the night playing like a soothing symphony through the trees. He heard the screech of an owl, a car's horn somewhere toward downtown, the pitter-pat of an alley cat running away.

Just a nice, normal neighborhood sleeping the night away, but the surroundings felt dark and menacing to Slade.

Dear God, don't let this maniac blow up my home and my family.

The door flew open before Slade could touch it. Dante dragged him inside, then centered Slade near the opening between the kitchen and den, obviously to protect himself from snipers. His gun pressing against Slade's ribs, he said, "Take a good long look, my friend. This will be the last time you ever see these people alive."

Kaitlin and Francine sat tied to dining chairs in the middle of the den.

Slade's gaze slammed into Kaitlin's. She looked defiant and calm, but he could see her knee twitching. Francine's big eyes widened but she didn't flinch.

Slade scanned the room. "Where's my father and son?"

Jasper shuffled out of the kitchen. "Your papa's sleeping, Captain McNeal. He'll wake up just fine in the morning."

Slade let out a breath. Was Jasper involved with Dante? "And…my son? Where's Caleb?"

Kaitlin's eyes held his and her chin lifted. Was she trying to warn him, or let him know something?

Slade turned to Dante. "I said where is my son?"

"We can't find him," Jasper said, his head down. "He took off when…when things got bad."

"Shut up," Dante said, his tone full of malice. "You are a big stupid goon and if you want to get paid, you will shut your mouth."

Jasper looked embarrassed. Slade's stomach roiled with a new fear. What had Jasper done to his father and his son? Slade shifted, the steel of the gun hitting against his Kevlar vest. "I want my son, Dante."

"I'd like to have my son back," Dante shouted, all patience gone now that he had Slade where he wanted him. Rage shook him, sweat dripped down his dirty face. "But Daniel is dead, Slade. Dead."

"I didn't know he was your son until this week," Slade replied, hoping to stall him. "I didn't kill him, Dante."

"Maybe not, but you went out that night to take him down and you did nothing, *nothing* to help him."

"Did you?"

Dante issued several choice words. "I tried. I gave his mother anything she wanted, tried to show them I cared. But they all double-crossed me—Daniel, Sierra, even Arianna and Gunther, and that conniving Jim Wheaton. Hiding my diamonds so they could go off on their own."

"So you just kept on killing anyone who got in your way?"

"I killed them because they betrayed me."

Slade felt sorry for his buddy. "Even Sierra, the mother of your son?"

Dante didn't seem so confident now. "She kept nagging me, man. It was an accident. Didn't mean to smother her, but I had to keep her quiet. I couldn't risk Yvette finding out."

Slade zoomed in on that, hoping to appeal to Frears's obvious love for his family. "Yvette and Emily, what will become of them?"

Dante shook his head. "I won't leave them. I'll send for them real soon and everything will be okay again."

Slade stared into Dante's cold, dead eyes. "I can get you some help."

"I don't need your kind of help!" Dante jerked Slade close, the gun digging into Slade's side. "That bullet-proof vest won't save you and it sure won't save these people." He shrugged. "I doubt any of us can be saved, huh?"

The man had a death wish and nothing to lose.

"How are you planning on pulling this off?" Slade asked, a calm steadying him each time he looked at Kaitlin. "You've confessed to a lot of things in front of several witnesses. The cops are all over the Lost Woods, gathering evidence, comparing notes. We have an evidence sheet on the diamonds. It's over, Dante. Why don't you turn yourself in?"

"I don't need to do that," Dante said on a sneer. "You'll all be dead the minute I shut that door. And I'll finally be free."

"You'll never be free." Slade wanted to shout that

Dante would be the one dead. He had to end this and if that meant letting Frears escape—

Slade's gaze held Kaitlin's. Now he understood why she had pulled away. He had to let Dante go in order to be able to get back to his family and her. He had to put them first. In a weird way, Dante had been controlling all of them, but mostly, he'd been in control of Slade's life. Not anymore.

"Give me the diamonds," Dante said, waving the gun in the air. "I know you've got people out there ready to dive in and save the day, but this is not the time to be a hero. So let's get this over with."

That sounded almost like a request instead of a command. Could Slade do this and save everyone, including Dante? Not until he knew Caleb was safe. "I want to see my son first."

Dante shook his head, sweat pouring down his brow. "I don't know where your boy is. Maybe he's hiding or maybe he ran away. That's the truth, Slade."

Jasper grunted, his eyes shifting to the old toy house in the dining room. One of Caleb's favorite hiding places and thankfully, the open handles on each side would give Caleb enough air to survive. If he was still alive.

Was the night nurse trying to tell Slade something? He glanced at Kaitlin. Her eyes went past him to the trunk.

Now Slade's whole agenda shifted. He prayed Caleb would stay in that trunk. *Dear God, keep him safe. Keep him hidden there.*

But it wasn't to be. Slade heard a little voice calling to him. Then the trunk's rickety plastic lid popped open. "I'm here, Daddy. Right here."

Kaitlin's eyes widened and Francine cried out. Slade

watched in horror as Dante rushed to the trunk and tugged Caleb out with one hand. "Ha, ha. What have we here? Hiding from Uncle Dante, huh?"

Caleb fought at Dante. "No, I want my daddy. You're a bad guy. Jasper told me to stay put."

"Well, you're right about that, little buddy," Dante said, holding Caleb up against his chest. "Jasper is going to regret that suggestion—hid you after my men left, did he?" He yanked Caleb up with one hand, gripping the boy around his middle.

"Daddy!"

Slade couldn't bear to see his son being manhandled by Dante Frears. He gave Kaitlin one quick glance then turned as fast as he could and shouted, "Dante, want the diamonds?"

Then he opened the box and threw the diamonds into the air. They lifted up with the flair of shimmering crystal fireworks and started falling like broken crystal onto the hardwood floor.

"No," Dante shouted, one hand holding Caleb, the other still clutching the gun. "No, no!" He put the gun to Caleb's head. "You'll pay for that, McNeal."

Slade rushed forward to grab Caleb, but in the same instant a large dog sailed out of the darkness from the hallway and flew up into the air, capturing Dante's gun arm with a growl and a snarl. Chief! And then he saw Papa standing there, holding on to his cane, his expression grim and determined.

Dante screamed and dropped the gun. Caleb wiggled out of Dante's grip, kicking and screaming. Slade heard the dogs barking in the truck so he grabbed Caleb and shoved him toward Kaitlin's chair. Jasper grasped a frying pan while Slade opened the front door and called, "Come. Attack."

Warrior and Rio hurled out of the open truck window and leaped up the steps and into the house, both of them tearing into Dante's arms and legs. Jasper pivoted around the dogs, avoiding bites until he was behind Dante. Then he slammed the frying pan down onto Dante's head.

Dante fell to the floor, the dogs still snarling around him. "Sit. Stay." Slade and Kaitlin both shouted at the same time. All three dogs sat back and stared down at Dante Frears. Rio let out one more growl for good measure.

Jasper put down the frying pan and started crying, then he hurried to untie Francine and Kaitlin.

Slade ran to Kaitlin. "Are you all right?"

She nodded as she swept Caleb into her arms. "We're fine, aren't we?"

Francine hopped up and hugged Jasper. "Better than fine."

Caleb reached for Slade. "Daddy, we got the bad guy. The one who was in my dreams."

That innocent declaration sealed the deal on this investigation. His son must have seen Dante the day he'd kidnapped Rio.

"We sure did. I'm so proud of you," Slade said, tears burning his eyes. He kissed Caleb and then kissed Kaitlin. "Take care of him for me. I'll be back."

Kaitlin touched a hand to his face. "You'd better hurry back."

As dawn lifted pink-faced and new over the horizon, Slade and Kaitlin stood over Caleb's bed, watching him sleep.

"I didn't think that could be done," Slade said, kissing the top of her head, his gaze on his son.

Joy shot through Kaitlin. They were all alive and together and she was thanking God. "What?"

"Three dogs and a boy all piled up in a twin bed."

"They deserve this special reward," she said, turning into his arms. "It's over."

"Yes." He glanced down at her, then tugged her out into the hall. "Before we go to headquarters to give more statements, I have a statement of my own."

Kaitlin stared into his tired, beautiful eyes. "Oh, what's that?"

"I love you."

She smiled, tears gathering in her eyes. Seemed they always had their serious talks in this hallway. "Really now?"

"Really. Now. And forever."

She wiped at her eyes. "I love you, too."

Hugging her tight, he whispered, "I finally got what you were so afraid of, why you couldn't watch what I'd become."

"It wasn't that—"

"I placed Dante above you and Caleb and Papa and everyone else. I had to take him down and I put you all in danger just to prove I could do it. If something had happened—"

"It didn't, in spite of everything. And I was wrong to pull away from you when you'd been working so hard for so long." She gazed tenderly up at him. "I know how things work with a lawman, but I pushed you away when I should have stayed by your side. I was afraid, Slade."

"You were amazing," he said. "I'll have to remember to stay on your good side."

She grinned at that. "You can now. You did it, Slade. You brought him down and we're all okay."

"*We* did it," he said, his smile etched with fatigue. "But I didn't make it easy."

She kissed him, then leaned back. "You're a police officer. No one said that would ever be easy."

"I'm going to do better now, though. I promise."

She laughed at that. "The only promise I need is that you will always love Caleb, and Papa and me."

"That's easy." He kissed her back. "And Warrior, and Chief and Rio, too."

"You have a lot of love to go around I think."

"That I do."

Together they walked back to the kitchen.

Francine was cooking breakfast. "What can I say? I'm nervous. And Mama is on her way over, too."

"Oh, boy." Slade grinned at that. "We'll have food for days."

A doctor came out of Papa's room. "He's fine," he said. "Jasper didn't drug him nearly as much as he could have. Probably what saved him. Just watch him for a few days and keep him quiet."

"Oh, boy," Slade said again. "Can we see him?"

"Sure, he's been asking for you."

Kaitlin and Slade went into the big bedroom. She stood back while Slade and his father had a quiet talk. His father was coherent and proud. "I slept right up to the good part."

"Be glad you did. And, Papa, thanks for saving the day."

Papa McNeal shrugged. "Chief did that. He kept

scratching at the door, so I knew something was going on." Then he turned serious. "What will happen to Jasper, son?"

Slade glanced at Kaitlin then back to Papa. "He did help more than he hindered. He sent the intruder away the other night, and he didn't give you too much of the sleeping drug. He also hid Caleb in that playhouse and he whacked Frears with a frying pan. I think he'll get a lesser sentence and probation. He's willing to testify so that'll be in his favor, too."

"The thought of Dante bribing and threatening that poor fellow into drugging me and planting a bomb." Papa shook his head. "But then, Dante did a lot we can't believe."

"Yes, he did. At least Jasper thought better of it in the end. And the bomb squad deactivated the bomb easily, thanks to Titan confirming exactly where Dante forced Jasper to place it under the kitchen sink."

Papa glanced over at Kaitlin. "Did my son do right by you, young lady?"

"He did, sir." She smiled and put her arm around Slade's waist.

"I hope Kaitlin will be around a lot, Papa," Slade replied. "But right now, you rest up."

"Do I smell bacon?"

Slade laughed. "We'll bring you breakfast, don't worry."

When they were back in the hallway, Kaitlin turned to Slade. "So you expect me to stick around, huh?"

He grabbed her close. "I expect you to marry me."

"Is that your way of proposing, Captain?"

"Is that your way of accepting, Ms. Mathers?"

"Yes to both," Francine shouted from the kitchen. "Enough already. Come and get some food."

"And that settles that," Slade said.

Then he kissed Kaitlin and together they walked into the kitchen.

Epilogue

A week later

Slade stood in front of the big white board that had "dogged" him for six long months. "We now know that Dante Frears, aka The Boss, had several underlings working for him. He bought a fleet of used black vans and insisted his team all wear black from head to toe. While he mostly wore the black silk jumpsuits and did some prowling himself, he rotated his cohorts so none of us, including our K-9 officers, could catch a scent. We had a few breaks here and there, but he finally got too desperate and he slipped up. He murdered a lot of people in the process. But we'll leave all that up to the evidence and a jury. We can clear this off the board now, boys and girls. This case is closed."

A round of applause filled the conference room. Slade glanced around at the five other human members of their team: Austin Black, Lee Calloway, Valerie Salgado, Jackson Worth and Parker Adams.

"I want to thank each of you for contributing to this investigation," Slade said, his smile real for a change.

"I know you all went way beyond what's expected of a K-9 officer and I will always appreciate that. We have some amazing animals working with us and I'm blessed that we have some of the best trainers in the country."

"Especially Kaitlin Mathers, right, boss?" Austin said with a grin.

"Right, Detective Black." Slade laughed and shook his head. "I have to say if there is anything good about this tragic case, well, at least we all found life partners. Can't figure that one out, but I'm sure we can all agree that God had a hand in this."

"Amen" came the shouts amid laughter and teasing.

"I can't keep up with who's married and who's engaged," Slade admitted. "But I promise I'll be there with those of you planning to get married."

"And we'll be there for your wedding, Captain," Valerie said, clapping her hands.

Slade nodded, then turned serious. "My former best friend, Dante Frears, will be paying for his crimes. He fooled a lot of us but we made it through. We became more than just the K-9 Unit of the Sagebrush Police Department. We were patrols, detectives, investigators and all-purpose officers, just like Warrior and Rio and the rest of our partners. I'm proud of this department."

After that, he went over the facts regarding the case, how Dante had used one of his businesses as a front for drug trafficking. The stable of black vans had come from an out-of-town business and so had the black silk jumpsuits. He'd bought the ski masks and fake contacts off the internet and Slade had receipts and records to prove all of it. Frears would go down for everything from drug trafficking to kidnapping to bombings and murders. He could get the final sentence—death.

Slade hated it, but justice was done. He planned to visit Dante in prison, maybe to find answers and maybe to give his friend one last shred of forgiveness. Kaitlin had taught him about forgiveness.

After the meeting ended and everyone had gone their separate ways, Slade started cleaning up the board. When he heard a friendly bark behind him, he turned to find Rio and Warrior standing at the door with Kaitlin.

"Hello," he said, smiling. He still couldn't believe he'd found this woman.

"Hello yourself. How did your meeting go?"

"Good." He motioned for the woman and two dogs to come over. Slade petted the animals then grabbed hold of Kaitlin and held her tight in his arms. "But I like this part better."

She laid her head on his shoulder. "I've been thinking."

"Uh-oh." He kissed her hair. "About what?"

She looked up and into his eyes. "I… I might be interested in returning to the force, as a K-9 officer, if that's not against policy."

Surprised, he drew back. "Are you kidding?"

"No, I'm not. I…thought I'd lost all my fears, but I discovered if you're not scared, just a little bit, you're probably still hiding something. I was afraid to put myself out there on the line with you, but now I think I need to be right there on the front line. Fearful but careful, and very sure."

Slade knew he couldn't talk her out of this and he had to admit, he was proud of her. "So…we'd be a houseful of K-9 officers."

"Yes, three dogs, two active officers, one retired officer and…maybe a future officer. Or two."

"Sounds like fun to me." Slade pulled her close and kissed her. "Wanna go out for dinner?"

She nodded, laughed. "Sure. We can talk about our engagement party."

"Engagement party? I have to buy you a ring first."

"You will. But…about the party. I'd like to have it right here out on the training yard."

He chuckled as they started out the doors, the K-9s right behind them. "Fancy. I like that."

She smiled up at him. "Yes, sir. Very fancy. Doggie treats and hot dogs, cupcakes and ice cream. Chew toys and barbecue. The works."

Slade leaned down to kiss her. "Perfect."

She giggled then touched a hand to his face. "For now, I suggest you go home and finally get some rest. Get a good night's sleep."

Slade tugged her back into his arms. "Don't you know, Trainer Mathers—I never sleep."

Then he kissed her to show her he had something else in mind. He wanted to cuddle with the woman he loved. Starting right now.

Behind them, Warrior woofed and Rio did a little tapping spin and gave them a big, happy doggy smile.

* * * * *

SPECIAL EXCERPT FROM

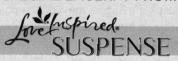

*A serial killer is after a military nurse. She'll fight to
stay one step ahead of him with the help of a heroic
soldier and some brave K-9s.*

Read on for a sneak preview of
Battle Tested *by Laura Scott,*
the next book in the Military K-9 Unit miniseries,
available October 2018 from Love Inspired Suspense.

Two fatal drug overdoses in the past week.

Exhausted from her thirteen-hour shift in the critical
care unit, First Lieutenant Vanessa Gomez made her way
down the hallway of the Canyon Air Force Base hospital,
grappling with the impact of this latest drug-related death.

The corridor lights abruptly went out, enclosing her in
complete darkness. She froze, instinctively searching for
the nearest exit sign, when strong hands roughly grabbed
her from behind, long fingers wrapping themselves around
her throat.

The Red Rose Killer?

It had been months since she'd received the red rose
indicating she was a target of convicted murderer and
prison escapee Boyd Sullivan.

She kicked back at the man's shins, but her soft-soled
nursing shoes didn't do much damage. She used her

elbows, too, but couldn't make enough impact that way, either. The attacker's fingers moved their position around her neck, as if searching for the proper pressure points.

"Why?" she asked.

"Because you're in my way…" the attacker said, his voice low and dripping with malice.

The pressure against her carotid arteries grew, making her dizzy and weak. Black spots dotted her vision.

She was going to die, and there was nothing she could do to stop it.

Her knees sagged, then she heard a man's voice. "Hey, what's going on?"

Her attacker abruptly let go just as the lights came on. She fell to the floor. The sound of pounding footsteps echoed along the corridor.

"Are you okay?" A man wearing battle-ready camo rushed over, then dropped to his knees beside her. A soft, wet, furry nose pushed against her face and a sandpapery tongue licked her cheek.

"Yes," she managed, hoping he didn't notice how badly her hands were shaking.

"Stay, Tango," the stranger ordered. He ran toward the stairwell at the end of the hall, the one that her attacker must have used to escape.

Don't miss
Battle Tested *by Laura Scott,*
available October 2018 wherever
Love Inspired® *Suspense books and ebooks are sold.*

www.LoveInspired.com

Love Inspired®

Save $1.00

on the purchase of ANY
Love Inspired® book.

Available wherever books are sold,
including most bookstores, supermarkets,
drugstores and discount stores.

Save $1.00

on the purchase of ANY Love Inspired® book.

Coupon valid until November 30, 2018.
Redeemable at participating retail outlets in the U.S. and Canada only.
Limit one coupon per customer.

52615926

5 65373 00076 2 (8100)0 12382

Looking for inspiration in tales
of hope, faith and heartfelt romance?

Check out **Love Inspired**® and
Love Inspired® Suspense books!

New books available every month!

CONNECT WITH US AT:

Facebook.com/groups/HarlequinConnection

Facebook.com/HarlequinBooks

Twitter.com/HarlequinBooks

Instagram.com/HarlequinBooks

Pinterest.com/HarlequinBooks

ReaderService.com

to the next time they could be together. In spite of his determination, his life was being linked to hers and her neighbors.

That would change once his coworker's trailer pulled up to take him back to Texas.

Sarah gestured toward the *kinder*. "They're hungry for love."

"You're worried they're going to be hurt when I go back to Texas."

"*Ja.*"

He wanted to ask how she would feel when he left, but he'd hurt his ankle, not his head, so he didn't have an excuse to ask a stupid question.

"The *kinder* will be upset when you go, but won't it be better to give them nice memories of your times together to enjoy when they think about you after you've left?" Nice memories of times together? Maybe that would be sufficient for the *kinder*, but he doubted it would be enough for him.

Don't miss
The Amish Christmas Cowboy by Jo Ann Brown,
available October 2018 wherever
Love Inspired® books and ebooks are sold.

www.LoveInspired.com

LIEXP0918

Though Texan cowboy Toby Christner was raised Amish, he has no plans to settle down in the new community along Harmony Creek. But when he meets Amish nanny Sarah Kuhns, he can't help but wonder if a Plain life with her is exactly what he needs.

Read on for a sneak preview of
The Amish Christmas Cowboy by Jo Ann Brown,
available in October 2018 from Love Inspired!

Toby was sure something was bothering Sarah.

He thought through their conversation among her family's Christmas trees. She'd been distressed by how Summerhays and his wife paid too little attention to their *kinder*, but she'd been ready to speak her mind on that subject.

So what was bothering her?

You.

The voice in his head startled him. He'd heard it clearly and, for once, it wasn't warning him away from becoming too close to someone. Instead, it was telling him the reason why there might be a wall between him and Sarah.

Maybe it was for the best. Every day he lingered was another drawing him into the community. Each moment he spent with Sarah enticed him to look forward